The Art of Always

by

Patricia Friedrich

The Art of Always

Cover Art by *Diana Carlile*

The Wild Rose Press, Inc.
PO Box 708
Adams Basin, NY 14410-0708
Visit us at www.thewildrosepress.com

Publishing History
First Edition, 2022
Trade Paperback ISBN 978-1-5092-3779-1
Digital ISBN 978-1-5092-3780-7

Published in the United States of America

A thin mist had covered the city. Inside the fog, cobblestone pavers and streetlamps gave the streets a dreamlike feel, which Ana experienced from the other side of her window. Watching the movement of neighbors hurrying to catch a train or walk to work, she knifed a small wedge of butter and slathered it on a piece of toast. The flavors of the morning, fresh coffee and jam, delighted her. It was a moment of perfection, a fleeting one, full of ideas about art and success, so she took full notice of it.

But soon the pleasure of warm French bread and sweet coffee was replaced with worry. Her morning with Joaquim and the strange intuition she had about it kept her heart prisoner and made her attention falter. The strange prophecy and the knot in her stomach alerted her to be careful. As she fell asleep the night before, she had made up her mind that the recent encounter would be their last time together. She reminded herself that no matter the powerful hold Joaquim had on her, she could do whatever she wanted.

Praise for Patricia Friedrich

"The quest for authenticity despite cultural norms and expectations—it's a timeless struggle for women, and a theme that takes center stage in Patricia Friedrich's breathtaking new novel, *THE ART OF ALWAYS*. Darcey is a self-doubting graduate student in 1990s Pennsylvania, while Ana is a free-spirited artist in São Paulo in 1922, but their stories—at times parallel, at times intertwined—together reveal what it means to want both love and self-fulfillment, and what costs that desire entails. A linguist and celebrated professor and dean, Friedrich evokes in her novel the rich beauty of her native Brazil, the political reality of academia, and the spellbinding appeal of romance and motherhood."

~*Barbara Josselsohn, author*

Dedication

for Carolina

Chapter 1
Darcey

Larryville, Pennsylvania, Christmas 1996

Darcey stroked the blue rug of the living room, cringing at how threadbare it had become since her childhood and how gigantic it looked in this much-smaller house. Her chest ached with the bitter-sweet memory of other times—the rug had once been lusher, seen better days. It now felt out of place, a feeling she knew all too well.

Around her, the air was laced with the clean smell of spruce, and at eleven in the morning, her family still rested in the half-light of the overcast winter sky. She was sitting cross-legged on the floor, where dotted wrapping paper scattered like make-believe flowers against a cobalt meadow. Her attention shifted from the floor covering to the small person in front of her, the one whose happiness and wellbeing were more important than anything else in the world. Just looking at Nina made her soul sing.

"Come here, sweetheart." She opened her arms and wiggled her fingers in anticipation of the moment when her daughter's hands would reach hers. She couldn't believe Nina was already three. Ever since her baby's surprise arrival, a love that had no match had consumed her. "Hey, missy!" she shouted, her hands at the sides of her mouth like a loudspeaker.

The little girl toddled over to her.

"Here, Nina, the new ball Santa brought you. Look!"

Nina squeaked in delight. Then she grabbed the ball, threw it in the air, and caught it. Looking at her mom with a smile, the little girl handed her the toy. Darcey tucked a lock of her daughter's dark curls behind the girl's ear. "Go sit over there. I'll roll the ball to you. Go." Nina grinned again and ran, barefoot, pink flannel pajamas, to the other side of the rug. She clapped her hands as if to say she was ready. Her giggles echoed around the room. Darcey blew her a kiss and continued with the game.

Under the Christmas tree behind Nina, a solitary present sat unopened—silent. Every year, Darcey's own mom performed the ritual with great dedication. For the last twenty-six years, Eleanor Mendes had bought a Christmas gift for her late son, Darcey's twin brother, whose shadow walked beside her every day of her life. This year, it was a five-inch-tall cube-like package, wrapped in red paper and tied with a green bow. It could be a mug or perhaps a puzzle. An action figure, maybe. Nina, now old enough to fully enjoy Christmas morning, had taken the edge off the gloomy rite but not completely eclipsed it. Eleanor would later, alone, open the present and tuck it away in a box of mementoes atop the antique armoire. Whether she had that right or not, Darcey would feel a sadness in her stomach, wishing in the very least she had been included in the ceremony.

"Her hair's long. We should take her for a haircut," Darcey said to Eleanor, examining her daughter's shiny mane. Nina's curls covered her eyes. While not fond of keepsakes herself, Darcey had saved a lock of her daughter's hair tied with a white satin ribbon inside one of her favorite art books.

Near the window, Eleanor seemed hypnotized, her gaze lost in the distance; the whiteness of the hills that surrounded their small country home outside Larryville always brought her to stillness. She wore her ash-blonde hair in a ponytail, revealing an angular profile, different from Darcey's softer and rounder features, which mirrored her father's.

"Mom?" Darcey insisted.

"What?" Eleanor turned to face her, as if suddenly awakened from the mesmerizing allure of the snow.

"I said Nina's hair needs a trim."

"Sure. Next time we're in town. I'll add this to my long list." She sighed.

The ball hit her leg. Darcey rolled it, and Nina chuckled, falling sideways to catch it. Darcey looked into her daughter's eyes, two onyx beads that shone with excitement. What wouldn't she do for that child? If only she could shelter Nina under her arm and never let go.

The simple game was interrupted when Eleanor spoke again. "Darcey, take Nina to watch cartoons with Grandpa for a few minutes, will you? I need to talk to you." She crossed her arms but remained seated. Her lips were tensed into a flat line, and her forehead furrowed, making her look older than fifty-five.

Darcey bit the inside of her cheek. They had spent Christmas morning opening gifts, sipping hot chocolate, but her mother had given one-word replies to questions and buried her head in tasks like baking more cookies than the four of them could ever eat. She always assumed her mother's silences on Christmas were about her brother, but there was something else troubling her. Something new. Another layer of preoccupation.

On the radio, "Fell on Black Days" by Soundgarden came on. It reminded Darcey of grunge and all the underground bars from the nights she had spent with Flynn, her child's father. She couldn't really tell anymore what led her to fall for the flannel-clad, long-haired drummer who left her when she was pregnant. Was it the fact that he liked to pluck flowers from people's front yards to give to her? Or that he said both she and her shaggy short hair were beautiful even though she had never felt that way?

She rolled down the sleeves of her shirt and let the lyrics play on her lips. It was time to lift Nina in her arms and take her to Grandpa. They dance-walked their way out of the room to scare away the anguish that had sprouted in her chest. She then returned to Eleanor and pulled up a chair.

"What's going on?" Outside, a layer of fog was forming, and it closed in on the house. It would be a perfect day to sit by the window under a blanket and read, if it wasn't for the trouble brewing. "Everything okay? Dad well? He seems a little quiet. Come to think of it, you do too."

Eleanor rested her hands on her thighs. "Yes, he's fine. I mean, as well as he could be under the circumstances." Her voice wavered, and Darcey's stomach tightened. "It'll be all right," her mother concluded with very little conviction in her voice.

"What circumstances?" She was picking a hangnail and biting on it. If only she could drop the habit.

4

"Mom?"

"Well, he lost his job. The main one, I mean." Eleanor stood up, collected the hot-chocolate mugs that had been on the table since early morning, and placed them on a tray.

"The accounting gig?" Her father was gentle and smart, even if not very ambitious. She loved his stories about being a child in Portugal, about the sea, and about making bread with his mother. It was ironic that her father kept other people's accounts while struggling to balance his own. She wanted better for him. "The job you moved here for?"

"Yep, that one. It kept us afloat…just barely. He's got some freelance work, but it's not much."

Darcey stood up and paced the room, needles pricking her scalp. This couldn't be happening. She was keenly aware of all they had done for their family. Now this.

"I'm so sorry" was all she managed to say. She collected a toy giraffe and the ball Nina had played with. She stared at the giraffe a little too long. It was awful to worry about herself and her daughter—after all, Nina was her responsibility, not theirs—but that's where her mind went.

"I know you still have one more year of school, and that's all right," Eleanor acknowledged, as if reading her mind.

Darcey should hug her mother and comfort her, but she couldn't. They didn't have that kind of relationship. "What're we gonna do?" she said instead.

"I'm not sure…start selling some bonds?"

Darcey nibbled at her fingers again.

"Ouch." The hangnail came loose, and blood

reddened the side of her nail. She brought her finger to her mouth and sucked on it. "Will that work?"

"For a while." Eleanor collected paper napkins and brushed cookie crumbs off the table.

"Good then, right?" Maybe it wasn't all bad. If they had bonds, they would be fine.

A long pause followed, and Darcey panicked over the silence that hovered in the room. She searched for a Band-Aid inside a drawer and didn't find any. At the back of the drawer, a spider was stuck in its web.

"Mom? Talk to me, please."

Her mother's delay made Darcey more anxious. "You and Dad have been so generous, taking care of Nina while I'm in school. What can I do to help? I could take time off my studies."

"And what will that do? Sure, you get to work, but what will that bring?"

"More than a teaching assistantship does."

"Barely, and in the end, it'll mean all our sacrifices were for nothing." Eleanor tugged on the corner of the tablecloth. "Darcey, I'll regret telling you this, but we don't see a way for us to keep the house much longer."

Guilt like a poisonous weed sprouted inside her chest. "Don't say that, Mom."

"What can I say? We have two mortgages. The money from the bonds won't carry us through much longer than, say, a year?"

"Then let me help. I can always finish the degree later."

"No. That's not why I told you." Eleanor rubbed her arms. "I guess I just needed to speak to someone. I thought you should know." She looked out of the window again. "And I know what happens to degrees that are left to be finished sometime in the future. Life happens. That's how come I never got mine."

Darcey felt as if she were sitting in a dunk tank, waiting for someone to throw the ball that would plunge her into the cold water. It was bad enough that, over three years before, they had given up her childhood home in Williamsport. Her parents sold it to fund a good portion of her tuition, to help care for Nina, and to move seventy miles away for a job that had now turned to ashes, like the wood in their inefficient fireplace.

"Oh, Mom. I'm...I don't know what to say. It's all my fault. If I had started to earn some of that money back...How about if I work retail? Commission could be good?"

Eleanor touched her daughter's arm gently. "Retail? In this place? And no one's blaming you." Her mother wasn't listening, and that frustrated Darcey. She wasn't a child. She wanted to help.

Nina's laughter filtered in from the other room, infectious and spontaneous. She loved cartoons and the calm companionship of her grandfather.

"Well, I *am* blaming myself."

"Then don't. Who could have predicted all those factory jobs leaving? No need for accountants if you have no accounts. I just thought to tell you. But you'll graduate in a year. Everything will work out. You'll give Nina a good future, and that's what matters."

Darcey's stomach churned, and inside it knots multiplied. On a typical day, Nina occupied most of her thoughts. The other few went toward her art history dissertation, her ticket to a stable job and a career as a professor. But not today.

"The day I can finally take responsibility for my daughter, I'll take care of you too. But if you won't let me help yet, what's the plan?"

"Beyond selling the bonds, I don't know. Maybe see if the bank will let us do a short sale in case we can't refinance. Rent a small place. Hope your father can find more work. I figured I'd try and cater a few dinners in town. But if we can't raise any money, the house will have to go. Don't worry. Nina will be taken care of no matter what happens."

But of course she worried, and while she listened to her mother, a germ of an idea started to form. At first it was a nagging voice in her pre-consciousness. But it grew louder, demanded to be heard. It called a name through all the mental noise: Aunt Lucile.

Not that this was an easy avenue. Why Lucile and her mother hadn't talked in years remained a mystery to her. The fateful misunderstanding was something they never spoke of. Her aunt had clearly stated money would come to Darcey by way of a generous trust fund later, and she didn't want to give Lucile the impression all she cared about was money because she really didn't.

"Mom, can you give me a couple of weeks and not do anything until we speak again? Can you do this for me?"

"Sure. What're *you* going to do? Don't tell me you'll ask Archie for a loan."

Darcey's heart thumped a little louder at the mention of his name. Why had he chosen the law school at her university when there were so many other options around the country? He had brought back with him so many emotions she wasn't ready to face.

"Of course not. I'd never do that. He'd offer if he knew, but I'd never tell him. And I still don't want him to know about Nina. She is my business and no one else's. If Nina's own father didn't care about me and his daughter, why would she and our troubles matter to Archie?"

"Because he's your friend. Because he is a different kind of man."

"That was a rhetorical question, but either way, I don't want Archie to know. Or Donaldson for that matter. The last three years, life at the university's been like a totally separate world, and it's worked. I weathered Archie's return a few months ago the same way. I wanna keep it as is." It seemed no matter how many times she and her mother talked about this, they would never really agree she had done the right thing.

"By the way, he called this morning while you were still asleep. Wanted to wish you Merry Christmas."

Darcey had to disguise the fact that her whole body felt warm at the thought of him. "I'll call him back later," she said as she moved away from her mother.

"I don't know how you manage. It's like you're two different people."

"It's not that farfetched." Darcey didn't know if she was trying to convince her mother or herself. "You live in the countryside, so our life can remain our own."

"It feels wrong. Secrets, double lives, I don't know." Eleanor rubbed her arms again.

"It may be a double life, but it's my life. Don't tell anyone about the mortgage either. Archie's return to Pennsylvania changed nothing."

Eleanor frowned, visibly dissatisfied with where

the conversation was going. "We still have a vestige of pride left. It's not like we're going to announce it about town. But Archie's different. You've known the boy for what now? Over a decade? You were inseparable, remember? Full of shared secrets. True, you didn't talk much while he was in D.C., but now that you're friends again, you should tell him about Nina. He'd be so hurt if he knew you kept such a big part of your life from him. I don't think it's right. I'll respect your wishes. I always have. But you know what I think."

Yes, her mother made it abundantly clear what she thought. "Well mom, thank you for your advice, but no. I don't need anyone's pity." The thought of his thinking about her in those terms was terrifying. Besides, Archie had been the one who left. A whole four years of absence. He couldn't expect to come back and find her waiting like the teenager he used to know, her heart aflutter at the mention of his name.

Darcey looked around, hands on her hips, her eyes stopping at all the wrapping spread on the ground. "Now I'm gonna clean this mess. I'm sure Nina is ready for a nap."

Once Nina was asleep and the living room in better shape, Darcey swathed herself in a throw and went to sit on a bench in the yard. She was numb to the cold that greeted her outside. The ground and the sky blended together in whiteness. When the snow melted, the rust and the tiredness of this small town, anonymous like so many others, would again be evident. But in the immensity of the snow-blanketed Pennsylvania countryside—all sounds muffled—she and her family were the earth's only inhabitants, and her problems were less urgent than they had been earlier. Her solutions seemed adequate, but she didn't let that temporary respite fool her. She would return to the house, and her reality would be waiting: she was a single mother, in a lot of debt, whose parents could become homeless within the year. Her love life was inexistent, and her thesis yet to be finished.

Her first impulse was to grab Nina's box of cheddar crackers, tuck herself into bed, and devour the treats while reading some impossible thriller in which the heroine ended up escaping despite very unfavorable odds. But she didn't have the luxury of time or laziness. Or believing in unlikely happy endings. She had to go back to school and finish her work on that French painter she had discovered. Their future depended on her ability to graduate.

A squirrel came to keep her company. Its tiny paws left indentations in the snow. What a blessing it would be to live the uncomplicated life of a small rodent, whose only concerns were food, shelter, and keeping its young safe. Though, ironically, she wasn't much different from the little animal. A moment later, startled by her sneezing, the creature disappeared behind a tree. The cold intensified. She loved the way clean, crisp air filled her lungs and calmed her.

The yellow glow of a lamp shining from within Nina's room gave her some comfort too. She thought of the little girl, sleeping in such peace, unaware of the problems that plagued her. One more year. She was so close. Maybe her mother was right to tell her to continue. And if Aunt Lucile understood and helped, graduating was still possible. It was awful to ask, but her aunt was rich. It wouldn't be a great imposition. It wasn't wrong to recognize a person needed support, was it?

For the same reason, sometimes she wished she could tell Donaldson about Nina. Her advisor was more than her professor. Did her reticence come from fear that he might make things easier for her because of her problems? Or did she fear he would be disappointed in her? As for Archie, the time to tell had passed. If she'd wanted to say anything, it should have been when Nina was born. Not now, three years later, when her family faced financial ruin. Besides, Archie would leave again when he finished law school. She would suffer if she thought otherwise or if she decided to stake anything on him. They didn't owe each other explanations.

The cold suddenly became unbearable. She went back in, folded the blanket, her mind already back to the university, back to the plan that could save their lives from ruin. She'd leave right after New Year's. Four hours on the bus, and she would be back in school and conveniently near her aunt. She made a mental note of her plan: visit the library to finalize her proposal, talk to Donaldson to get his blessing, and finally beg Lucile to be her patron.

That left six days to enjoy Nina's company and give her daughter all the attention she deserved. She and Nina would be fine. She kept repeating it like a mantra, until she almost believed it.

Chapter 2
Ana

São Paulo, Brazil, January 31ˢᵗ, 1922

Ana studied her naked lover, his glistening arms, strong hands, and his gold wedding band shining in accusation every time a ray of sun seeped through the waving curtains of their little alcove.

"Your pleasure now is your doom tomorrow," their dance was saying. It might have been a sign, a hint for her to release herself from his body and run from her studio. But she didn't. She turned her head on the pillow and saw her dress lying on the floor in a jumble of white and navy silk stripes.

It wasn't just a dress. It was the dress he always asked her to wear when he came to see her, on Tuesday mornings, at eight. Illicit love learned to wait. Illicit love had its own secret hour: a time to start, a time to be consummated, a time to end. She only consented because she had fallen in love.

The way those stripes on her dress overlapped resembled the way her legs were entangled around Joaquim's body. She looked for beauty and color in all she saw. The image didn't evaporate from her brain even under the burden of her lover's body, or in the reflection of their blended shapes in the mirror. Instead, it became fodder for her art.

The once-cool taupe bed sheets now clung to her thin, bare back. She shifted under Joaquim, and her stomach sank like decanted paint. Women only had the advantage of youth for a short time. She wanted to enjoy it while it lasted, expose her arms and wear a flirty dress like the one discarded on the studio floor.

But the impression of the dress wasn't the only thing she took in when she slid her hands down Joaquim's back. In the end, it was almost a relief to tune out and lend only her body to this act. Caring hurt too much.

Despite the comforts of the season and the leafy fertile exuberance of the tree that peeked into their intimacy through the window, things were no longer the way they once were. Love had smoldered in her heart, and the summer had overheated her body, making her too indolent. She became one of the people you saw in the tropics, languidly lying in squeaking hammocks, malaise making them unable to power their muscles.

If she could go back in time six months, to when they met, to the joy of visiting the market and eating fresh fruit, she would be braver, let their allotted time while away, ignored. She would head to the park and leave him waiting by her door that first morning. And he would give up. And life would be simple. She would paint, and art would be the only thing.

But she couldn't go back. She tried to overlook the faint and insistent hints of change all around: the telltale smell of an approaching storm, the distraction that had caused her to break her favorite teapot earlier in the day, and the disharmony of the shades of red in her most recent painting, the one she had tossed away in a fit.

If that wasn't enough, the recent prediction of the white magic lady, who sat at a street corner and dealt shells that told the future, hammered in her brain. Right before the art exhibit, she had shouted at Ana, "Deception, a swollen belly, a long trip." Ana threw coins at the woman and dashed off, grabbing both ends of her shawl, lest it tried to fly away.

Trepidation now lived in the pit of her stomach, a fluttering, an empty hole, widening, threatening to swallow the bedroom and all its contents. And the sensation lingered even during the customary carelessness of her forbidden morning. An affair was supposed to be liberating, wasn't it? But instead of happy, her heart was as tight as a sailor's knot, unable to set a rhythm, and beat like a favorite melody. Her voice was stuck in her throat, like a fishbone. And there was no one to rescue her, pat her back, unlock a life-saving breath.

Once, having a lover had been a declaration of freedom, an affirmation of art over convention, of desire over institution. Women could not subject themselves anymore to the rules of a world designed by men. Now, two decades into the twentieth century, she refused to be Victorian in Latin America.

She arched her back as well as she could, the soft sheets suddenly prickly and itchy, poking her and all her insecurities, the ones she convinced herself she didn't have. She focused on the ceiling but found no answers, only ever-growing lines where the paint had started to crack. She sank her head into the pillow, hearing the feathers readjust.

Noticing her unusual disinterest, Joaquim held her chin with determination. The faint scent of coffee escaped with his arduous breaths, his unshaven face against her skin. The taste of salt-water sweat beaded from his neck and shoulders, and the pleasurable but awkward heaviness of his chest against her breasts made her feel both trapped and guarded.

Joaquim smoothed her hair from her forehead. She tried to let herself be carried away by his rhythm and by the agreeable sounds coming from the gramophone, but she discovered she couldn't tune out the noise of people, animals, and industrial machines from the streets of São Paulo. Every bark, shout, and clank beyond their room seemed to intervene, creating an offbeat melody punctuated by the thuds of the wood headboard banging against the wall. And the words vibrated once more all around her, "deception, a swollen belly, a long trip." The broken china, the feeling of foreboding, the bad art—those had to have a meaning however unclear at the time. It was like a single-minded wind gust was pushing her away, and in truth she wished it succeeded.

By nine o'clock she had wrapped herself in her red Chinese robe and had brushed her black hair into its sleek, updated bob, while in the bathroom Joaquim erased all evidence of his morning. She was anxious to start work, to paint until she ran out of colors, to make something out of the void of the white canvas.

She gathered her brushes and her case, putting them next to a canvas. She inhaled deeply until her lungs felt cold. The air smelled modern. Living was daring. It was a good time to be an artist.

She had to leave him, ignore his charm, resist his burning eyes. It was easy for a person to want only a little before they got it. Once they did, they wanted more. They wanted tradition, family, constancy. She had begun to want.

A few minutes went by before she ushered her lover out of the studio. Because she loved him, she couldn't wait for him to leave and carry away the alarm and the prophecy twirling in her brain.

"Is today the 31st?" Joaquim stopped at the door making her almost crash against his back.

"January 31, 1922. Why? Is it a memorable day in any way?"

"No," he answered quickly. "Just a very boring meeting at the newspaper. Yet again. That's all."

But the date did stick to her memory. It was the day after her art exhibit. The day her life was supposed to start. A good day as any to break it off. To be free.

Joaquim blew her a kiss from outside the shutting door, his sideway glance more captivating than she could endure. And Ana wondered, grabbing her robe against her chest, if closing her heart and following the instincts that told her to leave him would be quite as easy as closing the door.

Chapter 3
Darcey

Summerford, Pennsylvania, January 1997

"Is this a joke, universe? Huh?"

Darcey slammed the heavy, life-destroying book shut. She never thought books could do so much harm, and yet she felt a pain in her chest that made it hard to breathe. She looked up at the cathedral ceiling of the university library, her arms stretched out in a plea. "Don't I have enough to worry about already? You wanna take away my dissertation too?"

Up until that moment, books had been objects of love, dear friends, no matter how dingy or yellowed. They had carried her through hard times: lonely nights when she was a child, restless ones when Nina was a colicky baby who wouldn't sleep. Books convinced her love was possible, even though Flynn had deserted her, pregnant and confused, and that dreams came true, even if she had forgotten what hers were. Books were safe, comforting, reliable.

Yet, that day in the library, sitting in front of a pile of modernist ideas, art history theories, and examples of good scholarship, she felt like the failure she always feared she'd be. She didn't want to envy the success of others. She tried to be a decent person. The effort took its toll. A wave of nausea hit, and she folded forward as if she were no more than a blade of grass, yielding to the whims of the wind.

Somewhere in the halls of academia a door was closing. Twelve months earlier, she'd promised herself she'd make a great artistic discovery. She'd planned to bring an obscure artist to light. After much work, she thought she had him. Mr. Walker-LeCarré, with his mustache and Panama hat. He was Nina's ticket to an easier life. But now, her plan was gone, disintegrated like old papyrus, made brittle by time and neglect. The artist, and subject of her dissertation, a genius scholastic find, had been written about before. She wasn't an original.

"You gotta be kidding me! All the time I wasted. What's the point?" She continued her solitary meltdown until a patron with chubby fingers looked up from her book. Conjuring all her strength, Darcey smiled at the woman. She had been taught to disguise disappointment with a pleasant veneer, and at almost twenty-seven, with a child to consider, she could pull off that pretense with calculated panache.

Once the lady left, she didn't have to pretend anymore. "I'm done with you." She skinned the colorful sticky notes off the pages and abandoned the favorite desk she had for so long considered to be her safe harbor. One whole year, fifty-two weeks, five hours a day. The distance from Nina. Financial hardship, house heading for foreclosure. All useless. Her topic was gone, and she was missing an alternative.

She'd imagined herself as a middle-aged professor, an Italian scarf tied around her neck and elegant leather shoes, instead of her current military-style boots, shining during one of her lectures. She would become someone special if she had a title. She could become that imaginary person her late brother would never be. Her little girl would look up to her. And maybe her mom wouldn't think of Darcey's brother so much anymore.

But when her real life from that point on reeled like a movie in front of her, she didn't like what she saw. A decrepit apartment, long days of low wages, trying to keep her family afloat. Financial strain would result in an inability to turn her confusing thoughts into anything concrete, like a few pages of writing—or money.

She scanned the library, looking for a place to anchor her distress. The colorful stained glass art— which probably cost twenty times her tuition—depicted men and women in cap and gown being anointed for their wisdom. The silence around her made her thoughts louder by contrast. She was about to lose herself in the beauty and sadness of the abstract panel behind the main desk, its yellows and greens beginning to soothe her, when her eyes met Abby's. Darcey marched, books in hand, toward the woman. The librarian, with her kind, familiar middle-aged face and soft-set crow's feet, had witnessed this scene a few times. Darcey hoped the woman would console her, like she'd done before.

Abby looked over her blue-rimmed glasses and tilted her blonde head in sympathy.

"Again? I don't like that face."

"I should've seen it coming."

"What do you mean?"

Darcey was on the verge of tears. "It was going too well, is what I mean. Great topic, full of romance, trips to Paris. Historical relevance. A great artist, you name it. I'd ensured no one in the US wrote much about him. Somehow, he had escaped. I'd even found a theme. It was a miracle."

"And then? What's the problem?"

"France. France is the problem. Two whole books dedicated to the works of Simon Walker-LeCarré. Published in Paris. So predictable. He had a French father. Here they are." She opened the work in question on the librarian's table and tested the first line of the text with a finger, as if it were burning evidence. "And they're good. See, the more complete of the two, is in English. Interlibrary loan just ended my career."

"Oh Darcey, I'm so sorry."

"Yeah," she agreed, her eyes glued to the floor, to the certainty of the patterned designs of the library carpet.

"You could still write about him. Find a theme, like you say."

"It won't be the same, you know? I wanna work on something special. A find that's my own. It doesn't have to be a major figure. Just someone really talented. And if it was the first time…but it's all dead ends. There must be someone I can write about."

"I know, I know. Hit an unlucky patch, huh? It happens. But you can always default to the masters, can't you? Perhaps write from a new perspective? Everyone enjoys the masters."

"No way, Abby. Can't imagine one more work on Dali, Kahlo, or Pollock. I refuse to be one of those scholars who makes stuff up to write about it in beautiful prose. You know, sometimes a red vase is just a red vase, and if there's anything left untouched in the work of these icons, trust me—it will be a meaningless red vase."

"A vase would be kind of hard in the case of Pollock, but point taken." Abby lifted her shoulders and then released them, sighing.

"Jeez, Abby. I'm sorry. I'm being awful."

The librarian patted Darcey's shoulder. "No worries. I get it. I'm sorry too. Really. But you'll get over this. You'll see."

She wished she felt the same, but in her experience when things started to unravel, they usually continued to loosen into oblivion, and she couldn't deny unraveling was a theme in her life right then.

"I doubt it. You know what's worse? I need to go tell Donaldson. I've been toying with the idea of dropping out. I've got a lot going on. I have to…never mind, I'm not going to burden you with the details. This seals it. I'd promised myself this was my last try. I've had it."

"What are you going to do?"

"Go back and help my parents. Find a job teaching children. Use my Master's degree for something."

"They'll understand, and if that's what you want…"

"It will have to be." She caressed the cover of the book she had cursed minutes before and thought of how much she wished the work was her own. Horrible envy caused her cheeks to burn, and, in her stomach, an uncomfortable anxious feeling settled. Donaldson would not be pleased to hear she was quitting. Neither would her parents. Archie even less. But she had to think of her daughter, of her unemployed dad. And it was not like she could count on Nina's father, the perpetually aspiring musician, for anything.

"Maybe this wasn't for me," she repeated to Abby.

"Give it some time. Think it over. Oh, by the way, we're doing a fundraiser to get books for local schools." Abby patted the lid of a large jar full of bills and coins.

Darcey reached into her pocket. Inside was a five-dollar bill she had put there the day before. Food money. She put it into the jar anyway.

The books needed to go on a shelf and the notes in the garbage. She would then speak to Donaldson. Gently. The idea filled her stomach with stones.

She rehearsed the least damaging words in her head while she said goodbye to Abby. She packed her things, looked around once more, inhaling all the dignity of writers and artists past, and left toward the department she was about to desert.

As she trudged back to school, she pictured her father and his benevolent face, the remaining white wisps of what was once a headful of dark hair framing the kind, droopy eyes. She could almost hear his words. "It isn't such a big deal you don't get to be a PhD. Lots of people don't. Did you know that eighty percent of people who give up on their doctorate do it at the dissertation stage?" Yes, she did. She loved that her father always tried to console her, but in this case, the thought didn't make her feel better.

On the other side of campus, the tan stone building housing the Art History Department of Mellenberg University looked at Darcey disapprovingly from behind the naked trees, so lush in the summer but now so vulnerable under a sky gray with winter snow. Those trees—it was as if they could guess she was about to crack under the weight of failure—and their branches reached out to her, encircling her limbs, and making her immobile. "You're losing your mind," she muttered to herself.

At the entrance of the Department's building, students climbed the steps beside her, as if it were the most natural move. She felt disconnected, tunnel vision taking over, making the university as immaterial as a puff of air. She wished she was home, telling her daughter a bedtime story, helping her mother with housework and her father with the bills. She missed her original home too, with all its hiding places and secret nooks. The den with the removable floorboard where she kept her diary. The tree in the backyard, with its protective top and dancing leaves tinted silver when the sun hit just right. She had fallen in love with art and its history under that tree, with the help of the books she got at the public library. Her bedroom, the one she had begged her parents not to paint pink, but blue. She got aqua instead. Her little easel had been in the corner, holding her beginner paintings so that they were visible from her bed as soon as she woke up.

She recalled her parents in the house too, in not-so-good moments. They were arguing downstairs. It was the last time she remembered her dad bringing roses home. They probably assumed she was asleep.

"We're not getting Darcey a puppy."

Her father responded with his melodic Portuguese accent, the one which became more pronounced when he was upset. "*Ora, pois*. She is an only child. It will keep her company."

"Damn it. This is not the way things were supposed to be," her mother retorted.

"It's been eight years!" her father said. "You get over it. You have a daughter." He was trying to contain his voice, whispering and shouting at the same time, but Darcey could hear. She sat at the top of the stairs, looking down on them.

"I know, but it's hard," her mother replied, picking up the photo of the twins from the mantel. "My little boy. He was so handsome, hardly cried at all. And Darcey's not always easy. She gets distant, as if she is in her own world."

"This is nonsense." Her father was often ready to defend her. "Darcey's a great child. Very smart. Of course he was a wonderful baby too, but he was so sickly." He paused, as if choked up. "Such a difficult month until he slipped away. You have to move on. His heart was weak. The doctors tried their best. We did everything we could. You know what? I'm not talking to you about this anymore. Darcey is alive. Just try to remember that. *Ora, pois.*" He walked away and turned on the TV, his favorite escape when things in the real world became too hard to bear.

Darcey was to blame for the fight. She never forgot it, and she gave up on the idea of the dog. Maybe it was just a need to name a date for their decline that caused her to think that after that night, they had become increasingly withdrawn, and her father had had trouble holding on to jobs. And Darcey never stopped thinking that maybe, had things been reversed, if her brother was the one with the aqua room, her parents would have been happier.

There were, of course, moments of contentment. Trips in the car to warm places on the coast. Her mother's sardine sandwiches and lemonade within arm's reach in the back seat. Dinner outside by the barbecue grill, after which her dad would get out his guitar and play the *fado*. Those moments were infrequent and far apart, though. Happiness only became more consistent in the household once Nina was in their lives.

"Hey Darcey, good class yesterday. I wish all my instructors loved their subjects like you do. Your class is a lot of fun."

Letting her memories fade, she smiled at the skinny student she recognized from a course she taught. He had his arm wrapped around a pretty young woman. She thought of Archie and the kiss he planted on her cheek the first time they met, so many years before. Archie would never have walked out on them. She felt a pang in her chest, noticing the shabby sadness of her red flannel shirt and the flowing oversized wrap she'd knitted when she should have been writing. Darcey wanted to say to the boy, "Help me out of this mess," but just said "thank you" and waved, watching him walk away, his head still turned, smiling at her.

When her toes started to numb inside her thin socks, Darcey reluctantly put one foot in front of the other until the snowy edges of the stairs disappeared, and she found herself under the golden light of the hall. "C'mon, Darcey. You can do this. You are stronger than you think. Just tell him you're leaving. It'll take only a few seconds."

The old entrance hall was heavily lit. It was like being inside a giant bulb. On the walls, alumni smiled at her from their polished frames. There were teachers, writers, artists, all posing proudly in their places of work, or surrounded by what they loved the most—books, brushes, and blackboards. She had often fantasized about being portrayed among them. She would bring Nina to school one day and point at her photo saying, "Look how young I looked." She sighed and climbed up to the second floor. Her boots trod the length of the hall as if they were keeping her from falling off a tight circus rope. Donaldson had a corner office, a perk reserved for senior professors. The office was alive with the sounds of Liszt, and she followed the music there.

Donaldson's office was always neat. Large wood crates kept records, canvases, and office materials organized. Dark-leather chairs at a corner gave the room a masculine quality. Behind his desk long shelves contained papers, books, the occasional art display, and a few Cézanne and Chagall reproductions. e dwelled in a universe of surrealism, modernism, cubism, and other -isms of artistic importance.

His face lit up with recognition and, from behind his white, well-trimmed beard, he smiled.

"Any progress this week? Did you settle on a theme for the French guy?" He wasn't one to waste time with pleasantries or pretenses.

Darcey hoped she would not break into high pitch, the kind she found hard to control when she was lying or nervous. She tried to make the words "I quit" form, but she couldn't. The finality of that statement caused her voice to falter. She went for the long road instead. "Not really. I have nothing concrete. Only some general thoughts that could perhaps turn into something."

Perhaps? The vagueness of the "somethings" and "nothings" pierced Darcey's own ears like little shavings of glass. She knew Donaldson wasn't a fool. Still, courage eluded her. If she told him about Nina, perhaps he would understand.

"I see." He brought his hands together and let the tips of his fingers rest on one another, holding on to the silence. The music in the background did not make up for lack of conversation. He rocked back and forth, causing the old fifties-style chair to whimper.

The annoying squeak prompted Darcey to speak again. "I mean, they're just thoughts for now." She guessed he wouldn't see more clearly through her if she was made of water.

He grabbed that silence again and used it like a noose. He wasn't going to make this easy, was he? He could be more incisive with that flat smile than a gangster with a threat. She was expected to speak, commit, contest, or simply make a decision. For a moment, she feared he would kick the chair, leave her hanging, or she would have to continue lying to fill the silence. Her ears buzzed, and Liszt murmured in the background, like the whispers of people issuing disapproving reviews at a play.

"I have a proposition for you." He sat back, looking away, and Darcey could finally breathe again. She almost thanked him. He reached into a drawer, which opened with considerable screeching, and produced an old pipe.

Darcey crossed her arms and rehearsed her most censorious face, chin down, raised eyebrows. He should know better, and she loved him too much not to care about his health.

"Don't give me that look. I know your mother doesn't approve." He played with the pipe in his hands. Donaldson and her mom had once, long before, been sweethearts. The romance had fizzled, but the friendship and the caring hadn't. Darcey felt guilty for not allowing her mom to tell him about the baby. She didn't want him to feel obligated to make things easy for her because she had a child.

"No, she doesn't."

"She would not approve of your procrastination either, and yet…"

"Touché."

Touché a million times. If she had finished her degree and found a good position, she could take care of everyone. It was a lot of ifs, and coulds, and yet knowing so did nothing to ease that weight on her chest. It was her fault that her life had gotten so out of hand. What was that compared to a little smoking?

Donaldson lit the pipe with the dexterity of many seasons of practice and the certainty of the upper hand. Smoke formed and disintegrated midair like her bad ideas.

"I don't know if you heard, but Browne might be retiring," he said.

He blew more smoke into the air. It jetted out of his mouth into a fast, white line. He seemed to be challenging her with these silent intervals.

"You need to be done, Darcey. I trust you."

He didn't know how right he was about the first part, and how misguided about the second. It was time to finish, to move on. Only she wouldn't be leaving with an actual degree. There would be no graduation cake with one of those silly plastic caps on top. Blue icing, the kind that stained fingers and tongues, would not spell congratulations on a layer of frosting. She would not be renting an oversized gown previously worn by PhD candidates more successful than her. She would simply pack and go, like a drifter.

She would be disappointing important people: her parents, Donaldson, Archie, her Aunt Lucile, Nina, who'd one day realize her failure. It wasn't an extensive list, but they were all people she cared about, whose opinion of her mattered. Worse yet, she would disappoint herself. Her stomach tightened, and her mouth became really dry.

"You understand what I'm saying to you, right?" he asked.

"That I need to be done. I get it."

"About Browne, I mean. In the department, there's talk of hiring an assistant professor. Cheaper and more teaching done. Still a good arrangement, with lots of time for research."

"That's nice. A good position for whoever gets it."

"If you were done, you could apply. Everyone likes you here, thinks you're a great teacher. My word counts quite a bit, too. But you need to write that dissertation. You need to defend your prospectus as soon as possible."

"Me? Work here, like permanently? But I study in the department. Isn't this against the rules?" A jolt of hope electrified her body.

"It's uncommon, but not unheard of. It's no secret Browne's not a people person. That has caused a lot of problems. Yet you are. People like you, but…."

"…but I need to finish."

"Yes, you need to finish. We might have even found a topic for you. That is, if you haven't settled on that other one yet. The French guy you always talk about."

The electricity vanished, giving way to a pang of surprise and suspicion. "No, I haven't. Who's we?"

"Me and Archie." He said it like it was the most trivial thing in the world. Like he and Archie were best friends, who planned everything together.

Her legs wobbled. Good thing she was sitting down. "Archie? What's he got to do with anything?"

Donaldson stretched his arms, like he was waking up from a nap. He continued in a casual tone. "He came to see me. He needs some help with a few family documents. He thought I could critique the art before he talked to you about his materials."

"What materials? What art? This is making zero sense."

"He can explain it to you better. It's about one, gosh, I'm sure I'll pronounce it wrong—Ana Valquíria Eça. A Brazilian relative. Active in the arts of 1920s Brazil. Some great works. Obscure, though, I'm afraid. Famous for only a season. But I guess you could play around with her story, see if there is any theme that can help you put together a thesis. I don't have to tell you that Ana lived in a period of great creativity and reinvention for Brazilian arts, a period any art historian should be happy to write about."

"The Modern Art Week of 1922. Brazil, Mexico, Argentina. New art was happening everywhere."

"Good. You get it. You can draw parallels. You can do cultural analyses. It is a great topic for a dissertation." His voice was like chocolate tobacco, masculine with steadiness and a hint of flavor. It carried the promise of an enticing treat, but in the end, it delivered the poison that would ultimately rust your blood.

It was impossible to argue with him. Let alone tell him she was quitting. But she couldn't allow herself to dream this was a lifeline. The temptation was great, and it made the promise of discovering a new artist exciting. The prospect of crafting a future for Nina even greater. But she had been down that path before. There was simply no more time. She had wasted a whole year, which meant she was a year behind. Her family needed her now.

"Be done, Darcey. Apply for the job when it becomes available. By then, five months from now, you can be at that stage we like to call 'all but dissertation,' and then six months after that, you graduate."

Of course she was excited about a new artist. She lived for the excitement of discovery, for the first time she saw a new painting, but this was different. She nibbled on her nails. "I don't know if all is as neat as you make it out to be. That's *actually* a very short time. Most people take at least two years. I just can't."

"Can't or won't? It is enough time if you really want this. Look, you are in need of a topic. These documents are in need of translation. Archie needs help. Unlike you, he doesn't know any Portuguese, and he's not an expert in art. But this is important to him. Something about his grandpa's legacy. You'll have to talk to him to know more. It is a perfect marriage of convenience. Just do it. We'll see where it all takes you." e tired of the pipe and threw it on the table with a sigh. "Are we good?"

The words "Archie" and "marriage" uttered so close together sent a funny feeling down her spine and undisguised warmth up her cheeks. It would be great to spend time with him, but the proximity would be dangerous. The attraction was still there, and she had it up to here with men. She was pretty sure his mother wouldn't approve if she knew they would be working together, much less if she was meddling with family affairs. And she wouldn't have anyone make her feel embarrassed for having Nina.

Donaldson stood up, walked toward the window behind his desk, and looked out into the yard, fogging the glass. For a second, Darcey imagined he would make a smiley face out of the moisture that formed, but that would have looked bizarre under the circumstances. None of the available alternatives would make her happy. There was nothing even remotely worthy of a smile in her situation.

"If you think it's a good idea…" she heard herself say while her mind tried to convince her to backtrack and tell him about quitting. Hope was a treacherous emotion to feed.

He came back to her, his shoulders loose and smile soft now that the business part of the conversation was over. "You know I worry about you as if you were my own daughter, right? I promised your mother I would look after you while you were here, but I have to say you don't make my job easy. Half of the time I don't know what you're thinking, and the other half I'm worried because I *do* know."

She looked down and played with her cuticles. He had no idea what was at stake here. For a moment, she let herself be lulled by the idea of sharing the weight of her secrets with him, having him come to her and put a protective hand on her shoulder and say, "It's gonna be all right." She finally lifted her chin. "I know. I'm sorry. I really think I need to call it a day." In her head, a tug of war was taking place. One side pulled her to quit already and start her life. The other tugged at her heart and demanded that she succumb to the dream. And truly what kind of life could she expect if she quit her degree?

"Good. Take the idea home with you, play some jazz or, if you want to be in the atmosphere of the time, some *chorinho*, make some nice coffee, and consider this proposition. How about getting back to me in a couple of days? That's all I am asking—nothing more, okay?"

"Okay." Heavy blinds now closed the truth-telling window of opportunity. She was tongue-tied. She placed a few books in her tattered messenger bag, running her fingers through the dry and cracked leather. The bag had seen better days. Everything was crumbling.

"All right," she finally said without conviction, letting her mind drift away.

Let Donaldson think she would look into this. It'd buy her time. But she had other plans to put in motion now. She needed to raise money, and her Aunt Lucile's was the only signature she could see on a check. Maybe she could save her parents' house. And maybe if the check was big enough she could stay in school and see this through. Or maybe she could leave grad school with a small fragment of dignity even if she was leaving without a degree. She could eventually help Archie as a friend with the translation—do it as a favor. And maybe, with any luck, she would be able to tell Donaldson—and Archie—that this time, the only time discovery had knocked on her door, fate was wrong: Ana Valquíria Eça's story was meant to be someone else's find.

Chapter 4
Ana

São Paulo, January 10, 1922

When Ana left home on that ripe summer morning, the month of January was almost half done. The street market already pulsated with the rhythmic hustle of maids and merchants, like the heart of a person freshly in love.

Today, Ana made her way through the stalls a little faster than usual. She had good reason to be cheerful, unfocused, and full of anticipation. Joaquim said he would be waiting by her studio at eight. He would bring his breathless kisses, his confident caresses, and she would lose herself in the dizziness of that affair.

She had once more slid into her outfit with the same care that she devoted to preparing her palette of paints. The dress, now a regular witness to their encounters, was fluid and loose around the waist, as fashion demanded. Her dark brown *garçonette* hair was adorned with a tan grosgrain ribbon and a clip that shone under the light of the morning sun.

She lived in a cul-de-sac near *Rua General Osório* where the market was located. She loved being close to the train station and the park, the place where São Paulo's pulse throbbed with activity. It was a city that now breathed new air, a city that had shattered

European art and collaged it back into a new whole.

"Olha a fruta, Dona Ana," one of the vendors hollered, calling her attention to the baskets of fruit. He stuck his chest out like a peacock, proud of his stall; the way he had cradled the apples in soft tissue and arranged the papayas over a bed of newspapers inside a basket was evidence of that.

Ana knew all the vendors—many by name, others only by face. She spoke to each of them like one speaks to friends.

The walk through the market was part of her work practice: the lush green grain of the acacia trees that lined the way, the colorful chirping of the morning birds, the close-to-unbearable pink of the azaleas— those were all sources of inspiration for her paintings. She caught herself in the fantasy that she could squeeze their colors out with her bare hands, letting them drip into paint cans for later use. Brazilian nature was so pregnant with color and texture that transforming it into art wasn't a job. It wasn't a chore. It was a responsibility, a commitment to be entered like a pact.

"Plínio, one day I'll turn this very street market into a brilliant painting," she said, accepting the invitation to get more fruit. "I will paint the beautiful fruit you sell."

Hearing those words, Plínio changed his posture even further. He became a rare bird now, engorged with self-respect and pleased that for the first time his little corner of that urban kingdom was worthy of praise. "Thank you, Dona Ana," he said.

She picked a persimmon and bit into its pulp. The red, ripe fruit overflowed with savory juice, and she only noticed she was squeezing it too hard when its contents ran down her elevated arm toward the exposed valley of her elbow.

Women now could free their shapely limbs. Two decades into the new century had been enough to extinguish some old notions of propriety. Nude arms were now as common at the market as tropical fruit. It was a welcome development given the early hours already announced the kind of heavy, damp heat to be expected by midday.

The incubating high temperatures didn't weigh her down. Ana felt as light as a fallen leaf, dancing suspended by the hint of a generous breeze. Plínio handed her the vegetables she bought. The produce was heavy in her hands, but her heart was weightless in her chest. If she let go of the bag, chances were she would float like a balloon all over downtown.

With a start, she realized she was late. Joaquim might have to wait for her. In her mind, she used that pretext to punish him for his guilt. For his part in their affair. Maybe he would have to sit in the square across the street and hide his striking, culpable face behind a newspaper and yearn for her. Good.

But a cloud of concern dimmed her little imaginary revenge. Maybe he would not wait, and she would find herself in the middle of the street, beleaguered with fruit, a sad orange rolling away from her feet.

She rushed from the market and into the little *vila* where her studio was located, nasty images, the stuff of nightmares, now plaguing her walk. She imagined him walking away, unaffected by her absence, already considering what to do next, what tasks he might have for the day.

None of it happened of course. She didn't have to

collect falling fruit. Joaquim had no newspaper with him, and he hadn't walked across the street to the square. He simply stood in front of her doorstep against the cobalt blue door, one hand cradling his hat and the other stretching the left side of his suspenders. He had the suave temperament of a radio star.

His smile was broad and inviting. He looked around to make sure the street was deserted before coming close. His forbidden kiss tasted as sweet as fruit. He took the heavy bag from her, trying to be gentlemanly as they disappeared behind the blue door. His shoulders sheltered her, and he placed a protective hand at the nape of her neck. He said the unnecessary endearing nothings that he liked to pass off as seduction. She was used to discarding any make-believe innocence one block away from the studio. No need for pretending this was anything other than an affair.

Or so she told herself every day.

She had been deliberate in seeking out Joaquim's attention, reasoning an artist needed life experience and emotional depth. He had been a fixture at the arts events of the city, and his masculine yet suave disposition had attracted her from the moment she first saw him. She hadn't considered how she might fall in love and how his inevitable leaving would make her feel. Sooner or later, all lovers left. That much she did know.

Five large canvases and two smaller ones displaying bright-color compositions of flowers and people greeted the couple when they came in. They were guests of a fancy, exclusive gathering, a party of disproportionate shapes and new forms which encircled them from the walls. Ana and Joaquim abandoned their belongings and residual inhibitions by the door and looked at the paintings as if their eyes brought the art into existence.

"I don't see anything new. These are all old friends. The gentleman with the purple cravat, the farmer drying his coffee. My favorite—you." He pointed at the largest canvas. "Is the still life not ready?" Joaquim asked.

"Not yet. Very soon."

A self-portrait hung from an iron nail high up near the ceiling. In the picture, Ana sat on a maroon couch and wore a strapless, bright green dress. Her face was made unrecognizable by the nature of her brush strokes—thick and angled—and by the asymmetry of features, her limbs and her chest. Her deep ebony bobbed hair, however, was unmistakable.

"Can't wait." He smiled, the double meaning of the comment evident, and took in his surroundings one more time.

Ana's studio was a refuge in a small and old building sheltered from the increased velocity of a city that grew like abundant ivy. It was hard to imagine that this quiet little street was just a block away from a busy avenue. Besides the maroon couch eternalized in her painting, the undersized alcove that served as a bedroom had an antique farm-style armoire, a dark-wood dresser with a mirror full of age spots, a side table carrying a gramophone on top, and a large luxurious bed with an antique-gold headboard. This last item, Joaquim kept eying while she, humming in the little kitchen nook, brewed fresh coffee. He chose a record, and a soft *chorinho* started playing. He finally sat on the couch.

"Can you stay through lunch?" she asked between songs.

"I'm sorry, we have a meeting at the newspaper, and I'm supposed to be there by ten-thirty. Big week for the arts."

She brushed off her annoyance almost as soon as she became aware of it. "More time for me to paint."

"Maybe we could do something later in the week. My wi—"

"Go ahead Joaquim. Finish what you were saying. I can hear the word 'wife' without fainting. You should know that by now."

"I know you can," he conceded. "My wife might visit with her sister this weekend. We could go out to dinner."

"Fine. But maybe I'll be busy." Maybe I will make myself unavailable, unreachable, unapproachable, she thought. "I had only planned for today, you see."

She gave him her back, and she scrubbed the little kitchen sink that was speckled with coffee. The rag in her hand moved around in fast circles, the kind she saved for big messes. Cups and saucers emerged from the little cabinet while she tried to keep her mind steady. On turning to face Joaquim, she realized he had quietly made his way to her. Her arms wrapped around his body, almost as if by their own deliberation, right before she was overpowered by the pressure of his lips against hers. His fingers undid the buttons at the nape of her neck, and the silky fabric of her dress caressed her shoulders as it slid off.

At that moment, someone knocked on the door, and Ana instinctively held her breath. She didn't bother covering her body, which his caresses had exposed, because she didn't anticipate opening the door.

She exchanged an inquisitive look with Joaquim and placed her index finger over her lips. He nodded. No appointments. No visitors. No clients. Not many people came to see her at the atelier, much less in the morning. That usual solitude was part of the reason they met there. But the reality of it was, nights were his family time—chicken stew, radio programs, a cigar in the *varanda*. It was an obvious scenario. The mistress got the odd hours. It shouldn't be the case, but she was mad, as if this foregone conclusion had suddenly and finally come to her.

After a couple of minutes, the uninvited guest gave up.

"You must go now, Joaquim. Leave." She would rather paint. The interruption had spoiled everything, caused her to think about his cozy evenings and life without her. It was her prerogative to change her mind and do as she pleased, even if it was just to prove a point. She was independent and free. No man would own her.

"What? We just got here, *coração*."

"I need to paint, to be alone. Leave."

He clenched his jaw, and the muscles in his face contracted. When he spoke, his voice was raspy and low.

"I won't be able to come back this week, not until my wife travels."

"It doesn't matter. I have a lot of work to do anyway. I forgot to tell you. I was invited to show my paintings in an exhibit, and I have less than a month to prepare. Go, Joaquim." She smiled even though her fingers itched to break a piece of china or two.

His face relaxed a bit, and his voice regained its usual velvety quality. "But you know I love you." He lit a cigarette and stared out the window. "Look, there is a handsome if serious woman walking away. I think the knock on the door was hers."

She brought both hands to her head, "Damn it. Eugênia. I completely forgot. And now it's too late. I'm not going to run after her with you here. Just go, Joaquim."

She left him for the small bathroom and for the red *robe de chambre* that she kept hanging from the door. It was spotless even though she wore it often when she worked. She was a neat painter, almost clinical.

Ana came back in time to see the door slowly shut and engulf the stream of sunlight that for a minute crept into the room and onto the wood floor. Of Joaquim, she only saw the hatted shadow, like the men's in the market, against the translucence of the closed curtains.

Better this way. Falling in love with him hadn't been in her plans and was now a liability. If only she could resist his kisses, forget his caresses. She picked up her brush and went to work. She wasn't going to waste the skill and talent she knew she had because of the courage and willpower she was starting to suspect she lacked.

Chapter 5
Darcey

Darcey left Donaldson's office, torn between hope and burnout. She couldn't afford either. She brought her hand to her head and fluffed her shaggy hair. She needed focus. So she walked across campus and concentrated on breathing, the rhythm of the activity finally calming her down. An hour after the interview with Donaldson, she entered a mammoth early twentieth-century house, built by an industrialist who wanted to impress his young wife. Had they ever guessed that one day it would serve as a fancy retirement community?

Inside, the mansion smelled of talcum powder and lilies. It had long, impressive aisles and deep burgundy carpets matching the patterns of the gigantic flower vases.

Darcey shook the snow off her shoes so as not to stain the immaculate floors.

A woman with hygienic-looking, sensible shoes put on her best business-like demeanor.

Can I help you?" said her deep yet gentle voice at the threshold of the main vestibule.

"Yes, please. I am here to see Lucile Bellevue. Am I too late in the day?"

"No, follow me, please."

The nurse walked a step or two ahead of Darcey.

She wore an equally sensible brown skirt and an old-fashioned silk blouse that made her look like a vintage schoolteacher. She talked without gazing at Darcey. "Are you family?"

"She's my aunt. Are you new here?"

"I have only been here for the last week."

Despite the initial boost in confidence, now that the time of the actual mission approached, tart angst rose from the pit of her belly. How she was going to broach what she had come to ask? When she first decided to see her aunt, she hadn't known how much worse her situation would get throughout the day.

Lucile's quarters were comfortable, more like a luxurious apartment. The lavish, golden wallpaper was yet another indication that retirement home could mean very different things to different people.

Lucile sat on a velvet sofa, with her back toward the door. She wore her silver hair in a low ponytail held together by a bone-colored barrette. Darcey's aunt was fifteen years older than her mother, the baby of the family.

"Book's on the side table where you left it."

"Hi, Aunt Lucile."

"Come here where I can see you better. You're here to read for me?"

Her aunt could be curt, but there was excitement in Lucile's voice. Darcey was always welcome. One of the nurses had once talked about how fondly Lucile spoke of her to others. "She counts the hours until you get here," the nurse had claimed. Not that the old lady would ever confess any of that to Darcey.

"Well, in a moment if you wish. Are you okay? This place still treats you right?"

Lucile stretched her arms. "Yes. It's the best money can buy, isn't it?"

"I wouldn't know." Darcey's voice came out more exasperated than she expected.

Her aunt tilted her head to study Darcey. "You're looking pale. Are you eating enough? Don't tell me you're on a diet. Young women are always dieting."

"No, not on a diet. Just overworked a bit."

"You have something on your mind, don't you? I hear it in your voice."

Good, it was better if Lucile could sense how tense she was. "As a matter of fact, I do. Can we talk?"

"We can always talk. You know you are my favorite niece."

"I'm your only niece. Uncle Bob only had nephews on this side of the family."

"Well, regardless. If there were more, you'd still be my favorite. You're profound and serious, with that crease in your forehead that tells the story of how you're always thinking."

"A fine trait that is."

"What's that?"

"Never mind." Darcey came closer. "Speaking of serious, I've got something to talk to you about." She fumbled and played with a pillow before delivering the short, dreaded word. "Mom."

"Oh." Lucile's shoulders sank, and her chest caved in. A second later, she puffed out her sternum. "I don't think I can be bothered to know."

"She's your sister. I don't care that you don't talk. She needs you now. We all do. She's going to lose the house, and it's all my fault. They took an extra mortgage because of me and Nina. They tried to ride the job crisis, but they can't anymore."

"Well, I'm very sorry to hear. I will, of course, help you with Nina. I always have. But about your mother…" Lucile walked toward the window and grabbed a watering can. There were five pots of daffodils lined to perfection on the sill; she watered each with surgical precision.

"But Nina lives with them. Help for her is help for them, don't you think? So technically, you're already helping."

"I don't see it that way. The money is intended for Nina, and I trust you to use it for that purpose. I can do nothing beyond that."

Darcey didn't want to show how desperate she felt, but it was impossible. Her voice trembled despite her effort to steady it. "Of course there is something you can do. They probably need about a hundred thousand. That amount is nothing to you but everything to us. I'll pay you back. You know I will. But at the moment, I only make ten thousand dollars a year from my teaching assistantship. What is that? A month here?"

"That's not the point."

"The point is I need you. Nina needs you. And trust me, it's not easy to ask. If you help me, I can help them." Darcey walked toward Lucile and her daffodils. She touched a leaf. It was cold against her hand. "I'll never understand what the deal between you two is."

"You don't have to understand." Lucile shrugged.

"Are you two ever going to tell me what happened? You realize that if I hadn't sought you out when I was a teenager, we wouldn't even have become acquainted? And even if she did something terrible in the past, does she deserve to lose her home now?"

Lucile smiled tenderly at Darcey. "Well, that you sought me out is one of the biggest joys of my life." Then she let the smile fade. "And she can tell you any time if she wishes. I have nothing to tell. It's not a matter of deserving. It just won't do."

"Urgh! You know that I love you and I respect you, but you two are like children!"

"The answer is no. I'm pretty sure she doesn't know you're here asking, does she?"

"No." Darcey scratched her head.

"See? What do you think she'd do if you showed up with that kind of money coming from me?"

Darcey sighed. "I don't even know why I tried." She walked back to the sofa but didn't sit down. Instead, she toddled around it, like a child playing musical chairs. "Let's think about it differently. You give me some of my trust fund money, and then I will be the one helping them."

"You'll get to do what you please with your trust fund money one day in the remote future. I'm still here, you know? You understand time is passing? You're turning twenty-seven, an event which if I'm not mistaken is happening in a month, isn't it? You should be focusing on finishing your PhD."

"How can I do that if all I have is problems to solve? You know there are mitigating circumstances outside of my control."

"Which are?"

"You know…on top of having no money, being torn between school and Nina, having just discovered I wasted a whole year on the wrong painter."

"Darcey, if you came here to try and make me feel sorry for you, you're wasting your time. There's a reason why Uncle Bob and I didn't just give you a bunch of money. Now if we were to sit down and list all the impediments that could lead us to fail, no one would ever accomplish anything, would they?"

"But you know I don't care about money."

"And yet you're here asking me for it. There are different ways of caring about money. It's not always about fancy cars or shiny jewelry."

"So your answer is no?" It wasn't fair, but she was desperate enough to play the Nina card a little further. "Not even for Nina?" She bit her lip. She hated using her daughter like that. Darcey paced the floor, trying to think fast. Was there any way to change Lucile's mind? She was not good at being deceitful. She would not fake tears or tell a lie to get what she wanted, but maybe the tears would come naturally given her great worry. Her mind went blank.

"I'll tell you what. How about I give you the hundred thousand if you finish your dissertation? You'll have to figure out how to get to that point. You can hate me if you want. I'd be sad if you did, but I'd survive."

"You'd do that?"

"Only because you're my favorite." Lucile smiled.

Darcey grabbed her hair at the roots, sliding her hands back from her forehead, and grunted. Was Lucile toying with her? In her mind, an image of Ana Valquíria Eça materialized. Of course, she didn't know what she looked like yet, but she saw a slim, elegant woman, with the face of a porcelain doll. She wore a red, silky flapper dress, loose at the waist and sequined at the bottom.

"So if I finish the degree, the money will be mine

to do what I want?"

"Yes, and that includes giving it to your parents, tearing it in a million pieces, or giving it all to a cat sanctuary."

Did Ana really have artistic merit? Were her work and her life worth studying? Would working with Archie be a good idea?

"Where is that boyfriend of yours?" Lucille asked, as if reading her thoughts.

The image of Ana vanished. A new one of Archie flooded in. She saw the two of them holding hands and looking happy. He had just bought her ice cream. Strawberry. Her favorite. She ran her fingers over her eyes and made it all go away.

"Archie isn't my boyfriend, Lucile, and you know that. He belongs with some rich heiress, a woman from his circle, at least if his mother can have it her way. Not someone who has to beg her aunt for money. Besides, I'm done with men."

"Nonsense. I may be going blind, but that doesn't mean I can't see what is in front of me. You two are bound to be together. I knew it the first time you brought him to me. I could hear it in his voice, and you know what? In yours too. You fought it the first time around, and what happened? Flynn. I'm not going to say horrible things about him, but only because he's Nina's father, and she is a little miracle. But if you're trying to prove something to yourself by keeping Archie away—that you're tough or independent—stop now. There is no virtue in this kind of sacrifice. It's not tough, and it's not smart. To love fully, you must be way tougher."

"I see." Perhaps if she stayed quiet, Lucile would

cut the lecture short. Only it didn't work.

"Let me tell you a story for a change. There was once this young woman, let's call her...Adele. Adele was in love with this young man, but he was going to war. Vietnam. So she decided it was best to let him go before he left. If he came back, well, that would be another story, now wouldn't it? But to wait and write, and hope...that, she didn't want to do. She didn't want to risk it. He came back, married her, and for over forty years, I had to hear him say again and again that I had been too spineless to put my heart where it belonged in the first place."

"I thought this story was about Adele."

"You know what I mean. What I'm saying is that you might not be so lucky. He might not be there when you finally decide to give it a chance."

"I guess we'll have to wait and see. And haven't you heard I am done with men?"

"Nonsense again. If you're waiting until you're a rich woman to feel some sense of equal footing with Archie, you risk losing him. He's a handsome and kind young man. And however charming, you're not the only fascinating young woman in the world. You understand at least that, right?"

"Yeah, I do. But I'm too busy to even think about that now. Besides, he wouldn't want a woman with a child when he can have anyone else."

"You are so stubborn."

Darcey finally smiled. "Jeez, I wonder where that comes from..."

"No need to be sarcastic. Now go. No need for stories from books today, either. You will come back soon, won't you? Or are you so cross you'll be giving me the cold shoulder?"

"No, no cold shoulder. How about next week? And about the money, it's a deal." She thought of Donaldson, Nina, and Ana Valquíria. She owed the first a dissertation, the second a good life, and the third…well, the third she would have to figure out. She lifted her arms and then let them fall to the sides of her body. "See you in a week. As it turns out, I'll be in town."

Chapter 6
Eugênia

Had she taken the train, Eugênia would only have arrived in São Paulo at lunch time. She would have been tired, covered in thin, red dust. But a neighbor and his daughter were going to a wedding and kindly offered her a ride in their car. She left Americana in the comfort of the leather seat of a Blériot-Whippet.

They traveled right before dawn, when the sky offered the first glimpse of hope for a new day and the roosters crowed their first songs. To Eugênia, the early morning air was like an embrace that suspended the world in a gentle peace, and so she enjoyed the ride, the fields filled with coffee plants and wheatgrass shining at first light, and the wind on her face. The changing scenery provided more entertainment than she had anticipated. Soon, the bucolic landscape gave way to the steel metropolis, and Eugênia couldn't wait to slide out of the car and look at shop windows and coffee houses.

After stopping at a bakery, where some mint tea revived her, Eugênia walked a few blocks to the cul-de-sac where Ana had her studio. She never understood why her friend didn't live and work in the same place. She spent most of her time painting anyway. But there was no point questioning artists. They were part of a different world of magic and dream. She was just glad she got to experience it all. Vicariously, of course.

Eugênia wiggled the doorknob of Ana Valquíria's cobalt blue atelier door. She had already knocked twice. There had been no response.

She mentally revisited the letter she had written to Ana a few weeks before and the reply that arrived in Ana's beautiful handwriting and personal stationery. She was sure she hadn't dreamed any of it. They were supposed to meet right there.

Dear Eugênia,

How wonderful that you are coming to town on the tenth. Please meet me at the atelier as soon as you arrive. I can't wait to see you. I have so much to tell you. I so wish we were neighbors or at least lived in the same place. This distance from you and all the secrets I keep...Have a safe trip.

Till soon,
Your sister and friend,
Ana

She loved that Ana always called her "sister" even though they shared no blood ties. It was Tuesday, January 10, and Ana should have been waiting for her. Eugênia was in town specially to see Ana and to buy sewing supplies. It was one of the inconveniences of the countryside that good fabrics and fine perfume were hard to find.

On the street, kids had gathered to jump rope and kick a soccer ball around. A street vendor carried a tray of *cocadas*, squares of shaved coconut and sugar. A large woman sang while hitting a rug with a broom, sending particles of dust to dance their silvery dance under the sun. Eugênia took her time observing people—such mundane joys that for a second she forgot she was worried.

Eugênia had left her shopping for later and hurried to the studio to hear news from Ana. She had informed Ana of her arrival, and, even if that wasn't the case, her friend should know she preferred traveling in the early morning.

Ana wasn't answering the door. Maybe she thought Eugênia would take the train. That must be it. A cascade of icicles prickled Eugênia's head and neck; she hated to think she'd made a mistake and was in the wrong place at the wrong time. But she knew she was right. She could swear it.

She put the small suitcase down for a minute and, looking around to check if she was alone, wiped her brow with the back of her arm. Maybe she should peek through the window? But she was afraid a gossiping neighbor might see and get the wrong idea. All she wanted was to find her friend.

Ana was the best of friends. Eugênia had proof: a scar in her arm from playing outside and climbing trees. The memory of afternoons telling secrets and brushing each other's hair. She had stored keepsakes from times of lying in the garden, on a blanket, reading poetry and stuffing books with little flowers.

In time, they turned into teenagers who dreamed of art, in Ana's case, and a husband, in hers. Now that they were grown women, they still dreamed of the same things. Maybe one day Ana would introduce her to a charming city man, one that preferred more timid women. Ana was so *chic*. So *nouveau*. Eugênia could never match her friend's charm, but it didn't matter.

She didn't have to. She was happy to be who she was.

Eugênia was traditional. She wanted honor, a house, and a living room worthy of guests. She hated being provincial, but she figured her usual agitation made her look just so. Modern women were supposed to be unmoved and detached. Languid and aloof. Sometimes they even smoked. She was none of those things. She got nauseous at the thought of cigarettes.

She checked her delicate watch, a present Ana had given her on her twenty-first birthday. She cherished that memento now more than ever because, with the distance, the times she could be with her friend were so rare. She put the golden object back in her purse and tapped her shoe on the stone paver. It was a new shoe, with a pointed toe and a pale pink color that matched her stockings and made her feel older and glamorous, even if for just an instant.

She brushed imaginary lint off the dress she had made, with the help of her maid, Leopoldina. It was a polished dress. Still a country girl despite the graceful veneer, she thought, with nothing of Ana's natural elegance, but she knew very few had it. That's what made Ana special.

Her face got hot. Had Ana found something more interesting to do, someone more modern to spend time with?

There was no use in pouting; she was simply going to leave a note, ignore those insinuating thoughts, and hope Ana would find the message in time to join her for the afternoon meal. They would have cake and jams.

Eugênia scribbled a few words in a piece of paper and slid the message under the door. She knocked one more time. Nothing. Picking up her things, she walked the short distance between the cul-de-sac of the studio and the busy intersection where a street cart had just arrived. Climbing on, she took one last look at the cobalt blue door and wondered what secrets Ana was hiding within.

Chapter 7
Darcey

By the time she turned the corner of University Drive and Malcolm Avenue, Darcey was running. Her feet blistered because of her boots. Light sweat beaded on her upper lip despite the cold weather. The university string quartet, a celebrated traveling ensemble, was to play on campus that Friday. The ballroom at the Union, with its etched-glass windows and dark-wood panels, looked festive and inviting. Instead of rows of chairs, the organizers had chosen small tables with chairs around them and flower vases in the center. This was the room that held books talks—favorite occasions for the two of them. Archie got two tickets for the event, and Darcey, after visiting Lucile and hurrying back to campus, was more than fashionably late.

Noticing with relief that everyone was dressed casually, and that her jeans and short-sleeved green blouse would not be out of place, she searched the area for only a second before her eyes fell on the heather-gray cashmere sweater that framed Archie's familiar shoulders. He let his light brown hair grow longer, and it was a becoming style. She pressed her hand against her neck, releasing tense muscles and conflicted thoughts. Since he had been back, his support was what kept her standing some days, but the reality was that she was poor. And now there was Nina, too. She had turned him down for pride before, when many of these problems did not exist. Now, unless she wanted to risk giving the impression she was a gold digger, she needed to keep him at bay.

But since he had joined the student body in the fall, they had been spending a lot of time together. Before that, while he spent his time working for political campaigns and traveling all the time, they spoke on the phone occasionally, but those were superficial conversations. Because her parents moved to the countryside and away from town, keeping secrets had been easier, and she never had the courage to tell him about Nina.

But here they were again. Back to the discomfited dance, the strange tiptoeing around love that had dominated their teenage years, before his short, sketchy relationships and her ill-fated romance that had resulted in the daughter she adored. She was too fragile, financially and emotionally, to even think of trying again, of bringing further instability into her child's life. What if things didn't work out and Nina already thought of Archie as family? What if they became dependent on his money and he felt used?

When it came to being a friend though, Archie was the best in the world—attentive and selfless. So many times on the phone had she tried to tell him the whole story only to have the truth about Nina and Flynn stick in her throat. The Darcey he knew had no baggage and no past. It was better that way.

Five minutes for the concert to start. Archie sat at a table in the corner, a place where he and Darcey had chatted over coffee and croissants several times.

Before approaching, Darcey watched him from a distance. At a neighboring table, three young women took turns trying to flirt with him—one crossed and uncrossed her legs as if unsure of which position made her look better. Another twirled her auburn hair around her finger, while the third produced high-pitched, annoying squeals she tried to pass for outbursts of laughter. Archie remained oblivious, and Darcey let out some air that had frozen in her lungs. Despite her immediate and unreasonable dislike of the three women, she tried to bury the jealousy that their flirtation had unearthed. She had spent the last six months attempting to conceal a lot of feelings.

She reached him from behind and covered his eyes with her hands. She didn't know how many years they had played that game. Letting go, she faced him.

He looked at her, and the whole room lit up. "How did it go? You spoke to Donaldson?"

"I did. He told me about your documents. *You* could've told me."

"I know." He gave her that smile that could melt snow. "Can we talk about this later?" He stood up and offered his hand. The quartet played Tchaikovsky's "Sleeping Beauty Waltz."

Darcey made a face and hid her arms behind her back.

"What?" You won't waltz with me?"

She wanted nothing more than to dance with him. "I wish I could, but you know that story about two left feet, right?"

"Nonsense. Look at all those people over there dancing. None of them is a bona fide Fred Astaire."

She closed her eyes and stretched her arms until

their hands met, sending an electrical charge through her. He was smiling widely now. She let her palm rest in his. They started twirling, giving her multiple chances to step on his toes.

"I'm sorry." She shut her eyes tightly, so as not to see her own ineptitude.

"You're doing fine."

"I'm doing terrible!"

He held her just a little more firmly. "Just trust me and have fun."

She let her body follow the rhythm and concentrated instead on the joy of being in Archie's arms. From that moment, the waltz would be her favorite piece of music, and the place where they danced it would be even more dear to her.

"You look…different." He squinted, as if he was having trouble focusing.

"Different how? Hair's the same. Clothes are old." She looked down, suddenly self-conscious of her outfit.

"No, I don't mean today. I mean, since I've been back. These last few months. I can't place it. There's just something new about you. Something softer."

Darcey could feel her cheeks blushing. Of course there was something new. She was a mother. Her body had changed accordingly. She had experienced indescribable love, intense anxiety, fear, and bliss, often all at the same time. How could she not be different?

"I'm sure I don't know what you mean. I'm the same old Darcey." She touched her short hair and shook it back in place.

When the waltz ended, Archie led her to a large sofa in the adjacent sitting area.

"So you're going to help me?" he said once they

were seated.

"What is this about? Who is this Ana Valquíria?" She placed a pillow behind her back.

"My grandpa Gus's mom. After Gus passed away last month, we settled the inheritance, and I received a box with letters, mementos, and a small diary. The papers are in Portuguese, and I need a translator. I'm super curious to find out what they say. Many are decrepit, with torn pages and dark stains, but others are legible. Over the years, Gus told me bits and pieces of the story of his mother, who was a painter and a flapper in 1920s Brazil. I was a kid, and a lot of it sounded mysterious and fantastical. I'm sure he embellished a lot. He made Brazil feel like a distant, magical land, and I didn't care what parts of the story were true and what were make believe. It was all so exciting."

"I sense a 'but now' coming."

"Yes. There's one. But now I've received this package, and there's a letter from him. It seems he wanted me to find out more—to finish getting to know where he came from. Here's where it turns weird: his lawyer has one additional envelope. My grandfather wanted me to take it to the person I find, in his words, 'at the end of the story.' It's sealed, and I can only open it once I tell the lawyer who the person is.

Darcey scratched her head. "This is all news to me. I loved how Grandpa Gus was a bit eccentric, but I never knew of this story."

"I know. It sounds strange and silly, but Gus was into puzzles and scavenger hunts. I guess everything was a game to him. In a way, he never stopped being a child. I have no idea what it all means, but being that you know Portuguese, and given your need for a dissertation subject, and Ana was one helluva painter, I hoped you might be willing to help me. You can publish anything you like. I just want to understand what Gus wanted. Honor his memory, you know?"

Darcey was quiet for a minute. This project had trouble spelled all over it. Family. Memories. Archie in her life. Could she end up worse off than she already was? She didn't think she could take any more disappointment.

"Are you sure you want to do this?" she asked.

"I don't like to leave anything unfinished. You would be doing me a great favor."

He was looking at her with those transparent eyes that glistened with honesty. She knew him too well. Like that freckle he had just below his left eye, or the way he ran his fingers through his hair when stalling for time.

She touched his hands lightly.

"Let me sleep on it, okay? It's been a long day. Way too long. I better not make decisions when I'm this tired. I promise I'll have an answer tomorrow. Now let's go back to dancing?"

"Do my ears deceive me?" His smile was back on display. "Now you want to dance?"

Her candor should make him happy. "Sure. It wasn't that bad after all." That would allow her extra time to be close to him.

"Darcey Mendes, I will never understand you." Archie led her by the hand back to the ballroom. When the next dance started, he twirled her around, and for the first time in her life, she was a ballerina.

Two hours later, well into the night, Darcey finally got home. Inside her apartment, she changed into sweatpants, turned on the radio, and rehearsed a few steps of the dance with Archie, aided by a pop ballad. She sang the lyrics she could remember. Then she lay on the floor, her stomach so glued to the wood planks that she could feel her insides throbbing.

A heavy South American art history book lay in front of her. It was a volume she had bought at a library sale. There might be references to Ana Valquíria Eça in it.

She opened the book to look at the satiny pages and was lost in thought almost immediately. The colorful modernist images jumped at her from the book. Green oceans and yellow boats. Working men and women, painted in various colors and shapes. Lively nature dotted by the reds and oranges of flowers. Life looked so simple back then, pure.

She was so involved, so utterly adrift in 1922, she didn't notice when the door of her small apartment— which she often forgot to lock—opened. She didn't even hear it creak.

"Busy?" A steady baritone voice called.

Darcey closed the book with a shriek, as if it contained forbidden stories.

"Archie! Don't creep up on me like that! Are you trying to give me a heart attack?" She brought her hand to her chest. To look at him she twisted her body, as if she was engaged in a strange yoga pose.

"Sorry…and no." Behind the box he was carrying, he looked annoyingly handsome, his scarf askew and his hair messy. "I didn't have any milk, and when I was coming back home, I noticed your light was still on. Music was loud. I know we said tomorrow." His excuses were completely forgivable because he gave them with such charm.

"Never mind that. Come here. Got something to show you."

Archie nodded and came over to her.

She jumped to her feet and flipped through the pages of the book. She placed it on the table. "Page one eighty-two. Some tea?" Darcey was already moving to grab him a cup. "Great," she answered her own question before he could.

She put the chipped yellow china next to the sink and continued talking. "Look. There she is. Your great grandma. It's kind of exciting."

He smiled at the first image. "No one's ever written about her, I don't think. Not in detail beyond printing a couple of images like these. Or describing how she vanished from public view. They wouldn't have had this." He looked down. "Here." He handed her the old carton box. It was heavy in her hands. The label on it read 'Silverton Boots.'

Her heart was beating fast, and she tried to convince herself it was all the waltzing or too much coffee. She looked at him with a dust of hope clouding her reason—a particle small enough for her to try to pretend it wasn't real. He was still grinning at her, and her knees were buckling. Maybe it was all right to try and fix this mess with his help. Maybe she didn't have to keep such a distance, although she was certainly not telling him about Lucile and her money.

"There are many ways to tell a story," he said so close that all he had to do was whisper. "And even more ways to understand it. I hope you find yours."

Her gaze fell to the coffee table and onto the picture of the two of them. Archie smiled at her from behind the fractured glass of a picture frame—one she broke when trying to slide a pile of books onto the table—where he sat with his right arm around her. They were sixteen in that picture. So much had happened since then. "Let's see."

"Speaking of telling stories, I think I will tell you this story in installments, at my own pace." She knew Archie was going to act dramatic when he pretended to cough and straightened his back. He also wore a pretend frown when he pointed at her. "And you, Miss Mendes, perhaps for the first time ever, will learn to listen and to accept help as it is given to you. Think of it as…a journey into the past."

"A journey? I don't have time for this, Archie. I have a deadline looming over my head." And Nina needed shelter, food, clothing. And mostly, her daughter needed a mother, she thought. "Hello. Dissertation. And by the way, I always pay attention."

"No, you don't. Please take my offer." While he waited for her answer, he moved to take the box away from her again. "Or give me that back."

"No," she snapped.

He offered a self-satisfied grin. She sat down next to him to examine the contents, spreading dozens of letters and documents on the coffee table.

The box was stuffed with yellowed pages, whose corners, and sometimes middles, had been eaten away by the merciless nature of time and the insistence of creases. A swollen collection of photos, displaying happy people and abundant foliage, was also part of the assortment. A few envelopes—some big, document-sized, others airmail, regular sized—which she imagined would contain letters and mementos, were inside. There was also a small diary with a red-leather cover, which Archie explained had pages missing.

Out of the corner of her eye, Darcey saw Archie prop his feet on the coffee table and place his hands behind his neck, elbows sticking out. She turned her attention to the documents.

"This is a mess!"

"You got something we can eat? I'm so hungry. Should I order in?"

"You never change. Food's always your main concern." It was heartwarming to see him focus on trivial things. She could learn from him, for sure. Unlike Archie, she had gotten used to living with one foot in the past and the other in the future. The present hardly ever existed. The present was a small apartment with bad insulation and rotting floorboards and a child she loved living almost four hours away.

"Of course I never change. Why would I change if you like me just the way I am?" He flashed an irresistible, toothy smile. Her cheeks caught fire, so she went back to safer subjects.

"I think I have French bread and some cheese. All stale, for certain. Warm the bread, melt the cheese if you want. You know the glitzy life at Chez Darcey."

"No worries. Will do." He levered his elbows against his knees and got up, upsetting her balance, since she had been leaning on him. After a few minutes, he came back with an improvised sandwich in each hand and sighed, pleased with himself. He sat down and offered her one of them.

"No, thank you." She split her attention between the documents and her visitor. "Archie, if you fall asleep on the couch after eating, I'm still gonna wake you up and make you go home. You know that, right?"

"You're the boss." He shrugged.

He had tried the maneuver before, and while she welcomed the thought of him there, of hearing him breathing next to her as she worked, she had to stop it. It was like fighting weeds. Couldn't give them any room to grow, lest her bed should become the next stop.

She watched Archie concentrate on the TV. His eyes were glued to the set, the indigo and green colors of the screen projected on the semi-darkness of his face, his blue irises almost translucent, entranced by the fast-paced action in front of them, until his trance became hers, and she could hardly think for a minute.

Returning to the documents, Darcey discovered the pile contained a clipped set of ten letters, written in different styles of penmanship. They didn't seem to be in any particular order, more like a stack that had been collected in a hurry. She set the diary aside and concentrated on them.

She would have to find some logic in this chaos. By sender, perhaps? Organize them from the oldest to the newest and read and translate them all? She continued browsing through the pages.

One letter commanded Darcey's attention because of the elegant and perfect penmanship. It wasn't for Ana but rather *from* Ana to a woman called Eugênia. She decided to translate that first, approaching the task with the kind of randomness that Donaldson detested. She ignored the things about methods she had learned in school.

Taking the two pages to the little red Formica table in the kitchen area, Darcey polished her rusty Portuguese, an inheritance from her Iberian father, as she translated the contents with a steady hand and increasing speed, writing sentence after sentence in a yellow legal pad. Archie remained on the sofa, looking content, with his hands on his stomach and his eyes on Darcey.

The bilingual dictionary sat in quiet hibernation. Words came back to her, shining with a familiar glow the same way old toys do when they are once again lifted from dusty boxes. She was lulled by the melody of the language playing quietly in her head, dancing faster and faster on the paper.

She didn't talk to Archie while she translated Ana's message. He didn't interrupt her, but she noticed him watching and waiting. She imagined hearing his heart beating; her own pulse accelerated.

When she was done, she prepared more peppermint tea and sat down to read the translation. She moved the pad away to examine her writing from a different angle, then brought the document closer and into focus. She squinted and read aloud, knowing she had Archie's attention.

São Paulo, January 17, 1922
Eugênia, my dear friend, how are you?
A thousand apologies for my having missed our reunion last week. I only found your note, lodged under the door, today. As it turns out, I was in the studio, but I couldn't open the door. I was in somewhat of a compromising position. Not having seen your note, I did not come to have the afternoon meal with you at your boarding house. I hope you come to São Paulo again soon so that we can spend time with each other. As always, I miss you very much and often think of our

times together, our confidences, and of you talking to me while I paint.

As a matter of fact, it would have been very nice to visit with you because I need to get something off my chest, and you are the person I trust the most. I ask that you please return this letter to me the next time you come to São Paulo, if you should come here soon, or else together with any reply you might send through the mail if you think it will be long before I see you. I am sure you will understand the reason for this request once you read the rest of this message. I might even regret sending it, but I was never able to keep anything from you.

You might think it is premature of me to write all of this in a letter, but you know me. I am impatient. Besides, I might lack the courage to tell you this, looking in your eyes. I have met a man, Eugênia, and it is becoming difficult to deny my feelings for him. His name is Joaquim, and that is all you need to know for now. No, in truth, you need to know more: he is married, and what started as something of a game now seems increasingly complicated. He was the reason behind my forgetfulness that day you came to visit. For I think of him all the time.

You most surely think me scandalous. I am certain you are shocked by my behavior. You often criticize me for the liberated ways in which I behave, but please, I ask that you do not judge me. I hope that I can count on your friendship even if I cannot count on your approval.

As for all else, I have been painting with much enthusiasm. Even if I am not completely satisfied with the new pieces, I must recognize that they improve with each passing day. I suppose a little drama is a good

*thing—emotion is after all the fuel that moves the artist.
I have an exhibition at the end of the month, and I am
very hopeful that it will be a good day.*

*Well, my dear friend, I must say goodbye with a
fond hug and wishes that you might not think too ill of
me. Come to see me soon, and maybe I can paint your
portrait once again?*

Saudades, Ana

Darcey rested the sheet on the table.

"I'm done." She looked at Archie. "I think I did
well. I left *saudades* untranslated. No good version in
English. 'I miss you' is close but not exactly it."

He nodded his acceptance of the linguistic
explanation. His calm made Darcey believe he already
knew what the contents of Ana's confidences might be.

A pang of anticipation sent a vibration through her
spine and her arms tingled as if she were about to take
flight. She was excited to continue, and yet it was
impossible to treat this woman she was just getting to
know as a stranger, as only the subject of a dissertation.
Archie was one-eighth this woman, his blood was her
blood. It was unreasonable that she worried she was
invading Ana's privacy—and Archie's by association—
when she read her letters, but she still felt that way.
These were desperate times, though. She needed a
premise for her dissertation and wasn't in a position to
fret or bargain. Scruples of that kind were for those who
could indulge them.

She browsed her brain for information on any
Brazilian artist of the beginning of the twentieth century
named Joaquim. She found none. Maybe he was a
musician or a writer; she knew less about those. But

why did he have to be artistic at all? He could have been anyone, really.

"This crinkle in your forehead." Archie had poured himself another cup of peppermint tea, and he tested the temperature of the beverage with his upper lip. "What is it for?" he asked.

"So, Ana Valquíria, the Brazilian painter, your great grandmother, had a lover?"

"Yes. You just read it. Ana had a lover."

She shook the crackling paper in front of him. "Just my luck. Archie, I didn't sign up for gossip. And are you sure it's all right for me to read these things? Even if you say it is, I'm going to ask the Office of Research on Human Subjects if I need any special permissions to do the work. This is deeply personal."

"Whatever eases your mind. In the meantime, it's actually a pretty good place to start. It's what caused all her troubles. Joaquim."

"What troubles?"

He evaded the question. "Ana was a true artist. A darn good one. Have you ever seen art without drama? I think personal letters are the right place to start. If you want to know about troubles, just continue reading."

Darcey walked around him, summarizing what she had read. "So Ana had a lover, she knew her friend wouldn't approve because he was married, and she was looking for a little compassion because the affair was getting out of hand. This letter should have a match, a reply from Eugênia if we are lucky and she didn't go to São Paulo to talk to Ana in person. Let's see."

Darcey, flipped through the brittle, aged pages which crackled under the urgent demands of her fingers. She used the dates to guide her.

"Here you go. There's a letter from Eugênia, from about two weeks later. And look at this sketch. So beautiful. Such a firm hand. Look at all this detail." Darcey had come across a graphite drawing, a languid woman reclined on a sofa, holding a letter in her hand and covering her eyes with the opposite arm. Had Ana recreated herself thinking of the letter that revealed her indiscretion?

Archie dumped the contents of his cup in the sink and rinsed it as if it was a job of some importance. He spoke without looking at Darcey. "It seems you are under Ana's spell already. Gus always said that was common. Will you help me? Will you go ahead with it?" He held on to the counter; his head dangled down as if he were going to dive into the sink. Was he afraid she would give up?

"With translating? If you say it's all right." She looked at him standing, elegant and strong, with no self-importance. How long until he realized she was no one?

"And what do you say to me? Thank you, perhaps?" He finally twisted his upper body to look her in the eye.

She pondered an answer for a second and regretted being so ungrateful. Why was it hard to concede that he might be onto something? And why have reservations about what seemed to be a gift from him?

"Yes, thank you. It is really nice of you to share this story with me. And I don't know...I gotta confess that I'm actually a *little* curious now. Who knows? Maybe you're right. Maybe some of this intrigue affected her art. Besides, Donaldson is already counting on me, right?" And pretty much my whole family, she thought.

"Ah, Donaldson. Don't you think you worry too much about what he thinks?"

Darcey didn't answer. She leaned over the next letter and waved goodbye to Archie. Then changing her mind, knowing she was being standoffish, she called out. "Archie. Thank you. I mean it."

Taking the hint, he placed a kiss on the crown of her head. It was only a peck on the head, but her heart thumped in her chest so loudly she was afraid he would hear. He left without a sound. At the Formica table, only the noise of Darcey's pen scratching the paper continued to disturb the silence. Darcey told herself she had hardly even noticed that Archie left, yet the spot where he kissed her still throbbed. She had the antidote to those unsettling feelings inside her, though. He cared now, but who knew what would happen if he knew the truth?

She tried to concentrate on the task of translating the second letter. It turned out to be more demanding than the first; she stopped often and relied on the dictionary. Portuguese was her second language, but in this case seventy-five years and a continent separated her dialect from Ana and Eugênia's. Where Ana's bold handwriting slanted in a continuous stroke, Eugênia's was careful and traditional, her letters straight and round, the dot in perfect alignment with the 'i.'

When done, Darcey edited the text for form and polish. The first draft sounded truncated and artificial, like most first drafts do, but the second was a lot better, flowing like an original letter would. Once the letters on the page started to look much like one another, Darcey put the paper away and dragged herself to the bathroom where the welcome comfort of a bubble bath waited.

By rereading the letters in her head, she avoided any thought of Archie until the perfumed foam of rosehips bubbles covered her whole body. Only then did she let memories surface.

The first one was of two nights earlier.

"Hey, I saw that your light was on." He angled his head and shuffled his weight while remaining in the same place, uncertain. When he let go of the door's threshold, which he had been anchoring as if the building's stability depended on it, he placed his hand in his jeans pocket, from where his white knuckles peeked out. "Thought you might want to watch a movie." He shook the greasy video box in front of her and lowered his chin in a plea. "It's a thriller. I know how much you like those."

They sat under a blanket, and she could hardly remember the plot because his presence absorbed all of her attention. When he got up to go home, she wanted to say "Stay, don't go. I don't want you to ever go." But she didn't because she was a coward where Archie was concerned.

Back in the bathtub, a pang of remorse filled her, a squeezing in her heart as if a frigid hand had slipped under the water and grabbed the vital organ. He tried hard, anticipating her wants, taking her mind off her problems, and in return she had kept the most important part of her life hidden from him. And it's not like they hadn't tried to have a relationship. He'd have to come back for the video. He was paying extra fees for having forgotten about it. She sank her head into the water.

When she resurfaced, her memories took her back

five years, when a little too much expensive cabernet had made her impulsive and bold. They hadn't even been dating then.

"I am not sure what I'll make of this tomorrow, Archie, but stay the weekend." She was housesitting Lucile's cottage, a vacation home a couple of hours away, and he showed up to visit. They didn't leave the house for two days, and her heart had been transformed. She was unprepared for the intensity of her love and petrified at the idea that his might not be as great. She had run from him after that, gone to spend time with Lucile and in the process applied to the PhD program in the same town. And in his confusion, he had accepted the job in D.C. A year later she had tried to turn her heart over to Flynn, who ended up being no Archie. The logic in that decision still eluded her. She had denied herself and Archie the happiness they both craved by succumbing to unfounded fears. Not that staying with Archie would have been easy.

Even then, Archie's mother would never have approved. Mrs. Northwood had always been very open about her hope that he find someone with a similar background. Scared enough to bury her feelings— because she never dealt well with being judged— Darcey asked Archie not to mention the weekend ever again. He had looked at her in disbelief, and she had feared she might lose his friendship, the most important thing she had in this world. She did lose him, for a while, but now he was back, and they didn't know where each belonged.

Darcey had tried her best to stay away, to cherish the memory of that weekend, and to believe that being friends was enough. She had Nina to think of, after all.

If things didn't work out, it would be two fathers to leave. But when he quit his job and came to the University, things had gotten more complicated. The physical distance had disappeared. If his mother found out how dire her financial situation was now, and even more serious, that she had a child, any romantic involvement would be considered a complete scam. Worse yet, she had no guarantee that he wouldn't think the same.

But Darcey didn't care a wink about his money. Or anyone else's. Except, as her aunt had coldly observed, to avoid a dire situation, and there was no denying that things were pretty dire.

As the water turned cold and her digits prune-like, sleep almost overtook her. She was so tired. She made a heroic attempt at standing up. The piercing night air that played around in the small hall of her apartment revived her, and by the time she made it back to the kitchen, she was awake enough to reread Eugênia's letter.

São Paulo, January 25, 1922
My dearest Aninha:
You can't imagine my worry when I read your letter. I don't care that you missed our date, although I knocked and knocked and looked at my watch and fretted before deciding to leave you the note. But the reason you give me, Ana, is unimaginable! The reputation of a woman is all she has. You are young, beautiful, and talented. Suitors will fall at your feet. Marriage proposals will come in waves. Why risk your good name for an arrangement that can never be profitable to you?

I know you think that I am old-fashioned and passé, but believe me when I say that you are yet to see full result of the choices you make on account of your temperament and desire for freedom. What if later you want a husband? What will people say if you are famous? Nobody is free, Ana. We are bound by social conventions and our own sense of right and wrong. Change your ways, my friend, before it is too late. End it now, before it hurts you.

I have already returned to Americana, and sometimes I wonder if I will ever get used to the countryside. Life here can be so morose. It is true that the village is growing and that we are already 4,500 inhabitants, but compared to São Paulo this place is like a little hole. In the end, people say that we will soon become a municipality. When that happens, it is possible that letters stop being lost on their way here. I always wonder if I am missing something of importance.

My beloved Ana, think about everything I have written. Stop acting like a child, come to visit me, and I will find you an industrialist or American farmer.

All my love,
Eugênia

Darcey put the translation away. She went to the computer she was lucky enough to inherit from a recent graduate and waited for the modem to connect. The dial-up tone and the series of electronic noises followed. It was unlikely that she would find anything on Americana, which she decided was a funny name for a town. How about Eugênia's reference to an industrialist or American farmer? She chose a browser.

Surprise overcame her when after clicking on 'Brasil,' following up with 'history," and after 'Americana,' she actually got results back. However improbable, the town was very real. She had never heard there was North American emigration to Brazil or contemplated American emigration at all. But the historical data was right in front of her.

It was an ugly story for sure. An attempt at still engaging in slavery once it had been terminated in the United States since Brazil was the last country to abolish it. Southern farmers from the US went into exile in Brazil in the aftermath of the Civil War, starting to arrive in that particular area of the state of São Paulo in 1866. By 1875 the São Paulo Railways Company had completed its expansion to the region and had built a station in what would later become Americana. With that, the place started to grow, new houses appeared. The square provided a public walkway.

"Americans in Brazil. Who'd have thought? A pity their original goals were not honorable at all," she murmured to herself.

In 1922, as Eugênia's letter had foretold, Villa Americana grew to hold a population of 4,500 and, in that same year, calls for it to become a city started to circulate. Finally, in 1924 the municipality of Villa Americana was created, and it became a very successfully textile hub, which was much better than becoming home to Confederates. She looked at all the present-day images on her screen—a large church, a beautiful boulevard, the skyline of a mid-size city.

She picked up the letter again. A little piece of history in her hand. She now handled it like one handles a precious memento. It had acquired new significance—it was precious. It had mattered to someone, mattered enough to be preserved, carefully folded, and tucked away.

Curious to skip ahead to the latter part of the century, Darcey learned Americana's current population was over 100,000 people. It had turned out to be a thriving city. She imagined few Americans knew about this. One more interesting thing for her to retell in her thesis and an opportunity to make a case in her work against the Confederacy.

She hung up, satisfied with what little progress had resulted from that night's work. Maybe it wasn't so little. It was true that she hadn't collected one shred of information on art or been able to establish anything about Ana's style or career. She knew there was something here, something irrevocably drawing her to this story. Snatching the diary from the table, she decided to find out what.

Chapter 8
Darcey

January 1997

Despite the stabbing cold and a gray sky that foreshadowed the arrival of snow, Darcey woke with an urgent desire to go jogging. She longed for the mechanical thumps of sneaker against pavement. The hypnotic road demanded her engagement and her energy. Besides, being physically tired was much better than being mentally exhausted.

She had called her mother early in the morning, and Eleanor put Nina on the phone. Upon hearing her mother's voice, the little girl started to cry, and Darcey's heart broke into a million pieces. She should be home, holding her daughter in her arms. She had cried too, alone in the apartment, once she hung up. The jog was supposed to cure more than one ill.

Protected by a thick fleece hat, sports gloves, thermal sweats, and a windbreaker, Darcey left her apartment. She chose a favorite route, one that took her through a long and quiet boulevard, behind the College of Arts and Sciences, on the way to the main library, and around the large stone fountain. It was her thinking road, where she could brainstorm and not be judged by knowledgeable professors and self-assured peers. She figured by the time she arrived on campus, her thoughts would be in order and her mind ready for work.

She considered inviting Archie to go with her. They could be in silence together without feeling awkward, and he was sensitive to the rhythm of his running partner. She'd rather he be there, telling her more family stories, helping her out with her work like he did. He would take the outer edge of the sidewalk in a protective gesture and would let her set the pace as she pleased.

But after some consideration, Darcey gave up on the idea. It hadn't even been nine hours since she had last seen Archie. He might get the wrong idea that she couldn't do anything without him. And once she got to campus, she would have to work. Work was of the essence now. So she filled her water bottle, made sure her muscles were ready, and embraced the road.

Yet something didn't feel right. What if she continued hiding and he gave up on her like Lucile had said? Her brain produced the image of Archie jogging with somebody else, laughing at another woman's jokes, realizing how much time he had wasted on her. Maybe he would even tell Ana's story to someone else. But she needed Ana's story now. She had started to feel a kinship to the woman, and it was hard not to fantasize about what Ana would do in her situation. Surely someone as bold as Ana would not struggle with mortgages and dissertations.

Thwap, thwap, thwap, her sneakers hit the pavement.

Thump, thump, thump, a week ago he'd knocked on her door. She'd put the books down. Oh Lord, what could Archie want so late at night? His living across the street made Darcey feel entrapped, claustrophobic, yet loved, comforted, and protected. She couldn't decide which feeling was the strongest.

"What is it, Archie?" she had shouted from her spot near the bookshelf, knowing her voice easily carried over to where Archie stood behind the old, chipped door. She wondered if he had his ear glued to the dark wood surface and smiled tenderly at the image.

"How do you know it's me?"

"I have X-ray vision. Who else could it be? It's eleven-thirty at night!"

"Oh, you want me to come back tomorrow?" He was sulking; there was muffled disappointment in his words. He could be such a baby at times.

"No, hang on." Darcey arranged her clothes and looked at herself in the mirror, combing her black shaggy hair with her fingers, before finally pulling the door open. On the other side of the threshold, he fidgeted for a second and the floorboards creaked. Before she could even blink, Archie had walked the eight-foot distance between the doorsill and the improvised living room, only to collapse on the futon. He smiled the same familiar smile. They chatted and ate the pizza he ordered, but he had said nothing about Ana that night. It bothered her he hadn't. Was he afraid to talk to her? She had played the scene back in her head, looking to see if at any point she'd cut him off, discouraged him from telling her he needed help with the letters, but she had come back empty-handed. He had given her no clue the project lay in her future.

On the road, Darcey stepped on a crack and twisted her ankle. She held her foot and made circles with it until the pain subsided. It was hard to do this alone. Had he been there, Archie would've come to her. He'd have looked more worried than the situation demanded. The thought made her heart swell with longing. She carefully put her foot down on the ground and tested its strength. All that daydreaming couldn't be good for her. She was clumsy enough without it. Marching in place for a moment, she warmed her ankle to health and returned to running.

From the opposite direction came a runner whose strong frame became more discernable as he got closer. Phillip, a graduate assistant from the Sociology department, smiled broadly, held both his arms out and asked, "What? Alone? No Archie?"

"You realize we aren't attached at the hip, right?" she said just as they crossed paths.

"Pfff, sure. A likely story. Just know I'd go running with you anytime, *Darcey Mendes*…Anytime!"

Nothing to say to that. If it weren't Archie, she would rather jog alone.

Invigorated by the brisk exercise, she sensed her body sweat under the many layers of clothing, until she was ready to tear them off. She stretched her arms above her head and breathed in the fresh air, falling into the soothing lull of the workout.

That's when she saw him across the street. Archie was at a corner café, a fishbowl with its insides visible through the all-around glass. He was standing, coffee in one hand, the other inside his jacket, and a tall blonde woman was right in front of him. Darcey had never seen her before.

A flutter in Darcey's stomach commanded her to stop. She jogged in place behind a large shrub, feeling idiotic yet unable to move on. Better leave. Nothing to see. And yet her feet wouldn't obey her. A man carrying groceries passed her by, and when he looked at her confused, she waved at him as if that served as an explanation for her current predicament. Her cheeks burned. Archie was smiling at the woman. From behind the leaves, Darcey saw him bend down, pick up a pocketbook and return it to the lady. She sighed. Always the Boy Scout, he opened the door for the blonde, who nodded in acknowledgment. He went back to his coffee, oblivious to Darcey's surveillance, looking like he had forgotten the woman already.

Darcey was still shaking a bit, not ready to resume the run. A window full of toys and baby clothes provided a distraction. A white crib with eyelet linens was displayed in the corner, and a couple stood right behind it, touching the fabric, smiling at the mobile butterflies that hung from an arm attachment. The very-pregnant woman touched her belly. From her spot on the sidewalk, Darcey squinted, imagining what it would be like to wait for a child's birth as a couple.

She thought of her parents. All the heartache and disappointment they had endured. Her sickly brother who, in the words of the doctor, had failed to thrive. She had added to their distress; she had no doubt about that. But she had suffered too, though no one ever brought that up. It was hard to experience loss as a child. That early notion that life might go wrong, and sometimes did, could tint a person's days forever. She couldn't explain loss to Archie. He wouldn't understand.

"Can I help you?" A saleswoman had come to the door.

"No thank you. I'm just looking."

The woman nodded and went back inside to fold

clothes.

Her brother's picture was in the house, on the mantel, a beautifully framed black and white portrait that made clear she was not really an only child. She had grown up listening to everyone talk about the things her brother, had he lived, would have done.

Her brother and his memory had all the qualities of an unfulfilled promise, the kind that results in limitless expectation fueled by imagination and no possibility of a reality check. He had been slotted for great things, and he couldn't fail in any of them. Maybe he would have been an astronaut or president. Maybe he would have changed the world, while she…she was just Darcey, the one with an unfinished advanced degree and a child she was yet to fully honor. Her parents had paid for most of her studies, probably putting aside any reservations they had about her. "Darcey gets so distant. She is such a strange child," she caught her mother saying more than once. The comment echoed in her head all the time, and the pain it caused was only compounded by the fact that she would love to have had a sibling, even more a twin brother.

When Darcey resumed her jog, her calf muscles started to stiffen, her stomach to growl. She moved steadily toward the university although it now seemed so distant. "Only a mile more," she reminded herself. "Everything is only one-step-after-another away."

She arrived to the usual campus scenes: professors shrouded in warm scarves walking to their classes and hauling rolling briefcases, couples sharing embraces and generating their own warmth, students reading on benches, despite the cold, forgetting the world outside the pages. Were they ever under attack by an avalanche of conflicted feelings like she was, or were their lives simpler, more linear, and their thoughts less scattered? She walked on.

At the library, Abby greeted Darcey from behind her desk. Her hair was cropped short, and she wore dangling colorful earrings that looked like they came from a crafts fair. "Back so soon? I thought you had given up." There was a knowing smile on her lips.

"Yeah, about that...there seems to have been a change of plans."

"So what'll it be today? Still European art?"

"No, Brazilian Modernism, as it turns out. I also called and reserved a book."

"That's new. Anyone in particular? Di Cavalcanti? Portinari?"

"A smaller figure. Ana Valquíria Eça."

"Never heard of her. But come this way. Let's find your reserve, and after that, I know where to take you."

To understand the artist, Darcey was going to live in Ana's time a bit, call those old spirits back into existence and let them take their time showing her around the stacks. She retrieved *Modernism in Latin America* and placed it on the desk near her but not before stealing a few glances at random pages of the book. She could hardly wait. While Abby updated the records, Darcey removed a couple of quarters from her pocket and placed them in the jar the librarian had shown her the last time. It was so padded with bills that the coins made no noise. She smiled at herself, content for having remembered this time. A second later, Abby alerted her to the presence of another patron.

"Browne is coming, and he is looking straight at you."

In no time, the bulky scholar was standing in front of her, squinting at the book. He had an imposing presence, and he towered over her by at least a foot. His round belly made him slant his head and shoulders back so that he wouldn't lose his balance.

An invisible thread tightened around her throat, making it hard to speak. Not only was he big like a giant, his presence always made her feel uneasy. His nose sniffed the air as if searching for an acrid smell he could complain about, while his eyes scanned the library, causing Darcey to hold her own breath.

"Conducting research for Donaldson?"

"Actually, no. My own."

"Really? Let's see. Modernism. Hmm."

As far as academics went, Browne was the scholarly antihero to Donaldson's protagonist, one leading by example, the other by vanity. Their novel-worthy conflict had endured a long time. Several years before, in front of colleagues at a university event, Browne had accused Donaldson of not being bold enough because he hadn't embraced the abstract art of a painter Browne adored. Donaldson in turn thought that Browne was a bully and told him so in unequivocal terms after one too many gulps of wine. So much for cooperation, she sighed.

"Where's the interest?"

She picked up the volume as if to protect it, and fanned the pages of the book, keeping her hands busy. She looked at Abby for support, but it was pointless now. Like a hunter and his prey, he was ambushing her, and she didn't want to end up caught in his trap, didn't want to contribute to the feud, recently reignited by allegations that Browne appropriated the work of students.

"Oh, you know, I just love that period. I'm reading about the classic figures of the movement."

"I see." But of course he didn't. His eyes were wandering about. He wasn't even paying attention. He only asked the question so that he could speak. She had no doubt he was a narcissist. "Listen, Darcey. I hear you're having some trouble coming up with a topic for a dissertation." That's what she got for confiding in a couple of other grad students. "Maybe it's not your fault."

"I don't understand."

"Students need good guidance. Strong guidance. Maybe you just need better advising. If this continues and you want to talk, you know where to find me. Modernism. Perhaps a radical take on Latin American icons? Now that's a good idea."

Beads of sweat formed on Darcey's upper lip. She disliked Browne's treatment of Donaldson, but that was just the beginning. Browne embodied all that could be wrong with academics. Dweller in the ivory tower, scornful of those still learning, believer in his own genius. Worse yet, in front of him, words deserted her, and she acted like a fool.

Once he was out of earshot, Abby, whose red face seemed ready to burst, spoke.

"I know I'm supposed to respect the faculty, but that man…Always supercilious. Arghh! Rumor has it he might be on his way out. Too many complaints about his attitude and lack of collegiality."

Darcey had heard this news from Donaldson, but she'd elicit more information without saying she already knew.

"That's not possible. He is a tenured full professor. He can't be let go."

"Yes, but he could be convinced that retirement is a good idea and offered a good going-away package. It'd be great, if you ask me. But come. I have books to show you."

Abby took Darcey through a narrow passageway. The books were separated in little alcoves, like those of a medieval monastery. The cave-like rooms on this side of the building smelled of mold, and cobwebs dangled from the archways as if the area had not been visited in years.

"Almost there." Abby cheered her on. They went up a few steps and down again, turned corners and cleared little recess areas, always followed by the faint smell of aging paper. The possibilities that only stacks full of books can afford surrounded them. "Here we are." They arrived at a little alcove where the shelves were distributed in a semicircle and the opposite wall was lined with small desks.

Darcey thanked Abby whose footsteps reverberated against the cement floor. She got the books from the shelves, spreading them over the largest table. Opening the first, an old photo-and-art volume, she was back in the 1920s, looking at pictures of young men and women posing at porches and wearing their best Sunday attire: lace-trimmed dresses for the ladies, suits and hats for the men. She could almost hear *chorinho* playing in the background, that delicious music style, aptly named "little lament," that filled Brazilian homes and ballrooms early in the century. She saw parks and lakes, and boulevards and squares, the train station and the *Theatro Municipal*. And she saw art and invention in bright hues and distorted shapes, the soul of modern art forever preserved in snapshots and explanatory lines.

She fell back into the pleasant pace of reading. Page after page of art and color nourished and invigorated her. She looked at the selection that she had in front of her—books by Brazilian theorists, biographies, a monograph by a professor from California—and she moved on to historical accounts, some literary, others more factual. She alternated between Portuguese and English; sometimes she didn't know which one was which unless she stopped to think about it, and that gave her a very agreeable feeling. Her second language was coming back to her like a gift from her family.

She was only browsing for snippets of life in early-century Brazil. She would have been happy with a picture of one of the best-known artists, or a few lines about the Modern Art Week, but it was in her destiny to find much more. The big discovery was a picture of three men and two women, Ana among them, with the subtitle "The Five Artists of the *Vernissage* at the São Paulo Cultural Center. January 30, 1922." She let out a little squeal, only to look around and make sure no one had heard.

She forgot about time, about hunger, about surveillance from behind bushes, and even dissertations when she saw Ana Valquíria Eça's name printed on the page. The accompanying picture showed the artist wearing heels and an embroidered sleeveless dress. Though everyone was dressed smartly, Ana was the center around which all else revolved. The woman had the posture of a queen and the dress and attitude of a flapper. Darcey couldn't take her eyes off the picture.

But in time the pull of real, present life became too strong, like an undercurrent that sweeps a swimmer away and throws him back to shore. As much as Darcey wanted to disappear inside the picture and the story it told, as much as she held on to the fantasy that she was starting to live a vicarious life better than her own, it was time to leave. She returned a hefty pile of books to a cart in the corner, a move appreciated with silent gratitude by the undergraduate worker on duty. She kept the one she had requested for checkout, and she told herself she could escape to that world anytime she wanted, anytime things in 1997 became too dry and without magic.

Darcey hadn't eaten all day, smelled of stale sweat from the jog, and was eager to shower and change, so, shielding herself with the book tight against her chest, she started home.

She hadn't been walking for more than five minutes when she realized she wanted to talk to Lucile and let her know she had decided what to do. If she was going to take the risky road of committing to a year of fast-tracked research, she should tell her aunt she would not shy away from the challenge. Knowing Lucile's propensity to like sweets, she stopped at a bakery for some treats.

When she arrived, she rested the blueberry muffins on a table and made tea in the functional kitchenette. She came back to find Lucile already devouring the baked goods. They fell into a comfortable silence only interrupted by the sound of Darcey slurping the hot drink.

"I wish I could have a cat here," Lucile said, breaking the silence. "But I guess it is good policy that they don't accept animals. A dog barking at night would not make me happy." She went back to her drink.

"Lucile?" Darcey hesitated for a moment. She wanted to ask a question without having to explain too much, and Lucile could not be tricked. If Ana wasn't related to Archie, she wouldn't worry, but this was different; the association made everything more complicated. She busied herself with cleaning the leftovers, trying to impart an air of insignificance to the question though it would sound awkward after the remark about cats and dogs. "Do you think the past is best left alone? I mean, do you think there is something to be learned from investigating the past?"

Lucile raised an eyebrow. For the first time since Darcey arrived, the old woman promenaded around the room, searching for the answer to Darcey's question in some hidden corner. She took her time before speaking.

"You wouldn't just ask me that for no reason. What's the catch? Spill it out."

"No catch. Just humor me."

"Do you think that just because I am old I have to answer questions like that?"

"Well…sort of. You seem to think you have an answer to everything, if you ask me."

Lucile snickered, the sarcastic honesty of the answer disarming her. "Fair enough. Because I have no idea why you're asking this question, I'll take the safe road and say that the past should be left alone. There. Happy?"

"Not really."

"Are you meddling with the past, Darcey?"

"Who, me?" She grinned at Lucile like a girl who

had stolen candy but was sure to get away with it.

"Oh, well. I don't know why you ask if you are going to do it anyway. And if I know you, once you've made up your mind…"

"Yes, I think I have. This is about an artist I'm studying. If there are any secrets in her life, they might come out. Do you think I'm wrong to investigate?"

"Not necessarily. Just don't forget the past matters. It's people's lives! You have to know it's more than words in a book or in a diary. Young people are really bad at that sometimes, the self-absorbed fools. Others might have reasons beyond what you know. Heartaches, and confidences, and regrets."

"Like you and my mom?" It was a cheap trick to bring up their feud, but she couldn't resist.

"Yes, like that. You can't just go airing other people's secrets without consequence. You of all people should know that. You best know what you're doing."

Lucile sat down, putting more weight on the bed than her fragile frame looked like it could produce. The bed groaned in response. She repeated, "You best know what you're doing."

Darcey tried to remain unphased by Lucile's repeat warning. She had a past too. She got it. But if this was a chance for her to change her *future*, shouldn't she take it? A few moments later, Darcey touched Lucile's shoulder indicating it was time for her to leave. Lucile held her hand and said, "Wait." She walked to a bureau in the corner and fetched an envelope. "I thought about what you said the last time, and I worry about you out in the world with little money. Here."

Her aunt's surprise generosity unbalanced Darcey. She had wanted the peace of mind of money, but she couldn't help thinking that between Lucile and Archie, she owed too many people an explanation and a positive outcome. It was not a comfortable position.

"Thank you, Lucile." She exited the room. She tried not looking back, but, in the end, there was no avoiding the question: in the future, would she wish ghosts to have remained ghosts?

And yet…there was this pull, one that told her to go on. She looked at the check in the envelope once she reached the corridor. Ten thousand dollars. Space to breathe.

She called her mother from the lobby of the retirement mansion.

"Mom. I have a plan," she blurted out even before saying hello. "Is it possible for you to make do with the money of the bonds for most part of this year?

Her mother hesitated. "I guess…Why?"

"If things go as I hope, I can be ABD in a semester. I promise I'll take over the mortgage as soon as I'm employed." And in possession of the money Lucile pledged, but that part she didn't say. It was scary and uncertain, but she had to try. "I'm also sending you five thousand dollars," she continued.

"Where in the world did you get that?" Eleanor said in a high-pitched voice reserved for surprises and indignation.

She thought fast to respond with an adequate lie. "I picked up an extra class to teach." It was a blatant falsehood given that TAs were only allowed two classes a term and payment was biweekly, never a lump sum, but Eleanor would not know that.

Her mother of course refused the money, saying they would not become a burden to her, that it was not what parents should do. Her father was going to work from home on a few freelance jobs. It would not be enough to save the house once the reserves were gone, but they would cross that bridge once they got there, her mother said. In the end, Darcey made progress in convincing Eleanor to let her help. She had just bought them some time. She would send the other five thousand next term, with the same excuse.

Darcey returned home and found Archie waiting for her, two lattes in his gloved hands. He sat against the front door and took turns tapping his right and then his left foot. "Finally!" he said standing up. "Where were you? I guess coffee's cold now."

Darcey gave him a look that said, "None of your business." Out loud she replied, "Did you come to tell me stories?" She turned the key and let him in. He just nodded.

She opened the door. He went to his personal spot on the futon.

"Okay. Ana. Lover. And then what?" Darcey asked just before she sat in the scruffy armchair, threw her legs up, and shook off her shoes, which pounded on the floor. She grabbed a pen and bit the end so hard it cracked.

Archie picked up where he had left off. "Around the same time, she started being noticed as an artist. The year was 1922, as you know, and the Modern Art Week was about to happen. She became quite a darling among the up-and-coming. Her paintings of people were distorted like Anita Malfatti's, but her work was even more vibrant with color: oranges, blues, and fuchsia. This famous critic came to see her and gave her his blessing. Ana was on her way to stardom. She was a little wild, a little reckless, and she had the kind of female attitude that would become more common as the decade progressed. Everyone talked about her. I think secretly, many wanted to be like her."

Archie continued telling his tale into the night, saying many things Darcey didn't think she could find in books: Ana's first *vernissage*, what she thought of her contemporaries, what he had learned about her art. If he suspected Darcey, the art history student, knew more and better, he didn't let that stop him. "Did you know Bruno Antonino Prada was the first to shine the spotlight on her?" he asked with enthusiasm. "She is supposed to have wowed everyone in a beautiful red dress that night." Darcey found a few newspaper clippings and a diary entry that matched the story he was telling, and she showed them to Archie, who smiled and ran his finger over the newspaper photos, now faded and fragile but still visible.

"Good." He abruptly stopped. He stood, rubbed his hands together, and turned toward the door.

"That's it?!" asked Darcey. She arched her back in a stretch and then affected some indignation. "You're just gonna stop almost mid-sentence?"

"Yep. But if you go out to dinner with me on Friday, I might tell you some more."

"You know this is coercion, right?" She was only half-joking.

"I do. Goodnight, Darcey." He walked away with a swagger.

Chapter 9
Ana

January 30, 1922

Later she would think she was so inebriated with the idea of becoming famous that she had romanticized everything about that night. Maybe it was all a dream. It felt like the air around the city center had stood still, hovering in anticipation of the event. No gusts, no winds, not even a waft. The invitation read "Modern Art Exhibit—January 30, 1922," and other details that by comparison she considered had no relevance.

Five young Brazilian artists, Ana among them, were exhibiting their art. Ana wanted to make a grand entrance, appear as if by magic in the large reception room ten minutes after the hour, wearing a daring red dress that, unlike most of the current fashions, accentuated the line of her hips before it went on and expanded into a tail of see-through fabric.

"A real beauty," she overheard men say when they believed she was out of hearing range. "A little bit of an extrovert," claimed a thin, maladroit woman whose black dress fell carelessly over protruding hipbones.

And so, her hair styled in her short, sleek bob and her bust adorned by an antique necklace with a ruby pendant, Ana walked around the art on display, examining everything she saw. A charming old man was all compliments saying to one of his friends, "An absent-minded visitor runs the risk of confusing her with the loveliest of statues." She smiled to herself, and she nodded at those bold enough to stare at her.

Not everything was pleasant, though. For several minutes, she had to endure Bernardo de Azevedo Pires, a fellow artist who spoke in platitudes, compliment her in his bizarre manner. "*Senhorita* Eça! You are a sight for sore eyes! You look as beautiful as a summer rose blossoming under the January sun." He arranged the sides of his hair in a failed attempt at being gallant. Ana had a sudden urge to take a bath and wash off his words and his gaze with soap.

"Thank you, Bernardo." She changed subjects. "So the event is going well?" She moved her feet backward to stand a little farther away from him. She wished for esoteric powers to shield herself behind an invisible wall.

"Yes, yes. It is magnificent!" He exaggerated. "And this house! It is a splendid acquisition that will enrich the lives and dwell in the very hearts of the city's residents! A miraculous epiphany!" She wondered if he had swallowed a dictionary.

The house whose praises Bernardo was singing was an old three-story mansion, painted in a tea-rose shade. It was located close to the *Pinacoteca do Estado*, the most important and oldest museum of the city of São Paulo. The hall where artists and guests gathered was the main area of what was a newly established cultural center.

Rich benefactors and patrons of the arts had decided that the city needed a space where new artists could showcase their work. Aspiring artists could also take lessons from painters and sculptors whose talent was already a matter for books. The inaugural event was to be an art show, an occasion of consequence for the city to take notice. Ana and her peers were selected to be part of the main show.

She could not stop thinking of the wave of good fortune that had carried her there, that had sent her on that fair sailing course. Her art was being exhibited. That's all that mattered. After word of her skill reached the diamond-adorned ears of Maria Pia de Alcântara, a rich, bored and rather large socialite, she knew she stood a good chance. With her alliance of wealthy housewives, Maria Pia had invested much of her social capital in finding a striking property for the cultural center and skillful artists to display therein.

The next step was to nag supporters just enough for them to open their fat wallets. But it was important not to annoy them. Ana didn't know whether Pia convinced rich people because they really enjoyed art, because they felt guilty for having so much money, or yet because sponsoring artists was *chique*. It didn't matter; whatever her strategy, it paid off. Now Ana could hardly believe she was looking at her own work, the long wall adorned with her paintings, and the first few guests admiring her art.

Several minutes had passed, and the tenor of Bernardo's praises did not change one bit. Trying to free herself from his rhetorical grip, Ana pretended to see a familiar face. "Always a pleasure, Bernardo." She grabbed a Champagne glass and looped her arm around a passing woman who looked at Ana with eyes bulging in surprise.

"Enjoying the evening?" she asked as if they were

friends.

The woman, not realizing Ana was one of the artists, simply replied, "This isn't art."

At the comment, Ana snickered a little and spilled her sparkling wine. The liquid ran shamelessly from her chin onto her clothes. The woman whose arm she had borrowed detached herself, and Ana didn't waste too much time feeling sorry for her outfit or for the woman. Instead, she went looking for the powder room.

It was on her way to the second floor that Ana saw Joaquim standing near the marble staircase, handsome as ever, doing what he did best: charming people. Charming women, more exactly, so she stuck around to inspect him, pretending disinterest and yet feeling her temples throb.

His hair had been recently cropped so that the sides were very short, and from the top, a thick heap of dark and straight strands occasionally fell over his eyes like a short curtain. Brushing it back into place was part of his luring stratagem. She knew that better than anyone else. She had fallen for it too. Now from a relative distance the move seemed calculated and artificial— even if she was the only one not being fooled.

Four elegant women and one not-so-youthful heiress took turns trying to impress him while he put on his best behavior to entertain them in return. From time to time, each of the ladies used delicate and freshly polished fingertips to select a *petit four* from one of the silver trays. They washed down the small treats with gulps of Champagne. One of them got a little bolder and selected a treat to feed Joaquim directly. Even he appeared to have been caught by surprise.

But despite Joaquim's rehearsed social

performance, Ana knew he had been assigned to cover the exhibit; it was hard to miss the obvious signs—the wandering eyes, the mental notes being taken when he spoke to others. No one looked more like a reporter than he did, even if he was engaged in charming the ladies. Maybe all men became their jobs after a while.

Ana was suddenly aware that she and Joaquim hadn't spoken since the day they were interrupted by Eugênia, her best friend's knock on the door waking her from his spellbinding charm. But today was about her art and not about their affair, so she vowed to avoid him. It would take a little discipline, but it could be done. Besides, her gut had been telling her to stay away, so she was bothered by how obsessively she had been thinking about him. A woman on the street, a white magic priestess, had seen trouble in her future, delivering the omen without having been asked. Ana was not usually superstitious, but she couldn't deny the words had affected her.

As if waking from self-hypnosis, Ana remembered the stained dress and hurried up the stairs. She let her new heels tap on the cold and expensive marble until she disappeared into the hall. In her mind, like an incantation, these words played again and again. "Close your heart, Ana. Save your art."

By ten o'clock most of the accidental visitors had left and were likely tucked in bed inside their long nightgowns and sleep bonnets. Some women were smoking in the winter garden away from the art. Others slid across the main room looking at the paintings; their movement was so furtive they seemed to have little wheels attached to the bottom of their feet. But no matter how much she tried to focus on art and interesting people, no matter how much she tried to avoid him, Ana had been spying on Joaquim from the corner of her covetous eyes for most of the evening. His whole body lured her in, invited her to get lost once again. It was a magnetic pull, and she found herself grabbing her chair with both her hands in an effort not to go to him.

She knew the little vices of his hands and his facial expressions by heart. She could predict when he would run his fingers through his tie, or play with his suspenders, or hide a crafty smile with the side of his hand. The effect was the same on other women.

"Joaquim, you write so well. I look for your articles every time I open the newspaper," said one woman loud enough for Ana to hear from her spectator seat. Another quickly intervened. "Your style is so distinctive. I would know it was you even if your columns were anonymous."

Why didn't they ask where his wife was? Why couldn't they see he was just toying with their hearts? She was so immersed in her own growing sense of jealousy that she hardly noticed a palpable change in the atmosphere when Maria Pia welcomed an important guest—a critic, whose word was known to make or destroy careers.

Ana would have respected the man regardless. He was said to be one of the organizers of the forthcoming Modern Art Week. She had no doubt—that week would forever seal the fate of arts and literature in Brazil and perhaps her own. Not even the planners and participants had as much faith in the power of their movement as she did. She knew it in her heart: to be modern was more than an ambition. It was a vocation, and they had been called.

She moved closer but stopped still several feet away. Prada was examining her self-portrait. His thick eyebrows lay flat across his forehead except for the innermost part, which curved toward the nose. He was pointing at parts of the picture, making invisible swirls in the air using his index finger. With much interest, he chatted with other guests.

"A great piece," he finally concluded.

"I think he likes your work," Joaquim whispered in her ear while standing behind her. His warm breath caressed the skin of her neck. His hand searched for hers in the folds of her dress. In the small crowd that had formed around her, no one could see he had wrapped an arm around her waist.

Prado then asked to see the painter of the beautiful artwork that made him think of Anita Malfatti. In no time, a legion of excited fans of the master came to collect Ana from where she stood. "He wants to meet you. Come quick." As they cheered her on, Joaquim only had time to suggest in a few hurried sentences that they should be together, that she should know their lives were intertwined. That it didn't matter that it was Monday. Or night. Or late.

In an instant, she was gone, dragged by an unknown hand in the famous critic's direction. He greeted her with a nod, and the two fell into a formal but fulfilling conversation.

After Bruno Prada left, roughly an hour after his arrival, the excitement around the young artist that everyone now knew to be Ana Valquíria Eça intensified. A multitude of art enthusiasts reasoned it was best to get to know her before she became too famous for acquaintances. Before she did what every celebrated person did and started thinking of herself as larger than life.

First there were enthusiastic hugs and congratulations from several guests—some loud, others whispered, as if important secrets were at stake. Champagne corks popped, and glasses were raised into the air in toasts. Next came small talk with the few remaining ladies-who-lunch, each trying to claim a part in the discovery of Ana. The first side effects of a little fame hit Ana like a hangover.

She was dizzy and off-center. There were plans to make and opinions to give. Did she like Cubism? How about Dadaism? Joaquim, with an amused look on his face, interviewed her for his newspaper article and then, as if he were conducting professional business, he wrote her a note, which he passed to her while others were distracted by the new developments.

"Here. *Senhorita* Ana, my information in case you want to know more about the article."

She hid it in her hand, inside moist fingers, somewhat dreading that the dampness might ruin the paper and erase the message.

Later, she excused herself to be alone and managed to escape to the little winter garden that adorned the center of the house. When Ana was finally able to read the message, which turned out, as expected, not to be professional at all, her heart turned both happy and heavy. The little crinkled paper simply read, "Tomorrow, January 31. Wear your striped dress." And omen or no omen, she knew she would be there to meet him.

.

Chapter 10
Darcey

"It is Ana's, isn't it? The large portrait of a girl, hanging on the wall of the living room in your parents' home?" Anxious for more answers, Darcey nibbled on her nails.

She and Archie were at the library, a place where Darcey now spent more time than in her own apartment. Sitting on a hard chair, hunched over books until her back hurt, wasn't an imposition. At the library, she was at peace. In the archival area, Darcey had been showing Archie books with images of the Modern Art Week of 1922.

"Yes, it's hers," Archie confirmed. "Grandpa Gus told me he could hardly remember a time when that portrait wasn't there. Our house was where they lived: Ana, Gus, and his dad Raymond. I believe the picture is actually a self-portrait of when she was a little girl. She must've painted it in the attic, where she had her studio. Maybe she was homesick. Once she came here, she never returned to Brazil."

"I remember looking at it for a long time when we were younger. I don't know why I never asked you who the artist was. It's not like me."

He brought his chair closer to her and spoke in a confessional tone. "I think when something is always there, we just take it as a given. I certainly have." He searched for her eyes, and Darcey could feel the skin of her face burning. Then, after a pause he continued, sounding more casual. "I've done that to the house too. You don't think about looking at it any different because it's always been home."

She breathed in deeply to recover from his stare. "I can understand that."

"My mom has another one of Ana's paintings in her sitting room upstairs, a convoluted composition of waves in different shades of blue. It's beautiful. But it's sadder, just like my mom. She sits and watches it, as if she was staring at the ocean itself."

Darcey had made her way to the stacks. She retrieved a book from the top shelf. "How is she doing?" she said when she returned to their table.

"Same. She is lonely and disillusioned. Wine ends up keeping her company. You know what she said to me?"

"What?"

His jaw tensed. For a moment, he wasn't his laid-back self anymore. One of his hands closed into a fist. "She said, 'Archie, I have one son and a quarter of a husband.' " His voice changed. " 'The quarter that pays the bills and goes to work every day and complains when his shirts aren't well pressed or dinner lacks a little salt. The other three quarters are nowhere to be found.' "

"I'm sorry, Archie. I don't know what to say." She actually did, but was afraid to mention that when it came to families, she knew the angst of trying to do your best and it not being enough.

"You don't have to say anything. I just wish I could make it better. You know I'll do anything to make her happy. I'm sorry. I don't know why I am saying all this."

"It's not a problem. I'm your friend."

A wave of pain flashed across Archie's face. Was it because of his mother's suffering or her last remark? Instinctively, she brought a hand to her heart. If only she could tell him everything that was stored in her chest. Why was it so hard to just be oneself, do what the heart wanted? She picked up another book. It was best to go back to work.

The book fell open at a reproduction of another one of Ana's portraits. This one was of a woman wearing a green dress, sitting on a lush burgundy sofa and resting her hands on her lap. Darcey pointed at it and tugged at Archie's shirt.

"See? Same brush stroke, thick yet elegant."

"This portrait is a powerful picture."

"I wonder if there's any of her in her striped dress?"

"What striped dress?"

"Oh, nothing. Just something I read in the diary."

Would it be bad to edit the translations a bit? Of course it would. And unethical. Darcey hoped the details of what she'd read the previous night could stay between her and Ana. It was the account of a love encounter with Joaquim, the man who had such a strong effect on her life. An instinctive urge to discover more befell her, but did she have to share everything with Archie? He already knew the gist. Joaquim was especially fond of a particular striped dress.

"What do you know of Joaquim?" she asked, happy to move on.

"Not much about his personality. Gus would only

tell me he was a mischievous character. Why?"

"Because he was a bit of a troublemaker and pleasure-seeker. A *malandro*, like they say in Portuguese."

"Is that your technical estimation?" He smiled that broad smile that made the world stop, the smile that made him look young and hopeful.

She tucked her hair behind her ears with both hands, unsure of what to do with them after. "Something like that. He's a lover and a rascal for sure." To keep herself occupied, she retrieved a bottle of water from her messenger bag and was taking a sip when he spoke again.

"You understand that Joaquim was Gus's biological father, right?"

Water spurted out of her mouth. "Say what?" A small puddle formed on the wooden table. She soaked it up with her long sleeve.

"I told you Joaquim was the beginning of all Ana's problems. As much as she came to love Gus, this was 1920s Brazil. Being pregnant with a married man's child wasn't exactly easy. And she didn't trust Joaquim to do the right thing."

"I hadn't realized. This will become complicated, won't it?" Darcey asked.

Archie just nodded.

"So this makes Joaquim…"

"…My great grandfather. Yep. Let me draw a family tree for you." He grabbed a pencil in her case and reached for the legal pad. "First there was Ana." He drew a circle. "She got pregnant with Joaquim's child." He drew a square and a line connecting them. From that line, he drew a vertical one and another square. "Their child was my Grandpa Gus, who, as you know, is my mom's father." He continued adding more shapes to the diagram. "But Ana married Raymond and came to Pennsylvania, where Gus was raised. Got it?"

"Oh, I'm sorry. I'm mortified." She covered her face with her hands. "I shouldn't be saying those things about Joaquim."

"Nah. I won't take it personally. I like to think I'm not like him. I prefer to imagine I'm like Gus and Raymond. With them, it was what you see is what you get. I like that. I never met Joaquim of course, and Gus had no concept of him. Raymond was his dad. Joaquim was only his father."

Darcey imagined how different Ana's life would have been if Joaquim hadn't been the bon vivant described in the diary. Maybe she would have stayed in Brazil. Maybe she would not have disappeared from public life. But the thought also took Darcey in a dangerous direction. Was Archie really not a version of Joaquim, with his captivating smile and natural charm? If Archie was like Gus, caring and solid, she was silly for not telling him the truth and hoping he would understand. Silly wasn't even the word. It was downright stupid. To recant love that was real and strong required a very good reason.

But it was not like he had ever been half of a steady couple, and he certainly had the captivating smile of a rake. Gus was stable and steady, but good sense could skip a generation. What if Archie turned out to be like Flynn? What if she introduced this father-figure to her daughter only to have to pick up the pieces once he left?

She was confusing herself, and her head hurt.

Would the actions of three generations, of people they had never met, matter so much? Researchers now believed memories got carved into one's DNA, changing the fate of their descendants forever. She couldn't remember where she had read that. Would the past in that way forever echo through the halls of the present? Would it take getting together with Archie again to find out? There was the risk of drawing a further wedge in the precarious relationships in his family, too. It would be for nothing if he turned out to be like Joaquim at heart.

"Darcey? You still there? Hello."

"Yes…sure…of course. I'm here."

She turned the page. There were many photos of the Modern Art Week. She found Ana in a couple of them. She was posing with other artists. "Look at her. So full of life. And I love her hair."

"The story goes, one day, she arrived at the fancy beauty parlor where her mother used to have her hair styled, took her long braids down, and told the hairdresser to cut them off. All the women stood around, begging her not to do it. But she was adamant. When the hairdresser had gone shoulder length, she kept yelling 'more!' After some hesitation, the hairdresser went on cutting, until Ana's hair was in a bob. Then Ana demanded bangs. You can imagine the furor."

"See? Same thing. Things we take for granted. No one thinks twice about short hair now. Look at mine." She pointed at her own hair, the wispy ends and long irregular bangs covering parts of her forehead.

She checked her watch and was startled by how late it was. "Archie, I'm gonna check out this book, and then I have to go. I'm sorry."

"Sure. I have a class too."

She didn't want to be rude, and she felt guilty for not telling him where she was actually going, but for the time being, it was better that way. Familiar anxiety made her stomach churn.

She walked toward the arboretum, thinking of the bits she had learned and the whole lot she still hadn't. The campus was quiet, and lamplights had started to light up even though it wasn't even six. Under their glow, rows of dark shrubs looked waxy covered in a thin layer of frost. She found Archie's mother sitting on a bench, looking elegant and influential as always in her well-tailored clothes, a heavy pashmina draped over her shoulders.

"Hello, Mrs. Northwood. You wanted to speak to me?"

"Hello, Darcey." The voice that replied was sad and sturdy. "I take it you're doing well? Come sit. Thank you for meeting me. I just arrived in town. Archie doesn't know yet. And your work? Tell me please."

When people had little else to lose, they focused on controlling that which they loved the most with a fierceness that neared obsession. In the case of Mrs. Northwood, that was Archie.

But Darcey wanted to protect him too. She knew that bitterness in the family could easily creep into one's own life, creating a curtain of resentment that didn't allow light and happiness to shine through.

"Yes, I guess Archie told you that I'm working on—"

"The life story of my grandmother. Yes, I know.

I'm happy for you. She was indeed a remarkable woman and painter, and I hope you find what you're looking for, that it helps you graduate. He said there will be some paperwork for me to sign?"

Darcey could feel the restrained politeness in the woman's voice. She came a little closer and uncrossed her arms, trying to look relaxed and friendly. She had expected Mrs. Northwood would establish boundaries for the research.

"So you don't oppose my working on this story?" she asked.

Mrs. Northwood adjusted her pashmina, further sheathing her body in the expensive fabric that now worked like a protective armor. "No, I don't. I guess Archie is excited about the project."

"Yes, I think so."

"And it will open doors for you?"

"It might."

"I appreciate that Archie must be filling you in on the story, and I have to accept that it's important for him to play this cat-and-mouse game that my father prepared for him. The two of them were very close, as you know, and even though I don't understand why it matters so much now, I know Archie cares."

"Yes, his Grandpa Gus meant the world to him."

The wind was turning nippy, and Darcey's long bangs swayed in front of her eyes. Her hair was short enough to make it impossible to tie back. She thought of Ana again, and how she would probably not feel this insecure if she were the one talking to someone like Mrs. Northwood. But she wasn't Ana. She had a lot to lose if this project was called off.

"How about you, Darcey? What matters to you

most?"

"How do you mean?"

Mrs. Northwood paced around, her high heels click-clacking against the stone pathway. "I remember when you were very young, seventeen perhaps, you said you wanted to travel the world. You declared you would never marry. You would be independent and free, and you would see all the sights and all the art you could possibly see. Are you going traveling when you finish? Is that still what matters the most to you, Darcey?"

The woman had no idea how unimportant traveling the world was now. "Mrs. Northwood," she started. She had never quit addressing her formally, the same way she did when she and Archie were kids. "Priorities change. I was just a girl then, you know, with many dreams and no sense of how the world works. Not so much anymore. When I finish, I'm going to find a job."

"To support Nina?"

For a second, Darcey thought she hadn't heard it right, but her stomach clenched.

"Nina?" Darcey froze in place. How did Mrs. Northwood know? She and Darcey were never close. Mrs. Northwood was simply a woman who always looked at her like she wasn't enough. The mention of her daughter's name in a secret meeting was the worst outcome she could imagine. No, there was another, worse yet. Archie would find out, would stop talking to her, and there would be no best friend and no dissertation anymore.

"Yes, your daughter Nina. Come on, Darcey. Your parents live in the countryside, but news travels. Your father is very proud of her and has friends in town."

Darcey swallowed hard. "So Archie knows?"

Mrs. Northwood shrugged. "I haven't told him. And if you don't want him to, there's no reason he must, is there?" She adjusted her earrings, as if holding Darcey's secret in her hands was the most mundane thing. "Once Archie graduates, he will want to settle down, maybe find a nice woman to marry…have kids of his *own*. And you, Darcey, you have your daughter to think of. If you need anything, I'd be happy to help."

Darcey knees faltered. She didn't want to believe what she was hearing. Mrs. Northwood didn't like her, and the feeling must have intensified once she learned about Nina. It was all very disquieting. She had come to the meeting expecting to explain her project, reassure Mrs. Northwood that she would be respectful of Ana and her legacy. She had rehearsed answers to all that. She had not anticipated having to protect her daughter.

Mrs. Northwood tapped her elegant shoe on the ground, expecting an answer, but Darcey couldn't string the words together. If she said something harsh, she could really damage things for her and Nina. Archie's mother saw that as an invitation to continue talking.

"Look, I know you're good friends, and now that he's here with you, it would be a great opportunity for you to advise him on his future plans. We're doing you a big favor letting you into our family history for your thesis. Wouldn't it feel good to reciprocate?"

"Reciprocate…how?"

"Talk to him when you have the chance. Speak of the advantages of having a plan for a life after this. He's your friend, so you want what's best for him, no?"

"Yes, Mrs. Northwood." She heard the words come

out of her mouth, but they were foreign to her and not what she wanted to say. She wanted to say she had a daughter she loved, and she was very confused about Archie, and whether they were best friends, once-lovers or mates-to-be was none of the woman's business because they were adults. It was also her prerogative to choose if and when to tell Archie about Nina. And speaking of Archie, he might not want to settle down yet, and why was she being set to the side yet again? Why was she so objectionable? Because she was poor? Because she was a single mother? Because she'd once said she wanted to be independent?

Mrs. Northwood had always told Archie that his father was unhappy at home. Was she afraid Archie would be unhappy too if she stayed in his life? Because of her wanderlust at seventeen? Archie was nothing like his father. It was true she and Archie were once young and foolish, and she was hesitant to embrace her love, and she had kept secrets, but that didn't mean it was Mrs. Northwood's job to decide she wasn't right for Archie.

"I have to go now, Mrs. Northwood. I'll advise Archie. Please don't tell him about Nina." All she wanted to do was hide in her bed, cover her head, and listen for scary noises, like the weakling she was. "And I don't need anything, thank you. I'll just work on the project, with your permission, of course."

"Good, you have it. I'm going to go find Archie now. I'll be staying for a few days. I think you'll agree he doesn't have to know about our meeting. Goodbye, Darcey."

The woman walked away, and with Mrs. Northwood's receding footsteps the arboretum grew silent. She had said 'yes, ma'am' to everything, and just like that, she had become a certified coward. To be fair, hadn't she become a coward anyway the minute she chose to hide Nina?

She wished with all her heart that she had Ana's boldness. Ana would have found something radical to do or say. She would have laughed at Mrs. Northwood, would have called her bluff. Ana would have said, "Go ahead! Tell Archie and risk him turning on you!" But she wasn't Ana. She was just her old self, who deep down didn't believe she deserved Archie's love, or anyone's for that matter.

When she got home, she went straight to the corner of her room where she kept her palette of paints. She uncovered the canvas on the easel, the one she returned to time and again when she needed to think. She didn't have Ana's talent, nor did she intend to make her art public. It already had a special place in her life. It provided her with a haven whenever she needed solace. Her paintings reminded her of everything good and beautiful in a world that often turned ugly.

She kept her work-in-process shrouded, especially from Archie. It wasn't the possibility of someone seeing an unfinished piece that scared her. It was the subject matter. She traced the lines of the image with her fingers. The face was like a song, one she could find herself humming without even realizing, the kind that got stuck in the brain and sprouted into life throughout the day. She followed the contours of that smile she knew so well, the dimples that formed on both sides of his mouth. His face was masculine, but the smile gave him the innocence of a child. She didn't have Ana's capacity for abstraction. She painted what she saw, but he would never see himself through her like that because she was too scared to show him the picture. Her raw feelings were on display in it. This was her diary, made only for her eyes. And yet, look what could happen to diaries. Ana's was now in a stranger's hands, ready to be used as Darcey pleased.

Ana's diary was right there on her bedside table. It called her from time to time while she tried to infuse light in Archie's disheveled hair. It was a magnetic pull, hard to resist. The volume was leather bound, and although the cover was cracked, it had held up well. The pages inside told a different story. Some passages were clear and complete—others were made illegible by brown spots, tears, and crumples. The night before, she caught herself inhaling the corky smell of the paper as if she could learn the tale and capture Ana's essence that way.

She prepared for sleep and changed into a nightgown, her mind still insisting on going back to Mrs. Northwood. Maybe telling Archie ahead of his mom would be the right thing to do, but she couldn't decide. She sat at the edge of the bed, looking at a hypnotic point on the wall. When the diary cried its mermaid-like cry one more time, she took it in her hands and dove in.

Chapter 11
Ana

February 1st, 1922

Two days after the *vernissage*, Ana was sitting in her atelier's small kitchen nook, enjoying a cup of coffee and feeling like specks of fame were still clinging to her clothes. Invitations and new exhibits were sure to follow. She dreamed of meeting new people, talking to the press, showing her art again. Those yearnings gave her a hunger that breakfast was unable to quench. Still, she prepared her meal with urgency, arranging her favorite things on a tray her mother had bought.

A thin mist had covered the city. Inside the fog, cobblestone pavers and streetlamps gave the streets a dreamlike feel, which Ana experienced from the other side of her window. Watching the movement of neighbors hurrying to catch a train or walk to work, she knifed a small wedge of butter and slathered it on a piece of toast. The flavors of the morning, fresh coffee and jam, delighted her. It was a moment of perfection, a fleeting one, full of ideas about art and success, so she took full notice of it.

But soon the pleasure of warm French bread and sweet coffee was replaced with worry. Her morning with Joaquim and the strange intuition she had about it kept her heart prisoner and made her attention falter. The strange prophecy and the knot in her stomach alerted her to be careful. As she fell asleep the night before, she had made up her mind that the recent encounter would be their last time together. She reminded herself that no matter the powerful hold Joaquim had on her, she could do whatever she wanted.

Absentmindedly, she picked up the newspaper. From the edge of her seat, she spotted his name while looking for any reports of the event. A small excerpt was printed on page five, written by Joaquim. He had written about her, generous with his words.

Tenderness flourished in her chest and withered almost as soon as she noticed it. It was true that if she asked him, he would say nothing had changed—they still met in the mornings, in the sheltered space of her studio. But to her everything *felt* different, almost staged, in a way that had become painfully clear as she watched her jumbled dress on the floor from the vantage point of her bed the day before.

She knew deep inside that she still enjoyed preparing the room for his arrival, smoothing her best embroidered sheets with scalloped edges over her bed. She would then trace the handcrafted flowers of the pattern on the pillowcases imagining that his head would soon lie there, his hair against the ivory fabric.

Yet it was now easier to deal with the idea of a lover than with Joaquim. The feeling brought clarity but also pain; she was a mistress—nothing else—and mistresses that cared were disposable and clichéd. They worried about each kiss that could be the last, they realized that they were always second to wives, and they eventually became needy and unwanted. She couldn't think of anything more awful than becoming that woman. If she had gone into the affair for fun, she now knew that nothing but complete surrender to love would do. It was either that or no lover. Under the circumstances, complete surrender was not an option.

She searched for and found some scissors, with which she cut off the newspaper article, careful like a doctor performing surgery. The clip went into her diary. Her hope was that there were many more articles to come. She needed to stay lucid and composed if she wanted to focus on her career. Going from a talented unknown to a star would take her full attention.

But staying clear was not always easy. On that particular Tuesday, she had forgotten to pick up fresh flowers at the market and considered that slip to be a sign of bad things to come. For a practical woman, she was becoming quite superstitious. Without the bouquet, her atelier, stripped of the paintings that were still at the cultural center, was just a hollow eggshell, devoid of its usual colors and textures. At that moment, her room was a depository of shadows and showcased only barren walls, whose coldness haunted her. It was nothing like in the previous weeks, when rivers and trees, vases and roses had provided the perfect background for their affair.

Wednesday morning found her returning to bed, unable to stay up. The surrounding ivory sheets camouflaged her naked legs, and she let her left hand rest on her messy hair. She was so tired. It was like someone was sucking all her energy and making it impossible for her to stay awake.

Her dress still lay to the left of her bed like a discarded, once-treasured object. She did not wish to pick it up and take it to wash. She had not gone home in two days. It was as if the studio would vanish if she was not there. Or maybe being away from it would make her feel like it never existed to begin with. And every one of her mornings with Joaquim would fade away, too, and hide in the dark corner where all forbidden romance went to die, the abandoned dress the only evidence it ever lived.

Ana once more caressed the pillow where Joaquim had lain twenty-four hours before, and its disloyalty, its insistence on still carrying his scent, gave her skin goosebumps. It was over. It had to be. She would write him a letter, and she would leave no room for second chances or negotiations. She only wished their last morning together had not been marred by her anxiety.

She had started feeling pity for herself, lost in those spiraling thoughts, when an insistent knock ended her self-hypnosis. Her feet glided quickly into high-heel slippers. Walking to the front of the studio, she wondered who could come unannounced at that hour, and she hoped, muttering a prayer, that it was not Joaquim.

On the other side of the door was one of her neighbors, Jussara. She was a hardened woman in her fifties, with a square face. Deep creases on the sides of her eyes added a leathery quality to her appearance. Her thin lips were pressed together as if intent on preventing a smile from blossoming. When she spoke, her voice matched her countenance: grave and hoarse.

"Good morning, Miss Eça. I was hoping to have a word with you."

"Sure." Ana moved out of the way, signaling that they could talk inside. From her vantage point, she could see that two other neighbors, women of about the same age, were observing her movements from the small square across the street.

"No, thank you. I will be brief."

"As you wish." Ana didn't like where that was going. She had nodded at this woman a few times, they had been introduced once at the market, but that was the extent of their acquaintance. She disliked surprises of this kind. Nothing good could come from them.

"Miss Eça, it has become obvious that you are.... emm…entertaining a gentleman here. At first, I thought it might be a client. I know you paint. But no client comes to visit every Tuesday at the same time. This is a family *vila*, a quiet place where good, God-fearing people live. We would like to keep it that way." The woman threw a look back at the other neighbors at the square, indicating this was not her opinion alone.

Ana could hardly believe what she was hearing. A sinking pain squished her stomach. As far as she was concerned, what she did inside her own space was her business. She didn't know what came over her, because the Ana she knew would tell the woman to mind her own life and would then shut the door. But instead, tired as she was of the whole affair, what came out of her mouth was the biggest lie in the world, one she crafted as she spoke.

"Miss Pereira. I don't know where you got this idea. That gentleman you speak of is a model."

"A model?" The woman, whatever she had anticipated, was clearly not expecting that.

"Yes, I wanted to paint a man, smoking and wearing suspenders and a hat, like those we see downtown going to work. So, I asked an acquaintance to pose for me. Would you like to see the painting? It's done." She prayed the woman wouldn't say yes, since there was no such work.

"That won't be necessary."

"All right then. Maybe you can explain the situation to your friends over there, and we can all move on with our lives, shall we?"

"Very well. Good day, Miss Eça." Without even a hint of a smile, Jussara turned around and went to join her friends across the street.

Ana did not wait to witness their reunion. She could hardly contain herself. The door slammed, and the heels of her house shoes clicked against the ceramic floor. She was angry. She could use anger. Anger was better than self-pity. Harnessing that energy, she opened the bedside drawer, reached for some paper, and found a fountain pen. Ironically, it was Joaquim's black pen that she found under an old sketchpad.

She wrote a first draft that didn't make any sense, so that was torn to pieces and dumped into the wastebasket. Breathing in fully, she started a new, more detached letter. If deep inside she knew that she was sending Joaquim away because she cared, she tried to convey to him the opposite, that because she didn't care, it was silly to waste any more time.

She considered saying that she loved another but was afraid he would see through such a blatant lie. She settled for a few decisive words of mock logic and a curt goodbye. She didn't sound like herself. Even her handwriting seemed brisk and uninvolved, quite different from the usually careful and refined penmanship she enjoyed using in her correspondence. With equal briskness, she stuffed the letter into an envelope. She would mail it later that day.

But it was time for other things. She was invited to a fancy *lanche*, an afternoon meal at Maria Pia's house, because of the art exhibit's success. Her plan was to coax an invitation out of Maria Pia so she could go to the Modern Art Week as a guest artist rather than a member of the general public. She had much to do before then. Looking her best was vital.

She stopped thinking and went into action, splashing her face with cold water, dressing quickly, styling her hair. A half-hour later she was ready. Outside, the fog had started to lift, and weak sunrays fought for some space. The cobblestones looked like graphite under the new light.

Maria Pia's *palacete* stood less than a block away from elegant *Avenida Paulista*, the most exclusive address in the city. There, coffee barons and industrialists built sumptuous villas inspired by French architecture and surrounded by flawless gardens filled with roses and begonias. Elegant ladies promenaded in front of the buildings, wearing the latest fashions consisting of boxy silhouettes, velvety shoes, and headbands.

A perfect line of trees flanked the three kilometers of the avenue. The buildings emulated the elegance of Paris, but Ana was not intimidated; as many other artists of her generation, she grew up affluent, studied in the best schools, knew her manners and how to behave at tea, was comfortable talking about clothes and culture. She also spoke French. She could pass for a blushing heiress any time, even if that kind of social conformity went against every part of her spirit.

A middle-aged woman in a dark blue uniform and

an immaculately white apron opened the door and smiled at Ana. Despite the maid's grin, circles darkened the woman's skin under the eyes. Those who needed a job had little time for such considerations as makeup or a good night's sleep.

"Afternoon, ma'am," the maid greeted her, rolling her "R" in a way that placed her unmistakably as from the countryside.

Ana held on to her beaded clutch and wondered how she was going to force an invitation. Should she bring up the Modern Art Week subject hoping Maria Pia would get the hint?

"*Dona* Pia is in the *varanda*, out back. Come on in, please. I am about to serve the *lanche*." She moved back slightly for Ana to go inside.

To get to the *varanda*, Ana walked through a cream-colored entrance hall decorated with a round wood stand, carved with a flower pattern. To the left was a large oblong jacaranda table surrounded by eight stately chairs.

For a moment, Ana had to fight the impulse to take her shoes and stockings off and stand barefoot on the soft surface of the thick carpet. The sound of a flute sieved through the house from the open glass-paneled doors of the *varanda*. This would be a musical meal, and the surprise was wonderful. As she progressed toward the patio, the maid appeared with a tray of treats.

"Ana. Delighted you could make it," said Maria Pia over the sound of the quartet, her eyes large with excitement at the young artist's arrival. The four musicians, two playing the flute, one the seven-string guitar, and one the *cavaquinho*—the very small ukulele-like instrument that Ana had once been told was native to the island of Madeira—did not miss a beat.

They continued playing the *chorinho* of Chiquinha Gonzaga, with its sweet, lively rhythm, so symbolic of the Brazilian spirit. Her hostess's walk was punctuated by the distinct cadence of the genre, known to be the antecessor of samba, as if she was quietly dancing.

Maria Pia introduced Ana to all her friends, society ladies who smelled of musky and expensive perfume just like Ana's great-aunts. Ana drew nearer to air kiss them by the side of their faces, realizing the smell resulted from a combination of perfume and *laque*, the hairspray that kept strands in place and heads looking expensive.

From the ladies' *coiffure*, Ana redirected her attention to the linen-dressed table that displayed a delectable selection of afternoon delights—cornmeal cake, pumpkin-coconut puree, figs in syrup, and *pudim de leite*, a Brazilian version of flan. All treats were cradled in expensive porcelain dishes with a charming hummingbird pattern. Art was everywhere.

For a second Ana wished no one would touch the food, that it would be preserved in its perfection as if on a canvas. But an eager, pearled woman, with chubby and nervous fingers, spoiled her fantasy by scooping up the plump figs and dripping their juices on the tablecloth. Maria Pia, in her aristocratic self-restraint, pretended not to see.

"Ana, may I say that the exhibit was a success? Today's *lanche* is my way of thanking you for your part in such a triumph. To Ana," and they all raised their glasses of Champagne punch; "*tin tin*," they said as the goblets touched, making a bell-like sound. "You will no doubt join me for the Modern Art Week. I've spoken to the organizers, and one of your paintings can be displayed if you wish."

There it was. A spontaneous invitation. One that was beyond her dreams. Ana nodded in consent while her stomach fluttered with excitement. "Of course I do. Thank you!" She took a long, sweet sip of the punch. Why had she worried in the first place? Everything was going her way.

"So it's settled. Oh, and I almost forgot!" Pia took a quick sip from her glass and put it down on the table. "Here he comes. The very man who can help you be known to all."

Ana turned her head to face the garden gate. Joaquim appeared, sporting a light jacket and a half smile.

"Ladies, good afternoon to you." He touched his hat and bowed. When he looked up, his eyes locked on Ana's. "*Senhorita*," he said, with that half smile turning into an open grin.

Ana's palms were so moist that she put her glass down before it slid from her hand. "How are you, Mr. Joaquim?" she replied. Brazilians often use first name honorifics even in more formal situations, and her mouth was so accustomed to his name that instinct spoke for her before she could think. "Would you excuse me for a moment while I powder my nose?"

Every time they were in public these days, she hid in a lady's room. It was becoming a compulsion. She knew it was best to just face him, yet her resolve faltered once he arrived. Of course she couldn't do that forever, and so after she stalled for a few minutes inside the gold-accented little cubicle, she opened the door to find him waiting for her there. She took a step sideways, only to end up cornered and partially hidden by a red brocade curtain.

"I hoped you would be happy to see me." His hand touched the side of her face, and he let it slide down toward her chest. His lips rubbed against her ear.

"Not here, Joaquim."

"What's the matter? They're all outside. No one around. It's you and me, *coração*." He brought the hand to the nape of her neck.

"I said not here." Annoyance was a hot wave flapping in her chest.

Ana had to think fast. She used the curtain for cover and cloaked her exit so she could rejoin the party. "You're here to interview me and make me famous. Do your job."

She returned to the celebrations and was immediately met with questions.

"So, what is it like? Being an *artiste*, that is." The woman with the pearls had introduced herself as Dulcenea, a stout lady who looked as if she was perpetually about to lick her fingers. Her expensive jewels, however, conferred on her a significant dose of importance as did her mixing of French words, a common trait among the Brazilian upper class.

"I wouldn't know what it is like not to be one."

"I think it is all so romantic!" intervened another lady, Aurora, this one almost the exact opposite of Dulcenea, with long, bony fingers and no corpulence whatsoever. Her thin back was arched forward making her look older. Her interest neared hunger.

"It is hard work, too, but of the best kind," Ana

explained.

"And you look so charming, with your fashionable hair and clothes. Look at that barrette," continued Aurora with undisguised admiration. The woman probably did not lead a very exciting life; her dark blue clothes were expensive and very polished to be sure, yet they lacked any interest or drama and fell lifelessly over her waif-like figure much like they would from a hanger. But she behaved in such a kind manner, with pleading eyes and fidgeting fingers, that Ana didn't have to pretend satisfaction.

"Well, thank you. That is very kind of you to say. Would you like to try the hairpin?" Ana was already removing it from her hair. Aurora's wide-set, green eyes looked ready to jump out of orbit.

"It is very beautiful indeed," Aurora's hands trembled with nervous admiration as if she had been given the chance to play with one of the Crown jewels.

At this point Ana noticed two other women at the corner. Their faces contorted as if they smelled something putrid. Ana snickered to herself. She had that kind of effect on some women. Outright contempt. Oh well, she sighed. Things were what they were. To try to please everyone was impossible and extremely time-consuming.

In a while, one of them walked toward Ana, her expensive black shoes hammering the floor in an audible threat.

"I don't understand modern art. Honestly, to me it's just scrawls. Corruption. No wonder Monteiro Lobato, a truly talented writer, was so mad and critical of it."

Ana should have been taken aback. Criticism

directed at her art was usually hurtful. But between the nosy neighbors, Joaquim's insistence, and now these spiteful women, she had had enough for one day. Instead of angry, she was strangely amused.

"Adélia!" Pia was livid. "I'm sure you don't really mean that." Her tone was firm but polite. She was trying to send a secret message that was painfully clear to everyone.

"Oh, but I do. Ana will certainly understand my position. It's clear I'm not the only one. And this Modern Art Week idea, I could bet my diamonds it will be nothing but a fiasco."

Ana examined Adélia, starting at her curled hair and ending at her shiny shoes. She made the action look quite deliberate, as if she was examining a canvas in a museum. Then she widened her smile and delivered the blow.

"I'm certainly not surprised. It takes a special person to understand change before it happens, and we cannot all be special, now can we?"

At this, Joaquim, on a bench smoking, lost his composure and chuckled. Adélia's face turned pepper red. To avoid the destruction of her idyllic afternoon, Pia took control of the party.

"Ana, I would like to announce that I am buying one of your paintings. That beautiful flower composition. I love those oranges and yellows. Can I have it?"

"It would be my honor." Ana turned her back to Adélia and engaged Pia, Dulce, and Aurora in pleasant conversation. Pia sighed a loud breath of relief.

At the end of the afternoon, a photographer appeared in the *varanda* with lights and tripods.

Joaquim, who had behaved the rest of the afternoon, despite his piercing stare and constant surveillance of her, gave the young man directions. The women, preoccupied with looking their best and with how they would be remembered by posterity, arranged their hair, reapplied make up, and grinned to the camera until their cheeks became numb.

After the photos, Ana escaped the afternoon meal dizzy with punch. She had managed to elude Joaquim, though her heart ached with the prospect of never lying with him again. She chose to walk for a while. As she reached the *Parque Trianon* with its classic belvedere, Ana thought of the central role of the "Trianon Intellectuals," so named because they always met in the park, in making the upcoming Modern Art Week possible. The events they had envisioned were only a few days away, and her art would have its place there. What an exciting time to be alive.

The excitement and the fatigue of evading Joaquim's advances finally got to her, and she sprawled on the grass with her hands supporting the back of her head. People frowned at her as they walked by, but she didn't care. The women were the worst, with their judgmental gaze, as they clung to their cloche hats with one hand, their husbands' arms with the other, and urged their spouses on. From the men, she could often get a smile—never from the women. She remembered Adélia at Pia's house and Jussara the neighbor. She figured she gave women reason to suspect her. It was like each of them knew of Joaquim.

Embraced by the fresh aroma of the park, Ana decided she should go home to air up the place, start anew, leave her studio and its memories for a while.

But there was something else she wanted to do on the way home. She put her shoes back on, disregarding how constricting the leather was against her stockingless skin, and went in search of a streetcar.

****

Ana had chosen to go to the place she knew would change her life. The *Theatro Municipal*, a large Baroque-inspired construction completed in 1911, stood majestically facing the *Praça Ramos de Azevedo* in the downtown area. It was one more symbol of the wealth that coffee plantations produced for the state of São Paulo and its namesake capital.

Ana had passed by the area many times before, but the building now took new meaning; it was to become the site of the Modern Art Week. She looked up at its ornate façade and wondered if she was witnessing history unfolding before her eyes, like the red carpet that was sure to be unrolled at the beginning of the event. She had an uncanny feeling about the year; she couldn't tell if it was about the life of the city or her life, but something was coming. Something big.

As if a wind had whispered in her ear, Ana turned around to face the square. She was grateful for the premonition, for it allowed her to prepare herself, when she saw the familiar silhouette of Joaquim come into focus a few meters from her. Again. The sight of him caused a familiar swishing in her belly, which she chose to downplay. With the event so close, and the newspapers crowded with news of the occasion, it was no wonder that he might be there. But he could also be looking for her. Had he actually followed her?

Ana's first reaction was to hide once more, this time in the shadows of the building. With the letter still burning in her purse, it was useless to cause a scene in front of the theater; drama should be reserved for the inside.

Her knees were weak under the weight of her heart. She used the hard wall for support and waited in silence until his footsteps became indistinguishable from the noises of the city. She tried to cling to the excitement of the upcoming event. She breathed in and looked to the sky, conjuring up the joy she got from her art, but her eyes melted into a scattering of tears. Mercifully, only the walls saw her cry.

That night at home, over a light meal of cold chicken, soft cheese, and coffee with a splash of milk, Ana took stock of things. She found herself alone, neglectful of her friends and family because of Joaquim and painting. She hadn't visited her parents in such a long time. Like the art of her contemporaries and her own, she was at a crossroads, wanting to take charge yet feeling unable to deal with the love she had to leave behind to get what she wanted.

They were all swimming in contradiction: fighting the bourgeoisie while being bourgeois themselves, embracing the national while finding inspiration in all things European, breaking social rules while deep inside keeping old-fashioned morals. Being modern was not always easy. Sometimes it required more than lobbying for women to vote or cutting one's hair short. It took surrender and patience. It also took time. And while a little voice inside of her kept telling her to be careful, like most young people, Ana figured she had plenty of time.

Chapter 12
Darcey

The burnt-red table linens at *La Fleur Rouge* were embroidered in black. Darcey traced the etched designs with a finger and dreamed of how her house would look one day. Fancy fabric like the one on this table would be involved. She would set the table with the antique silverware that had belonged to her grandma, and she would bake orange cake with sugar frosting, which she could decorate with candied fruit.

While she played with the graceful shapes, and waited alone at the restaurant for Archie, she wondered what this dinner invitation meant. Did he think of it as a date? Should she act like they were on a date? It wouldn't have been the first—dinner or date. With the excuse of talking about Ana, they had eaten Chinese food, vegetarian, and now they were having French. She would begin with baked Camembert. With each new meal, they were getting closer, the conversation more intimate, her guard down. Last time, she had almost uttered Nina's name by mistake.

With anxiety and alertness rising in her stomach, Darcey sipped on the water, her throat constricted by thirst and her lips dry with winter. She let her fingers touch the petite pendant hanging from a gold chain around her neck. It was a four-leaf clover for luck, twenty-seven years old this year. The good fortune was bound to kick in any minute now, she thought to herself with little conviction.

The words of Mrs. Northwood still echoed in her brain, though. Archie would arrive, and she was supposed to advise him on life matters, as if she had any expertise on them. He came in a few minutes late and unbuttoned his coat as he walked into the room. The effect, charming and irresistible, was redolent of the classic movies she and Archie often watched together. He wore gold cufflinks trimming a butter-colored shirt that peeped from underneath a chocolate-brown wool jacket. Archie looked happy all the time, as if being content was his vocation. He smelled of soap and cologne. By contrast, Darcey felt underdressed in a short-sleeved black top and a white linen-blend skirt too lightweight for winter, with her scuffed boots to make it worse. She moved the chair closer so as to obscure them underneath.

This is not a date, she kept reminding herself. She tucked her hair behind her ear and smiled back at him. She'd used a flatiron to turn her shaggy hair into something smoother, and she had parted it on the side, letting a soft strand fall over her eyes. She clipped one side of the hair with a small comb, allowing a dangling leaf earring to show. Ana had been her inspiration.

"Sorry I'm late. If you'd let me pick you up, we'd have arrived together," he said. "I like what you did to your hair." He gave his coat to the waiter before he sat down. She blushed. He was looking at her in a special way.

"Thank you. I was on campus anyway—not home."

"What are you drinking?"

"Water." She raised the glass in a toast.

"How adventurous. Can I pick something else out for you? It's Friday after all."

Darcey twisted her lips. "Are you trying to get me drunk?"

He leaned forward and rested his right forearm on the table. He whispered, "No, I am trying to make you lighten up, Darcey. That's my only agenda."

Most days, she didn't notice how much she picked on him for no reason. She sat back and tried to relax. She would prove to herself she could be nonchalant if she tried, even if that took all her energy.

"Fair enough." She gave in. "Order something I'll like."

Archie nodded at a young, freckled server.

"Can I offer you something to drink?" The waiter had a full, baritone voice that sounded as if he'd been voiced-over.

Grinning, Archie looked at the server and gave him precise cocktail instructions involving strawberries, lime twists, and maraschino cherries. "And I'll have just a glass of house red, thank you." He turned back to Darcey. "This might be a little too sweet for you, but who knows?"

She raised her brows and refrained from answering.

The drink turned out to be delicious. Apparently, bartending was yet another of Archie's annoying hidden talents. As she sipped the syrupy beverage, she looked for cues that it was all right to chat about Ana. She didn't want him to think that all she cared about was the story. She cared about him too.

Archie noticed her vacillation. "I promised I'd tell

you some more, and here I am. Wanna order their lemon and butter sauce chicken with early potatoes? It's my recommendation, anyway. We will get right down to Ana after." He closed the menu and pushed it away.

Darcey agreed and in no time the young man, order in hand, big voice tucked inside, went to take care of other customers.

"So Ana was on the verge of being discovered, she had some great supporters, and she had an affair with a married man. Her exhibit was a success, and she decided to focus on her craft and let Joaquim go," Darcey summarized. "Can you tell me more? Maybe something not from the letters, something from Gus?"

"You have to understand that women like Ana were pushing the boundaries of propriety. It was 1922 after all. At first she didn't care. Her audacity was paying off. Her paintings got disapproval from more conservative people because of the distorted shapes she created and the themes she focused on. But the more modern loved it, which was exactly what she wanted. She was a star. She could get away with anything. Her first exhibition was more than she hoped for, drawing critics to rave about her. And then came the week that changed so many lives."

"Modern Art Week, also known as the Week of '22."

"Exactly. Brazilians until this day consider it to be one of the most important moments for art in the country. It was also the year of celebration of one hundred years of independence from Portugal, so you can see the symbolic meaning in that too. And Ana was right there. But although many things were going her way, she was learning that having it all had its price.

Exciting times, don't you think?"

"Unlike today."

"What do you mean?"

She tried to find the right words. "Do you sometimes have the impression that nothing exciting happens anymore?" She circled the glass with alternating fingers, as if she was trying to make music. In truth, she was being a little flirtatious.

"Don't be dramatic, Darcey," Archie scoffed. "That's because you're here, in this moment in time. You are the little mouse in the maze, can barely see what's in front of your nose. I'm sure many people back then were thinking the same. Those were the days. Things were better before. Where is this world going, and all that."

"I don't know. It's work and pay bills, and work again. Where's the passion in that?"

"Asks the queen of skepticism," he added before gulping his wine. "Besides, didn't people have to pay bills back then?"

She put her own drink down. "Stop that. I am not cynical!"

"*Right*," he took his time injecting the word with mock condescension. "Listen, Ana, just like everyone else, could only see so much. Hindsight is great, isn't it? You don't have to go far into the past to see that— just watch a movie from the 1970s and the concerns of the time are obvious, the same way ours will be to someone else in the future. We are all blinded by our own cultural experience. Our time is our box."

He finished his wine. The waiter came to pour some more.

"Not for artists, though," Darcey said. "Artists are

different. They don't have to be ruled by conventions like you and me." She thought of Mrs. Northwood and her own inability to break free from expectations, live fully in her own terms. "But that's the reason why they are so often misunderstood. Take your cinema, for example: movies by real geniuses survive the test of time. Truth be told, artists are the only ones who can see beyond social niceties. But we often try to hold them back, we judge their visions. They should be allowed to be carefree, to be like children."

Archie's laughter caused fellow dinners to turn their heads. "Darcey Mendes—do my ears deceive me? Are you a romantic after all?"

She didn't give up. "If believing in art and artists means I am a romantic, then I'm proud of it." She drained the rest of the drink. Her head was floating in a cloud of strawberries.

"I don't think that's the way you're supposed to drink that," he teased.

"Shut it, Archie," she said putting the glass down and running her fingers zipper-like across her lips. She was starting to feel a little wobbly and had to make an effort for her words not to slur, for her eyes not to bat in continuous flirtation. And Archie was starting to look really good, even better than when he arrived looking like a 1950s heartthrob.

"Anyway, I brought something to show you." He reached inside his jacket. "This is a picture of an afternoon tea at Maria Pia Alcântara's house. Pia was a very wealthy matron of the arts, and she loved Ana and her paintings. This photo was taken right before the Week of '22. Look at Ana." He moved his chair and positioned it so that they both could see the photograph.

"She really was quite the looker!" Darcey held the picture and took everything in—the delicate clothes of the women, the nice tea set, the abundance of desserts and pastries, Ana's charming smile, the ivy that crept on the wall behind them.

She smelled Archie's scent—he sat very close, twisting his neck so that their faces would not actually touch. For a second she wished they would. A moment later, she felt as if her personal space bubble burst, could not shield her any longer. From what, she wasn't sure. She brought her hand to her face and then to her hair. She tried smiling and then looking serious, as if she was focusing on the picture. She straightened her skirt and her necklace, and she sensed his breath on her neck.

In her confusion, she moved sideways, and her arm hit his wine glass. The red liquid stained her skirt and destroyed it. A shriek came of out her mouth, causing those around her to turn their heads.

She got up in a jerk. "I need to use the restroom." Disappearing into the next room, Darcey was oblivious to the fact that she held the old picture in her hand.

When she returned after blotting her skirt with a million useless paper towels, Archie's chair was back to its original place. She gave him the picture. Maybe soon he would realize how unfit she was, even for dinner out, if he hadn't already. She thought of Mrs. Northwood. In her imagination, the woman was shaking her head in disapproval.

She covered her lap with the fine restaurant napkin and talked nonstop to mask her embarrassment. Maybe if she didn't give him any time to think, he wouldn't arrive at the conclusion that she was a fool. She hoped to survive the humiliation by focusing on the story. After two hours of conversation and questions, talking of Ana and Joaquim, of Brazil and art in the year 1922, and yet another two rounds of the delicious strawberry drink, Darcey accepted Archie's offer to take her home.

"It's not like I'm driving you far. You remember that I live across the street, right?" She tried to take no notice of his teasing remarks, but the alcohol made it more difficult because it caused her to relax.

In the car, Ella Fitzgerald sang "The Man I Love," and Darcey let her head fall back on the headrest. She ran her hand down her throat, feeling the delicate skin of her neck. She imagined Archie pulling over, touching her face, until her thoughts eclipsed the great singer's powerful voice. She returned to an upright position. "I enjoyed tonight," she confessed before her brain could censor her mouth.

"Me too," he replied.

When they arrived at their street, Archie ignored his garage and stopped the car in front of Darcey's building. She prepared to exit the vehicle, looking for her things under the low light of the car's interior only to realize he had come to the passenger's side to hold the door for her.

"Mademoiselle," he kidded, extending his arm as if to show her the way.

The air, which smelled of woodchips and night, was fresh and fragrant. It had a sobering effect on Darcey, but not enough to put an end to her clumsiness. She held his hand and improvised a few steps, as if she were dancing a pas-de-deux. When their eyes met, she lost her grip of him and landed against the red front door.

A young man exited her building. He nodded at Archie and Darcey. She stood there, watching the swirls of mist that broke away from Archie's mouth, so close. She knew the texture of his lips, their firm feel, the calm with which he engaged in a kiss. The memory of it, of her buried experience, came back to her, waking her from months and months of denial. She forced the recollection back

How would she prove her love for him had nothing to do with his money? How would she argue she wasn't simply looking for a father for Nina when she had hidden the little girl from him all this time? How would she explain not having told him about her daughter? His mother would be the first to point at how perfect her timing was. She couldn't antagonize Mrs. Northwood by saying she loved Archie instead of advising him to pursue someone from his circle, no matter how wrong the woman was. Family came first and, as much as she wanted to be in his life, she wasn't family. It was easier to live in solitude, removing its mysterious layers until it became almost kind. Until she could stand her own ground, be financially independent, if that day ever came, Archie was out of the question.

She looked down, rummaging for the key in her pocket, and the moment, the one that might change everything if he tried to kiss her, was gone. He was her best friend. That was it. Dreaming of what else could be just wasn't practical.

"Thanks for dinner." She offered him a grin, a bittersweet force tying her stomach in knots.

"Sure." His hair was tousled from the wind, but he didn't try to put it back into place. "Maybe next time we can have Greek food? I know you like that." He played with the keys that jingled in his hands.

"Next time?" Her heart beat a little faster.

"You…want to know more, right?"

"I do. Yes. In fact, I'm going upstairs for some reading." She wrung her hands together. "We have Donaldson's party next week, no?"

Archie stared at her. What could she do to make him stay, even for a little longer? She wasn't ready for the night to end. She had come to rely on Ana when she needed an excuse to be around him.

After a drawn-out, deliberate breath, he started back to his car, but Darcey stopped him. "Wait!" He turned around. "Sit here on the steps near me, and tell me stories." Using all she had left, she enticed him to come back with a shy smile.

And come back he did.

Chapter 13
Darcey

February 1997

There were reasons to look forward to the month of February. Opportunities to enjoy new exhibits at the university museum were far apart, and so Darcey had been counting the days until the Women of Latin America show opened. The cocktail party to launch the event was scheduled for the evening of her twenty-seventh birthday. Was the coincidence prophetic? Did it signal her fate was linked to the story of these women and of Ana in particular?

February had also brought fresh snow. The layer of crispy white frost was a relief: without it, black ice made the roads slippery, unsafe. Not a great feature. As it was, being outside was a pleasure, the air as pure as a loving wish.

Ana's art wouldn't make it to the exhibit—she was a small, forgotten figure—but some of her contemporaries, with their ideas about independence, the meaning of womanhood and art itself, were sure to grace the well-lit halls of the gallery, which, in its whiteness, was almost an extension of the snow around campus.

Darcey turned down most attempts by friends and family to celebrate her birthday. She had taken a bus home to spend time with Nina the weekend before. That was a perfect gift. Or would have been the perfect gift if her parents hadn't looked so worried.

When Darcey got home, Nina had run from her grandmother's side into her mother's arms, and Darcey lifted her child for a tight hug. Every time she went home, the surprise over how much Nina had grown hit her, spreading its bittersweet taste. She was missing out on milestones, discoveries, and smiles. She reminded herself it was for a good cause.

Nina put her head on her mother's shoulder only to remove it a second later and cry out.

"What's wrong?"

Eleanor came closer. "She has an ear infection. I already took her to the doctor."

Darcey's insides twisted into an anxious knot. "Is she all right?"

Eleanor sighed. "She'll be fine. She's on antibiotics. The doctor prescribed that expensive kind, though. The one that doesn't need to go in the fridge?"

"Yes?" Darcey replied, already thinking of what was coming.

"And the insurance company doesn't want to pay. Another seventy-five dollars plus the twenty-five of the co-pay."

"I'm sorry, mom. I will reimburse you."

"Only if you can." Her mother's answer was a clear sign that things had gotten worse. She would otherwise have brushed it off.

Darcey had seen a campus call for Portuguese tutors, to help a couple of athletes who were falling behind on their language studies, and decided there would have to be enough hours in the day to add that job to her schedule. She would call on Monday.

Upon her return to campus, all her pending problems caused her to feel even more guarded than usual. She walked around shielding her chest with her books and making mental lists of all the parts of her life that needed juggling. Everywhere she went, there was an issue. The ones that were small were getting bigger, requiring her attention. Dissertation, love, mortgage, child. She could take her pick.

Lucile was a good example. As usual, her aunt couldn't take no for an answer and had insisted Darcey stop by at lunchtime to share a small ice-cream cake. It was a nice gesture except that Lucile replaced real meals with sugar whenever she could, causing Darcey to worry terribly about her aunt's health. She had many risk factors for developing diabetes and should've been eating much better foods. Yet how was Darcey supposed to make sure a grown woman ate properly? When she tried, all she did was sound like a grouch.

Her parents had called with good wishes and sent a card through the mail. They put Nina on the phone and she shouted, " 'Appy Buday, mama!" which made Darcey smile. They had avoided talking about money even if concern was obvious in their voices. At least Nina's ear infection had cleared.

Finally, she hadn't yet heard from Archie on her birthday. Had Mrs. Northwood said anything? If he could at least stop by for a hug, her night would be saved. Though what right did she have to expect anything when she constantly pushed him away? He was still helping her with the work, and that was more than she deserved.

Darcey was going to the exhibition by herself. She

dressed with extra care that evening, something she'd neglected to do in the last several months. She wore a black woolen dress and combed her hair back, styling it with spray for hold. She finished off with large dangling earrings and a touch of eye shadow. It was a departure from her usual no-nonsense beauty routine. She was elegant and bold, cloaked by the perfumed night air and protected by the soft glow of the streetlights that lined the way to the museum, a few short blocks from her apartment.

The museum gallery looked bright and inviting, all its lights on and large bouquets at the entrance. Large canvases were on display, showcasing common modernist themes—people, nature, objects, often distorted, collaged, or reassembled.

Darcey waved at a few people she knew. A couple of students were volunteering that night, and others, herself included, would take turns during the week. The result was worthy of any big-city museum, and Darcey marveled at all the work she loved and all the history it told. After a little while, one of Browne's few remaining graduate students came over to her. He wore a black tee and black pants, their uniform when they hosted an event.

"Enjoying yourself this evening?"

George was a tall blond man in his early thirties, and although he often nodded at Darcey when they met at any of the long halls of the art department building, they had never exchanged more than a few words.

"Yes, it's beautiful, isn't it?" She couldn't help but talk in big arms and a voice that came out louder than she intended. Art made her happy that way.

He crossed his arms. "I'm partial to Mexican

modernism, in no small measure because of the work of Frida Kahlo but also of Rosario Cabrera. How about you?"

"Brazilian. I've come to love Brazilian modernism. I love the colors, the lines. The pictures are almost architectural." She drew a triangle in the air with her finger.

"I can't say I know much about it at all." He shrugged.

"I think you'd like it. Let's see if we find anything for me to show you."

They walked the white-walled extension of the museum's main room until she found one of Tarsila do Amaral's paintings, a primitivist rendition of blue and pink puffy flowers. "This is not one of her best known, but I like it very much."

"Yes, I can appreciate that. And I can see what you mean by architectural. You know what?" He turned to face her. "Hey, maybe we could sit together one of these days, discuss some works. I could stop by, and you could tell me a bit more about Brazilian modernism. I can talk about my work on Mexican art."

Darcey didn't know what to say. She wanted to be friendly, but her first loyalty was to Brazilian art and her scholarship. She had no intention of going out with this man. He had no reason to want to be her friend now. Yet she wanted to be civil.

"I'll be working in my office tomorrow." If they were to meet, better make sure it was at school. "It's a group office, so there might be students around, but my desk is near the window, and there's good light to appreciate some art."

"It's a deal then. I know where it is. I'll be there

after class in the late morning." With that he said goodbye and went back to distributing leaflets about the exhibit. Darcey was free, and relieved to be able to explore the rest of the art unencumbered.

There were images from diverse parts of Latin America, and because modernist art often focused on reimagining local beauty, the geographies and the flora depicted were varied, too—seas, jungles, hibiscus, palm trees. The work was well received; visitors talked about the pictures with enthusiasm, pointing at favorite scenes and providing their own interpretations. The small artist photos that accompanied the art showcased strong women: penetrating eyes, powerful faces, and the certainty that no matter what the world thought of them, they knew what they were doing.

Two hours later, after looking for him from time to time, checking her watch compulsively, she approached a stranger from behind, touching his shoulder thinking he was Archie. She could only imagine the disappointment he saw in her face when he turned around. After that, Darcey accepted that Archie had not shown up. She'd hinted at her excitement over the exhibition and gone the extra step of mentioning the details of place and time more than once. She never invited him directly, and that had likely been a mistake.

At nine o'clock, after having been in the gallery for two hours, she decided to leave. Everything seen, inspected, and admired, she grabbed her coat and concentrated on tying her scarf while her eyes traveled through the glass panel of the gallery to the courtyard. Outside, the glow of little specks of fire, suspended above a nearby garden table, ignited her imagination. Curious, she made her way outside. Warmth filled her belly despite the low temperature, and she couldn't help but tear up. Archie was lighting the last few candles on a frosted cake.

He stood up straight and spoke, pretending royal affectation, "I made sure to ask the powers that be for a night with no wind. It would have spoiled the surprise if the wind blew out the candles before you could. It's a carrot cake. Your favorite," he said with pride.

"I can see that. It's beautiful." She grabbed his arm in an awkward but genuine hug.

"Are you going to blow the candles or what? I have managed to keep the wind at bay for now, but my level of influence over the forces of nature is not that great yet."

She walked closer to the table, leaned in, made a wish, and blew the candles with all the power in her lungs.

"What did you wish for?"

"If I say, it won't come true." Despite her fixation on the dissertation, she had wished for him. It was always him.

"I see. Well, my wish for you is that you get your wishes. Happy birthday, Darcey."

He produced a couple of plates and plastic forks. He cut a piece of cake and gave it to her. They ate in silence for a while, enjoying the still night and the luxury of being able to not speak. Even their occasional awkwardness was natural and familiar.

"I was afraid you had decided to skip the exhibit altogether," she said. It was her birthday. She could afford to tell him he was important.

"No, I thought of coming, but figured the cake was more important." He nudged her shoulder with his, and she enjoyed the brief moment when their bodies touched.

"My two main meals today were cake."

"Then you had a successful birthday."

"I suppose. I was thinking…"

"What?"

"Wouldn't it have been lovely if Ana's art had been exhibited here? There was a beautiful Tarsila do Amaral. The two would have gone together perfectly."

"Yeah, that would've been great. Maybe one day." He ate a large forkful of cake and started slicing another piece.

"I was thinking of the Modern Art Week of '22." It was her way of entering Ana's world again. In Ana's world, she was by default always close to Archie.

"Did you know that in the end she actually got to exhibit there? It was the highlight of her career, but it wasn't without controversy. It *is* Ana we're talking about."

"Tell me." She removed a speck of cake from the side of his mouth.

The night felt like early spring even if the calendar indicated otherwise. They sat outside the museum for a long while, and Archie entertained her with stories about Ana. His enthusiasm was contagious, and she succumbed to a bittersweet pull to agree with him, no matter what he said. She could listen to him talk for hours. But that desire was tinged with sadness. His censorial mother, the awareness of her pile of problems, the feeling of guilt for not having told him about Nina, all those ghosts intruded in her wonderful night. The more she wanted Archie, and the closer she got to surrendering to that love, the bigger the obstacles became.

When she started yawning under a shielding hand, Archie offered to walk her home. He placed the cake inside its pink box and led the way to their street. In front of the apartment, feeling emboldened by the night and the art, she held his head with both hands and gave him a peck on the lips. It was a small gesture, yet a wave of heat overtook her. He kissed back, as timidly as she had, looking afraid that if he made any bolder moves, the magic would dissipate midair. The way his eyes shone in return didn't leave her all night.

The next morning, she remembered with a jolt that she'd made an appointment to meet George in her office. She collected the correspondence she hoped to work on that afternoon and stuck it in a manila folder. Then she packed some lunch, including an apple to offset all the cake, and hurried out the door.

Another teaching assistant was holding office hours in a corner when she arrived. She tried not to make noise, sat at her desk by the window, and flipped through the correspondence she wished to read, paying special attention to the dates. She came across a letter from Maria Pia about the Modern Art Week and flagged it with a tiny sticker tag. A minute later, when George arrived, she shut the folder and stood up to greet him.

Once he sat down, he rummaged inside his backpack and produced a set of papers and a volume. "I brought you a book and a few pages of text I recently wrote. Here."

They talked for a while, and she flipped through the pages of the book, noticing the differences and similarities between Mexican and Brazilian art in the early 20th century.

"I'd be eager to hear what you think of my work. Perhaps we can even have a little study group."

Annoyance rose to her cheeks and made them warm. She was now certain she had made a mistake by inviting him to the office, which she had done out of misguided politeness. Many students had study groups and peer reviewers, but they didn't have Dr. Browne looming in the shadows. She was annoyed by this offer and at the sudden familiarity George seemed intent on establishing. Until that very day, none of Browne's students had wanted to have anything to do with her, and she liked things that way.

"Thanks. I'll take a look, and I'll let you know," she said.

One of Darcey's students arrived looking for a graded test. Hesitating to leave George behind but feeling under pressure to help the young man, she stood up and spent a few minutes chatting at the door. More than she intended. The student was contesting his grade, and it took some time to convince him it was, in reality, a fair score. When she came back, George was looking out the window with great concentration as if he was following some activity outside.

A second later, he was in a hurry, putting his work away without care and avoiding eye contact. "Darcey, I gotta go. I just remembered an appointment. Great talking to you. We'll talk some more later." He shoved his papers in his backpack and left without looking back.

She sat and held her chin in her hand, wondering if she had done something wrong, until her eye caught a color, something of interest. On the ground lay the sticker she had attached to Pia's letter, in silent affirmation that he had been through her things and now knew about Ana.

The episode upset her more than she cared to acknowledge. Was George a spy for Browne? If so, what would lead a senior professor to snoop on a grad student? Whatever his original intent had been, George had tricked her. She was a naïve fool. Confronting him was an option, but that would only make her look desperate, and if she told Archie he would likely confront George, making it seem like she couldn't fend for herself. All that the incident proved was she shouldn't go around trusting people. They had ulterior motives, and they lied and schemed to get what they wanted. Browne, George, and Mrs. Northwood were good evidence of that.

What if someone stole her dissertation? At the moment, it was all she had going for her. Unable to stand the idea of being alone at the end of the day, after having taught and graded and held meetings with students, Darcey sat at a coffee shop and ordered a pot of tea. The beverage sent a pleasant wave of warmth down her chest, and she made an effort to breathe deep calming breaths. She had Ana's diary with her.

Ana's hopes for and fear about the modern art event were evident on the pages, which were illustrated with beautiful sketches. Ana was not common. Not in the least. Yet she was guarded. Her diary didn't make Ana ordinary, for that would have been impossible. Yet it made her human.

Darcey asked for a second pot of tea and read on. Portuguese had become a comforting and familiar language now, with its musical quality and multisyllable words. Darcey mouthed them for practice as she read. She learned about Ana's hope for the Modern Art exhibition, about how modern art was received, and about the future of Joaquim. And she was less lonely because of the musing of a woman transported through time from seventy-five years before, a woman who now kept her company.

Even if she succeeded in crafting a coherent account of Ana's art, would people be interested? While she would never showcase her own art, how would her academic work one day be weighed? Would it be shredded to pieces? Would people think she was an imposter standing in for a scholar? Would they prefer the work of the likes of George Pearson? Or maybe her thesis would be a worthy contribution. She imagined the best-case scenario: speaking to a large and interested audience about her findings, and then receiving their compliments in a reception afterward, knowing she had made Ana shine again.

"Would there be anything else?" A kind-looking young woman behind thick glasses came to check on Darcey. She had been there for almost an hour. The image she had concocted disintegrated.

"No, thank you. I'd better be going."

"I'm sorry if I took you out of your concentration. You were so immersed in the reading." The young woman placed the bill in front of Darcey.

"I probably needed that. I can be pretty focused. A little too much."

"If the subject is interesting, why not?"

"Yeah, let's hope I can *make* it interesting before someone steals it from me." She paid for her tea and walked home thinking about George, Archie, and trying to ignore the gut feeling that she wasn't safe just yet.

Chapter 14
Ana

February 1922

February the thirteenth took forever to arrive. Ana received a letter from Maria Pia, which explained what would happen at the *Theatro Municipal*. There would be many concurrent sessions going on: poetry readings, lectures, art exhibits, music. It was paradise for the modern soul. Ana was as excited as a child who had been promised a carousel ride. She had left her clothes ready and hanging from the front of the armoire since the night before, but not without having tried a dozen outfits before settling on one.

The opening ceremony was scheduled for eight. She dreamed of meeting the exhibitors, fellow artists who had inspired her. She dreamed of making this night a landmark in her life. These were the most important artists of her generation, the ones bound to end up in history books. Invitations for her to exhibit would follow. News articles written by journalists, other than Joaquim. Trips to events abroad.

But despite the dream, Ana had no illusions. Even if modernism was an intellectual pursuit, not all thinkers approved of the ideals of the movement. Some were especially upset at the call for a break from more classical patterns of art that until that moment, ruled twentieth-century Brazilian art. Constricted emotion or its absence altogether. That's what some wanted.

It was widely reported that the events would not be without controversy and opposition. Some of the defenders of academicism were sure to make their voices heard, *maybe even in contrite verses about Greek vases*, she thought sarcastically, imitating Greek statue poses with her arms in the air. And she wasn't sure which side critics and the general public would take. The former could make her career, so yes, critics mattered; but the public…the public was the reason for art in the first place. Sometimes people were scared to embrace the new. It was just easier to stand with the crowd. Tiresome, but easy.

She applied red lipstick deliberately and sprayed her body with a vanilla mist. She put her clothes on. It was such a new design she imagined heads would turn as she walked through the elegant halls of the theater. She dressed to be seen. It would go well with her bold art. She would not side with custom for custom's sake. Never. To nod in agreement was simply too vulgar and trivial; it was better to be wrong than to be one more. Of that she was sure.

She looked at herself in the mirror once again. Her black, beaded dress shone back at her. She adjusted her embroidered stockings, a high fashion item. Like modern art, she was bound to attract acclaim and disdain. She was fine with both.

On that summer night, the entrance hall of the theater was the site of the inaugural exhibit. The night was cloudy, and the high temperatures required light clothing. A soft breeze welcomed guests to the entrance of the theater, where an international visitor, a man talking in English, wore a suit more appropriate for American autumns. He was fanning himself with his hat. Ana was sorry for him. Maybe no one had told him that in the southern hemisphere, the seasons were reversed, and that February was one of the hottest months of the year.

By the time Ana entered, knots of anticipation tying her stomach, the most conservative members of the public were already booing Graça Aranha's speech even though the writer was one of the organizers of the event. Aranha, the famous intellectual, believed the arts should not be subjugated by scholarly pursuits, to the dissatisfaction of many. Ana stood by a middle-aged couple who alternated shouting, shushing, and making animal-sound imitations, like the barking of dogs, the neighing of horses, and clucking of chickens.

"Some people simply don't know how to behave in public!" Maria Pia looked personally affronted as she spoke to Ana. "You can expect to find some of these same individuals at elegant restaurants eating with the right pieces of silverware! And yet here…they bark."

"Don't worry, *Dona* Pia. I'm quite sure the organizers expected nothing different. The things people do when they feel threatened…" Ana patted Pia on the shoulder for comfort, but she couldn't help but be amused. Modern art evoked such deep emotions in these people that they were willing to neigh.

With the speech and the booing, Ana was already invigorated. Of the works on display, she particularly enjoyed those of Anita Malfatti and Di Cavalcânti, the first marked by their reliance on bold yellows and human forms that looked almost like melted wax on the canvas, and the second alive with people and their round shapes and piercing eyes. She also took a special liking to the sculptures of Brecheret depicting men in their clean and simplified lines, their strong presence.

She was introduced to some of the artists later in the evening, and her hand trembled a little every time it reached for theirs. "Your art will make the day after tomorrow even more memorable," said one of them from within a broad smile. "Don't you think?" She might faint. She looked at Pia, who grew an inch taller, proud of her artistic find.

"It's all wonderful, thank you. That day will be wonderful too."

The tenor of the rest of the evening remained tense, the audience booing the more sweeping statements by the artists, but Ana was too occupied with taking everything in to be bothered. Art was all that mattered.

"For many of you, the curious and suggestive exhibit that we launch today, is an agglomeration of 'horrors,' " had been the first words of Graça Aranha. Later she recalled the inaugural speech the most. The first impression. There was always something unforgettable about the first stroke of the brush, the first word of a speech; like a first kiss, it might not be the best, but it held the promise of a beginning. Ana loved beginnings. A new painting, a new dress, a new love. They sent pleasure waves through her body, the memory of which kept her alive.

****

No night events were scheduled for the next day, and so Tuesday provided quiet time that allowed Ana to do the things she loved the most. Simple things—the market at first light, the time when the fruit was the freshest, even if the most expensive.

A large sisal bag held her purchases. She craved peaches and figs. She would buy some vegetables too. Perhaps turnips and okra, the first for a salad, the second for a stew with tomatoes and onions. She was so hungry.

The usual people were at the market. Their day had started several hours before with the loading of produce at a distribution center. They were the invisible pulse of the city—workers of the market, construction crews, bakers, factory workers, tired in their early-morning unsung glory, as they attempted to sustain a metropolis. Though some people thought of São Paulo as provincial, it had engorged itself to home almost 600,000 inhabitants.

The market kept the city alive by feeding it. That fact didn't escape Ana, who always had a kind word for its vendors, a smile, an understanding look. In return, the vendors, the little boys selling lemons, smiled back; they gave her flowers, and they helped her pick the sweetest fruit. Each side was grateful for what the other provided in this symbiotic relationship. That is what made the market beautiful, what made the walk there joyous.

After the ceremonious selection of produce, Ana took her purchases to a square where she sat with a book. She also drew sketches in her little notepad and ate tangerines and walnuts. She rejoiced in the touch of the cool breeze, the chirping of the *sabiá*, the smell of white oleanders.

She found new inspiration for her art in the simple world painted before her, in the manner in which the light made even floating dust shine like precious stones, in the beautiful things she witnessed on her way to and from the market: birds, smiles, generosity. And for a while she forgot Joaquim.

Sitting at the square and closing her eyes that were suddenly overwhelmed by the joy in the sights she saw, she missed Eugênia and figured she should plan a visit after the exhibit. It would be good for Eugênia to breathe a little of the urban air of São Paulo even if it were only through stories. The countryside was probably very unnerving at times, with its long silences and pitch-black nights. Ana was sure she couldn't stand the country for long. She would be doing her friend a favor.

Wednesday brought a light rain. The cooler temperatures allowed for charming shawls and pretty cardigans to parade the halls of the theater. Ana's own shawl was a majestic composition of reds and bright yellows, a color scheme that agreed with her perpetually crimson lips.

Loud voices and long bouts of applause intermingled across the palatial chambers of the second floor. The antagonistic mood the audience displayed on the first day intensified as different artists took center stage to showcase their music, their paintings, and their words. Red was the right color to match the passions running wild in the corridors of the theater. If the first day had brought loud booing, the second witnessed raised umbrellas and fists and heard hard terms and profanities.

Ana had anticipated that not all members of the public would be ready for modern ideas, but to see men and women voice such disdain for innovation was daunting. Some of them seemed so mad that it was as if the additional energy could not be contained in their bodies, and they walked the corridors weaving like drunkards.

A small woman bumped into Ana while the young artist was stepping backward trying to better appreciate a painting. The lady, wrapped in a severe and unbecoming brown suit, looked at Ana with contempt, perhaps reading in her eyes her appreciation for the canvas, and walked away muttering improprieties under her breath. If at first the contempt of these amateur critics had been amusing, it had now started to irritate her. Modern art was there to stay. They better get used to it.

Ana took a deep breath and went into the room where her paintings were. Heads turned to welcome her, and she could tell who the modernists were because they were smiling and making room for her to walk toward the paintings. She stood in front of her work as a spontaneous round of applause erupted. Right at the moment, out of the corner of her eye, she saw an object fly toward her self-portrait and crash onto it with a splat.

It was a tomato. It had landed on the dress depicted on the picture, and it ran, in an indecorous pale red, toward the ground. Still dazzled by the act, because it had been both bold and unexpected, Ana looked for the defacer of her picture, and her eyes found those of a round and stout older woman who held her fist up in defiance.

"We don't want your art. It's ugly."

"That's right," said a diminutive man next to her. He wore a black, ill-fitting suit, and when he raised his hand, loose threads hung from its seam. He was unraveling, as were his clothes. "Go back to where you came from."

A small commotion, with pushing and yelling, followed. The artists had vowed to dialogue with the audience, so they didn't want to escort the woman out. At the same time, they couldn't permit the work to be ruined. In the end, the woman chose to exit of her own accord, and was followed by the man who was still shaking his fist up in the air.

Ana was shaking too, her whole body trembled, but soon friends of her art were all around, consoling her and making sure she was all right. She thought it best to use a rag and remove as much of the stain as she could until she had a chance to evaluate the damage. Someone had already had that idea and was cleaning her dress, the one forged in oil paint on the canvas. It was not that she doubted the need to stay on course and be modern. It was that the reactionary ways of fellow Brazilians were wearing her out. What did they have to lose to be so afraid of art?

As always, Pia remained enthusiastic and chose to see the incident as evidence of the passions art caused to rise. At the end of the day, she took Ana by the arm to a corner. "I'm going to tell you something very important, Ana, and I want you to remember it." She paused for effect. "I can tell you have real talent, and your art is met with ardor of all kinds. You are blessed with great talent, but the rest is up to you." She gave Ana a hug and left. Ana vowed to herself never to forget those words.

After the event, Ana joined a group of artists that were going to continue their intellectual pursuits at a café nearby. She was still energized by the exhibit and by the controversy she had created. She thought to herself, *An artist has not arrived until someone throws a tomato at their work. I've arrived!* Her companions were bewitched by her work. Over drinks and cigarettes, they asked her questions, discussed art, humanity, and love with the superciliousness of those who know just enough not to know any better. They laughed out loud as if to reassure themselves of their wit, and they broke into spontaneous recitations that seemed to have been fully rehearsed.

A tall, blue-eyed, curly haired, and altogether handsome sculptor, whose insinuations she pretended not to notice, walked her home afterwards. She didn't have any desire to invite him in. Joaquim had done away with that kind of impulsiveness in her. And so, she didn't. He walked away looking down, disappointed.

The final day of the festival arrived with the anticlimactic personality of endings. It was a night of music and, as a result, the least controversial of the events. The compositions of Villa-Lobos echoed in the halls of the theater; they did not provoke in the attending public the primeval reaction of the earlier nights and of her own art. If anything, their beauty and their themes brought people a little closer together.

Maria Pia's car was set to take her home at the conclusion of the event. Ana could tell that the woman was eager to share her opinions, to gossip. No matter what Pia said, Ana would forever remember that week. She had become more widely known; she had her life ahead of her, a life of inspiration, of beauty and art. She was the luckiest woman in the world.

Before they left, she asked if she could have a moment to go outside and stare at the theater, to see if it looked any different from a few nights before, to draw in her memory a picture of what it looked like on that day.

****

The air was fresh and the temperature moderate outside the theater, and Ana stared spellbound at its majestic construction.

"Are you going to paint it?"

Ana's head prickled as if cold needles had been inserted all over as she recognized the voice. He was always sneaking up on her. He had turned into a haunting ghost. She had never mailed the fate-sealing letter. She wondered if somewhere deep inside her brain was the buried wish that he would be waiting again, at the same place, and maybe it was that subconscious desire that had taken her there and caused him to follow.

"No, I'm just admiring it, thinking of what will be." She gave her back to his seductive voice. She knew the contours of his face well enough.

"And what will it be?" He came a little closer. His confidence was at times irritating. He traced the curve of her arms with his fingers. She wished he hadn't.

"Joaquim, this was never a good idea. I've already told you we must stop seeing each other." She felt a little cowardly for not saying it eye to eye.

"We cannot stop seeing each other," he replied with a smirk. "You seem to always go to all the events I cover."

"You know that is not what I mean. And those will be the only times you will be seeing me."

"Don't you think this is a little drastic, *coração*?"

"Stop calling me that." She cut him off, this time

turning around to face him.

"Easy, easy! What is going on with you?" He lit a cigarette and inhaled its smoke with careful deliberation. "And on such a beautiful night."

Why was his tone always so patronizing? *All the better*. It makes breaking up easier.

"Let's not end this badly, Joaquim. It was what it was and nothing more. I'm sure you will find many willing arms to console you, if this is in any way difficult for you. Or maybe this time you can fall in the arms of your wife for a change." She regretted her sarcasm; it usually conveyed more than it should. Cynicism was often a desperate ploy from those who had something to hide or to lose.

He brought the cigarette to his lips again.

"You will come back, Ana. I know you. I'll see you soon." The ease with which he had let it go made her think he didn't believe for one moment she would actually leave. He bowed to her holding his fedora gallantly and walked away. She saw him disappear into the square. So much for writing goodbye letters. So much for forgetting to mail them.

With those endings—the art week, the affair— daily life became motionless. Yes, the exhibit had propelled her career, but something that big would take a while to happen again. By the end of February, the feeling of stillness had become almost comforting, a state of awoken dream. It did not tell any tales. It did not give away the many ways her life was about to change.

Chapter 15
Darcey

February 1997

Professor Donaldson's February party was an event Darcey looked forward to every late-winter, a time of the season when everything stopped being fresh and promising because the New Year wasn't new anymore, and the everlasting sea of snow started to get on everyone's nerves.

Pierre-Auguste Renoir, Donaldson's favorite painter, was the frayed excuse for the tradition: the party was always held on his birthday. Much like the master's paintings, the event was a repeated success. The atmosphere inside the professor's arts-and-crafts home was informal, but people dressed up for that occasion. Donaldson played period music from different eras and served old classics like canapés, artichoke and shrimp appetizers, olives in garlic dressing, and deviled eggs. For starved graduate students, it was a treat not to miss.

Darcey wore a second-hand, dark burgundy velvet dress she'd bought with money saved from her birthday and a black silk scarf, a present from Lucile. She had also bought a bold, red drugstore lipstick, and she blushed while she applied it. Then came the finishing touch: a thick bracelet in an old-gold tone that she'd found in a flea market. Archie had bought it for her when he saw how much she liked it. The design was of fish and turtles, made more evident by the darkened crevices around the etchings.

"I can't accept that, Archie. It's a little expensive," she had told him at the time.

"Nonsense. You might not have another chance," he'd said, already paying for the item. She had cherished the present ever since. After enough hesitation, she slipped the piece around her wrist once more and snapped the clasp closed. Beautiful things were made to be worn.

Darcey took a look in the mirror. Would Nina one day look just like this, or would she end up taking after Flynn, a man who was little more than a stranger to them now? She thought of Ana, too. Was the artist right to sever love at its root when it became an inconvenience? Was it ever convenient, though?

Playing with her bracelet, hearing Lucile's voice claiming her fate was sealed, she waited for Archie to pick her up as the little mechanical alarm clock next to the futon tick-tocked the arrival of eight o'clock. Donaldson had invited Archie to the party when the two men met by chance on campus. She was so happy to be spending the evening with Archie.

When she tired of watching his door from her window across the street, she reached for the letters and found one whose date made sense. It was from Eugênia. She turned on the lamplight and went to work.

Villa Americana, March 31st, 1922
Dear Ana,
I am concerned about you. Your last letter seemed

somewhat incoherent and rushed. Your beautiful penmanship was so transformed I could hardly tell it was you writing the words. Why do you want to come here so urgently? Of course you can come, but I wish you would tell me what is bothering you so much. I thought things were going well for you, with your art and exhibits being such a success. I hope this has nothing to do with that man. I believed you would really leave him. So what could be happening? I will be waiting for you at the train station as you asked. You certainly can stay here for as long as you want. But ease my concerns and send me some explanation. Please be well.

With all my care, Eugênia.

Darcey tried to put herself in Eugênia's place, to imagine how she would feel not knowing what was happening with her friend. Ana's life was suddenly unfolding right at that moment rather than seventy-five years in the past. Darcey had come to regard both Ana and Eugênia as her own friends, even though they were separated by the two extremes of the same century. Now she was worried too. Her throat constricted, and her hands turned clammy. If only Archie could arrive soon and tell her about Ana. It was naïve to expect the letters to tell everything. There were two keys to the story: Archie and the correspondence, and one didn't unlock the mystery without the other.

But that wouldn't be fair, would it? To quiz him on a night they were supposed to have fun and relax? Maybe Ana just missed her friend. Maybe she was still recovering from having left Joaquim. Yet Darcey's intellect insisted on looking for problems and enigmas.

But tonight, she'd control her mind. The topic was bound to come up in conversation, but not from her mouth. She'd focus on Archie and on impressing her potential colleagues. If things worked out as Donaldson had outlined and she applied for the job, it should help if these professors already thought highly of her. She sat by the window and read from the diary while she waited.

The ride to Donaldson's cottage in a remote area north of the campus took a pleasant turn. Archie had been late, twenty minutes and no excuses, but when she opened the door and saw the way he took in her dress, the wait was suddenly worthwhile. For once, he had been the one to blush, right before saying, "You look...radiant, Darcey." She couldn't remember ever receiving a better compliment.

In the car, she swayed to the songs Archie offered by changing mixtapes swiftly. She sang off-key the lyrics she remembered, but it didn't matter. In time, she started teasing him:

"Oh please, 'romantic rock?' " she said reading from the tape case and drawing invisible quotation marks with her fingers. "Give me some real rock'n roll!"

"What do you know of rock'n roll?" he scoffed.

"I know you wouldn't recognize it even if it wore a neon T-shirt in front of you."

"You wish," he said as he looked at his watch. His tone grew sober. "I'm sorry I was late. My mother called right when I was leaving."

"Not a big deal," Darcey said.

"Why don't I make up for it with some information on Ana and her show?"

He started speaking of Ana. Family must have been on his mind. She let him talk about the exhibit, about Ana's dress, and the Theatro Municipal.

The bits and pieces Archie narrated matched what she had read in the letters and in parts of the diary. But Ana was not always consistent in her journaling; sometimes there were lots of details, other times a rushed line left Darcey hungry for more, so it was good Archie could fill in some of the gaps.

At the party, a well-lit living room was alive with the sounds of conversation and the satisfying laugher of the guests. Donaldson's house smelled of warm spiced drinks, wood, and mold. In the mudroom, where boots, hats, umbrellas, and firewood fought for space, Darcey removed her shoes, feeling her cold feet inside her delicate black tights. Archie followed suit. Like a traveler to a faraway land taking the hint from a more seasoned voyager, he trailed her around the house.

Darcey laughed at his socks, striped in shades of orange and dark green, and Archie's cheeks reddened. Donaldson came to them smiling. "Great! You're both here. Go find something to drink in that large tin cooler by the kitchen counter. There's plenty of food, too."

In the dining room, a professor of literature was making a toast. "If something should hurt, may it be your cheeks because of how hard you smile!" Students laughed and raised their glasses.

Archie gestured for Darcey to join her colleagues. "I'll get drinks." He headed to the kitchen acknowledging people he knew with a wave or a nod. Soft jazz played quietly enough not to interrupt conversations. The saxophone was especially soothing, and, when Darcey watched Archie go, her heart fluttered.

He stopped near the stove, grabbed a handful of pretzels, and munched on them. A minute later, someone shoved two bottles of old-fashioned soda into his hands. They exchanged pleasantries, and soon he looked ready to rejoin her, stepping out of the kitchen. Looking at him, Darcey caught herself happy, and she broadened her smile for him to see. But her excitement was short lived: a second later, a hand was on his shoulder, and he turned away. Darcey positioned herself where she could see and hear what followed.

"Hey, stranger," said a raspy, put-on voice. "Were you planning on not saying hello?" The woman speaking threw a lock of red hair over her shoulder. It took a couple of seconds for him to connect the face to the voice. But Darcey knew who it was right away: Dominique Saunders, from Archie's International Law class. He'd once told Darcey about her eying him during long lectures. He'd said her commentaries in class were plagued by logical fallacies. Inside, Darcey rejoiced at the little detail, as if it indicated a major character flaw.

"Dominique? You know the Professor?" He sounded surprised and a bit uncomfortable, but Darcey could not tell if the last part was true or just wishful thinking.

"I like art. Took one of his classes when I needed an elective, then took another one just for fun. You?"

"Oh, I'm here…with a friend," he said.

From those few feet away, Darcey felt the words pierce her chest. She leaned against the wall, pretending to listen to Browne in the next room fall in love with his own voice. It was like trying to read a book while

173

someone else watched TV.

"You look quite dashing tonight, Archie. This green sweater looks good on you. May I?" Without waiting for his assent, she slid her fingers down the front of the garment as if determining the exact texture of the wool was vital. "Really nice." She grinned.

"Thank you," Archie mumbled. He removed lint from the front of his sweater and tried a faint smile. "You're here…by yourself? I mean…you're here with friends?"

"Alone—till now," she said shifting her weight repeatedly from her heels to the ball of her feet and back again. She was short and stood several inches below him. "Thought the worst that could happen was recognizing a familiar, friendly face. I was right." She lifted her eyes toward him.

Feeling guilty for eavesdropping, Darcey scrambled to sit on the floor under a string of lights and listen to Dr. Browne, who was clearly enamored of his academic brilliancy. He made a statement about art in the 1960s and the effects of changing world politics on artistic expression, and he held his chin up like a hunting dog sniffing the scent of its prey. "One cannot really separate artistic, journalistic, and political activity at that time in many parts of the world. Art was an outlet for what could not otherwise be said, written, or spoken about." His right hand set the pace of his voice. He was the conductor of a verbal symphony, and his forehead shone under the glow of a large iron chandelier.

When the professor paused to take a breath, Darcey offered a comment.

"Is your assumption that when political undertone

invades the arts, the actual artistic merit of the work diminishes? But it's hard to generalize," she said. "Take Brazil in the 1960s and early 1970s. Some of the most brilliant music comes from that period. A lot of it was political."

The professor looked at her with Medusa eyes. "Yes. I wasn't finished, and it's a bad idea to interrupt a senior professor."

Condescension flourished in his small but loyal cheering squad. He had said she needed better guidance, but it was clear that what he wanted was just another feather on his cap, another student because very few wanted his guidance anymore. Was he disappointed when George told him she was making progress after all?

The night was quickly offering much less than it had originally promised—Archie's undivided attention, professors thinking she was smart. Instead she was feeling so small, she might as well have turned invisible. Did Browne have to shut her off that way?

Scanning the room, Darcey focused again on Archie who held on to bottle necks with one hand and dried the free hand on his jeans to disentangle himself from Dominique's grip. His eyes caught Darcey's. "Excuse me, but I was about to take these to Darcey over there. I guess I'll see you later?"

Darcey grinned, experiencing a moment of levity in the middle of frustration. A second later, Archie handed her a bottle of orange pop and offered a hand to pull her up. She looked at him with relief.

"Sorry, I was looking for a bottle opener and people kept making conversation."

"No worries. Thanks for rescuing me. The situation

turned a little awkward in here."

"That guy?"

"Yeah, I'll tell you about that some other time."

After chatting a bit with his students, Browne restarted his speech.

"Never mind that man. Who cares what he thinks?" Archie put his hand on her shoulder. "You're probably too smart for him anyways." He gave her that smile that made everything right.

She drank the soda, aware that people were now speaking around her. Intelligent conversation was welcome, but small talk was beyond her. And then most of what was said would be relinquished at the door, discarded like the blue plastic cups everyone was drinking from.

What would Ana have done at this gathering? Would she have had a sharp retort for Browne? Darcey could see Ana here, the center of attention without even trying. She probably didn't have to chat at all, able to shush an inconvenient guest with a stare. In Darcey's imagination, men fell silent in front of her beauty. Ana's perfect little face would be framed by perfectly behaving hair and secured by eyes that knew it all. Her own eyes probably revealed all her qualms and the fact that she knew nothing.

Donaldson came over. "You'll wanna grab a glass of the Argentinian Malbec I just opened for the two of you. It's outstanding."

Archie thanked him. "I'm driving, but I'll take one for Darcey." He looked at her for confirmation.

She nodded.

Once Archie left, Donaldson motioned for her to sit down. "Enjoying yourself?"

"Sure." She spoke with little enthusiasm. She didn't have to lie to her advisor, but the words came out of her mouth, beyond her control so she wouldn't disappoint him.

Archie came back with the wine. "I'll leave the two of you to chat," he said before exiting the room again.

"The work?" Donaldson asked.

"Progressing. I'll update you in the office. What a fascinating woman. I love this story. This project."

"Well, I am glad to hear it. We'll talk on Monday then. I'm still confident you can finish and find a job here. Do your best, all right?" His eyes were pleading now. He was a straightforward man, but he was also kind.

"I will. And thank you…for standing by me. I will see it through," she promised.

At the buffet table, Darcey refreshed her drink. She used a small plate to gather a chunk of cheese, a soft roll, a couple of deviled eggs, and some fruit. She was just considering adding some potato salad to the mix when a shadow appeared on the table and engulfed her frame.

"Darcey Mendes, how are you? I haven't seen you in a while." Victoria, one of Browne's grad students, took her time enunciating the words. She was cultured and polite.

"Good. And how are you?" Darcey looked up and tried to sound equally appropriate. Her gaze rested on Victoria's tall figure, embraced by a teal cashmere shawl over which her long, ash brown hair cascaded. Long fingers, with impeccably polished nails, rearranged the bangs that fell over her eyes. She smelled of gardenias. She looked expensive.

"Very well and very busy, you know, the last stages of a dissertation are always so demanding. I'm really excited, though. Dr. Browne says I should be ready to defend soon."

"Right." Darcey examined the dish of olives and hoped to discourage any further conversation.

Victoria did not take the hint. "Oh, you will see, the time will come for you very soon. I just know it. And we'll all celebrate." She touched Darcey's arm.

A wave of heat rose to Darcey's face. Guilt gurgled in her throat. The condescending tone she read in Victoria's words could have been a product of her imagination. Her arms were wobbly and her voice strained. "Yeah, maybe one day soon." Her classmate was lovely. Perfect in every way. If Victoria had succeeded in grad school, good for her. It was a feat to be cheered, not envied. Unaware of its taste, Darcey looked for consolation in a cold deviled egg.

As if part of a procession, different students walked by her at the buffet table, saying hello. She grew so accustomed to their rhythmic walk, she was startled when Browne approached her.

"Have you given it any more thought?" He stuffed his mouth with an egg, licked his fingers.

"To what?" She covered her own mouth.

"Switching advisors. I hear you are working on some secret documents. Maybe you found a topic? Something to do with Brazilian modernism?"

Darcey squished a soft roll in her hand. He wasn't supposed to know that. George, the spy. This just confirmed it. "Dr. Browne, I am very content with the mentorship I get from Dr. Donaldson. I'm sure you have a lot to offer your students, but I'm already committed to seeing this through under his guidance. Thank you."

He shook his head. "You know that's an error of judgment on your part, especially because I provided you advice on the value of studying modernism and practically spelled out what your research should be about. Others could, I don't know, misconstrue this refusal to acknowledge my contribution as a form of academic dishonesty. And since you're going on the job market soon..." He let his words trail off and looked around as if expecting applause.

She could hardly contain her disbelief. Spelled out what? He'd said one sentence to her and suggested she defaulted to French icons. What had she done that even remotely drew on that? He was not going to make a fool out of her. She gulped down her wine for courage.

"Dr. Browne, you don't care about my work. You know nothing of Brazilian modernism. This is *my* work, *my* find, and...and..." She saw Archie, talking to a stunning middle-aged woman in an elegant red wool dress. Browne faded in the background, no more than a passing cloud.

"And what?" Browne was red in the face, ready to explode.

Archie touched the wall and leaned forward, giving the lady all his attention. He was always the good listener. Holding on to her every word, letting her savor the moment. He was making her feel special without even trying. Her fingers touched her collarbone and then trailed the path of her necklace toward her chest. Women said so much with their bodies. Darcey was ready to scream.

Perhaps it was the wine. Or Archie flirting with

another woman. Or her habit of taking a step back instead of standing her ground with the likes of Browne. Whatever it was, Darcey stumbled on the leg of the table and fell backwards, breaking her wine glass into a thousand pieces and twisting her ankle. The floor was cold against her back, and all eyes were on her. She imagined how she must look: ripped tights, wrinkled dress drenched, utter astonishment on her face. Her shoulders hurt as she calculated whether she could move. Her lower back was tingling, and her pride as shattered as the shards on the floor.

Mercifully, no one giggled. Browne ate another egg.

Archie was first on the scene. "What hurts?"

"Left foot."

"Here." He wrapped her arm around his neck and pulled her up. "Don't put any weight on it." He opened the door to Donaldson's studio, dark and quiet in comparison to the smells, chatter, and clattering noises of the party beyond it. "Can you hop to that sofa?"

"Yes. Oh, God. I'm so embarrassed. No one will take me seriously now. What a mess I made." She couldn't stop her head spinning.

"Never mind that. By now someone has already fetched a broom and a rag. And your reputation can survive a tumble."

Archie kneeled in front of her. She was shoeless and certain her delicate and slippery hosiery had been partially responsible for the fall. Her clumsiness too, and the lovely lady who was receiving all of Archie's attention, and the stupid table, and Donaldson who had placed it there. Yes, there was plenty of blame to go around.

He reached for her ankle. "Can you move it?" Without waiting for an answer, he grabbed the leg with one hand and the foot with the other, rolling it first inward and then outward. He looked up waiting for a reaction. "All good? Does this hurt?" His hands burned her skin underneath the hose; her pain vanished. "Do I continue?" His hand traveled up and down her leg, warming it up, reminding her body of what it already knew.

"It's fine, Archie. You can stop now." She bent down toward her foot, as to retrieve it.

But he held his ground, looking at her, their faces so close his breath caressed her lips. If she moved just a little closer, if she breathed just a little deeper, their lips would have no alternative but to meet. "Is that what you want me to do? Stop?"

She tried but couldn't hold his gaze. Why was this so difficult? Why was this final space before a kiss the longest to bridge?

He placed her foot on the floor without looking down. His arm rested on his knee. "What do you want, Darcey?"

She smelled soap and the scent of his clothing detergent. His free hand was ready to cup the back of her head and pull her in. All she had to do was ask.

She could taste it now, the kiss yet to happen. Giving in to Archie was the obvious thing to do. He was right where he should be. But this friendship was all she had. Friends had a much better chance of standing the test of time than lovers.

Images of the unfortunate accident invaded her brain once more.

"Darcey, do you want me to stop?" His voice was

firm. He wouldn't ask again.

And just like that, ignoring what could be, what she knew to be right and good, and what would make her whole, she pushed him away.

And it only took a nod.

****

By eleven o'clock, Darcey was ready to leave. More than ready. She wanted her small, cold apartment, her bed, and distance from that train wreck of a night and needed to find Archie to discover whether he would still take her home. She had made such a mess of things. And to think that just a few hours before she was happy and carefree in Archie's car.

She looked around. He wasn't in any of the downstairs rooms. Unless Archie was submerged under the sea of scholarly articles by the credenza, there was no place else on that floor where he could be: she had left no corner unvisited and no chair unscanned. She wondered if he might be upstairs. The second floor only housed the professor's bedroom and a bare guestroom besides the full bath, so she took a cursory look, conscious that she was invading Donaldson's personal space. Could he have left? Donaldson walked in her direction.

"Darcey, you okay? Can you believe I have already run out of wine? I brought so much to the kitchen earlier today. How's your foot?" His eyes kept scanning the room. He looked overwhelmed, hair messy and collar crooked. He scratched his head and gave her a feeble smile. "I can't possibly ask my guests to go to my basement and witness the chaotic state of the laundry area whenever they want some Chianti, now can I?"

"My foot is fine. I'm sorry for the broken glass. Such a mess. I'll get the wine. It's the least I can do. By the way, you seen Archie?"

"Last time I saw him he was talking to Donovan over there." Donaldson pointed to a corner where an older man sat immobile.

"But Donovan is sleeping." Darcey looked at the octogenarian scholar who had his head tilted back, supported by the armchair's hefty padding.

"Oh well. Thank you so much for the wine. Don't want people thinking I am stingy with the drinks."

Darcey found the door ajar. The smell of fresh laundry traveled up from the semi-darkness of the basement. She walked down the steps carefully—she'd had enough accidents for a night. She whispered the lyrics to the '80s ballad playing upstairs, which became more distant as she moved farther from its source. Something about broken hearts and new chances.

As she descended, rustling sounds made her think of mice and other critters she had no desire to come across. It was an old house.

But she didn't find little mice, crickets, or spiders downstairs. She found a web of hands and arms and red hair. It took several seconds to decode what she was seeing, because her eyes were unaccustomed to the dim light and because what she saw went against everything she knew to be true. Her heart pounded. Her stomach sank.

For from behind the entanglement of long, blazing hair, Archie's eyes suddenly recognized hers.

Chapter 16
Ana

March 1922

A devastating wave of nausea overcame Ana when she tried to slice a tomato. She had a notion that she could identify every smell in the world, that she had the odor-detecting power of a hunting dog locked in on the scent of its prey. This time, she almost didn't make it to the lavatory, and when she did, she sat on the floor exhausted, her neck pounding from the effort her body made to reject food.

She took a towel to her forehead.

It had become impossible to deny what this was. She was exhausted all the time, so sick it was like perpetually living on a boat over restless waters, and so on edge that any meaningful thought or scene could trigger interminable tears. Sitting on the cold bathroom floor with her arm wrapped around the latrine, as if it were a floating device after a shipwreck, she considered what to do.

Her first impulse was to call Joaquim and yell at him. Demand that he take responsibility for his part in the affair, for this child. But then what? Was it right for him to leave his wife and take her and their unborn baby? Ask that he initiate the destruction of another woman?

Bad idea, most certainly. She had made enough mistakes as it was, had risked more than she was willing to lose. This nausea, this anxiety was all she had now.

She had managed to hold her dream inside her palm and close her fingers around it for a second, her dream of being an artist, of living freely. And then she let it fly away, swept by spontaneity. In truth, she had been drunk with arrogance, believing that the rules of the world did not apply to her.

And now she needed a decision. She was going to do what she had never done before. Running away to Eugênia, who was logical, more centered, was her plan. She would find shelter in the countryside and wait, hoping that a solution would come to her.

She would witness her stomach expand in awe and terror. She'd cry and smile at every new flutter from inside until running from this responsibility became impossible. And maybe she would be forever sad like *Pierrô* who lost his beloved to the dark and unfeeling *Arlequim* in the centuries-old story that had been transplanted from the *Commedia dell'Arte* of Venice to the Brazilian festival of the people.

It was a fitting fancy for this time of the year, this time of so many make-believe *Arlequins* and *Pierrôs* parading the streets. But in *Carnaval*, an *arlequim* only pretended to be sad, a single tear drawn with *kajal* on his cheek standing in for the real thing. Instead of sulking, they took to the streets dancing and singing, rejoicing at the biggest Brazilian celebration, the one which made all of the troubles of the year bearable.

They were in the boulevards and alleys right then. She could hear them, the many *Carnaval* dancers with their vibrant costumes made of colorful satiny fabrics and sequined masks. She knew their hands would be full of colorful paper confetti, and they would be moving their feet in a rhythmic march, chasing the beat of the *bumbo* and the razz of the trombone, singing about the love triangle between *Pierrô, Arlequim* and *Colombina*.

Maybe Joaquim was out there with them, having fun, oblivious to her predicament, unscathed as always. He would be drinking beer, looking at beautiful women, dancing till sunrise. Her cheeks burned in anger.

She could also hear the melodies in the air and the happiness of the street party beyond the walls of her home. She looked out of the window. Children were playing in the *vila*. Her little cul-de-sac would be littered with colorful paper confetti in shades of pink, blue, and green. She could see herself in years past playing with them too—dressed as a sailor or a ballerina, the music of Chiquinha Gonzaga, dancing in her ears. During *Carnaval*, she and everyone else could be whatever they wanted, leave problems behind for four days, pick them up at the exit, and maybe look at them from a different angle then.

But this time she was not a part of it; she was the shadow of a woman, invisible inside her little bathroom where the black and white floor tiles accused her like little beady eyes. Her hair was plastered to her sweaty forehead, and her stomach felt as thin as a linen sheet. She couldn't wait for night to come; the only respite she got was through sleep.

To revive herself, Ana splattered some cold water on her face. She avoided the mirror, afraid of what she would see, and before sickness took hold of her again, she went to her bed and wrote a hurried letter to Eugênia.

The letter did not reveal much. It asked for shelter and company. It stopped there. It glossed over the fact that a fissure had opened between the pair of them, mostly because Eugênia had tried to help, had warned her to leave Joaquim, and in doing so had resorted to all of the societal clichés about matrimony and proper behavior for a woman that Ana was unwilling to entertain.

Ana, sick to her stomach and almost succumbing to the sensations of her own body, knew she couldn't wait any longer. That pregnancy was real, and it would make itself evident in no time. One morning, she was walking through the market. When she saw tomatoes, she became violently nauseous. It took the taste of lemons to recompose her and the help of a cool breeze to carry her through to the post office.

After mailing the letter, she returned home in a daze and slept until she lost track of time. When she woke up, the morning sickness was still there even though it was dark outside and definitely not morning.

As *Carnaval* ended, Ana saw *melindrosas*, pharaohs, and pirates start to slowly undertake their daily obligations again; they dragged themselves to work with their partying feet making swooshing sounds on the ground, too heavy to be lifted. People leaned against doors, walls, and lampposts as if the effort of standing up straight was too much.

She had trouble standing up straight as well, but for different reasons. She was hungry and afraid to eat. She often settled for dry toast, which helped ease her queasiness. The relief was always short lived: when she was not sick, she was worrying about her baby and her art, and most of the time she was both.

In the brief intervals between one of her bouts of nausea, Ana arranged a few of her things in a leather suitcase. She chose loose-fitting items that could hide her condition for a while once she started expanding. She had little thought for embellishments, but she still took her favorite barrette, the one everyone admired at tea in Maria Pia's house, as a little talisman.

That day and that existence seemed very far away now, impossible to recover. At the very last minute, she also packed a gold-toned etched necklace, one of the very few presents Joaquim had ever given her.

When her suitcase was finally ready, Ana sent word of her impending trip to her mother. They hadn't talked often recently, but she still believed she needed to provide some sort of explanation.

She lied by implying that Eugênia was lonely and that she, Ana the good friend, was going to provide much needed solace. The notepad accepted her fabrications as if they were true.

She walked to the market once more and found a boy who would, for a couple of *réis*, happily make the delivery. And then she sat and waited until her room grew cobwebs but was in reality only a few days. Eugênia's reply arrived.

****

The train was reaching the Americana station when Ana started seeing little stars in front of her eyes and knew she was about to pass out. Her knees buckled. Then came nothing, followed by her eyes opening.

She woke up feeling a cold cement floor against her back. At first, it was hard for her to tell what had happened. She noticed the sky, blue and dotted with the lightest clouds. It was so hot, and she tried to wipe rolling beads of sweat from her forehead. Her arms were too wobbly even for that small task. Finally, Eugênia's face came into focus, a look of concern and suspicion in her eyes, and everything else came rushing back to Ana—the train ride, the nausea, the oppression of the weather. The anguish.

"Thank God, she is coming to," said a female voice she could faintly make out.

"Give her some space to breathe. Here. I have some smelling salts." She didn't recognize that particular woman but saw in her the universality of the worried housewife who would have a story to tell that night at dinnertime.

"Oh, Ana, don't scare me like that," said Eugênia.

Ana sat up and gave Eugênia a weak hug. Looking from the vantage point of her friend's shoulder, she observed the scene around her. Beyond the concerned passersby, the dirt road disappeared in the distance. Women, whose shoes were covered in dusty red powder, whispered to one another. The train chugged away.

Men with sweaty brows, who carried pails, shovels, and rakes and had their eyes glued to the ground, were set in their obstinacy to make it to work on time. The nascent town with its humble houses, their walls half-stained in mud from the frequent rains, fell quiet. Worry wrinkled Eugênia's mouth. When Ana revealed her predicament, the worry would only intensify rather than go away, she thought. She hadn't written of the pregnancy in the letter. Her courage had once again faltered.

For a minute, she wished she were one of the townswomen, sitting inside their simple quarters, darning socks, stirring pots, or simply watching the movement on the streets from the safety of their windowsills. She wished she hadn't tried to be modern. She wished she hadn't tried at all. The same attitude that had brought her fame had now lost her everything.

She must have looked awful—her hair in disarray, her face devoid of the crimson lips she liked too much. Eugênia had taken the handle of her suitcase and was carrying the luggage herself. They walked to a parked car, where a man, no doubt one of Eugênia's father's workers, awaited. She vaguely remembered the trip afterwards, and Eugênia putting her to bed and explaining they should talk when she had recovered from the trip.

When she woke, she stood on steady legs and opened the door a sliver. She could see *Seu* Jacinto Pereira's concertinaed forehead and his almost silent whispers to Eugênia, the father and daughter duo still thinking Ana was asleep. But she was fully alert now, and her secret had a due date. She dreaded Eugênia's reaction. The sermon she would get would be tough to swallow, but it was her friend's disappointment in her that she really couldn't take.

"I am concerned for Ana," Seu Jacinto said to Eugênia. Ana, although within listening range in the bedroom, moved closer to the hall to hear even better. "You know I care for her like a daughter. I want to see her well."

Ana was soothed by that paternal love, a partial substitute for the bond that never truly existed between her and her own father. She could not keep her hosts in the dark. She owed them honesty.

So, at night when she was a little stronger after spending most of the day in bed, she threw a shawl around her back and went looking for Eugênia. She found her friend on the back porch, gazing up at an impossibly starry sky and humming a song.

"Making a wish?" Ana tried to sound cheerful.

"Maybe I should wish that you tell me what is going on."

"I know. I am sorry. I invited myself, provided no explanation, and then proceeded to faint in front of the whole town. I'm a bad friend, Eugênia. You deserve better."

Her *mea culpa* appeared to mollify Eugênia, so she continued.

"You were right about everything. Joaquim, me. I am…I am…Gosh, I don't know how to say it."

"You are with child, Ana. Aren't you?"

Ana looked down and nodded. She waited for Eugênia to start preaching, to remind her that she had been warned and that her reputation would be forever tarnished.

But the sermon never came; instead, Eugênia's arms clasped around her, and she rested within the embrace as if she had been swimming for a long time and had finally made it to shore. And the tears came hot and plump, dotting Eugênia's silky blouse. It felt as if they would never stop; they would flood Americana and turn its main street into the bed of a river, and what a great idea a bed was because then Ana would lie down and sleep until all this sorted.

"I made a grave mistake, Eugênia."

Eugênia was quiet for a while. Maybe she was

debating with herself and deciding what to do. Or maybe she was just searching for the right words. When she finally spoke, it was with the affection of a sister, and that measure of love was exactly the kind that made Ana fall apart. "You are my family, Ana. I love you no matter what." Sometimes love is all it took for a person to come undone.

"Hush, hush. It's all right. I'll take care of you, and who knows? Things have a way of working out when one least expects. You trust me?" Her friend spoke with the same calm and control used to console a child. Eugênia would make a great mother someday. And like a child, Ana allowed herself to be walked back inside and be served some soup. The warm liquid awoke her nausea, but her stomach accepted its sustenance.

While they ate, Eugênia made a suggestion. "Let's keep my father out of it for a while longer." They would tell him it was an illness. Eugênia was all questions: had Ana told her own parents? Did Joaquim know? Was she going to tell him?

Ana's head was spinning. She didn't have any answers, to these questions or any others. At that moment, she was merely thankful that she had someone to talk to and that her stomach was settled enough to tolerate soup. *The things we take for granted*, she thought.

In bed that night, for the first time Ana brought her hand to her belly in an instinctive and protective gesture. In those few weeks, her body was changing already—it was full and fecund even though she hardly ate. She imagined she was floating, suspended like a balloon, swinging to the lull of a breeze.

The moon, as round as she would soon enough be,

made the whole bedroom blue, and she stayed in awe of it all for a long while. The ways life could change in a sudden stroke, making what once seemed important rapidly feel distant and unreal. There was only her stomach now, the night and a hunger only matched by the constant queasiness.

When Eugênia shifted on the bed next to her, she spoke of her fears. "This will be complicated." The calm of the moment eroded. "Joaquim will eventually know. I don't have the skill to lie to him about this baby's paternity. And my parents, they will be livid and mortified. The social repercussions will be all they care about." Their ideas of propriety were expected and superficial and yet very resilient. No scenario in which they would accept this grandchild existed.

"We will figure it out…tomorrow," Eugênia murmured in her sleepiness.

The truth was, without her family's money, Ana was just another struggling artist, a dreamer, a woman. Almost at the same time that the idea crossed her mind that she could not have this child, it dawned on her that she already loved its being.

She slept dreamlessly. And she woke up feeling better because at least she was not carrying this secret alone anymore. She even mustered enough energy to stroll the town arm in arm with Eugênia, running errands and buying soap, fabric, and a couple of pencils for new sketches, while the looming fear of what was to come followed and stalked her from a distance.

The town was so small, Ana's arrival was known to all its inhabitants. As she paraded the boulevards or sat under the shade of a tree in the square, men greeted her with a quick lift of their hats, and women issued demure smiles. She felt welcome, as if she belonged, and she almost forgot the worries of the previous night.

There was no judgment in their behavior. Would that change if they knew? She shushed the thought and scared her apprehension away. She didn't need their additional weight. If there were repercussions once her belly grew, she would worry then, and only then.

With each passing day, her nausea intensified until she was afraid of leaving the bedroom. She stopped bathing with soap because she could not take the familiar scent of lavender. She avoided the kitchen and its many combined smells—onions, garlic, basil—until thirst overcame her. Sometimes, she was at the edge of a breakdown, unable to do anything without awakening her nausea. And then one day the morning sickness disappeared as if by magic, and Ana could finally sit outside and enjoy the smell of wet grass and of morning dew. The relief was so intense it drove her to tears.

Those were pleasures she would never take for granted again, not after feeling her whole existence was wrapped around the sensations from her stomach.

But her newfound health brought concerns too. When nausea subsided, an expanding waistline would soon follow. After all, three full months were now behind her, and she would not be able to live in denial anymore. She needed to make a decision very soon.

"Let's go to the Saturday *sarau*—lots of music, readings, good food. My friend Pedro is hosting it." Eugênia's invitation jolted her back to reality. They were sitting in the living room. Eugênia was sewing.

"A *sarau*? With poetry, guitars, dancing? They have those here?"

"Oh, this is the countryside, Ana, but the year is

still 1922."

"I'm sorry. I didn't mean to insult your town."

"Yes, you did. But that's fine. There's still a party, and I still want to go."

To make up for her tactlessness, Ana agreed. Besides, the *sarau* might be a good idea after all. A time to see people, hear poetry and music, talk about art and literature, meet kindred spirits and wear something other than a brown sack-like dress.

"So who is going?"

"It's not like you know anybody, so what does it matter?" Eugênia was frowning and her voice lowered, and she had not let go of the slight.

"Just making conversation, Eugênia. You will need to lend me something pretty to wear. I'll style my hair."

"So that all eyes can be on you? Deep inside, Ana Valquíria Eça, you'll never change."

Later Ana fumbled through Eugênia's armoire, looking for something colorful and fun. She needed to shake the feeling of dread, the fear of the future that insisted on gluing itself to her skin, and some color might just be the best medicine for that. It would not cure it, but it would numb it, if only for a night.

She sulked as she confirmed what she already knew—her style and Eugênia's were completely different. Her friend was attracted to rosy hues, antique blues, and light yellows. Eugênia was lilac while Ana was red. As she discarded delicate lace trims and intricate embroidered collars, she came across a maroon dress that mercifully had a *ton-sur-ton* red trim around the waist, neckline, and at the bottom of the skirt. It would have to do. It was probably one of the last chances of highlighting her thin midriff, and, carried away by that thought, she didn't even worry that the dress's high waist was the opposite of all modern fashion in vogue right then.

Once they were ready and groomed, Ana and Eugênia visited Eugênia's father for a few minutes, and amidst his many compliments and good wishes, made it to the front door in high spirits, chatting, laughing, and anticipating a fun evening.

But when Eugênia opened the door, all color and fun left her face. The pretty dress that a minute before had made her happy lost its power, and for the first time that day nausea rose up her throat while a shiver made it down her spine.

Right outside Eugênia's door, looking as debonair and relaxed as ever, stood Joaquim, wearing his smile as a greeting card.

Chapter 17
Darcey

February 1997

Archie joined Darcey upstairs. Her legs were still shaking. Seeing Archie with Dominique had been a horrible shock. She had run back up the steps, her ankle throbbing again, but not before issuing an "as you were" to a goggly-eyed Archie and his giggling companion.

Back on the main floor, she regretted drinking so much wine—it made her grumpy, not happy. In a daze, she watched him approaching, noticing him a little more than before and how handsome he really was. She tried to lie to herself; she'd said again and again it was good he was pursuing someone else. Truly. They were not a match, and if he was involved with Dominique, all the better. There would be less complication and more focus to finish the project. But a prickling in her head and needles in her stomach told a different story.

Jealous was a gross understatement. If she had been able to get away with it, she would have walked around sobbing, bent forward, a hand on her heart protecting it. Yes, she was jealous, but she was so much more. She was disappointed in him for getting tired of her, and in herself, at expecting that he wouldn't. For a moment, she wished she was the red-haired woman:

free and brave, unafraid of consequences. Ana and Dominique were alike. They knew what they wanted, and they let nothing stand in their way.

Archie came to join her. His light blue shirt was wrinkled. A flap of it hung out of his pants. His nice sweater had disappeared, and his hair was tousled and covered his brow. He walked at a steady pace, and his arms swung from side to side. His eyes were laser beams piercing through hers, challenging her to a duel. She wouldn't have been surprised if he had pulled a fencing sword.

But of course, he didn't. What made it tougher was that he looked so attractive. So masculine. He was alone, and that gave her a little bit of forbidden hope.

By the time he reached her, his shoulders were lowered and his face more relaxed. He could never be angry for long. There was the usual tenderness toward him but muddled with the new emotion that swirled in the pit of her stomach: loss.

"You ready to go?" he said as he looked down at her purse resting on the carpet, next to her seat. Her mother said purses on the floor bring bad luck; maybe she was right.

Darcey nodded, looping the bag around her shoulder. She wanted to say something, but had no idea what. They waved a silent goodbye to Donaldson. The sounds and the warmth of the party grew distant. The ice-cold wind outside greeted them. The snow muffled the sounds like cotton balls inside ears.

The first part of the ride was quiet. Archie concentrated on the road, and Darcey looked from the window and focused on how winter transformed everything.

In the passenger's seat, she toyed with her bracelet and pulled its sides apart. When the silence was ready to avalanche, Archie asked, "What's wrong with your bracelet?"

"Clasp broke. Don't know if it can be fixed. I bet it can't. Sometimes things just break." What would the ride have been like had Dominique been with them? Would he have asked the redhead to sit up front? Would Darcey have been relegated to the back seat from where she would only get crumbs of conversation and laughter?

As if reading her thoughts, Archie intervened. "Look, about Dominique and me—"

"Archie, that's none of my business, really. I'm actually happy for you." She faced him and tried to produce a relaxed and noncommittal expression, but her muscles were frozen.

"I know, I just wanted, you see, I wanted to say that I was caught in the heat of the moment. She was so…so…forward."

"And so you ended up in the basement with her by accident?"

He fell silent again.

"Like I said, it's none of my business. Maybe something good will come out of it, you know?" She put the bracelet in her purse.

He didn't reply. After a few minutes, he asked, "Music?"

She didn't want any music. Who knew what new emotions, what memories it could evoke? She shook her head and looked out of the window again, to eliminate any prospect of further conversation. She didn't want to cry in front of him. Or for him to console her. Park the car, take *her* face in his hands, say it was all a grave mistake, and kiss her. That's what she wanted from him.

What a ridiculous idea! She had to stop those fantasies. Between his mom, her debt, and good old pride, there was enough to keep them apart for the next thousand years. She had chased him away because it was the right thing to do, and now it was too late for any of that. If they stayed friends, she would be grateful.

The country road turned into the almost-urban environment of the university's neighborhood. The houses that lined the street were quiet and agreeable, with fake candles at the windows, their yellow glow making the snow outside look blue.

On another day, she would have walked and focused on the scents that those houses exuded— French fries crisp from the fryer, drier sheet fragrance escaping from the vents, the things that made a home a little factory of efficiency and activity. But today, they had no appeal. She thought of a novel she wanted to read to distract her, but on the cover was a beautiful redhead in front of a manor, and that made her think of Dominique again.

Any brief, soothing feeling inside her soul vanished, giving way to intense fatigue and watery eyes, as if she was overtaken by the flu. She couldn't wait to get home and crawl into bed. She would sleep all night and most of the following day.

In front of her apartment, she exited the car quickly without saying goodbye. She didn't look back but waited to hear the sound of Archie's car as it made its way to his driveway. Behind her door, she started to cry.

She did sleep most of the day, although the night was restless. When she finally woke up, not relaxed, not clearheaded, she was bitter and achy all over, with a heavy head.

If sleep didn't cure her, maybe work would, so she reached for the stack of documents beside her bed. Darcey reread the letter she had translated before the party. She'd captured Eugênia's anxiety quite well.

Searching the other documents, she found a newspaper cutout from the same month in 1922.

NIGHT OF ART AND LITERATURE A SUCCESS

An evening of art and literature took place at the patio of the Pinacoteca on the 15th of March. It was a night to remember, with both young and established painters and writers sharing the stage and their accomplishments. Young artist Ana Valquíria Eça was particularly well received. The poet Edgar Ramos Souza read his verses in front of one of her canvases. Many celebrated artists and intellectuals were present. All in all, the night was a success. More than two hundred visitors came to support the artists. Many paintings were sold.

Darcey scratched her head. Ana had reason to be happy. Her art received the recognition she'd longed for. She looked for more clues and evidence of other shows but didn't find anything that advanced that line of research.

Darcey sighed. It was a day of dead ends, of unfulfilled promises. Without realizing, she walked to the window and observed Archie's house across the street, the garden with large trees, the flawless white of the paintwork. It was silent. The shutters enclosed it as if warning the curious to keep out. All the things not said. The present in the past and vice-versa. Was she like Ana, a victim of social obstacles? If Ana really loved someone like she did, and he wasn't married, wouldn't she have done anything to be with him? Would she have cared one bit about what his mother thought?

No one came to her apartment. Why would they? Her only companions were the steps of residents and their friends arriving at other apartments and causing the floorboards to chatter. By eight o'clock she was again ready for bed. Her body fell onto the mattress, and the old coils squeaked with the strain.

But sleep would not come. Not surprising since she had slept so much already. She made tea but didn't drink it; it cooled off next to the sandwich she didn't eat. The music coming from a neighboring apartment didn't help. It reminded her that somewhere else people were living. Feeling stifled, she decided to open the window and let the cold air stroke her face.

With eyes that threatened to release a flood of tears, she watched Archie as he locked the door of the house. He wore the perfectly-tailored brown jacket he'd sported at his cousin's wedding and a white shirt. His leather shoes shone like the lustrous pavement, still wet from melted snow, under them. Did he have a date? The idea only made her mood worse, but she refused to cry. Archie could do whatever he wanted.

He focused on his path, not looking up toward her apartment even once. He got into his car, started it, and disappeared around the corner and into the night.

Darcey closed the window and sighed, fogging the glass pane. Ana, missed opportunities, and her own discontent weighed her down. She wouldn't have the chance to tell him about the latest of Eugênia's letters. He wouldn't clarify what it meant. Not tonight.

The next day, Darcey knocked on the door of Archie's pretty house. He had always come to her in the past, but she needed to talk. Her excuse was Ana, but this was about so much more. She waited with borrowed patience for him to open the door, her throat hurting from the pride she swallowed to be there, her hands as fidgety as ever. When he did, surprise flashed in his eyes.

"Will you tell me some more, Archie? What about Ana after the Modern Art Week? I found a letter. Is it the baby? Is it the reason I can't find anything else about her art?"

"First of all, hello. I'm glad you're talking to me."

Darcey looked down. He was hurt. When it came to making a mess of things, she and Ana had both become big-time experts.

Archie stepped back. "Come on in." He didn't smile.

Darcey closed the door behind her. The icy-cold air gave way to the toasty atmosphere of Archie's front room. And for a moment she didn't care that she would now be the bargaining one.

Chapter 18
Ana

Americana, 1922

Joaquim stood at the door holding his hat. He was wearing a brown suit that would have looked threadbare on most anybody, but that on him looked worldly.

"*Senhorita* Eugênia, *Senhorita* Ana," he bowed. "I believe you were on your way out, and by the looks of it, a special event awaits you," he said, referencing their clothes. "But I hope you can spare me some time."

Eugênia blushed and looked down.

"Come in and sit down, please," Eugênia offered.

Ana held his gaze. A part of her was surprised to see him there, but mostly she was mad at his attempt to claim territory again.

"We are pressed for time, Eugênia." Ana tried to disengage from the reunion, but Joaquim had already walked into the main room of Eugênia's colonial house, with its wood floorboards, big windows, and dark furniture.

"I'll bring some coffee," Eugênia said before disappearing into the kitchen.

Ana took the leather armchair opposite the sofa, where Joaquim sat, lying back with a half-smile on his lips.

"Little town square, quaint train station, big rustic

house. This place is the opposite of you," he said, as soon as Eugênia left.

"I happen to like it very much. How did you find me?"

"You seem to forget I am a reporter and darn good at my job."

"Joaquim, I've told you there is nothing between us anymore. I don't know why you're here."

"And I told you that I know you will come back. No time like the present." He smiled again. He always looked like he had never been turned down, like he expected the world to follow his lead.

"Well, you are wrong. And Eugênia and I are indeed late. I'll check and see why coffee is taking so long. If you would *excuse* me."

In the kitchen, Ana asked Eugênia to hurry and not leave the main room anymore. When the two returned, they found Joaquim leafing through a poetry book that had been lying on the coffee table.

"It's so quiet here."

"We like it," Eugênia said.

"So where are you going, and can I join you?"

Eugênia and Ana exchanged conspiratorial looks.

"No, it's a women's poetry reading group. I don't think you would be welcome. That book you were browsing? That's the one we are reading from," she lied, feeling witty and resourceful. This time, he could try all he wanted, and she would find a way around him.

"I see. Well, I'll be brief then. I came to fetch you, Ana."

Ana stood up and held two clenched fists by the sides of her body. She noticed Eugênia cross and uncross her legs and run her palms up and down the arms of the chair.

"To fetch me? Fetch *me*? I'm not a hat you left behind. I can't be fetched. I came of my own volition, and I will leave of my own volition."

"Heavens, I certainly didn't mean it that way. I meant that I would like to escort you back into the city, if you are ready to go back."

"If and when I'm ready to go back, I will."

He raised an eyebrow. "Does that mean there is a chance you won't?"

"It means I will do what I want. Excuse me...again. I'll reapply my face powder and then, Eugênia, if you please, can we go?"

She left for the lavatory. When she saw herself in the mirror, she was mad. He still had the ability to drain all the color from her face and bring anxiety to her eyes. She reapplied some rouge. She could not wear perfume, but she powdered herself with talcum. If he thought she would obey him—obey, because that is what it felt like—then he was sorely mistaken. He would never know about the child. He would never have power over her again, and he would never, ever tell her what to do.

She counted to a hundred before she made it back to Eugênia and Joaquim, who were chatting like old friends. Joaquim made a joke, and Eugênia laughed with abandonment, her head tilted back, exposing her long neck and porcelain skin. Ana's impatience overflowed.

"Eugênia, I'm leaving. We're very late now, and I don't want to be rude to your friends." She gave Eugênia a meaningful stare, lowering her chin and looking up.

"We better go," Eugênia finally agreed.

"Wait!" he said as they walked out. "Don't forget your poetry." He smiled.

At the door, Joaquim said goodbye, kissed Ana on the cheek, tipped his hat, and bowed his head to Eugênia. He left with them, his hands in his trouser pockets, and then, as they watched, he walked on, toward the train station. His silhouette became undiscernible in the distance, and they headed for the town square and the civic center where the *sarau* was being held. Ana detected the sound of a flute playing. Eugênia held her hand, and Ana squeezed it hard. She touched her stomach, where a firm, low bump was forming. She looked ahead and swallowed a single tear. Somewhere in the depths of her heart, she knew she would never see Joaquim again.

****

Through semi-opened eyes, Ana saw Leopoldina, Eugênia's maid and former nanny, open the heavy curtains of the bedroom, making tiny specs of dust and lint fly into the air. Dina, as they had called the woman since their childhood, clearly wanted to inspect the room, which after her three-week absence was sure to be looking frighteningly messy to her. The old woman looked surprised, but it was not by the appearance of the dormitory. It was the presence of Eugênia that startled her, still sleeping so late in the day, her feet sticking out of the covers as had been her habit ever since she was a girl, and of Ana, who was rubbing her eyes and sheltering her face from the assaulting sun.

"Dear Lord! Aninha, *Geninha*, I didn't know you two were here. And sleeping still. I'll come later." She started closing the curtains again, but was interrupted by Ana who sat up and threw a light shawl around her shoulders.

"No, no, Dina. You're fine. We overslept. We went out last night. I'm sorry we surprised you. How are you?" Standing up, Ana went to hug the woman's hefty figure. Leopoldina was particularly large around the middle, and her starched apron was tightly tied behind her back. Her face carried soft wrinkles. She had spent a lifetime in service, and the years had been long. On her head, she wore a handkerchief with tiny flower embroidery. It tied at the nape of neck. Her round eyes looked at Ana with open tenderness. What a precarious situation it was to live in the in-between that employment at a house for one's lifetime created, a house that became so familiar but never one's own. Ana had vowed to never treat anyone differently because of their position in life, especially in a society with still so much classism and so many race divisions. Weren't artists supposed to fight all forms of injustice? And yet, here she was, once again benefiting from Leopoldina's hard work.

"Back from your trip already?" Ana asked.

"I missed this one too much," Leopoldina said, pointing at Eugênia, her eyes misted with affection, until Eugênia herself came to hug her.

"Oh, Dina, I missed you so."

After her mother passed away, Eugênia had slowly become like a daughter whom Dina fed, dressed for school, consoled after falls, and worried over constantly. She never married or had her own children, and Eugênia occupied most of her time. How could someone give up so much?

The years passed, mostly smoothly if one could

call it that, between the chores of the house, the darning of socks and the stirring of pots, until Eugênia grew up and roles were slightly but surely redefined. The house had a new grown woman to make decisions.

Leopoldina had known Ana from the time the young artist was a schoolgirl and Eugênia's mother was still a part of this world. "Yes, three weeks was too long to be away from home." Leopoldina let her eyes scrutinize the room, as if looking for reassurance that she was indeed needed and missed.

Eugênia's family had rejoiced at the chance to be back in the countryside, and to Ana it was upsetting that she was there too, not to visit, but to disrupt that calculated peace with her troubles.

But she loved all of them like relatives. They were her true family, always supporting her without asking for anything back. And the truth was that she had never given much back. She had only taken, and she was about to take some more.

When Leopoldina left them to dress for breakfast, Eugênia sat down on the bed, still dazed by sleep. Yet she was awake enough to start a conversation about Joaquim.

"So, do you still feel as aggravated by Joaquim's insistence as you did yesterday?"

Ana was straightening out her blankets. "Can you blame me? I could have ranted the rest of the evening, but that would have spoiled an otherwise perfect night."

"You mean because of the American?"

"What American?"

"At the *sarau*. Don't play coy. I saw how he kept coming to talk to you any chance he got. His eyes couldn't help but follow you around. And he wasn't pushy like Joaquim. Are you going to see him again? Hold on a second. I'll be right back."

There had been a loud noise down the hall. Eugênia left to check on it, and Ana traveled back to the events of the previous evening.

After Joaquim left, Ana and Eugênia had found an animated event at the civic center, the music of a flute, a piano, and a cello playing cheerfully. A table of desserts, with corn cake, *quindim*, and banana pie was set at the back. Free conversation flowed all around. The music stopped only for the poetry readings, and Ana reminisced about the Modern Art Week, the last time she had fed her soul with the art she so craved. She was lost in the words of a long poem about the beauty of nature when a tall man approached. His name he said was Raymond. He had a beard, which he touched lightly when he spoke. Originally from Pennsylvania, he was unrelated to the US southerners who came to the town, which was a relief. He had a large farm in Americana, where he lived alone except for a housekeeper. He was kind and gentlemanly, but also a little insecure, almost as if he was afraid of her. He had nothing like Joaquim's perpetual self-assuredness.

Her mind, without her consent, gravitated toward the latter. Wasn't it typical that Joaquim had turned up demanding attention? Not because he cared or worried, she figured, but rather because he had been turned away and now his ego was bruised and his reputation as a heartbreaker tarnished. And she, pregnant, alone, and now courted by a man that wasn't the father of her child. Her modern sensibility should've been able to stomach that. Maybe she was more provincial than she thought. Joaquim must never know anything. He wasn't a man whom a woman could rely on. And as for Raymond, well, that too remained to be seen.

Raymond was different from Joaquim in other ways too. Raymond was attentive and polite, anticipating her need for a drink and her desire to sit down. He wasn't half as dapper, of course, with his ash-blond hair cut a little too severely and his clothes so traditional they would have been antiquated in a man twice his thirty-two years. But he was not bad looking, and given some sound advice, his big-built and rugged shoulders could be stately rather than awkward.

And those blue eyes, so clear you could see all the little flecks of dark in his irises, were rather inviting. You could look into them without blushing too much, without having to look down to rearrange a skirt or twist a bracelet. Maybe he wasn't to be taken for granted. Maybe he was a silver lining indeed. It was fortunate she had sent Joaquim home, ignoring his rather tired, "You'll be back" retorts. They were getting old.

But who was she kidding? She was almost four months along. If it weren't for loose fashions, Raymond would have seen the bump. What kind of reaction was she to expect when she expanded a little more? Americans could be quite traditional that way.

"Do you think Dina was listening in?" Eugênia was back.

"What?"

"Dina. The noise. I think she was listening in, and she dropped something. There's a broom. Right outside the door. I don't like it one bit. She is smart, my Dina. She can piece things together and tell Father." Eugênia brought her hand to her mouth and bit on the sides of her index fingernail. Had she been a child, a parent would have rushed to cover the tip of her finger with pepper to prevent the habit from forming.

"I know. I will have to tell him. You keep reminding me time and again. Just give me a few days, will you?"

"Fine. Your secret, your choice."

"Eugênia?" She was just going to ask what she was thinking. Eugênia was reasonable: she could use that. "Tell me honestly what you thought of Joaquim yesterday."

"What do you mean?" Eugênia blushed.

"I mean how does he strike you?" Ana simply wanted her friend to confirm how right she was to keep him out of her life.

Eugênia looked like she was hand-picking her words. "To be honest with you, I think sometimes you paint him to be worse than he is. He came here, he seemed really concerned, and while you dismissed him and went into the bathroom to powder your nose…again…he talked to me, and he was kind."

"Talked about what?"

"He mentioned his wife a couple of times. There seems to be nothing left there but his guilt. He seemed worried about you too. He also asked about me; let me talk for a bit. I understand his ways are bad sometimes, but your keeping him at arm's length does not help much either. He has the right to know he will be a father. You can't predict what he would do."

"So now Joaquim's ways are my fault? I don't have to predict. I know him. Even if he offered help now, it wouldn't last." This was not the kind of support she was looking for from her best friend. Her only true friend.

"That's not what I said. Look, I don't want to say anything anymore. You shouldn't have asked."

"If I can't ask you, who will I ask?"

"I don't know. You will do what you please no matter what I say."

Did Eugênia resent her? This was hard to take.

"Don't say that, Eugênia. Don't defend Joaquim." She was almost begging. She needed to know she was doing what was right.

"Fine. You're right. He's wrong. End of story." Eugênia stormed out of the room showing in very plain colors how she really felt about the matter.

Chapter 19
Darcey

March 1997

Darcey had fallen asleep on Archie's couch. She only woke up the next morning. A simple enough occurrence. Two friends who talked into the wee hours of the morning until one of them got really tired. No big deal. Except it was. For as long as she could remember, she'd warned him not to fall asleep on her couch. In the past, she'd threatened to throw him out at the slightest sign that he had dozed off. She scoffed at the irony of her situation. It had happened while he told Ana's story. The more she heard, the more she thought of her own life. Her mind traveled between the present and the past, Brazil and the US, love and loss, Ana's situation and her own. At some point her brain just shut off.

And there she was, her hair flattened by the denim pillows on his sofa and her face mirrored on the television screen, puffy with sleep. The air smelled fresh, and yet she had trouble breathing. She experienced some sort of panic, a dread, regret. If only Archie had woken her up and walked her home, she wouldn't have had to face waking up in his living room, not knowing where he was.

As entitled as he would have been to wake her up, given how clear she had been about the transgression of sleeping in each other's houses, Archie didn't make her leave. Instead, he had covered her with a soft blanket while she slept, and he had left a night light on, which she now, since it was a new morning, stretched to switch off.

Shocked at the stealth of the idea, she caught herself in a daydream of the goodnight kiss he might have placed on her lips or forehead while she snoozed. She let the thought remain for a while because it helped calm her. If only she been forthcoming about her love from the beginning. About Nina, whom she missed so much. About being a good, imperfect person.

She smelled fresh coffee and spotted a large croissant smothered in strawberry jam strategically placed on the coffee table where she could not miss it. Her stomach growled. Her heart sang.

Archie joined her a few minutes later. He moved like a cat, and he sat at the edge of the couch, where she was still stretched out. She collected her feet in a timid and slow choreography. He lingered there, cautious, dressed in last night's gray sweatpants and white tee. His hair was disheveled, and he reeked of cigarettes though he never smoked. When he moved closer, it became obvious his T-shirt was inside out.

Besieged by images of his hands over another's body and consumed by a sense of injury she could not justify, Darcey blurted out, "So you were with Dominique?"

"No, I was in my bedroom. What makes you say that?"

"Your shirt. It's inside out."

He raised one eyebrow. "And that means I must have been with Dominique?" He grabbed the T-shirt by the collar at the back, pulled the garment off, turned it the right way, and put it on again. "There. Better?"

Darcey looked away, her face hot at the sight of his stomach.

"Your hair smells of cigarettes."

"What is this? After you fell asleep I felt restless. A bunch of guys invited me to play pool, so I went. When I came back, I collapsed in bed, and this morning I grabbed the first T-shirt I saw. Any objections?" There was irritation in his voice. He'd stopped being cautious or patient with her.

"None whatsoever." She took the croissant. It wasn't warm any longer, but its flaky texture and comforting flavor were perfect. After a few bites, she changed the subject. "Can we continue last night's conversation? I'm sorry I fell asleep."

Archie stretched and put his bare feet on an ottoman. She hardly waited for him to settle down and drink from his mug.

"So can we talk about what I know?" She crossed her legs.

"If you like…" He turned his head toward the window, like he had become indifferent to her.

"So Ana got pregnant. Did she eventually tell Joaquim? Did he leave his wife? But there was the American too. I'm sure she would rather Joaquim left his wife, but would he? And then she ended up here…I mean…you are her descendent and you are here, so—" Darcey stuffed another piece of croissant in her mouth as if it were the only way to shut it.

"Will you slow down? Jeez." He stood up and walked to the window.

Who could blame him for his impatience? "Sorry.

216

I'm just intrigued." It was best to ignore his behavior. Maybe this irritation would go away if she left it alone. "Tell me something else. Was she painting during that time?"

He sighed and paced around. "Oh, yes. More than ever. It was her one outlet. When she painted, her head was clear. While she painted, she could dream."

"Maybe I should do the same," she mumbled under her breath.

"What's that?"

"Nothing. Just thinking, talking to myself. Ignore me."

He continued, "In this phase, her pictures were very dreamlike. She took to softer shapes and lighter colors than her typical greens, reds, and blues. She also worked on watercolors. My father found one that he gave my mom several years ago. You might have noticed it back home, in the entrance hall. I really like it."

"I see." She played with the rim of the coffee mug, tracing circles again and again. Her mind drifted far away, in Americana with Eugênia, Leopoldina, and the young artist who brought her closer to Archie. *What do you want from me, Ana? What are you trying to tell me?*

Archie's voice pierced her thoughts. "I don't mean to be rude, and you're welcome to stay, but…" He was being formal for a reason, and it was all dreadful. "I have to go."

"Ahh, Dominique?" She had to stop saying the first thing that came into her mind. It made her look weak.

Archie sighed. "No, I actually have a group meeting. I go to school here, remember? What's with you today?" From the side of the couch, he produced a pair of loafers and proceeded to untie the shoelaces. A minute later he had changed his mind. "I'm gonna go take a shower."

"Sure, sure. Go. Have fun." She placed the mug back on the table, knocking over a candle in the process. Its waxy body broke, and the two resulting parts remained attached by the wick alone. "I'm sorry. I am such a fool! It's like I ruin everything."

"Darcey," he said, somewhere between chuckling and scoffing. "It's just a candle."

He headed for the bathroom, leaving her contrite, tangled, and wishing away the growing sensation that she'd made an awful, perhaps irreparable mistake.

"I'll be going now. Thanks for everything." But he had already exited the room and did not respond.

That same day, the library turned icy-cold because the heaters malfunctioned. Darcey sat in a far corner away from the circulation desk and kept her gloves on. She went about the documents while her mind went back to Archie. She had to make an effort, focus on the task at hand.

Darcey took her time arranging documents according to their dates. She'd organized about half of them before she ran out of clear plastic folders. She zoomed in on Ana's mother's letter.

The penmanship was weak and slanted to the left. The lines were not straight, and the writing went downward as it progressed toward the right of the page. Given the sloppy handwriting and the content of the letter, Darcey's antipathy for the woman grew. She sighed and reminded herself this was work. She translated the text with objective efficiency, although she kept wondering if her lack of enthusiasm was a result of the woman's unpleasantness or the increasing tension between her and Archie.

Repairmen arrived in the library to try and fix the heater. Within an hour, warm air flooded the stalls, and she finally removed her gloves and scarf. She picked a comfy armchair and read her translation.

Ana,

Your father and I are surprised at the long time you are spending with Eugênia and wonder if you are imposing on the family. I thought that you wanted to paint and be serious about art—as serious as you can be about that anyway. Are you there to work? Paint landscapes? I don't really understand what you mean to accomplish. Honestly, I think it is time you settled down. Most of your school friends are married, and a few are already taking children to the park. If only we could expect the same from you. Instead you are wasting your life. Typical of you.

We just received the invitation to the wedding of your cousin Amália. We expect it will be a very elegant affair. By the time you receive this, you will have a couple of weeks to come home. I hope you will return to São Paulo for it. It is not like you are doing anything important at present anyhow. Your father and I cannot continue to support your pastime, so we will need to have a conversation once you are back in town. Not only is your cousin getting married, her sister Rosa is about to have her third child. Her husband was promoted again, this time to vice-president of the bank. You should be thinking about your future in those terms. Please send my regards to Eugênia and Jacinto.

Your mother

The air of the library was not cold anymore. After all, the heating was back in full force. All the same, Darcey was trembling. While her own relationship with her mother wasn't always the warmest, it was certainly nothing like Ana and Mrs. Eça's. Darcey's mother had suffered trauma, the loss of Darcey's twin creating a hollow space between them, a distance that was hard to transpose. That ache sometimes spilled over Darcey's own life, making her afraid to connect to people. It was understandable, even if unfair, but it was nothing compared to what the letter gave away in the young painter's case.

Ana's mother was as cold as an iceberg. It was hard to convey it in her translation, but Brazilians were often warm and inviting. This level of directness was not common, even if English readers might simply disregard it as a little stern. Darcey could imagine Ana, a young dreamer full of hope, trying to speak of her vision, of all the emotions that she felt and all the beauty that she saw, only to be met with condescension, only to hit an unclimbable wall of ice. She had just unveiled a reason for some of Ana's rebellion.

Guilt over her behavior in the last year overwhelmed Darcey. It was easy to cast herself as a victim of circumstances until she realized that nobody lived unscathed. Her relationship with her family was hard; so was Ana's. Life could be unpredictable; Ana's had certainly been. Most of the time, people were just trying to get by, and they dreamed too, when life allowed. She had made it her business to build her own misery brick by brick, feeling sorry for herself, discarding all the good that had come her way—Archie's devotion, her parents' support of her, Lucile's friendship and sass. She was a fool. A naïve fool, expecting the world and people in it to guess what she needed and change accordingly. The world owed her nothing.

Putting the letter aside, Darcey looked for other documents. When she saw another letter with the same disquieting penmanship, she resisted the urge to put it away. It was dated a few weeks after the first.

Ana,

Your last letter was extraordinary. It is a relief that you are coming to your cousin's wedding, but the fact that you are bringing an unnamed man with you is the kind of irresponsible behavior we have come to expect of you. I hope you do not embarrass yourself or us, especially when the whole family will be present. I ask that you use your best judgment, or else it is best you don't come at all.

Your mother.

A rising sense of rage assailed Darcey, as if some of the wrongdoing had been directed at her, not at Ana. She hated warnings. She couldn't stand manipulations, like the one Archie's mom was responsible for. She wanted to go outside and scream, and to go back in time and tell Ana's mother to back off. Or maybe, time travel was not necessary. Maybe what she needed was to tell Mrs. Northwood she would not give up on Archie's love for the sake of the woman's convenience although there might not really be any part of Archie's heart that was hers to claim anymore.

It might be too late. Dominique might turn out to be exactly what Archie's family had dreamed of, in which case there would be nothing for her to do. Just like her house, fully mortgaged, and her degree, unfinished, Archie would become a promise—unfulfilled.

****

Not knowing what else to do, she found herself walking toward Lucile's. Her aunt was sure to have a word of comfort disguised as back talk. The familiar path to the mansion calmed her. Leaving her own troubles aside, she conjured an image of Ana. Who was the man she was taking to the wedding? She doubted it would be Joaquim, but wasn't it too soon to introduce Raymond to the family? What was the purpose behind that move? She had an unnerving feeling that things were about to become very complicated for Ana. As curious as she was, she didn't read ahead. She wanted an excuse for Archie to have to fill her in.

Lucile was slicing an apple pie when Darcey arrived. The smell of it was so enticing Darcey forgot to say hello.

"It seems every time I come here you're indulging your sweet tooth." She tossed her coat on the armchair.

"I am an old woman, Darcey. I'd rather enjoy what I like sooner rather than later. What reason could I possibly have to wait?"

"It wasn't meant as criticism. Just a thought."

"I know, I know." She placed two delicate plates adorned with birds next to the pie. The old woman had parted with so many items from her previous existence, but not those. Her husband had bought them during their honeymoon in London, and the gift reminded her of that wonderful time and place.

Darcey stole a little slice of apple and sucked the gooey filling from her fingertips. "Too much criticism going around anyway. Wouldn't wanna add to it."

"Excuse me?"

"It's nothing. Just stuff that is coming up with my research."

"Still meddling with other people's lives?" Lucile offered Darcey a generous slice of pie. "Wait. Here." She curled a dollop of whipped cream next to the dessert. It looked like a flower. "You can't have pie without cream, you can't have progress without strife, and you can't dig into the past without trouble. Simple as that." Lucile offered her best know-it-all smile and sliced what looked like half the pie for herself.

"Lucile, my work is in art history. The past is all I have."

The old woman snickered and, being that her mouth was full of pie, she had to make an effort not to send fragments flying into the air. "You sounded older than me when you said that. *The past is all I have*," she mocked.

"What's wrong with that?"

"It is too melodramatic. Despite your occasional insecurity, I always thought you'd go after what you wanted and would leave the past behind. That you'd know what that is, and you'd do what you could to succeed."

"What if I can't? What if that's not in the stars for me? How long do I keep pushing? It seems what's meant to be should come a little easier, you know?"

"Where did you get *that* idea?"

"People. I mean look at Archie. He goes to school

and does his work. No drama."

Lucile put her plate down and, smiling, batted her eyes at Darcey. "Archie, huh?"

"You know I am talking about my professional life. I mean, he's a part of that now."

"*Right*." Lucile looked victorious, like she often did when she tried to hit a nerve and succeeded. "And your professional life and your personal life are colliding, aren't they?"

Darcey let her body be swallowed by the soft couch. "Well, sort of. I'm just wondering about the choices people make, you know?"

"What do you mean?" She shoved another forkful of pie into her mouth.

"So I'm studying this Brazilian painter, right? I read her diary, I translate her letters, and I know what she should do next, what the easiest way out is, but she always takes a different direction. I'm living seventy-five years in the future. It's like trying to direct a movie that has been made already."

"Like that would ever work." She put her fork down.

"Do people realize the consequences of their choices as they make them, or do we only see them in retrospect, like I'm doing right now? Am I as clueless as the people I'm reading about? Do they lie to themselves to try and feel better?"

"You again asking impossible questions. Eat your pie."

Lucile was employing diversion tactics. They ate in silence for a while.

"So how is Archie, anyway?" Lucile's question danced on sly, grinning lips.

"He's fine." Darcey didn't dare reply with many words. The more words, the more revelations.

"Do you ask him lots of questions too?" Darcey didn't doubt for a second that Lucile was thoroughly enjoying her discomfort. If only she knew where the uneasiness stemmed from. As if on cue, her mind delivered an image of Archie putting his T-shirt on, unaware it was inside-out. Maybe it was time she did the opposite of what she usually thought to do, and that meant opening up to him.

"No, Lucile. I save them all for you." Breaking protocol—they could both be a little standoffish—Darcey placed her arm around her aunt's shoulder. "Besides, he's busy kissing other women."

"I beg your pardon?"

"I caught him kissing someone else."

"Well, I never. Is this some sort of karma in this family? Kissing the wrong people?"

"What're you talking about?"

Lucile collected the plates and pie crumbles. "Nothing."

Lucile's demeanor, her hand nervously touching her neck, meant it was something quite important rather than nothing.

"Is this about you and my mom? Did one of you kiss someone they shouldn't have? Does it have anything to do with this never-ending feud?"

"Forget I said anything."

"Aunt Lucile?"

"I said forget it. What are you going to do about Archie? If I were you, I'd act quickly."

"No. There's nothing to do. Anyway, I gotta go. Thanks for the pie."

"Anytime."

Darcey was already down the hall when Lucile added, "Bring Archie next time!"

As Darcey walked back through deserted streets, she organized her ideas about the research. It was a ploy not to think of Archie. She'd studied Ana's available paintings, but most of her thoughts wandered back to the artist's private life when she was not watchful, and Ana's private life made Darcey think of her own.

Ana had the makings of a great painter, yet she had suddenly vanished from public sight because of an untimely pregnancy and a destructive love. But Darcey had a feeling that her life and her craft were closely connected in other ways too. She needed to see it through. But the documents only went so far. The prickly truth was that there were holes in this story— and one way or another, she needed Archie.

Chapter 20
Ana

April 1922

Under better circumstances, Raymond would have been an interesting new development: an American, shy and courteous, who looked at her like a queen. But under her actual circumstances he was more than interesting: he was a godsend. Ana didn't forget for a minute that the courtship had happened too fast and that it was rushed because of the impending birth.

A few days after the *sarau*, at a big luncheon at his house, he made his intentions known. The most important citizens of Americana had gathered to enjoy good food, conversation, and ultimately a dance with live music. It had all been for her, he made sure that much was clear, and he walked around the large patio, looking for ways to please her—providing her with cool passion fruit juice and a delicate hand painted fan so that she could feel refreshed even under the heat of that unusually summery April afternoon.

While his luncheon guests chatted, he came to talk to her outside. "Are you having a good time?" He usually spoke in Portuguese, but with her he tended to revert to English. She didn't know why.

"It's wonderful. Thank you for inviting me."

"Inviting you? You are my guest of honor." He put

his hands inside the pockets of his summer suit only to remove them a second later. "I mean, sure. I'm really glad you are here. Really glad."

She was overwhelmed by the attention. She was used to men openly showing their admiration for her, but it was often in superficial ways: stares, gallant words, insinuations. Raymond was different.

That day, she lacked the courage to tell him she was pregnant with another man's child. It was too nice an occasion to spoil. And Beatriz, the housekeeper, had pressed his clothes with such commitment and prepared all the food with such care. But it wasn't all noble consideration on her part. To acknowledge Raymond's feelings for her with a revelation was to close the door on Joaquim for good, wasn't it? She swallowed her words and just commented on the great food and wonderful fruit.

She couldn't be silent forever, though. A few days later, sitting at the same patio where crickets provided nightly music, consumed with guilt and dread, she told him the whole story. Of how she tried to lead the life that befitted an artist. Of how her independence came at a high price. Of how she still could not be certain she had extinguished her feelings for a man she knew to be a *Don Juan*.

"I am sorry I didn't tell you before, but it's not a really good conversation starter, is it?" She drew faces on the ground with a stick, clouds and mountains and random stars too. "I just thought you needed to know because it's clear you are thinking of this as more than friendship, I mean. Not that you must. It was the right thing to do. Tell you, that is." They had switched places, and she was suddenly the awkward one.

To her surprise, Raymond didn't flinch.

"I have a feeling about this child."

"Oh?" Given his usual shyness, she was surprised at how upfront he could be.

"It's going to be a boy. Strong and kind. A real blessing in your life."

She was very grateful for that sentiment. She had so many doubts about this baby's future and her own.

"This just makes it more urgent that we marry." He looked ahead toward the mountains, as if he had said the most trivial thing in the world. As if he had said the sun was setting, or the afternoon was turning cold.

"You want to marry me? Knowing I am pregnant with another man's child?" Her heart pounded in her chest. It was an impossible notion. She didn't know this man. What was his favorite dish? His biggest fear? His most impossible dream? She knew nothing of his life or his heart, except that he was crazy enough to ask her, practically a stranger, to marry him.

"The timing will be a challenge. If people do the math, well, at least we will be married already."

As if he felt he needed to further sell her on the idea, he said his family would be overjoyed at the thought of a male heir produced by him, the eldest son. And did the man know he would be a father? Because if he didn't, then it should all be perfect.

"I can take care of you, Ana. I can make it all fit in."

At first, the thought of it dizzied her more than the pregnancy hormones did, but over the course of a few days, the idea became harder to resist—it was beyond anything she could dream under the circumstances. It was a door, a way out of this muddle. While she debated it with herself, thoughts of Joaquim kept intruding, and she dutifully silenced them. Raymond was charming and nice. She would grow to love him. Her love for Joaquim would be muted by the passing of time, the demands of motherhood, married life. She needed to believe that.

She confided the news to Eugênia one afternoon when the two were alone.

"He's a good man. I'm sure I can grow to love him. Besides, it's not like I can hide in your house forever. I have to think of this baby."

Clearly the right thing was to accept the proposal, and why wouldn't she? Eugênia could go back to her life, Joaquim could continue his farce of a marriage without ever knowing about this child, and she could go from outcast, tainted woman to respectable lady. It was not like she had a choice. And so she convinced herself it was good and proper.

She didn't accept the proposal right away. She didn't know how to bring it up. Instead, as a token of good faith and to see how her family would react, she invited Raymond to Amália's wedding. He accepted, nodding once, twice, switching his weight from his toes to his heels, as if he was preparing to jump for joy, and knowing that this was a step in the right direction.

****

The *bem-casados*, macaroon-like sweets, were ready at the back of the church. They had been carefully wrapped in lavender and cream crepe paper and then tied with shiny white satin ribbons. Displayed on a large oblong table, together with antique metal buckets of chilled bubbly and a tiered white cake frosted with meringue and silvery confectioner's sprinkles, they patiently awaited the end of the religious ceremony and the arrival of the posh guests.

Ana had never made *bem-casados*, the traditional wedding treats that consisted of *doce de leite*, Brazilian caramel, inside two delicate butter cookies stuck together to symbolize the perpetual union of the bride and groom. But she loved eating them, so she was happy her nausea had subsided. It was the first time she had enjoyed a favorite treat in weeks. It was the first time she was happy since Joaquim's visit.

As expected, the wedding of her cousin Amália to a rich heir and future owner of acres and acres of productive sugar cane plantation was an event to remember. The church of Santa Cecília, always so sought after by the expanding elites of São Paulo, was regally decorated with orange blossoms. The nave smelled like an orchard and looked like the Garden of Eden.

Equally perfumed were the bouquets of the eight flower girls whose lemon-chiffon dresses were decorated with a delicate butterfly pattern at the hem. The girls' twinkling eyes revealed the importance the little ladies attached to the wedding and their role in it. The one that carried the rings seemed unable to contain her pride and smiled profusely at any guest that made eye contact. Smiling at others too, Ana walked carefully, as if any sudden move could highlight her shape and give away the changes taking place in her body.

The bride's sister, Rosa, looked so pregnant Ana worried she wouldn't make it through the ceremony. Everyone had been looking dotingly at her, touching Rosa's stomach as if they had some right over it, and

Ana had to control herself not to touch her own belly, the belly which was to receive no attention because no one could know of the secret it contained.

With her enlarging waistline, Ana had chosen a fluid dress that did not squeeze her midriff. Instead, the pattern of blues and greens of the dress, with its drop-waist, were gathered only at the hips, where a strip of solid color was tied in a knot to the left.

The dress was a gift from Raymond, who in his discreet style, adorned her arm at the church, looking at times uncomfortable under the gaze of so many strangers who no doubt wondered who the tall, unknown foreigner might be.

"You look beautiful," Raymond had said when he first saw her, turning her around by the arm like a dancer. "No, actually you look radiant." He then covered his mouth and whispered, "Poor bride's about to be overshadowed."

When Anna first wrote to her parents, they were not at all thrilled to learn she was taking a guest with her to the wedding. However, once they discovered Raymond was a rich American whose family's land ownership cut across both ends of the continent, their demeanor suddenly changed. They more willingly expressed, albeit with their customary lack of enthusiasm, their readiness to meet him and welcome him to the upcoming family gathering. The episode left her disenchanted and sad. He deserved better. She could have been better to him too.

Eugênia didn't want to go to the wedding even though she had been invited. Ana wondered if deep inside her friend resented her for the attention, the drama, and, most of all, the proposal. In recent weeks,

Eugênia had more than once said, "You go, thanks" to Ana when she suggested activities. It was probably not easy to play best friend to a woman who, for better or worse, managed to find herself the center of attention most of the time. In her polite way, Eugênia simply said she would rather stay in Americana than go to the wedding. "Really, I want to stay. You go and memorize everything so that you can tell me later."

Ana didn't insist. She spent the next several days trying to be a friend for a change, and she asked Eugênia many questions about dreams and plans and fears. "How about you? Tell me all you want. I'm better now. I don't feel so sick. I'd like to hear."

It turned out she had much to say when prompted, when given time. "I think I want to travel. You will think I am silly, but I want to go to Egypt and Morocco. Can't you just see me wearing a hat and a scarf dancing in the wind?"

Eugênia entertained dreams of learning languages too, preferably French and Italian. Covering her mouth and erasing the smile from her face, she also confessed, "Maybe I can even find myself a husband sometime. I'm good at taking care of people." And Ana kissed her cheek and held her hand in gratitude. Ana and Raymond went to São Paulo and promised to tell Eugênia everything about the festivities upon their return.

Ana kept mental notes on the church, the gowns, and the delicious *bem-casados* waiting for them in the grand salon. Keeping her mind occupied helped. It ensured that the nervousness of introducing Raymond to her parents and hiding her condition would not overtake or overwhelm her.

True to herself, Ana's mother first saluted Raymond outside the church with frigid politeness. She extended a firm hand while her upper lip contorted in an attempt at smiling. Ana's father took Raymond to see the beautiful architecture, leaving Ana and her mother to fill an uncomfortable silence.

"He seems adequate." Mrs. Eça said when the men were out of hearing range.

Ana wanted to run despite her heels. "He is a lovely man," she retorted instead.

"Is it serious?" her mother asked while examining her nails.

"I suppose."

"Ah, Ana! What could that possibly mean?"

Ana's face was burning. "It means, mother, that I suppose it is serious. That he is a wonderful man, and that I hope you don't scare him away with your chilliness and your judgment."

Ana marched off, clutching her silver mesh purse so hard she could feel the little mirror inside it poking at her skin. Her legs were trembling, and her vision seemed blurry. She could not remember ever daring to speak to her mother that way. Maybe the pregnancy had destabilized her. Some women wanted to eat endlessly; she just wanted to put her mother in her place, say the things she had never said before, like "Treat me with kindness" or "See me for who I am."

She searched the church looking for Raymond as if he were a lighthouse in the storm. Her life was indeed a storm, and right at that moment he was all she had. *Uma tábua de salvação*, a lifeline.

She found her father explaining patiently to Ray the *rococó* details of the church, and once again she was aware she and Raymond were strangers to each other. She didn't even know if Raymond was a Catholic. She expected that if he were Christian, it would be of a Protestant denomination. She would ask him later, even if she wasn't too concerned, just to know more about him.

Upon seeing Ana, Raymond smiled broadly. She tucked her arm inside his and was immediately comforted by the warmth of his body. Being taken care of by a man was like nothing she had ever experienced before. It was great to be free, but it was even more wonderful to be sheltered in someone's love. She basked in that feeling until the changing dynamics around the church brought her back. Like a busy little colony of ants, people started to line up and hurry back to their pews. The ceremony was about to start.

Ana and Raymond reached the bench where her mother was already seated, looking even more acerbic and resentful than usual, while organ music mercifully filled the air with its calm.

The bride entered the church wearing an embroidered gown with an elevated neckline and a bodice embossed with the tiniest pearls. Her bouquet was a cascade of the same orange blossoms that beautified the church, intertwined with white swan roses and baby's breath. As usual, no one noticed or cared about what the groom was wearing. When Amália reached the end of the nave, Raymond searched for Ana's hand, and before they sat, he squeezed her fingers, marking the moment by smiling at her.

Ana caught herself enthralled by the wedding, the music, the gaze of the groom and bride, the pomp and the admiring eyes of the spectators. She noticed an aunt whispering in her friend's ear while looking at Raymond. No doubt people had been wondering. He took everything with ease, the curiosity and the subtle pressure. When a cousin commented on Ana's rounder face, he came to her rescue, remarking how beautiful and healthy she looked, and Ana sighed with relief.

At the end of the ceremony, after drinking the expensive champagne and eating cake in the grand salon, everyone gathered outside the church for the traditional farewell to the newlyweds. Ana, her hands full of rice, was feeling refreshed, vindicated even. Raymond had sealed their future together a few minutes before, still inside the church. It had been the moment that she was waiting for—a sign, an unequivocal indication that he was the man for her, who would stand for her when she needed.

As they left the pew, Ana's mother leading the way with her chin up in the sky, Raymond had lightly touched the woman's arm, causing her to turn in surprise. When she did, she was met with his disarming smile.

"I want to thank you for raising such a wonderful daughter," he said overtaken with sudden emotion. "She is the most wonderful woman I have ever met. She is different from everyone else, and I cannot help but think that you had something to do with her uniqueness. She is creative and beautiful. I just wanted to say this to you. Thank you for Ana."

Ana could have kissed him right then, forgetting all notions of propriety. Her mother, without any possible dignified alternative, thanked Raymond.

"How kind of you to say this. I am so pleased you were able to come to the wedding. Would you like to come to dinner with us at the house? I don't think your hotel is too far, is it?"

Raymond gave Ana a nervous look, and seeing her nod, accepted the offer.

Three hours later, in the large living room, traditionally and uncomfortably kneeling, with the two senior Eças for an audience, Raymond looked official as he re-asked the question that would change the course of all else.

In a flash, Ana saw Joaquim's sly face. She wondered if the baby would look like him, if it would be a constant reminder of what could have been. Before, she had scanned the church wondering if he was there, ready to whisk her away and take responsibility for the child he didn't even know she was carrying. Now, involuntarily, she looked out of the window, half-expecting to see him outside, touching her belly and yet knowing the idea was absurd. And then returning to the one reality she had, feeling teary-eyed and a little off balance, Ana said yes.

Chapter 21
Darcey

April 1997

It was Saturday. Darcey woke up to a familiar rattling of silverware in the kitchen, things being shifted around, dropped, shaken, and washed, and cupboard doors opened and shut. She felt no fear, as she considered Archie the usual suspect. But wasn't he too restrained for all that noise?

When she arrived in the kitchen, her mother was standing by the sink, her back to Darcey. Eleanor wore slippers and an apron. She spoke without turning around.

"You don't lock your door! You're lucky it was me and not some criminal in your kitchen."

Nina came running in from the couch and jumped on Darcey. "Mooooom." Panic made Darcey's neck warm. Had anyone seen Nina? What were they going to think? What if Archie had seen her? But she couldn't say anything. Her family had made the trip to see her, and her heart was joyous—and a little guilt-filled for having second-guessed their presence. She got to see her daughter unexpectedly. That alone was a great gift. "Hello, sweetie! What are you all doing here? Where's Dad?"

"I am here." He shouted from in front of the TV.

Darcey walked halfway toward him. "I'll be right there, Dad." She headed back to her mom.

Eleanor inspected a spoon and made a face. She threw it in the sink and came over to give her daughter a hug. "Are you happy we're here?"

"Of course. Oh, Nina. I miss you *so* much."

Nina smiled and tilted her head, happy with the attention.

"So, what're you doing here?" Darcey asked.

Eleanor brought her hands to a kitchen towel. "You don't call enough. We came to make sure everything is fine."

"Everything is fine, Mom." No, she wasn't fine, but her mother didn't need to know.

"You sure? When you say fine, I hear overworked, not eating enough."

"Mom, I'm fine, really."

"Go get dressed. I'm taking you out to breakfast." Darcey's anxiety must have been apparent because Eleanor continued, "Just you and me. Dad will stay with Nina. She needs a nap anyway. You can invite Archie if you want." Eleanor folded the kitchen towel and placed it on top of the microwave.

"Archie's busy." Darcey tried for noncommittal instead of irritated.

"Oh? That's new." She had Eleanor's full attention now.

"What's new?"

"Don't play coy with me, Darcey. That boy's been after you from the day you met. Or do you think I ever fell for that 'best friend' silliness?" Her hands were positioned above her waistline, her elbows sticking out like the handles of a sugar bowl.

"You forget it's impossible." Darcey gave Nina a bittersweet smile. "And for once you're wrong. He even has a girlfriend." She crossed her arms and looked toward the window. The glass was smudged and thus liable to attract her mother's attention. She went back to the word "girlfriend" in her mind and experienced a tightening in her chest. It wasn't just paranoia. She'd seen Archie and Dominique together on campus while the woman fed him ice cream. She was caught by surprise. What was even more surprising is that she and her mother were talking so openly about this.

"Really? Well, I stand corrected then. Good for him, I guess. I can't say that I'm not a little disappointed, though."

Darcey shrugged her shoulders. She didn't want to fall apart. "It is what it is."

"Which means it's not what you would want it to be?"

"I guess not. I miss him." It was strange to say it aloud like that. It made the feeling more real, but it also gave her a strange sense of relief.

Eleanor gave her a timid smile. "You know what? I think it is the first time you've said something so heartfelt about him. I wish he could hear you. Maybe you should tell him." She picked up her purse. "Now let's go. Pancakes await."

Darcey thought of Ana. She was thankful Mrs. Eça was not her mother. Her heart filled with sympathy for her mom and for her suffering. She had become guarded—that's all. A person's first instinct is always to protect their own heart.

"Where are we going?" Darcey gave in, feeling guilty for having been unfair to her mother often enough, for having thought Eleanor would've preferred her brother.

"You pick."

"Okay." Darcey fluffed her hair.

"And what's with this haircut? Is it a bob, is it layered? I can't really tell." She smiled, teasing her daughter. Her disposition was more relaxed than Darcey had seen in years.

"Mom. Leave my hair alone. Come on. We could stay and make breakfast here?" Darcey picked Nina up and held her tight. She went into the living room and kissed her father on the head. "It's good you're here, Dad." He pulled Darcey in for a hug. He was a good man.

At an eatery near the campus, the waiter placed a large serving of blueberry pancakes in front of Darcey and a couple of slices of dry rye bread with a splotch of orange marmalade for Eleanor. On the other side of the glass, the neon sign of the *Café Bon* buzzed unsteadily as if it were not sure whether the store was open or not.

"How's Dad?" Darcey asked once the server left.

"Dad's fine. Dad's dad. You know. He's back to working a bit. Freelance. Between the bonds and his pay, we have been able to make ends meet. For now." She drank her coffee and raised her eyebrows, like the beverage was actually acceptable. It was like her inner-perfectionist had gone on vacation despite all the problems.

"I promise I will change our situation soon, Mom. These last few months have been productive. This year will end well—I promise."

"I know, Darce." Her mother hadn't called her that in a long time. "So many people lost their houses. We, your father and I, should've known better. But what's done is done. House or no house, we'll be fine. Chances are we will put it on the market soon."

Darcey's stomach tightened. "Mom…Don't do it."

"We'll see. Let's talk about something else. How's work?" Eleanor rested her chin on her intertwined fingers.

"Work's good. Really good."

"Finally! Something to celebrate. You never give me details of what you are writing about."

"I don't wanna jinx it, but…Brazilian Modernism. Putting my Portuguese to good use."

"Your father will be delighted to hear that."

"Yeah. Don't tell him, though. I might try and surprise him when I'm done. My Portuguese has improved so much I wanna try and write something for him."

"That's a great idea." Eleanor touched Darcey's hand and said, "You're a good daughter." There was a calm between the two of them now, made more obvious by the fact that Eleanor hadn't pushed to find out more about Archie and his new friend. Darcey was grateful for both the compliment and for her mother's discretion.

"And that will be soon—the end of the project, I mean?"

"I think by the end of—" The door had just chimed with the arrival of new customers. Looking at it was one of those unavoidable natural reflexes—turning if someone shouts "help!" or honks a horn nearby.

It was Archie. When he saw Eleanor, his smile broadened. He was always able to make her smile too. Darcey avoided his eyes. He wasn't alone. From behind

Archie's well-dressed body, Dominique's irritatingly polished figure, in a lilac cotton blouse and a pencil skirt in stark contrast to Darcey's flannel pants and T-shirt, caused the latter to feel even more inadequate than usual.

Darcey shoved a giant forkful of blueberry pancake into her mouth and angrily minced it between her teeth. At least they weren't holding hands. She nodded at them and turned back to her mom. Nervousness rose in her throat and turning away was a strategy too. She would see him later for research. No need to make this excruciating encounter any more painful. Except that Archie, being who he was, came over to say hi to Eleanor, and he brought Miss Fancy Shoes along with him.

The breakfast had started out so well; it was disappointing to see it go downhill. Dominique whispered "Hello." She looked as uncomfortable as Darcey felt. Archie and Dominique bought croissants and left. Darcey shuffled her food around the plate until the pancakes were so soggy that they turned inedible. Eleanor drank from her cup. Her eyes traveled from her daughter to the couple on the street.

Darcey left the café despondent, the beauty of that street, with its old, well-kept houses and stores lost to her.

Her mother, who had avoided any comments about the situation, didn't stay much longer. She had planned to visit a school friend two hours away, and they had tickets for the theater. The whole family was gone by four. Nina waved from the backseat of the car, and Darcey, her heart small in her chest seeing her daughter be driven away, was left to count the minutes to the appointment with Archie, to go over more research. She was happy about her family's visit, though. She had opened up and as a result felt closer to them than she had in a long time.

When she arrived at Archie's house that evening, five minutes early, sweet perfume dabbed behind her ears, he avoided her eyes and stepped aside for her to enter.

"Tell me about Ana's mom." They sat on the carpet of his living room. It was a little past seven. Darcey reclined on a large pillow, drinking chamomile tea, and Archie stretched out on the sofa above her. He offered her a space there, but she took the floor, as the chair was too uncomfortable. She was bewildered because he was usually such a gentleman.

"What do you want to know?" he asked and looked up toward the ceiling, his hands behind his head and his legs extended and crossed.

"I know she's your great-great grandmother and all, but Mrs. Eça seemed cold and unfeeling." She slid back a little farther away from him. Not her finest comment. This was Archie's family she had just criticized.

He took his time before speaking. When he did, his tone was impatient. "She was a traditional woman, born and raised in the 1800s. It's not hard to imagine that the early twentieth century, all that change, scared her. She wanted what she knew and understood. Don't we all?" He raised his head and looked at her intently, like he was talking about her. He sat up and poured some wine. "I'm sure she felt she didn't understand those new, liberated women, or how Ana had turned out to be one."

He drank from his glass of Zinfandel. Darcey knew it was too sweet for his taste, but he'd probably bought it because she liked it. He preferred dark, rich Cabernets. She would have felt better if he had bought a Cabernet. She wouldn't even take a sip. The memory of drinking too much wine at Donaldson's party made her shiver with embarrassment.

"Is anything wrong? You seem a little off." She moved closer to him. She wished they could go back to being sixteen, to the smiles and hugs like the ones in that picture in her apartment.

"It's nothing. I just don't think I'm in the mood for this story today. In fact, I haven't been in the mood for a while now. All this family drama." He gulped the wine down. "I have things on my mind."

"Like what?"

"Like it doesn't matter. Not worth your time."

"Well, if you tell me, I can decide if it's worth my time." She should have stopped there, but she didn't. "Do you tell *Dominique* now?"

Her barren resentment surprised her. But he'd been different, had allowed Dominique to anchor herself on his shoulder at the coffee shop, as if she'd already claimed him like an award.

"I just don't know if I care about this project anymore. It's messy. People always get hurt. That's all." He said it so casually, she thought she had misunderstood him. But as soon as her brain wrapped itself around the idea that he might give up, her spine prickled with fear. Her degree depended on this, her whole life possibly. How could he act like it didn't matter? The diary and letters were incomplete. He was the glue that held it all together.

"Oh, great." She stood up. "And you expect me to do *what* now that I have told Donaldson that I got this, now that I have spent a million hours doing research on Modernism and the backdrop of this story?" She walked back and forth, tripping over her words as she enumerated her frustrations. "Now, now that I like Ana as if I knew her? Now that I feel she deserves a place she never got among the artists of the time, huh? Now that my parents are about to…" She didn't finish. Her voice cracked, and her pitch soared so high it hurt her own ears. "What do you want me to do? Just tell me. Tell me and I'll do it."

"I don't want you to do anything, Darcey."

"Then please, let's continue. You gave me the gift of this story, set it up for me. Please don't leave me in the lurch now."

He thought for a minute. His breath went from labored to more stable, although still accelerated.

"Fine. I'll continue." He stood in a brisk, sudden movement.

"Thank you." She faced him, eyes locked on his, her fists clenched, and her mind wavering between relief and anger.

"Sit down." His voice came out sharp, but after he issued the command, his body relaxed. The person who looked back at Darcey after a couple of minutes was more like the Archie she knew. She grabbed on to that, to the scraps of what she still believed existed between them.

He sat beside her, his forearms on his thighs, his torso bent forward, as if he'd run a long distance and needed to recover. "Ana decided, for obvious reasons, to have a short engagement, and her mother wasn't happy about it. Amália's wedding was a memorable event. She wanted her daughter to have something even bigger and better. She wanted all her friends to be jealous when she told them about Ray's fortune. But Ana wanted to marry quickly, within a few weeks of Amália's wedding, and in the countryside of all places. It was unthinkable, especially given the wealth of the groom. The two women almost stopped speaking altogether."

"So Ana didn't tell her mother about the pregnancy?"

"No. Would you have said anything, in her position?"

Darcey thought of *her* position, and how she'd lied to Archie for three years already. Her cheeks burned in shame at her own behavior. "Probably not. I'd avoid calling attention to my condition at all costs. That must have been hard for Ana, don't you think? Not calling attention to herself?"

"Yep." He was distant again, stretching back, his eyes searching for some elusive sign on the ceiling. If only she had the courage to reach for his hand and tell him she was there for him, for whatever he needed. But she was still angry too. He'd given her quite a scare when he almost quit the project. She realized how generous with his time he'd been. Two thirds of the work were done. If only he'd stick with her a little longer. *Forever, maybe?*

Darcey stood up. "Maybe I should go home. It's clear you need some space, or time. I ordered some texts through interlibrary loan. Let me know when you are back to normal." She put on her jean jacket.

"Back to normal? You mean available, at your

disposal? What if this is the new normal?"

"No, this isn't normal. Not for you," she shouted, packing her things in a hurry. She shoved her notebook in the messenger bag and folds formed on the cover. This wasn't good. Her Archie was gone. Yes, she was being selfish, but she couldn't help it. She was so scared.

"Darcey," he called, making her stop. His voice was broken and weak, all the anger vanished. "I'm not trying to be difficult. I just need a few days without this. I'm going to visit my mom."

"Is everything okay?" It took her that long to realize the extent of her self-absorption. This wasn't about her thesis or her at all. Something else was hurting him.

He looked at her as if deciding what to say. He breathed in and spoke. "My parents' marriage fell apart. She's going to divorce him. I don't know how I can help either one of them."

He was like a wounded animal, scared and wild at the same time. Darcey approached carefully and sat beside him. She waited for him to react. His head rested on her shoulder. He was tired; he looked like he didn't care what she thought of him. He was crying, and her heart overflowed with love. She put her arm around him.

As he lifted his head to look at her, his hair caressed her cheek. She stayed still, not daring to hope. She wanted to touch his face, to say she was sorry for all the pain he was feeling, that she wanted to make it go away. He looked at her with those piercing eyes, and her skin burned under his gaze. The kiss, stored away for such a long time became so necessary that it hurt.

She could tell he felt it too, as if the idea had been planted in their heads at the same time. They'd taken different paths but had arrived at the same intersection. Darcey pulled Archie even closer and held his head a centimeter away from hers.

"Ask me again. Pretend we are back at Donaldson's party. Pretend I wasn't stupid."

"Darcey, do you want me to stop?"

"No, Archie. I don't."

Her mouth recognized his in an instant, with relief. His lips were as soft as she remembered. Darcey and Archie lingered there, engaged in that kiss forever, lost and away from the walls of his house. This wasn't the inconsequential kiss of years before. This one carried the weight of so much longing and so much denial. This was what she had always wanted.

She was home.

His arms reached for her body. For a second she worried the moment would pass, and he would retract his embrace. She'd gotten so used to second-guessing. But soon his hands were inside her jacket. He helped her remove the garment, which fell to the floor. She stood still while he unbuttoned her white shirt. She wanted to savor that moment. An instant later, his own shirt fell to the ground, and when his skin pressed against her body, all her worries dissolved. Her heart throbbed in her ears. Archie's breath quickened, and his palm cradled the back of her neck like all of her belonged to him.

"Darcey Mendes, you never make my life easy, do you?"

She smiled and looked down. "I guess not."

"Come here. We'll have time for stories later."

He took her hand in his. There was no other place where she needed or wanted to be.

Chapter 22
Ana

May 30, 1922

Ana had asked for simple flowers, hydrangeas and other hardy foliage that grew without being coached in the fields around the house. She had chosen the patio of the farmhouse for the site, and the maids had placed little vases on the tables where people were going to enjoy lunch after the ceremony.

"I'm not wearing my mother's dress," she said to Raymond. "It's antiquated. And it would never fit around my waist. Even worse, it wouldn't be mine. Ours." Raymond had ordered a dress in São Paulo. It was loose-fitting, with the silhouette that was so in vogue in the city.

Besides her parents, the guests of the wedding were few: Eugênia and Jacinto, Leopoldina, Marina and Letícia (two friends whom she had met during her stay at Eugênia's), a couple of friends of the groom, and some politically significant townspeople who would have minded being slighted. While she waited for the ceremony to start, Ana looked out one of the windows to see the guests arrive. Ana enjoyed seeing Raymond talk to those men of prominence. Around them, he was so steady and secure. His posture changed, he stood very straight, holding their attention, and being as charming as he could be.

The parish's Catholic priest had agreed to preside over the wedding not knowing of the complication that would have likely caused him to leave. Each day she got a little bit more confirmation, in episodes such as speaking to the priest, that their decision to keep the truth and the paternity among the five people who knew—herself, Raymond, Eugênia, *Seu* Jacinto and Dina—was the right one.

Raymond's parents didn't come. His mother was too incapacitated to make the arduous trip from Kentucky, where they owned a second home. They sent best wishes and conveyed their hope of meeting the bride soon. Ana was relieved. She could meet them later, at a time her life was not in such a state of ebullition.

May had been plagued with showers that all but tore the plants from the ground. Yet on the day of the wedding, everyone woke up to the splendors of a cloudless morning and mild temperatures that matched calendar expectations.

Ana didn't walk down the aisle, as there was none. She strolled regally from inside the mansion's main room. Raymond's devotion was written in his eyes, in his careful hiring of a string quartet, in the beautiful wedding bands he bought, a little line of white trapped inside the dark, expensive yellow gold. He held her hand in his cold palm, and he said, "I hope you know that from now on, it will be all in your honor, everything to make you happy."

He told her she looked beautiful many times, and that he would work hard to bring her joy for as long as they both should live. The child too. The boy, as his conviction went. He stole discreet glances at her stomach. It must have been an uncomfortable thought, her body being inhabited by another man's child. He had a few hours to overcome the feeling before conjugal duties took place.

"She looks like a princess," Ana overheard Marina, a tall woman of about thirty, say as they prepared for the vows. Raymond turned his head toward his mother-in-law, and Ana followed his gaze, searching for signs of emotion, contained or otherwise. As always, she found only moot civility. If Raymond had stereotyped Brazilians as the emotive kind, Mrs. Eça defied the typecast.

"…in sickness and in health, *na saúde e na doença*." In Portuguese the words were reversed. "*Na alegria e na tristeza*, in happiness and in sorrow." *Please let there be happiness*, she wished silently.

When he slid the ring on her finger, she experienced instant relief: it fit perfectly. She looked up, straight into his eyes, to convey gratitude with her gaze.

As soon as the wedding ceremony was over, a light lunch and champagne were served.

"Is everything to your liking?" Raymond wanted to know.

"Yes, it's all beautiful, thank you." There was still too much politeness between them. No intimacy, nothing done without words.

"Would you like to cut the cake now?" And so they did, and they danced to the sounds of the quartet that was still going strong, and they received the compliments of the guests who had brought colorfully wrapped gifts, breaching the tradition of sending them ahead of time.

When night fell and they were alone, nervous since they were strangers to each other, they found ways of overcoming their shyness by making plans and dreaming up a future that they didn't yet fully comprehend.

"I'll work, and you'll be able to paint and care for our son."

"Yes, I'd love to exhibit again, but in the US? Who knows what Americans will think of my art. It's so Brazilian."

"They will love it. You'll see."

She smiled at him, unsure of how things would turn out, but thankful for this love.

It was only later, tired of dawdling, that they let their wariness melt into a discomfited and still tentative form of intimacy. There was no music to it yet, no rhythm or harmony. There were legs and arms that moved, but it would take time for their bodies to recognize each other.

The months that followed were happy and sleepy and quiet for Ana. Americana, with its friendly squares and tranquil dwellers was a good place to start life, to take in the changes that the whirlwind wedding had brought.

Raymond was no surprise. At least not at first. He continued to be the gentleman he appeared to be before the marriage. He spoke often of the son they would have, and when enough time had passed for their pretense to stand scrutiny, he was the first to announce to everyone that he would be a father. She was four months pregnant, and they had known each other long enough for people to assume she had gotten pregnant by him while single, which was a better alternative than if they were to suspect the child wasn't his.

By then, the weather was turning cold, as happens in June in the tropics, and the extra layers of fabric allowed Ana to relax a bit and enjoy her growing stomach privately under the safeguard of coats, shawls, and capes. She decided she liked winters. At least she didn't dislike the Brazilian ones.

Eugênia came to visit almost every day. Ana welcomed her to the house with lavish lunches and quiet afternoon coffees. The two women had traveled to São Paulo to close both the atelier and Ana's house and to sell unneeded items and pick up the necessary ones.

Ana avoided old acquaintances. She later sent wedding announcements, as tradition demanded, to Maria Pia and her society friends, and to all the artists she had started to befriend. It was a message both elegant and vague, offering the house that she knew she would only have for a few months to visitors that would not come.

Raymond had suggested they make a life in Americana. Ana didn't agree.

"The distance from São Paulo and Joaquim isn't big enough. I want to start anew, in the United States. Better for everyone, including you."

So when Raymond was presented with a business partnership that would take them north, an opportunity to salvage a failing textile factory in Pennsylvania, she begged him to take it. They could wait for the birth of the child and spend a few months in Brazil for the baby to gain its strength, and then they could embark on a ship and make a fresh start where they wouldn't be bothered.

Raymond agreed with some reluctance. "Are you sure?"

"Yes, very much so," she said with more conviction than she actually had.

"Won't you miss everyone? Your parents?"

"Ray, you've met my parents. I think some distance would actually do us good. Let's just wait for this child to arrive." Surely, she would miss Eugênia, Jacinto, and Dina, but they could come to visit. And in a few years, the family might come to Brazil for a vacation or even to stay if the situation was different by then. What different meant, she wasn't exactly sure. She hoped it would involve her child being older, and Joaquim having forgotten about her.

"My son. You will always think of him as my son, won't you?" He held both her hands in his. She thought he already loved the baby so much because it was an extension of her, and she laughed at what was becoming a sort of obsession for him, frankly because it made her a little uneasy. He spoke with absurd certainty and wouldn't be dissuaded otherwise.

"What if it is a girl?" she asked delicately from time to time.

The tenor of the answer was always the same. "Nonsense. I know in my gut it is a boy, and he'll grow up to be a learned man, a leader. You just wait and see."

And so she would change subjects and hope not to crush his dreams. He wouldn't let the subject rest for very long, though, asking the village women to knit blue blankets and little socks, commissioning a rocking horse at the local carpenter's. A son was all he ever talked about, and he was to be raised like a prince.

The day she really worried was the one when Raymond, on all fours, played around with two new toy trains he had ordered in São Paulo in anticipation of the birth, and in between crashing the vehicles together and inspecting the parts, he looked up at her and asked, "Do you think he will look like me?"

Ana didn't know what to say. She worried that to cope with fathering another man's child, he had created a fantasy, a delusion, and she didn't dare imagine the consequences of bringing him back to reality, for him or for her. Would he leave her? Would he be mad?

She smiled tenderly when he asked impossible questions, and at night she held him close, listening to him talk about all the things they would do in the United States, about where they would live and what places they would visit.

"I'll buy you a big colonial. I'll furnish it and hire help so that you can paint to your heart's content. Maybe Beatriz would like to come and be our governess. Our little rascal playing in the yard, you creating the beautiful things you always create."

"A small house will do, Raymond."

"Why? Let's have a big house! And parties—let's have parties that everyone will remember, like the ones you told me about, with artists, musicians, and avant-garde people. Is that what you call them?"

He blushed a little, looking self-conscious, maybe worrying that he didn't have any glamour, which indeed he didn't, although she really liked that about him. For now.

"If that'll make you happy," she would say without much conviction, and would then change subjects because, honestly, what else was there to say?

Sometimes she thought of Joaquim, and a panicky feeling overcame her, a prickling in the back of her head, although she never spoke to her husband of those things. She resorted to confiding in Eugênia instead. "Do you think it is really bad of me that I'm not even letting him know I'm having his child?" she would ask.

Eugênia always took her side, but Ana wondered if it was because they had fought over the matter in the past. "Do you believe he would honor his responsibilities if he knew?"

Ana couldn't imagine he would, but a part of her kept searching for a good reason to tell. Maybe he would have a change of heart? Or perhaps she had misjudged him all along? These questions went around in circles in her head, without providing any satisfactory, matching answer.

It was a self-perpetuating cycle of doubt that only left her more ruffled. Her changing moods coincided with periods of affection for her husband and phases of rejection. One day she would shower him with attention, helping Beatriz bake his favorite cake, and bringing Raymond to see the toys she bought, only to lock herself in her room the next.

One day she fetched pen and paper onto the table and went as far as to write the first line of a letter to Joaquim, only to tear it into little pieces. She convinced herself that her life was meant to be spent with Raymond and never tried to write again. After much agony, she discovered she had to live with the guilt and uncertainty of not having told. The thought finally helped her move on.

When the nine months were almost up, Ana started feeling an urgency to be done with the pregnancy; a nesting instinct caused her to clean and organize everything. Laziness was punctuated with bouts of vitality.

Yet, she persuaded her husband that the birth couldn't be that soon. "Go on the trip. Visit those lands. It's your property, and you need to check on it. It's only a day anyway." She'd stay with Eugênia, making plans, knitting the final rows of a blanket, too warm for the month of November.

"No, I'll stay. My son could arrive any moment now. I want to be here when it happens. I'll be the first, no, the second to hold him in my arms." He paced the room and spoke as if he was talking to himself.

But Ana could be so persuasive when she wanted. She experienced great relief when he finally agreed. In all honesty, she was trying to be alone for a while. The moment she put the baby in Raymond's arms, she would have transferred the paternity from Joaquim to her husband. There would be no turning back. If Raymond was the father on paper, he would be the parent in life too. She needed a moment alone to acclimatize to that idea.

"I feel nothing yet. Really. The baby will wait." Contrite and afflicted, he left for the fields promising to be back the next day.

It didn't take long for the misery to start. Raymond had been gone for only three hours. She was folding baby clothes that smelled of sunshine. Dina had just brought a basket of them from outside. At first, it was a dull pain, almost an afterthought. But soon, the contractions came strongly, in unpredictable intervals. They had their own caprices, and they acted out with her body's control.

Ana told nobody. Now that the event approached, she was filled with denial, wishing she had more time. She stayed in Eugênia's room where her friend found her contorted and pale a couple of hours later. She could barely talk by then.

Eugênia wanted to call the doctor, but Ana refused. "Dina has played midwife so many times that she's better than any doctor," Ana argued.

Jacinto paced the living room as a sort of substitute father, Dina and Eugênia boiled the water, cleared out the bed, and positioned Ana on her back, supported by a few soft pillows. Dina found a spool of thread, with which she would cut the umbilical cord, and placed it on the nightstand.

Ana's screams pierced the heavy, humid air. They made her shiver despite the oppressive weather, the early heat of that tropical day. Ana could hardly breathe. It was as if her insides were being pried open by the branches of a tree. Everything in the world right then began and ended in her uterus. She was a planet herself, round and bountiful.

Dina looked worried. "She's so small. She doesn't have the hips of a *parideira*," a woman born to give birth. "Eugênia, sit behind her, cradle her in your lap, and when I tell you, help her by telling her to push toward me."

"I can't do it," cried Ana, almost running out of power.

"Me neither," whimpered Eugênia.

"That's what everyone says, Aninha. But you have to. There's no turning back now. And you, Eugênia. You are here to help, not to make it worse," Dina scolded.

Ana held tightly to the sheets, twisting them in her sweaty palms. Everything started to feel like a hallucination, a nightmare—the bedroom that suddenly looked dark and cold, Eugênia's face upside down in front of her, a horrible need to bear down, a baby's cry, and Dina running back and forth and then pausing to look at her.

Then came a long wait, as if she was crossing a tunnel. She closed and opened her eyes again. She was unsure of what constituted reality and what might be a hallucination.

And then voices and more little screams, and Dina that would not stand still, and were those little legs in the air she saw moving as she turned her face? A mother. Could she possibly be seeing what she was seeing? She was still lying on her back, her body exposed and her feet painfully cold. Everything else was different. Incredibly different. Motherhood, uncertainty, surprise. More than she could have imagined.

When it all finally stopped, Ana could not tell if she was awake anymore. Her body felt empty of blood, but also drenched in a cold sweat. Her limbs shook, powered by a release of adrenaline. She noticed Eugênia sliding away from her, leaving her bed and looking to approach the newly arrived baby.

****

Raymond had found the fences of his property torn and invaders threatening to take possession of it. He had to stay longer to fix the problem. He galloped back to town two days too late to hear that Ana had already given birth.

From the stupor of the poorly slept post-birth night,

and the closeness of a front room, Ana heard his voice down the hall.

"I'm sorry for the intrusion. I heard!"

"Congratulations, Raymond!" said Jacinto. "No apologies needed." He then shouted toward the rooms "Dina, is Ana decent? Ray's here."

Leopoldina took her time getting to the sitting room to fetch Raymond, and when she did arrive, she used all the formality she knew. "Ana is ready for you now, Mr. Raymond. This way, please."

Ana heard the cooing of the baby and saw her husband looking emotional and unable to take his eyes off him. The next instant he was sitting next to her, the infant in his arms and his lips parting to utter the words. "A boy!"

This was it, the moment she was dreading but which now provided some relief.

"Your son, Raymond," Ana stressed. "I'd like to call him August, if you don't mind."

"No, I like it. It's a strong name. Unusual for a Brazilian, but I cannot expect anything common from you, can I?" He laughed. "We'll call him Gus while he's little." He paused. "Now that he is here and he's actually a boy, I might as well tell you that I am relieved. I mean, I think of him as mine now, but the fact that it's not a girl helps very much too. I cannot explain why. It just seems like it would be harder. I always dreamed of a boy."

His candor was a grave mistake. His love for her and the child should come with no conditions, but she was not in a position to demand anything. It shouldn't make a difference. She managed to smile feebly, but he had hurt her. He didn't know about her conflicted thoughts, about everything she was compromising by having married him. And how could he? How much had she shared with him, and how much did she continue to hide? All he saw was this child, this boy, and his own adoration of her, not as a person but as an ideal. Maybe she was just a fantasy he had created, and now she had to keep up that make-believe.

Like a giant who has broken a fine china cup with his clumsiness, Raymond looked awkward and unsure of how to fix things. "Ana, I'm sorry. I didn't mean to upset you. I don't know what I am saying. And after all, here he is—our boy. There's no need for this kind of speculation."

She changed the subject. "I'd like you to go and fetch a few things for me in the big house. We will be ready to head home when you come back with them. Then we can start planning for our journey to the US. I would like to leave within the month."

He crossed his arms and uncrossed them again. He walked toward the window.

"Don't you think it's too soon? We had agreed on a few months."

"That was before. No, a month will do."

He came back to her and touched her face lightly. "Ana, I'm an ogre for saying what I did. I'm sorry."

"Raymond, as you said, it's immaterial. Gus is here, and we are leaving in a month. End of story. Go now. I cannot impose on this family any longer. If you could also send word of the arrival to my parents, I would be grateful. Tell them he was early but is well. I don't know how many people will believe he was conceived after the wedding, but I'm sure that, since we are married, no one will say anything." As if by design,

Dina appeared at the door to take the baby.

"Aninha, you need your rest. Mr. Raymond, she is very tired. I'll take the boy now." And bending over, Leopoldina removed the bundle from Raymond's arms.

Devoid of anything to say and slumping his shoulders, Raymond left to do as he was told. A short while later, they were ready to go home.

****

A month can pass very fast when one is in a haze of semi-slumber, waking up at all hours for feedings and learning to be what they never were before. There were little clothes to be washed, bottles to be boiled, and a perpetually needy mouth to feed. There were also opposing emotions to be tamed and tears to be cried.

Ana hardly saw Eugênia anymore, her days filled with taking care of Gus and making preparations for the long trip ahead—packing, making lists, buying items she was sure to miss abroad: her favorite soap, a bottle of an expensive perfume. When Raymond challenged her on Eugênia, she always blamed her absence on her new responsibilities. She didn't want to tell the truth, to speak of the heartache that leaving would cause, and of how Eugênia and everything she represented would soon belong to her past.

"Why don't you go and visit with Eugênia? Beatriz and I can watch the boy for a few hours," he would insist, to Ana's despair.

But Ana argued she should do everything herself. "I'm a mother, aren't I? It's my duty to take care of him. Besides, Eugênia is busy." She disappeared behind blankets and bottles. She never took a break.

And she never painted either. Painting made her think of Joaquim, of her beautiful Brazil, of the dreams and the treasures she was leaving behind. Of the future of her baby.

When a month was up and the tickets for the ship at the *Porto de Santos* had been bought, Raymond took charge of the final preparations. And this time he insisted.

"Go and spend a good long time with Eugênia. We are leaving, Ana. She deserves a little time with you." Ana could think of no excuse not to go, even if all she wanted was to stay and only spend time with her son. He now filled almost all of the spaces in her heart. She dressed in the first thing she saw lying on a chair and combed her hair dispassionately, hair that was not bobbed anymore but rather fell carelessly over her shoulders, and she went to Eugênia's house.

When she came back two hours later, she went into the bedroom, locked the door, and slept for a whole day.

Chapter 23
Darcey

Summer 1997

Archie had been gone for three long, ghostly days. His mother needed him. Darcey distracted her mind—a mind that insisted on believing Archie would leave when she told him the truth—with the narcotic allure of Ana's life and problems. Reading her diary was an anesthetic, and it made the distance tolerable because Ana was now a link that connected them in new ways. Her story now belonged to both of them.

Before he traveled, Archie had filled her in on Gus's birth, the plans Ana and Raymond made for leaving Americana, and the fact that upon Ana's departure, Eugênia had decided she too would leave and go back to São Paulo, to forge a life for herself. With that information in hand, Darcey went to look for matching documents and details on their new lives.

During those days, nature tried to cheer her up by allowing white blossoms to appear in shrubs and the sturdiest trees to regain their leaves. A fresh breeze blew new air onto every corner of campus, and she opened the windows to refresh the apartment. But despite her curiosity and the light atmosphere, she found the task of turning book pages daunting. Everything around her reminded her of Archie's eyes, their kiss, his hands on her body, his smell on her hair. If she ate a croissant, she thought of him; if she heard an '80s ballad, she thought of their banter in the car. And of course, Ana's story was what caused him to exist.

His kisses still scorched her lips, his fingers burned her clothes, and the memory of him went around in her brain like a fixed idea. Did that mean they were together now? And if they were, could she afford one more moment without telling him about Nina?

"You always feel like home. I'm distraught and confused, but you bring me back to what I know," he'd said in bed, the morning before he left.

Could she trust his feelings were real, or was she just a comfort at a time of need?

He'd left with so many matters unresolved. She didn't think it was prudent to call, and she wouldn't know what to say anyway. His being home meant Mrs. Northwood could tell him about Nina anytime. Foreboding dwelled at the edge of her consciousness, and she didn't know what to do with it.

She went to work, playing with the specters other people had left behind in books and notes, and the diary. Like the sweetheart of a sailor, all she could do was engross herself in stories and wait. The living room futon looked ragged and uninviting, its black fabric faded and spent. Archie's spot on it was empty, and the room was somber and gloomy.

Darcey sat on the floor with a blanket over her shoulders. She fanned out documents which she'd organized chronologically and marked with tabs. It was almost like reading an epistolary romance, with the gaps between missives creating an aura of mystery and interest. Just as with love, it was what one didn't reveal that kept the interest alive.

She'd found some pictures too, a few of Gus in Ana's and in Raymond's arms. In a particularly striking one, Raymond held Gus, lifting him up for the camera. They were in front of Archie's house, Raymond and Ana's house at the time. It was sunny, and Raymond beamed. He wore a crisp, white shirt, and Gus held on to the collar. There was another where Gus took his first steps. Dina's benevolence shone through a picture of her and Eugênia, who were making what looked like a birthday cake. The back read, "The São Paulo house, November 1923." But other pictures were more obscure, with no inscriptions on the back and faces of people she didn't recognize; she would ask Archie about them once he returned. She set them aside. Then she walked to the library because she just couldn't stand her apartment anymore.

Once situated in a study area, she took out the last set of letters. Another researcher might have thought it best to translate everything first and then go expanding the research around all letters. But that had not been Darcey's method. She had chosen to take each letter as an event, and to build Ana's story around it as if it were the only one. She thought she'd gotten more depth, but the downside was, several months into the project, she still had letters to work on. She translated the first of Eugênia's letters to Ana in the US.

São Paulo, December 20, 1922
Dear Ana,
I hope you are adapting to your new life. I am certainly trying to get used to the new reality here, with

all of you far away from us. I am now in São Paulo with Dina, and I plan to be here for the next several months at least. We found a little place in a vila, *a very calm, dead-end street, lined with* sobradinhos, *these cute two-story houses of all colors. The neighbors seem to take care of one another, and a kind old lady with lots of time in her hands who lives across from us is teaching me to sew elegant gowns. I should start thinking of that as a profession. She says I have a special talent for it. Besides, I like the idea of becoming self-sufficient even though I don't know if my father will approve.*

Don't worry about anything. We are managing better than I imagined. I hope you are too. I have received what you sent. It will certainly do. I miss little Gus, but I'm sure he is well and protected. I'm not certain how long a letter takes to arrive there, but I hope you will write back as soon as you get this and tell me you are at peace. Till later,

Eugênia

The prickly sensation came back. The letter was strange and distant. Had they fought? What had Ana sent? Why were things as expected? Unlike earlier communications, this one wasn't paired with its reply. Had Ana sent one? Darcey feared there would be no more returned letters. She still had a few small envelopes to open, but she doubted she would come across what she was looking for. The letters weren't dangerous anymore. They didn't speak of forbidden love.

For the three next days, courses dragged themselves through hours of assignments, lectures, and presentations. The clock as good as stopped. She kept worrying about the classes Archie might be missing, and by Thursday, she found herself walking toward Benson Hall, where most of his classes were held. She walked down the main hall, examining the beautiful wood floor and inconspicuously peeking through the glass panels of doors. She gasped when she saw Archie sitting in the second row of desks, scribing in a notebook and then playing with a pencil, unaware of the lecture going on in front of him.

A pain pierced through her stomach. Why was he there, and why hadn't he let her know he'd returned? His mother must've told him about Nina. That was it. Her legs buckled in a manner that perplexed her. Would she even be able to move? She found she could use the extra surge of adrenaline to fly away from the hall. With any luck, he hadn't seen her.

She ignored the people walking on campus. Tears ran down her face, cold against her skin, as she dashed through the calm boulevards and blooming gardens. This was all stupid. She dove into that family's life as if it were her own, as if it was her legacy. But it wasn't, was it? It was Archie's and he could detach himself from her at any minute, and she wouldn't have him anymore. Or Ana. Perhaps it had already happened.

Darcey arrived in the library, a place where she felt safe. She paced the area around her cubicle as if she wanted to wear down the floor. What other explanation could there be? She had proved a horrible lover and an even worse person. He would take it all away from her. She wouldn't graduate. Her doubts multiplied like wild mint in an unkempt garden.

She found the next letter and held it between her fingers. As if outside her own body, she saw herself tear the letter into pieces, while it was still inside the envelope. "Stupid project. Stupid letters. Stupid everything," she said to herself while sobbing.

The pieces fell on the table, like dry leaves from a tree. The sender's name became visible, and Darcey froze in place. "What have I done?" The envelope was still sandwiched between the layers of the yellowed document. She brought her hand to her mouth; she had destroyed a piece of history and someone else's property. She brought together the fragments—a jigsaw puzzle.

She tried to regain her composure and took the bits of letter back to the desk. She asked an assistant librarian for a roll of tape and started sticking the pieces back together. Maybe her career would be hampered by her defacing a document, but she would discover what this letter said. How Joaquim had found Ana's address, she could only guess. Eugênia had probably caved in. In time, the message shone back at her. Each new scrap that was reattached eased the pain in the pit of her stomach. Once each of the two sheets was reattached, she read the text, translating it without difficulty.

São Paulo, December 24, 1922

I want to tell you a story, Ana. Being that I am a journalist, isn't that what I do after all? But this is a different story. This is the one where against all odds, my heart gets broken. Maybe this is my punishment, and I am sure it will stay broken for all time.

This is the story of when I ran after you and lost you forever.

I knew the Porto de Santos was a nautical city, busy as a tavern in the evening. I knew it would be

271

populated with workers, ship officials, and rich sojourners. To look for a person in that sea of heads, suitcases, crates, and packages was equivalent to searching for the proverbial needle in a haystack.

But I had an advantage. I am a reporter. I know how to ask questions and extract information, sometimes in ways that trick the person into revealing more than they initially intend. That's how I discovered where you'd be in the first place.

Don't blame Eugênia. I realized that if I worked on her emotions, she would talk even if against her better judgment. If she were to talk, it would be because of my insistence and because she has your best interests in mind. She is a wonderful woman, whom I'm starting to admire. Don't think she ever betrayed you.

Talk she did, ultimately spilling out the time of your departure as well as the name of the vessel and its likely location at the port. Armed with that information, I hurried to find transportation away from Americana, where I had gone looking for you again, and toward the coast. I had less than a day. Once I shook a few bills in front of the noses of a couple of townspeople, finding a willing chauffeur to take me to Santos wasn't all that hard. Percival, a skinny middle-aged man, became my driver for the day.

Scanning the port was a different story. So many faces blended together that in a while I didn't know what I was seeing anymore. All the way, I kept wishing, "If I could only speak to her one more time."

Suddenly I found a uniformed official. I had a glimpse of hope. The name of the ship. A finger pointing in the right direction. Then a slight jog with a bit of desperation. I didn't want to believe I could be too late.

The image of your face guided me.

I actually made it to the farewell. There were white handkerchiefs flying in the air and tears of joy and longing streaming down powdered faces. And suddenly when I looked up, I saw your familiar silhouette. Longer hair but the same curvy, graceful shape and the ethereal gait I had often taken for granted. I didn't anymore.

My heart was pounding. I considered shouting. But I was hypnotized, frozen in time and place. From behind your delicate shoulder, a blondish little head bobbed carelessly. I can count, Ana. Ten and a half months. Us, in the secrecy of your studio. Stolen moments. That boy, no more than a couple of months old, could only be my son. Everything made sense. My whole world crumbled into pieces.

I know you are married now. You have chosen a different life. I wish I had known. You may consider me a coward, but I would have claimed the child as my own. I would have stood by you. I hope you live in peace with your decision. I have little hope that I ever will.

Joaquim

He knew. Joaquim knew he was a father.

"You weren't home. You weren't with Donaldson. I figured you would be here."

Darcey's back stiffened as Archie stood behind her, and she folded the letter. "You're still speaking to me?" she asked without turning to face him. Her heart was lodged in her throat.

"Why would I not be speaking to you?" He threw his hands up.

She wouldn't look at him, not yet. Relief ran through her veins. Still, in the back of her mind was the notion that she would have to tell him about Nina. Perhaps that day. In her mind, her world came crumbling down at the thought of his face, pale and disappointed. He would take a step away from her, while he listened in disbelief.

His voice pierced through her daydreaming. "I went to class right away. I was going to call you in the afternoon." He sounded worried.

He sat next to her. They looked at the shelves, as if searching for a particular book. Darcey searched for the right words with which to fill the silence between them. As stealthily as she could, she hid the letter under other papers so he wouldn't see what she had done to it.

"Archie?" Her voice came out in a whisper. She was surprised it came out at all.

"Yes?" His whole body bent toward her, waiting.

"I don't know how to do this, but I have to tell you something." She was a coward, but she didn't want to burden him with the truth. He deserved an uncomplicated life.

"All right?" There was a tinge of concern in his voice.

"The thing is..." She wrung her hands together. She couldn't do it. She gathered her things. "I gotta go."

"Darcey, what is it?" He looked up at her, his eyes pleading.

"I can't. I have to go." She turned around, sighed, and walked away.

He called after her, but she didn't stop and didn't look back. A weight in her chest made it hard to breathe. She kept wishing for the door of the library. Just a few steps more, and the threshold would be right there. This was so much harder now. Harder than she ever imagined, but still easier than staying and waiting for him to leave. Or being really mad when he discovered she was a liar. She walked in a daze and arrived home, unaware of her surroundings.

When Darcey opened the door, the phone was ringing. She dropped her things on a chair and hurried to catch the call. On the line was a voice she didn't recognize.

"Mrs. Bellevue has been calling for you. She hasn't been well."

Darcey didn't let the woman finish. "I'm on my way." She ran out the door carrying only her coat.

At the retirement home, Darcey found Lucile resting on a chaise, covered with a warm blanket despite the spring-like weather.

"Who is the gossip of a nurse that cannot keep her mouth shut?" She didn't look up from the magazine she held in her hands. She pulled the green wool blanket closer to her face.

"I've been so inside my head that I neglected you. I'm sorry. But you…when I arrived, the nurse said your sugar levels were through the roof!"

"Pfft. An exaggeration, of course."

"No exaggeration. I worry about you. I should've kept an eye on you. To make it worse, every time I come here, I eat dessert with you. I'm an enabler."

"And dramatic. Jeez." She looked at Darcey as if she was studying her. "Still meddling in other people's business?"

"Can we please *not* change subjects? We need to

talk about your health."

"Where's Archie?"

"Can we *not* talk about Archie? Did you hear what I just said?"

"You choose…"

"I'm sorry, but I'm worried enough about you as it is. What's going on? What did the doctor say? Will you understand that you're sick?" She picked up a chair, brought it close, and stood there, holding on to its upholstered back.

"Darcey, get over it. I am not sick, I'm old. That's what is going on with me—old age."

"I'm tired of worrying about losing those I care about."

"Are you still talking about me?"

Darcey sat down. "Yes and no. There's Archie too. I don't know how to care. All I do when I care is worry. And then I turn selfish, trying to make people do and be what I expect. It should be about you. And Nina. And Archie. Not about me. How am I supposed to live this way?"

"The only way to learn is by doing it. I think you're smart enough to realize that. Or was I wrong about you? Was I wrong to trust that you could see things through?" This time, she raised her head and waited for Darcey's reply.

"Is this the reason why you put me though this game?" Her hands felt moist and cold. "Archie's grandfather sets him up with a game. You set me up with a game. Why?" Darcey opened her arms in a plea for an answer.

Lucile offered a cunning smile in return. "It's not a game. Maybe in a very selfish way, I see in you the young woman I once was, stubborn and headstrong. Is this a horrible thing to say? I figured you needed a push. That's all. Maybe Archie's grandfather believed the same. You don't open yourself to others, and you don't face your fears. And you certainly don't trust."

Darcey took a long, deep breath. "No, it's not horrible. But did you have to make it so hard?" She took Lucile's hands in hers. They were warm and soothing.

"Perhaps I should have been easier on you, but you know what? You need to have a spine if you want to be like me. Be more adventurous too."

"Be like you?"

"Yes, when I was your age, I jumped without looking. Went after what I wanted without second-guessing."

Darcey turned around to see Lucile better, incredulous at what her aunt had just said. "So that's your advice? Jump without looking?"

"Every so often. Especially when you already know there's a safety net below you."

"Safety net?" Darcey's arms were open and pleading again.

"Archie, my dear. He's your safety net." Lucile took one of Darcey's hands back and held it tight, making any further response impossible. He was her safe harbor, wasn't he? She was a fool for not having grabbed on to him to never let go.

They stayed like that for a long time, until Lucile fell asleep. Darcey placed the woman's hand under the soft blanket.

As Darcey left, a nurse was putting away a few toys in a box, surely the entertainment offered to a small child visiting grandparents. Her beloved Nina needed toys, clothes, everything. Would she be able to finish her project? Would she not be able to help her parents? She had been burning bridges and destroying her chances through her own self-sabotage, just like she did with the letter.

At her apartment, Darcey went back to the papers she had left scattered on the floor. A great historian she was, tearing antique letters to pieces, leaving documents on the floor as if they were litter. Once she stopped admonishing herself, she recognized Eugênia's neat writing on a letter she hadn't seen before. She sat on the ground.

January, 1924
Ana,
You know I never had much ambition. Life in the country or managing a home would have suited me well. Yet sometimes life comes at you with other plans—we both know that well. So today I am writing to you to tell you the good news. Great news, I think.

It seems incredible but I was hired by a fashion maison here in São Paulo, to design dresses for society ladies. I have a group of seamstresses working for me, and my dresses are bought by the city's crème-de-la-crème in elegant fashion shows. I cannot believe it all happened in a few months. To think that not long ago, I was sewing the afternoon away with Dina in my father's house!

I wish you would write more often. I have so much to tell you. Please write back and let me know how you are doing.

Your sister always,

Eugênia

Darcey was happy for Eugênia, who for so long had played the sidekick to Ana's lead. Maybe there was hope for people who weren't larger than life like Ana. It was encouraging. Perhaps she would find her own place in the world too, even if she wasn't shiny like Ana—or Dominique. As for the thesis, she would write about Ana's artistic temperament, Brazilian society in the early twentieth century, and the tension of having money but rebelling against it. That day the final structure of her work came to her very clearly—a combination of biography and art analysis set against the cultural background of the country.

But she needed him to fill in the gaps. What happened to Ana and Eugênia's friendship? She dialed Archie's number. When he didn't answer, she reached for the diary and buried her disappointment in Ana's own despair.

Chapter 24
Ana

December 1923

The windows of the attic studio in Ana and Ray's Pennsylvania home were fogged, so Ana used her palm as if it were a rag to wipe one of the panels. The gesture was useless; outside a sea of snow greeted her. She thought of the sunshine she had left behind, the sweet smell of fruit from the market. The birds singing as she walked the streets of her neighborhood. The sound of summer rain. She closed the curtains in acute misery.

She then returned to the unfinished painting resting on the easel, her cold soles cracking against the wood floor at each new step, as if she was about to break like an icicle.

Gus, barely a year old, was playing at her feet, moving the ubiquitous trains and cars that he loved so much. On a side table was Joaquim's letter, the one that had arrived only a couple of months after they set up residence. It had never left her side since then.

Ray was away at work as usual, engorging the already bloated bank account that allowed them to live like kings. Beatriz, Raymond's housekeeper who came with them from Brazil, labored in the kitchen, and the aroma of citrus cake sieved through stairs, vents, and corridors, bringing solace to the higher and colder levels of the house.

Ana examined her unfinished work; the blood-like color of the girl's dress was overwhelming, as she had intended, and contrasted brilliantly with the softness of a lilac ribbon. "This might be my best creation yet," she said to the empty space, "painted in my own gloom and sorrow in this distant land that I don't understand, a kingdom of perpetual whiteness and unnerving calm."

Ana's soul was frozen. She was dressed in a gray-wool tweed dress, so different from the bright and ethereal colors of yesteryear. Yet the weighty layers never seemed to be enough to prevent her from shaking inside. Nor were the infinite cups of tea that she drank piping hot throughout the day. Their effect was fleeting, and once empty, she was left colder than before.

"I baked an orange cake." Beatriz interrupted Ana's thoughts. "Gus, come eat. *Dona* Ana, have some. You look so thin."

"I'm fine, Beatriz. I need to finish this painting."

The maid walked backward to look at the work from a distance. She stumbled a little given the unevenness of the wood planks. "It's beautiful, *Dona* Ana. But the girl's so sad."

"Yes, she is, isn't she?" Ana muttered more to herself than to her companion. "Gus, go with Bea. Mom needs to work." And the boy wrapped his arms around the woman with the familiarity of a child who has gone through the same motion far too many times.

Ana was left alone with the haunting feelings that never deserted her. She touched the locks of the girl in the painting as if she was caressing the hair in real life. She then added a few strokes of the brush, enhancing the shine of the strands, transforming the pinkish color of the skin, making the face more abstract and genuine at the same time.

She was weak and unsteady, but she had to finish the work.

When she did, she collapsed on the attic's little velvet couch drained of all energy and all color, as if the hue of her lips and the blush of her cheeks had been poured onto the dress of the little girl like a hot liquid, leaving behind only the faintest of stains.

It hadn't always been like this. When they first moved into the house, she had hopes she could be happy despite everything. She had played the devoted wife. She had cooked and made beds, wiped windows and darned socks.

She shopped for beautiful new china with a delicate flower pattern. She had some local people over for dinner. She roasted meats and caramelized pears. But then the letter arrived. And little by little, her resolve to forget him waned, and she found herself more drawn to her attic and less involved with the family. She slept a lot and ate very little.

And then there was Ray…

In the haze that her day had become, Ana heard a door shut in the distance. It was a heavy door that closed the impressive, wood-beamed, solid old house Ray had renovated for her. She knew he was home because she could discern Gus's little giggles, the ones he saved all day long for his father, for the time Ray would press his lips against the little boy's forehead or blow raspberries until her son was red in the face and breathless from so much laughter. Their tight connection offered her a bit of consolation. Not enough though. It would never be enough.

Ray's steps gave away his intention of visiting her in the attic. He was doting to the point of being suffocating. She didn't get up to greet him. She waited like one who waits for a fate already decided. It was easy to blame him for all her woes: her distance from Brazil, this coldness that never ended, the large house she had not wanted. It was certainly a lot easier than her taking responsibility for her own choices.

Every time she looked at him, she went through a laundry list of her pains and how they all connected back to him. It didn't matter that, in reality, all he had wanted was to help and make her happy, that he wasn't privy to one half of what haunted her. While now she reserved an unmerited role of victim to Joaquim, Ray was a convenient scapegoat. Her contempt for him grew stronger, fueled by illusions of blame and responsibility, until it took hold of her whole being. In those times, she was rude to him, curt and condescending. She disliked who she became when she told herself those stories and when she acted unkindly.

"Ana. How's your day been?" His eyes were generous as always.

"Fine." She had no right to shut him out like that. Some days she could hardly look at him, and then possessed by guilt and angst, she would try and be generous, but her efforts looked contrived and ridiculous. She was a good painter but a terrible actress.

Yet she never thought of going back and taking Gus with her. The decisions she made the day he was born were irreversible.

"I see you finished another painting. It's wonderful." He touched the corner of the canvas, and she wanted to intervene, to make him stop. At least this small universe he shouldn't be able to penetrate. This was her private world, where she nursed her private pain. She wanted him to go.

"Thank you," she offered instead.

He paused for a while, as if calculating the risk of making a suggestion. "Beatriz tells me she baked a cake. You should eat a bit. You look a little thin."

She could guess the two had been talking about her in the kitchen. They always did. "I'm not hungry."

He sighed. "You are never hungry. You are wasting away."

She shrugged. If it weren't for Gus, she wouldn't care about eating at all. For him, she made an effort. Making another mistake, anything that would make her boy suffer, would hardly be justified. After all, Gus was the reason for everything. He was what remained.

"Ana, tell me what to do. Do you want to go visit Brazil?"

She shied away, hurt, as if stung by an oversized bee.

"No," she whispered, knowing deep inside she would never go back. She couldn't possibly go back. Her errors still ached in her. "Just leave me be, Ray. I beg of you."

He looked down in defeat, his arms hanging next to his body like useless appendages. "Shall we call you later when dinner is ready?"

Ana nodded without looking at him, and he left, probably to find Gus.

After what felt like a long time but could have simply been minutes, Ana got up and went to the picture. It was finished; she knew it in her gut. She knew many things viscerally: one never recovered from what Joaquim had meant. A mother was never at ease unless her young were under her watch. A colorful, hot weather bird like her would wither in this merciless weather. She knew too much to ever be happy again.

Dropping her thin body on the couch once more, she reached for the small red box where she kept her correspondence. She found what she was looking for without much trouble. It was one of Eugênia's letters, a few months old, with the little bracelet, one of the many mementos Eugênia liked to share. Eugênia, now a self-made woman, probably even had a professional greeting card to her name, she thought.

Ana had never expected that. She didn't think Eugênia had expected it either. Her friend designed fancy dresses and had the city's socialites at her feet. She imagined it all with a flush of the face and a strange sensation at the pit of her stomach. Some of her former matrons of the arts were probably now worshiping Eugênia's dresses, like they had once revered her paintings. It was ironic that Eugênia was the successful one; Ana had wanted the world, and Eugênia seemed to be getting it. Who was the modern woman? She took the little bracelet between her fingers and let it slide in, toward her palm. She was being unfair. Eugênia, who had always been so selfless and loyal, deserved this and a whole lot more. She clenched her fingers around the piece of jewelry.

A couple of nights later, Ray was munching his dinner with little enthusiasm as if the texture of the roast beef Beatriz had prepared discouraged him. Given her frequent acerbic moods, made even more frequent by the arrival of Eugênia's letter, Ana wondered if she, and not the meal, was responsible for his disposition.

Propped up in his wood highchair, Gus was squeaking with delight at every new spoonful of soft potatoes the maid inserted in his mouth. Ana just played with her food. Much like other pleasures of the body, eating was now absent from her inventory of priorities.

She heard Ray's voice from a distance, as if he was outside the house and his speech was muffled by the snow.

"You and I are going to take a trip," he said still looking at his plate.

She didn't respond at first, unsure of what the words meant, like listening to an unintelligible foreign language.

"Ana, did you hear? I decided we must take a trip."

"I don't want to go. It's too cold here to even leave the house." She continued playing with her food.

"Well, that's just it. It's too cold *here*. I will take you to warmer climates, and you will feel better. You'll see."

"I won't go." They seemed to have the same conversations all the time, and she was tired of it all. What would she do alone with him, without Gus, without her canvases and her paints?

Beatriz, probably feeling trouble would ensue, picked up little Gus and left for the kitchen.

"Ana, I hardly ever make a point of something, you know that. But this time I'm adamant. We're going. It's settled."

"How about Gus?" She was trying to buy herself time, to find the right argument that would leave him without an option.

"Gus will be fine with Beatriz. He adores her."

The commentary was like an icicle from one of the

windows through her heart. Was he implying she was not a good enough mother? Maybe she was imagining things. She couldn't tell anymore. She often had the feeling he could read her mind and all the secrets it contained. Reality and fantasy had long become one entity sheathed in a veil of absurdity and hurt.

"Fine, have it your way." She pushed the plate to the side and let it slide off the table, almost on purpose. The china hit the floor and scattered into jagged pieces. She wondered if stepping on them would take some of the pain from her chest and redirect suffering to her limbs. She didn't apologize. She got up and went to her room without looking at him. She paused long enough to hear him sigh, but in her own suffering, she had stopped caring.

Chapter 25
Darcey

Someone knocked on the door. It wasn't a playful knock. It was a demand, heavy and decisive. It couldn't be Archie. She had learned to recognize how each person knocked in a distinctive way. A knock was like a fingerprint.

She opened the door.

"Archie?"

He was a different man, his features hardened, his brows creased. His shirt was wrinkled, and his hair was not carefully disheveled, but accidentally messy. His fists were clenched, not in violence but in protection.

"You gonna invite me in?"

She took a step back and motioned with her arm, offering him the room.

He didn't take his usual place on the futon. He stood in the middle of the room facing her as she walked toward him. When she stopped, he spoke.

"What do you want from me, Darcey?"

The constriction in her throat was a sure warning to tread carefully. She needed to study him a little longer, discover exactly what he was asking.

"What do you mean?"

"When I'm around you, you push me away. Then when I'm away, you reel me in. Expect me to be available. What gives?"

I love you Archie, so much I'm frozen with fear. "I don't know what you're talking about."

"Oh yes, you do. I'm tired of this game."

"What game? The one Gus set up for you, or the one Aunt Lucile imposed on me?" She hated her own sarcasm. She was being unfair to all of them, Lucile and Gus included, but she suffered such anguish that she couldn't help it.

"What has Lucile got to do with any of this?"

Darcey covered her mouth with her hand.

"Nothing," she said, but it was too late.

"Darcey, I'm not buying it. What of Lucile?"

She let out a long breath and braced herself. It was time for the charade to be over anyway. She was so tired of juggling all those pieces of her life. "Aunt Lucile has a very large trust fund set aside for me."

"Sounds great. What's the big deal?"

"She will give me one hundred thousand dollars from it when I finish my PhD."

"Then finish your PhD."

Yes, but that's not all."

"What else?"

"My parents can lose their house any minute now if I don't make it."

"What?"

"They've been struggling for months. That's why I accepted to work on Ana's file. I had to take a chance."

His face was red, but his anger transitioned into something much harsher. "And you didn't think to tell me any of this? You didn't think that I would've liked to know and help?"

"That's exactly why I didn't tell you," she said. And she hadn't even said anything about Nina. Her stomach sank.

"You really are something else."

Please don't leave, Archie. "Oh yeah? What would you have thought of me if I had come to you for money?"

"That you trusted me and that you realized I was in a position to help?"

"Oh, your mother would have loved me for it."

"Why are you bringing up my mother?"

"You know she doesn't like me. She doesn't think I'm good enough for you." This was as far as she was willing to go, and it was plenty. If she told him his mother had tried to bribe her with post-graduation presents, and was blackmailing her with her knowledge of Nina, she would lose him forever. She couldn't ask him to take sides.

"You know, I've tried supporting you any way I could. I have no idea where you got this sense about my mother, but I've always been honest with you, and I would've liked the same in return."

"In your perfect world, I'm sure that's easy, isn't it?"

"What's perfect about my world? The fact that my parents can barely be in the same room together? That my father was always absent and too busy for me? That the woman I love is always finding ways to push me away?"

Love! He had actually said he loved her. She was lightheaded, and she had to reach for the back of a chair to steady herself. No other word was as powerful, more anticipated, and more destabilizing.

"Love?" she repeated, still dumbfounded.

He looked incredulous, his arms hanging to

indicate the obviousness of her realization. "Have you ever had any doubt?"

She didn't know how to respond. It wasn't his love that she doubted but her own worth and her ability to love him back without fear. So she became her own worst enemy. She did it time and again.

She shrugged.

"Then why do you reject me?"

"Because." If she told him she would look as weak as she felt. No one cared for weak people.

"Because what?"

"Just because." Because she had always doubted herself, since she was a child. She had always wondered if the loss of her brother had caused her parents to see in her the pain of their reality, the incompleteness of their family. She had built her whole identity around the idea of not being enough. Not for her parents. Not for Archie. Not for anyone.

He came close to her and lifted her chin with his index finger. She hated that he saw her crying. She felt small and petty while he was noble and fair.

"We can't continue this way. I can't do it." He spoke clearly and slowly, as if wanting to make sure she understood.

She took a deep breath. She was a second away from divulging she had another reason for living—the love for her child. A love that didn't ask for anything back. A love that could never be disappointed, diminished or replaced. She shut her eyes and wrung her fingers. She had nothing else to lose besides her pride, did she? If she didn't say it, she would lose him anyway.

"What if you get bored? What if you get tired?

There's also my—"

"As if you and your temper would give me a chance at boredom."

"I don't know. What if some redhead comes along? It's been known to happen." At least everything was out in the open now. Everything except the biggest secret of all. She sat down, her shoulders tense.

"I'm not perfect. And can you blame me?" His eyes were begging her.

"No, but it hurts."

"Darcey, do you push me away because you don't love me back?" He looked down.

Her heart ached in her chest. *I love you so much, Archie. You and Nina are my world.*

She looked down too.

"I'll tell you what. You probably have enough to finish your project. I will not impose on your time anymore. Maybe I wasn't meant to discover what Gus wanted me to discover. So far nothing earthshattering has really happened."

"But I'm not done. There are little envelopes I haven't opened. There's a lot of stuff." She wanted to cling to their project, cling to his presence.

"Or maybe there isn't anything to know, and he was just suffering from boredom and decided he needed a project. You can finish what you started if you want. And you know where to find me if by any remote chance you might think you need me."

Her relief turned into renewed panic. He was slipping away from her. And it was her own fault.

He didn't say goodbye. He just walked out.

"Archie!" she called after him.

She sat on the futon, drained of all emotion and

energy.

"I've always needed you, Archie," she said to the walls of the now-empty room. And she remained there, stunned. If only she could have made him come back, sit on his worn spot on the sofa, where he was meant to remain for all time.

****

Later, she managed to find tears. She didn't give Lucile any chance to react before she was in her arms sobbing.

"This time I really did it."

"What?"

"Archie. I don't think he'll come back now." Darcey buried her face in Lucile's shoulder.

"There, there. I have no idea what you're saying." Lucile made large circles on her back, as if she was a crying baby.

"He's tired of me." She had moved from anger to frustration, and now to self-pity.

"I don't think that's true."

"It is. I blurted out a bunch of things." She used her fingers to enumerate them. "Trust, mortgage, his mother. I sounded selfish and horrible. Oh, Lucile, I just made a mess of things."

"Nina?" There was anxiety in her aunt's eyes.

"Not Nina. He doesn't know."

Lucile sat her down and patted the seat of the sofa indicating where Darcey should rest. She nibbled on the tip of her finger, looked down, and then at Darcey.

"What is it?"

Lucile fidgeted. "I'm going to do something I didn't think I would do," she said. "I hope I'm right in talking to you about this."

Darcey dried her eyes with her sleeve and sat up in attention.

"This is about Mom?"

"Yes."

"Go on." Darcey moved her body forward while her hands clutched the edge of her seat. She had waited a long time for this.

Lucile hesitated. "I don't know."

Darcey touched her shoulder lightly. "I imagine after all this time it's hard to speak of it, but please, tell me."

Lucile looked at her and smiled feebly.

"Please. I need this, Lucile."

Lucile began.

"We were at a party. Me, your uncle Bob, your mother, and Stewart."

"You mean Donaldson?"

"Yes. We were already married, Bob and me. They were dating." Lucile faltered. "I don't think it is right for me to tell you all this. It's your mother we're talking about."

"Now that you've started, go on. Please help me, Lucile. I'm lost here."

Lucile sighed. "Donaldson and your mom were once very much in love, but at this point they were not like they once were. He was too focused on his career. She was feeling sad and insecure. Bob invited her to dance, to cheer her up. She'd been grumpy all night and had tried to pick a fight with me. In those days, people slow-danced at parties, and Bob loved to dance. Stewart was outside smoking. Bob had asked me if he should dance with her, and I said it was a good idea. Only she was not thinking straight, and by the end of the dance she tried to kiss him."

"That's not possible!"

Lucile looked down and nodded. "Unfortunately, it is. When I confronted her about it, she said I didn't want her to be happy, and I told her she was a spoiled child, a traitor. By the time we were done, we were like enemies."

Darcey paced the room, unsure of what to say next. She couldn't believe her mother had done that. But then again, when they hurt, people did unexpected things. She had hidden a daughter from the man who loved her. "Why are you telling me this now?"

"Because I often wondered if, had we managed to clear the air right then, we would have avoided decades of estrangement. The support I could have given her. The hours of companionship I missed out on. It was a silly thing, really, but at the time it felt like such a big betrayal. Resentment has a way of weeding itself into our hearts, Darcey, and from there it grows disproportionately large with no concern for reality. Your mom and Donaldson broke up; she and I stopped speaking. I was young and proud. I only thought of the moment. Two or three years later, she found your father, but our own relationship by then was too frayed to fix. It all feels pointless now, a real waste."

At the word "waste," a sharp pain pierced her stomach. So much love that could have been. Lucile's sisterly kind, Ana's passionate one. Archie's steady, loyal devotion. Should she insist that they clear the air? But who was she to lecture Lucile when her own life was a series of missed opportunities and misunderstandings?

"Your mother was wrong. It should have been

possible for me to see it, disapprove it, but not abandon her. Don't let regret be the defining element in your life," Lucile said. "Let it be love. And trust. It's up to you. What could be more important than love? Pride? Fear?"

Of course not, but Darcey felt trapped in a maze, where every new step toward a supposed exit left her more lost. "What if it's too late? I don't know if I can fix it."

Lucile came close and looked into her eyes. She didn't look like the strict aunt anymore, coaching Darcey to be tougher. She was an older woman, who had learned the hard way. "It would be wise to at least try."

Chapter 26
Eugênia

1923

She let him use his hand to caress the length of her arm and stop at her wrist. He then placed her hand in his and raised it to his face so he could kiss it.

In the space between the north and south of her limb, his fingers were like a feather flirting with her skin, and they gave her goose bumps. She kept her eyes closed, imagining the two of them at a different place, under different circumstances. In her fantasy, this romance was at least licit. But she didn't fantasize he was her husband; that would have been too banal. She was not that kind of woman. Not anymore.

He had an infectious laugh that resonated against those four walls. Maybe he could tell she was half present but also far away, lost in daydream, and he teased her with naughty jokes to reel her back. She didn't blush. She was not that kind of woman anymore either.

Instead she opened her eyes, looked firmly into his, and took him to the bedroom, that dingy alcove with the rusting iron bed that squeaked. She had sunk rather low.

Not that she had a choice. Not at this point any longer. Was she becoming Ana? As it was, he had been like a gradual addiction, the most dangerous kind, inoffensive until it was too late.

And like an addict, she had accepted this shabby room, the inordinate hours, his cancelations and excuses, as long as she could get a bit of him. She had given up fancy restaurants, strolls in parks, expensive gifts, or maybe even a matrimonial proposal. Instead, she had the dubious honor of a few afternoons a month.

He undressed her with little care for her expensive fabrics. Her beautiful, luxurious dress with gold threads was hanging precariously from the bed, and for one split second she had to fight the urge to go and fold it. It was a favorite garment, and she would've hated to see it destroyed or even soiled.

His hand perused her body knowingly, stopping at the right places. His decisive kiss caused her to fall into the bed. At times, he was an egotistical lover. At others, he would caress her face like it was made of silk, knowing that made her smile. Maybe she didn't know any better. Maybe she didn't know enough to require any different or any more.

She covered her body when it was all over, suddenly self-conscious of her nudity. He wasn't paying attention. He was standing in his shorts and undershirt near the window shifting through some notes and smoking a cigarette.

She took her time observing him, looking at his legs, taking in his muscular calves. He noticed and gazed at her, smiling, and she melted under his flaming stare.

"It's late," she said grabbing the watch that had been resting on the *criado-mudo*. What a perfect name for a piece of furniture, "silent maid," a bedside table that witnessed everything and said nothing. "I have to go. Lots of work to do at the *maison*."

She didn't wish to move from the bed, feeling languid and slothful, but she needed to go back to the world outside those shabby walls. There was only so much time she could pretend to spend in search of expensive fabrics. She didn't want any more complications than she already juggled.

He put on his pants and crinkled shirt. His clothes were so wrinkled, he looked like he had come out of the hamper, yet he still kept his good looks, his sleek hair falling carelessly on his brow. Women could never get away with any of that. Women got away with very little. Except Ana.

"I'll see you next week." He planted an absentminded kiss on her forehead, and she made for the stairs.

When she reached the corner, Eugênia caught a last glimpse of Joaquim as he stood by the second-floor window observing her. She headed for a busy intersection and back to work.

At the *maison*, she handled the heavy scissors with the same agility she managed her lover. She was designing a nightgown of fluid emerald-green silk, but her thoughts were on her dangerous affair.

It had started quite innocently in the spring of '23. Joaquim had tracked her all the way from Americana to São Paulo, and one day knocked on her door. She couldn't let him in, of course, but he looked so damaged that she took him to a café, and they talked for hours. In a way, they had both been deserted, and they both had healing to do. After that, they started meeting at inconspicuous places—an out-of-the-way restaurant, a bakery far from her neighborhood, nameless fabric shops—so that he could exorcise his ghosts, and she could do what she was born to do: take care of others, discover what they needed from her. Under the veneer of nonchalance, he was a good man, one who could feel affection, guilt, and sympathy.

When he first arrived, all he wanted to do was talk about Ana. Many too were the questions about the baby he thought he had seen in her arms. He would sit next to Eugênia and look into the distance as if he could see Ana there. And Eugênia was grateful for his presence, for extracting a smile from him with her kindness from time to time.

Eugênia lied dutifully about the child. It wasn't her secret to share. She sinned more by omission than deception. If he assumed Ana married quickly because she was carrying Raymond's baby, she wasn't going to contest it, but Joaquim couldn't be fooled. That her own stake in the situation had suddenly gone up significantly now that they were together was a notion she chose to brush away, like one buzzes off a bothersome bug.

In time, he spoke less of Ana, he became a little more jovial, a little flirtier. But Eugênia feared that soon there'd be no more reason to meet. At that point, several months later, she was already catching herself thinking about him during the day, anticipating the occasional rendezvous that would bring them together, planning what to wear. Who was she kidding? She could trace her infatuation all the way back to Americana, when he went after Ana and, given her coldness, ended up sitting with Eugênia and paying her some attention instead.

Eventually came the apartment, a cheerless family property that Joaquim had promised his uncle to put on the market to be leased. They would eventually run out of time, just like they had run out of shame, but for as long as they had the place, she could not turn him away.

Had she been able to think clearer, she'd have minded that the apartment was the least inviting place for an affair. The paint on the walls was chipped, and the old green sofa had a hole in it. The street below was loud and busy, and noises came from adjacent rooms.

But when he issued that smile, the room changed. All she could see were the flowers he brought to put in a vase next to the bed and the sunlight shining on the bed, warming it. That seasoned man had chosen her, so plain and common, and she was falling in love with him. She'd have never fathomed anything like that could happen. Not while she was under the shadow of Ana and the protective gaze of her father.

As she was starting to feel a certain excitement over her audacious rendezvous and her new-found forbidden pleasures, a nasty thought crossed her mind and stuck to her brain like molasses—what if she was the only connection to Ana he could have? What if she was a proxy whose only attractive trait was her association to the woman he really desired?

That first time, his voice had interrupted the painful reflection.

"Are you sure?"

She issued a whispered yes and then managed to nod, but she did so in an unequivocal manner. For once, she knew what she wanted. She was changed beyond recognition, and she would have to keep a secret from Ana, the only person from whom she kept no secrets and to whom she was bound forever. Yes, she felt guilty, but she was also ready to convince herself she owed Ana nothing. They were the pieces of life Ana had left behind, and if they tried to patchwork a precarious joint existence out of disappointment, sadness but also desire and a growing fondness for each other, Ana should be the last allowed to pass judgment. Still, Eugênia was afraid she would turn into the kind of woman she once condemned. Maybe she would simply have to cover her dishonor and her hypocrisy with lots of expensive silks and chintz.

Chapter 27
Darcey

1997

It was Spring Break. To go home and see Nina was all Darcey could think of. They would eat popcorn, watch cartoons, play outside, and read books together. Nina's company and easy smile would make her new again. Nina was the love that asked for nothing in return.

Darcey sat dutifully in her seat for the whole four-hour bus trip. A biography of a Brazilian musician of the early twentieth century kept her company and gave her ideas for the necessary modern-era details of her thesis. The beautiful Pennsylvania landscape rolled by outside her window with its fertile meadows, dotted with yellow flowers, and farmhouses with cows grazing nearby. When there was only about a half hour left, careful not to disturb her seatmate, she looked over her shoulder toward where Archie slept, still wearing his headphones. He had, as he promised after their fight, kept his distance. Coincidence or not, they ended up on the same bus headed home.

He hadn't tried to switch seats with anyone in her row, having only stopped momentarily to chat with her when they boarded the bus. It was good that way. She wouldn't have known what to say if they had longer.

But a flurry of tiny, invisible ants still prickled her head when she realized he would not attempt to be near her.

Eleanor was waiting at the bus station when they arrived. She wore a peach blouse and a pair of brown slacks that made her look younger.

"Did you have a good trip?" Eleanor asked, already looking at Archie. She was always a little nicer to him than to the general population.

"Yes, it was fine, thank you. It's not that long," he replied.

"So what are the plans for the holiday?" She turned her attention to Darcey, then back to Archie.

"I thought I'd—" Archie started.

"I'm going to work, that's all. No time for anything else." Darcey intervened before Archie could finish.

"She's going to work," he repeated, charging ahead of both women and ending the conversation. His rolling carry-on made hollow noises on the ground.

Darcey rearranged the bag on her shoulder and smiled weakly at her mother. She had responded too quickly. Lucile popped back into her mind. They had spent a great long time talking, and she still hadn't figured out how to fix what was broken.

"Can I stop by later?" she called out to Archie a few feet ahead.

He gave her a thumbs-up right before his silhouette disappeared at a corner.

****

The next morning, Darcey sat at the kitchen table hiding a yawn. The dissertation had kept her up most of the night. First it was the writing itself. Then, when she least expected it, she opened a tiny envelope to find a photo of a young girl and a gold bracelet. She turned them over in her hand again and again, knowing immediately what the piece of jewelry was. A tradition among people of Portuguese descent, a golden initial or a name bracelet was often gifted to celebrate the birth of a girl. She had one herself. It had been a present from her Portuguese grandmother. She had lain in her bed for hours, admiring the darkened gold of the piece and the mystery of the initial etched on it: R. The whole time, her heart thumped in her chest, telling her this find was important, that the night had brought a breakthrough.

Later, she drove her father's old station wagon seventy miles to Archie's, rehearsing what she would say when she got there. "I'm sorry Archie, for being an idiot." She was still murmuring that kind of apology when she knocked on his door and when the maid took her to his bedroom. She stood before him—while he sat on the bed—embarrassed to be so dependent on him. "Would you look at something for me?"

It took a second or two for Archie to register the question. "All right," he said with a bit of reservation. His ecru sweater made him look young and preppy. He would help her; he still cared. And his mother hadn't said anything about Nina, or else he would've acted very differently.

She changed her mind. "Okay, but first, I need to say something. I've been rehearsing it all the way here." She walked toward him and stood a couple of feet from where he sat. "I'm sorry, Archie. I'm an idiot. I don't deserve your friendship or your help, but I'm glad you give them to me so selflessly. Here."

She showed him the picture without giving him any time to reply. "Look at this. Do you know who's in this photo?"

Archie examined the image.

"Did you find this in the box?"

"Yes. An envelope inside another. There are so many little scraps, each day I find something new."

"It seems to me it's Ana, when she was still a toddler, maybe?"

"That was my first thought, too. I wanted to confirm it with you."

"Come here." Archie led her downstairs. They walked in silence, fast, concentrating on not bumping into the heavy furniture of the first floor. When they got to the living room, Archie opened the curtains so that they could get a better view of the canvas, a large painting of a girl in a red, velvety dress, hanging prominently above the mantelpiece.

"See? Of course you can't see the features the same way you do in the photo, but look at the hair, the eyes. It is clearly the same person. Even the composition is similar. I bet this is the photo that inspired the portrait." He looked from the picture to Darcey, to the canvas, and back again.

"Why do you suppose this photo was with the letters?"

"I don't know." He was still looking at the large painting; one Ana had painted in the attic of that very house, the house Raymond had bought for her, the house Gus had given his mother and where they had lived for so many years. "Maybe something to remind her of Brazil, of her childhood there."

"I guess," Darcey took the picture and examined it one more time. Something wasn't right. Ana would have been a toddler in the late 1800s. This girl was wearing 1920s fashions, the low waist tied with a ribbon reminiscent of grown-up styles.

"Oh, and there's something else. Look at this little bracelet." She removed a small object from her jean pocket. "It has an 'R' etched on it. I found it together with the photo. I almost missed it. It's so tiny." She extended her palm with the shiny trinket in evidence.

"'R' for Raymond?" Archie conjectured. "It is too small, though. "Maybe Ana had it made for Gus, in honor of Raymond? He sounded unsure of his hypotheses.

"A little bit of a stretch, no?" Darcey retorted.

Archie frowned. "Do you have a better explanation?"

"What if Eugênia had a child?" She gathered the items and put them into a folder she had brought with her. "Can you ask your mother? Would she know? Perhaps there's someone else in the family whose name begins with an R." The thought of asking Mrs. Northwood for help filled her with more anxiety than hope, but she couldn't think of how else to discover.

He assented. "So, you're going to lock yourself at your parents' and write?" They walked to the front door.

"Mostly." She wrung the sleeve of her red sweater. "But I hoped we could have dinner tonight?"

Archie looked at her as if she had delivered the last bit in Russian. They stopped in front of the imposing door, his hand on the doorknob. He shifted his weight, let go of the door, only to hold on to the knob again.

"You know, I haven't been to Maggie's Bistro in ages. Just thought we could get a bite there? Around seven?"

Archie found his self-possession this time. "S-Sure.

307

I'll see you there at seven."

"Great." She smiled broadly, hoping he'd see her genuine enthusiasm.

"Great." He adjusted his sweater.

Darcey heard the heavy door close behind her, a smile on her lips.

She returned home in time for lunch. She cooked and fed Nina, who gave her the best hugs. She wanted to freeze time and stay with her daughter for days without end. In the afternoon, she fell asleep cuddling Nina, with the envelope full of documents and an assortment of plastic sheet protectors beside her.

She dreamed she was a painter in the 1920s, young and full of confidence. Everyone was young. After the war, the air was fresh and new and filled with hope. The clothes were colorful and flowing, and smoke of interminable cigarettes twirled around in cafés and restaurants. Darcey felt free, unencumbered by the past or future, and she danced the Charleston with fun-loving partners until dawn. Everything was sleek, slight, and streamlined, from mustaches to silhouettes, from sculptures to buildings, from ideas to ideals. In her dream, she didn't hide her own canvases. She displayed them at bars and took in the compliments from customers.

She woke up with a tear rolling down the side of her face. Had she cried for Ana? For the women she knew? For herself?

The thought of dinner made her stomach flutter. She would dress up. Be pleasant. No reason why she should only be brave in dreams.

Careful not to wake Nina, she picked up a letter without realizing what she was doing.

The missive was a little folded paper, unimpressive and so water-damaged, so brittle at the creases, it could've fallen apart at any moment, turned into dust in her hands. It was from Joaquim to Ana. Darcey unfolded it with supreme care,

She sat up, not believing her eyes. Her hand trembled. His mother would not be pleased, but she had to tell them, without thinking of her own stake in the situation. She checked the clock. It was almost seven, but she had to read it once more, capture all its details and write a translation.

Darcey arrived five minutes late. Her hair was tousled and her face devoid of makeup. Her lips were pale. She still wore the same clothes she had fallen asleep in. No time to say hello. She pulled a chair next to Archie and grabbed his arm.

"I think you need to see this."

Chapter 28
Ray

From 1924

Ray didn't know when it truly started. For his own benefit, for the welcome possibility of marking a date on the calendar with a red-ink circle around it, he was inclined to think it was the day she threw her plate on the floor, scattering it into a thousand pieces. It was January 1924, and a snowstorm raged outside, coating the town with white nothingness.

But he knew episodic memory was flawed, and he couldn't be sure. And maybe it didn't matter. He had become the main chronicler of Ana's story, the one who remembered, because for the most part she herself could not evoke it anymore. And so it was: translator, spectator, and narrator. He became Ana's sentinel and protector. Most days these weren't easy roles, but for reasons that could only amount to love and devotion, he was there, picking her up at every fall.

At first, her demise was so subtle, so intermingled with her bad moods and outbursts that it was indiscernible from what everyday life had become. He had learned to recognize the calm periods, when she was kind to him and affectionate, when she allowed him to kiss her slowly, when she undressed him with deliberation.

Then later, if the weather were good, they would walk the area of the garden not saying anything, just living in the moment. He longed for these periods. The cyclical nature of their arrival gave him reason to look forward to the times ahead and strength to cope with the intervals in between.

But then something changed in her eyes, the way they became vacant, glassy even. While her body had been slight for a long time before, it gradually turned lifeless, its contours embedded in the armchair, as if all its energy had gone to live elsewhere.

Her hair, once glossy and lush, started turning ashy; her skin lost its vigor, and her voice became brittle, as if heard over a radio that was too far from its transmitting station.

Yet, year in year out, she painted feverishly, at all hours of the day and of the night. Her paintings were increasingly convoluted and abstract, even if they retained the gift of color. She focused on blues, but now they hinted of dark gray, of purple and black. Ray was particularly taken aback by the grays, so sad and one-dimensional, their meaning unequivocal and their vibration so solemn. She burned many of her paintings after they were done. He always smelled soot on her when she did.

She demanded to work alone. Her few hours of daily interaction were devoted to Gus, to reading for him, listening to him talk about his studies, teaching him about art. Ray was mollified by the fact that she sheltered Gus from her downfall; she did it expertly so that her son could have a notion of his mom to carry him through life instead of hampering his future. In that, she succeeded brilliantly. In everything else, she seemed to be failing.

To make sense of the strangeness that had become Ana, Raymond categorized her downfall in terms of episodes, little or large explosions after which she would be more markedly changed. He knew these were somewhat random, but such is the human brain that it needs milestones, little white wood sticks hammered into the ground to make things real.

In early 1924, the ill-fated trip that was supposed to take Ana away from the cold foreshadowed things to come. She spent her days complaining about the food, the rain, the schedule, and her nights tossing in bed and missing Gus. Raymond breathed in deeply and slowly at each new protest, this way hoping to deflect more serious clashes.

Ana was always plotting additional objections to instigate a fight, but such was his temperament, and he consciously cultivated it, that he resisted and avoided these traps, perhaps further aggravating her. She ended up *accidentally* breaking a few items in their hotel room in Florida. Many days later when they were back at home, the imaginary monster in her head already tamed, she took both his hands in hers and begged for forgiveness. He, as usual, assented. He had become obsessed with healing her.

A few years later, Raymond bought Ana a beautiful powder-blue satin gown. She looked ethereal in the cold, liquid fabric, and he took her for a night out on the town in Philadelphia. But she wasn't there. She was nowhere near the concert hall, and she was but a shell in the French bistro afterwards. Her body had traveled in the car with him, it had sat in the designated seats, but her mind was lost to the world. Maybe it had traveled south to Brazil, had taken an out-of-body vacation, and nothing he said or did that day was able to bring her back.

Once they got home in the early hours of next day and Raymond had already had a chance to drown his frustration in whiskey, he found Ana sitting on the floor, wearing her nightgown and cutting the dress into tiny pieces that fell around her like fresh snow. He ushered her to bed and collected the little rags as if they were precious stones.

The next decade brought hopes that Ana might actually be on the mend. She gained a bit of weight and when she thought no one was looking, she surprised Raymond, who took to spying on her, by humming a tune or singing in her native Portuguese.

Gus, by then a teenager, convinced her to learn to play chess, and some nights they would sit out in the porch and he would let her win just to see her smile. Yet Ray's optimism was soon crushed by a trip down the Mississippi on a steamboat. The confinement of the ship made Ana restless, and she paced the deck making empty sounds with her heels. After a few days, he couldn't sleep anymore, engaged as he was in watching her near water.

When she had a bad fever sometime later, Raymond feared the worst. Ana sat in bed and in her delirium spoke of people who did not exist. She created outlandish scenarios and stories of betrayal. Not even Eugênia, her good and loyal friend, escaped the role of villain. Ana recovered from the fever in the end, but as for herself, Raymond was not sure she could even convalesce.

By 1941, Raymond was running out of ideas. He

had tried gifts, vacations, and the simple offering of love. He didn't know which had failed more unequivocally.

One night, he was sitting outside in a blatant attempt to avoid the conflict zone that his home had become. He had started smoking and was playing with a cigarette between his fingers, wondering whether he should light it or not.

That was when the plan hit him like a shoofly pie. He clicked his tongue, annoyed with himself for not thinking of such an obvious course of action before. Then he tried to shape the idea a little more, turn it around in his brain until he could almost touch it and retrieve it with his hand. He lit the cigarette after all.

There had to be someone interested in buying Ana's paintings! They were good. Even a layman, an unrefined common man like him could see that. All he had to do was make them known. He wasn't a professional, but he could try a few tricks. He was a man of some influence, to be sure, and he was used to having to convince people in his own line of work.

It wasn't such a complicated process in the end; he was turned down several times but figured that it was mostly for his breach of protocol rather than for the quality of the work. He must have looked plain silly in his first attempts during his trip to New York, too pleading with his hat in one hand, the portfolio and a small painting under his arm, as if he was a traveling salesman or something. In the end, Raymond left Ana's file with a small but reputable gallery in Greenwich Village that was willing to showcase a couple of watercolors and oils from her most recent, blue and gray phase. He sent the work by post and waited. The neighborhood was so filled with artists that Ray expected nothing would come of it, yet not a whole season passed before he heard word that all paintings had sold.

Upon being told the news, Ana seemed a little excited, a little like her old self. At first.

She put her old red dress on, and she danced to the music of Carmen Miranda, grabbing Ray and Gus by the hand and making their awkward feet move. She asked Gus, "Do you have Brazilian blood in you or not? Where's your rhythm? I should have taught you to dance years ago!"

She looked at Ray with resurrected eyes, and he was filled with tenderness for her. She kissed him. He felt alive again. He lived for those little crumbs of affection, the ones that reminded him of the reasons why he had wanted her in the first place. So many years had he been dependent on these fleeting expressions of love that his life now seemed full of blank in-betweens. She put his head to her chest and played with his hair. And then, after Gus went to sleep, she took Ray to their bedroom, so foreign and unknown to both of them like a distant, unexplored land.

But the days that followed saw her increasingly confined to her bedroom. For even her upstairs atelier in the attic was now only inhabited by little spiders whose webby art had replaced Ana's own. She was refusing to paint. She said she was unworthy of success.

Raymond insisted for a while even if he knew that when Ana decided on a course of action, it was almost impossible to make her change her mind. The gallery wrote a couple of times but soon moved on to other artists, more willing ones. Loyalty to Ana had become a business for few.

After the incident, the years became predictably bleaker. By then a mature and always collected Gus had left the house and was studying in Philadelphia. Ray missed him, his benevolent smile and those dewy eyes that reminded his father of the boy he once was. If Ana was a whirlwind of emotions and frustration, Gus was the calm after the storm, a young man capable of bringing tranquility to a room just by walking into it. And while Ray had many times selfishly wished he could keep Gus in the house, he was also relieved that Gus could be somewhat shielded from Ana's erratic ways, and that he had not only survived intact but had even become a better person for seeing struggle and love in equal measures.

But Gus's departure must have also accelerated Ana's demise, as if there was little in her waking hours to motivate her tenuous grip on reality. She spent long days looking out of a second-floor window, resting on pillows that Ray made sure were made of the best goose feathers he could find. He and Beatriz often brought Ana soups and other easy foods that they could trick her into consuming. Many times they failed.

And so the days dragged themselves with the laziness of creatures who have nothing to either win or lose. Months became seasons, and seasons folded into years, a quinquennium, to be more precise, of silences, of stillness, of spectral whiteness.

In 1949, Ana took to her bed. After that Ray knew, like men know what truly occupies their soul, that she would never really leave her bedroom.

Chapter 29
Ana

The house, always cold…her heart, always cold. Gus, so small and beautiful. And then growing fast, like corn in the fields. She loved him so much. She didn't deserve him. *Close my heart, lock it away from all the love I might receive.* More wood in the fireplace. *I need to paint. Maybe this pain will climb out of me, will jump onto the canvas and stay there.* Ray growing more exasperated. *Let's walk in the garden. Let's live for today.*

The years were passing; her life was passing her by. This inability to act. Feet like blocks of ice, stuck in the ground. And the cold. More wood in the fireplace. *Going back to painting. The girl on the canvas. No other place to go.*

Gus, so grown and handsome. Not unlike his father. Joaquim smiling at her. Ray smiling at her. A hole the size of Pennsylvania in her heart. Her hands shivering. *I can't paint while my hands are shaking.* More wood in the fireplace. More spent canvases into the fire in the backyard. Back to painting. Expunging the pain. Eugênia's little mementos. She was always good at keeping them. The little bracelet. Her heart could not mend now. This stone-like feeling in her stomach. No use in putting more wood in the fireplace. No use in painting.

One day Ray came to her with the letter in his left hand. Stole it from her box in the attic. He looked pale. In shock, maybe.

And then he said the words to her. She wasn't sure if to hurt her. Perhaps to redeem himself. The words that sealed her fate.

"You know, we could've brought both. I would've kept both."

And after that, there was only darkness and despair.

Chapter 30
Darcey

1997

Darcey trembled when she shoved two pages in Archie's hands. One was the original letter from Joaquim—the other the translation

Ana,

I'm going to tell you of Eugênia and me and of the day my life changed forever—yet again. The first part you must know by now: we are a couple. After what I have discovered, I think we are even.

At first, I thought it would be one of those romances doomed to self-consume in a few months. It had everything to go wrong. She and I are very different, and my feelings for her developed slowly and caught me by surprise. The years passed, and I was not able to leave Eugênia. She became a part of me, like a second skin.

For the first few years, I accepted Eugênia's offerings as they came: a stolen weekend at the coast, my wishing the hands of the clock would freeze in place, the rare evening spent in an out-of-the-way restaurant where the waiters had become our co-conspirators.

I like to see her change with the seasons. Her

outside appearance, always conservative, but also fashionable and up-to-date, matching the time of year and the new trends: tubular sleeves in 1925, short knee-high hemlines in 1926, "shocking pink" in 1929 before the crash of the stock market made the 1920s feel like a holiday in paradise.

Her innermost self changed with experience, and experience brought her a serenity that made her as appealing as an afternoon on a quiet beach. Instead of tiring of her, I became captivated. That man I once was, proud and shallow, had to make room for someone more trustworthy, someone worthy of her.

My marriage crumbled, eroded as it was by lack of nurturing, arid and infertile like a patch of wild desert. Though like you predicted, I didn't leave my wife. I felt too much guilt. But in the end, it didn't matter. I didn't have to, anyway. She left me.

As I aged, I decided to shed the pride that had first brought me to you and had later found penitence through Eugênia. I wanted more. I wanted all her days and nights. For the first time, I wanted a life together. I knew she could see it. She silently wanted it too.

So as 1929 unfolded, I gathered courage. I took it in small doses until I was strong and confident again, as if bravery was a powder in my coffee, a smell in the air that I could inhale and absorb. I walked the streets of São Paulo, noticing the people a little more, the store windows displaying women's shoes, the pharmacies with their pristine marble floors and the bars with their constant melodies. The world was new to me. I headed for Eugênia's house.

I was almost running, sure of the words I wanted to say, hopeful of her answer. I could already see the façade of the building, the well-kept garden with azaleas and dark greenery framing the windows. And I knocked on the door unable to tell if the sound had been loud enough because my heartbeat was throbbing in my ears.

It was not Eugênia who opened the door. It was a little girl. The world came to a halt. It wrapped itself in silence. I angled my head down as my eyes adjusted to an image I couldn't decode well. Seven years old, maybe. Long, dark hair tied with a ribbon. Flowery dress and matching shoes.

She looked just like you.

Archie looked at the leaves of paper. He was in a trance. Darcey remained silent, waiting for his response, which took an eternity.

Of course the letter changed everything. Darcey's heart grew small and withered, like a peach left too long in the sun, like a flower dried and crushed inside a book.

Ana had a daughter.

Darcey thought of Nina. Living a few hours away and seeing her only on holidays and long weekends was almost unbearable. What mustn't this have been like for Ana? Thousands of miles away, no contact whatsoever. It was unthinkable.

"Does anyone know about this?" she asked once he had finished reading. She played with a fork, scratching invisible lines on the tablecloth.

"I—I don't think so. I mean, I was told the whole story, and this is the first time I've heard of this. Apparently, it wasn't the whole story after all." He scratched his head, looking lost.

She buried her face in her arms, which were folded on the table. "Is it bad, that I found all this?"

"How could we know? Besides, I was the one that gave you the letters."

"What do we do now?"

He paused for a second.

"Order more wine, I guess?" He searched for a server and, meeting his eyes, tapped on the bottle. "We'll need a minute to take this in."

"You seem to be taking it in really well already. Better than I expected."

"I'm surprised, but freaking out will not help, will it?"

"There's more," she said, holding Archie's hand. "Here. I knew Eugênia would not have allowed Joaquim's words to be the only ones." She produced one more letter. "I'll translate out loud from the original." After mentally translating it three times at home, Darcey had the words imprinted in her brain.

"Dear Ana,

"I won't know if I have the courage to mail this letter until I actually do it, but I can't lie to you anymore, my sister and confidante, who has entrusted me with her biggest secret and the ultimate blessing in my life. I hope enough years have passed to soften the blow of my actions and that you will forgive me if this causes you pain. But certain things need to be said, certain secrets cannot be kept forever or else they will consume us.

"Several months after you left for the US, I met Joaquim again. I never allowed him into the house, so he never saw his daughter. Your daughter. Yes, Ana,

your daughter grows more beautiful each day, and each day she looks more like you. She is equally headstrong. I hope the pictures and the little memories of her that I have sent you over the years, like her baby bracelet, have helped keep her in your heart as she has lived in mine and has given purpose to my life. Renata is indeed the perfect name for her, since it means 'born again.' For she is born to me each day when she rises, and I get a chance to enjoy this life with her. Because of her, I am reborn too.

"I shielded her all these years as I had promised you I would, and I tried to resist the temptation that eventually lured me toward Joaquim. As you know, my efforts were eventually overpowered by my heart.

"As our friendship progressed, I fell in love with him. I know it is grave and unfair, but you of all people should understand. I couldn't resist him, and our lives became tangled, but I never allowed him near Renata. Sadly, I was never blessed with another child, so the privilege of caring for yours was not lost in me.

"I imagine what you are thinking; my righteous ways led me straight to my downfall. The irony of telling you to stay away from him, only to fall into his arms myself.

"So the years passed, and if I never burdened you with this, it was because I always expected each of my moments with Joaquim to be the last. I never thought of months, let alone years with him.

"It was a few months ago that, in his own terms, Joaquim gathered the courage to come to the house. I wasn't in. It was a Saturday, in the middle of the afternoon. I was out shopping, and Dina was at the back washing some clothes. Renata opened the door to

welcome her father! Immediately, he knew. It would have been futile to deny it. She looks just like you.

"I finally told him everything. How you gave birth to twins. How one was a boy and the other a girl. How you were afraid that Raymond wouldn't have wanted a girl—yet another baby who wasn't his—and how you had suffered, regretted your decision ever since.

"I told him I had been good to his daughter, that I loved her with everything I had. And I asked him not to judge you because all of us had contributed in many ways to the complicated reality that our lives had become.

"He was without words for a long time, pensive and quiet, and then he went to look at Renata who had fallen asleep. He touched the tips of her hair with his fingers. For the first time, I saw him cry. Ever since that day, the two of them have become really close, as if she knew it in her heart that he was her father. We haven't told her. We wanted to hear from you first.

"I am writing in hope that you allow me to tell Renata about her father, and that in the scale where you weigh my virtues against my shortcomings you remember to place the sisterly love I have for you and the unconditional dedication I have offered your daughter. It is all I aspire to from you now, and all I dream you give me.

"Yours always,

"Eugênia"

Darcey drank a glass of water, swallowing the cold liquid with difficulty. She couldn't stop thinking of Nina, of how much she wanted to hug her and keep her safe. Her throat was constricted. Her voice cracked when she spoke again. "Do you think Renata is…?"

"…still alive?" It's possible. Gus had a long life."

"Should we look for her? Tell your mother? What do you want to do, Archie? It's your call." She reached for his hand once more. He lifted his eyes to meet hers when their fingers touched. He held her gaze before speaking.

"I can't think. She deserves a visit, right? An explanation?"

"We don't know the extent of her knowledge, though. Do you think we should potentially shatter the memories of an old woman?"

He took his time thinking about it. He looked at the translation of Joaquim's letter again and again making the paper crackle in his hands.

"Can you give me a few days? If it's waited this long…" But then something changed in his expression. His eyes widened, and a flush of color tinted his cheeks. "Darcey! She is the person!"

"What person?"

"The one Gus said I'd find at the end of the story. The one the lawyer is waiting to hear about. This is it!"

"Do you think?" She played around with the idea in her head until it was completely plausible. "You must be right. Then we have work to do. We need to speak to the lawyer, and we need to find Renata."

Archie nodded and then smiled at her. With his index finger, he swept a strand of her bangs off her face.

Darcey ironed out the wrinkles from her sweater, suddenly aware of the appearance she had neglected all day. She tried to smile pleasantly. "Do you still want to eat?"

"Yeah, I still want to eat. This can wait until tomorrow." He rested his elbow on the table, made a fist, and held the side of his head against it. He looked at her with that disconcerting half grin that made her knees feel like jelly and sent electricity to the pit of her stomach. "Come on. It's your turn. Today you choose the food."

She chose salad, with red and yellow pear tomatoes, basil, and olive oil. After that, she ordered risotto with mushrooms and black olives. Archie held his gaze on her. When they left the restaurant, a little inebriated given the good wine, a little lighter given the good company, Darcey reached for Archie's hand.

In front of her apartment, she still didn't let go of him. "Would you like to come upstairs?"

Let him perceive it for what it was, she thought—an affirmation of life, a regard for missed opportunities, a lesson from other people's past mistakes that she didn't want to repeat. He must have realized all that, because when they reached her apartment, he asked for the keys, opened the door, and led her inside.

****

They sat side by side on the plane, a subtle and calm intimacy between them while they sipped water and flipped through in-flight magazines. Archie had taken only two days to decide they had to go to Brazil and track down his great-aunt Renata.

First, he hired a detective. Then he booked tickets to coincide with the upcoming end of semester. When he surprised Darcey with the trip, she had little room for saying anything other than, "Where do we meet?"

The aircraft's engine produced its reassuring hum. Darcey put away her magazine and grabbed the São

Paulo book she had borrowed from the library. She'd marked the pages that described places she wanted to visit: the *MASP*, São Paulo's museum of art; the *MAM*, modern art museum, that was holding a Portinari exhibit; and the *Museu da Lingua Portuguesa*, a whole gallery dedicated to the Portuguese language, located at *Estação da Luz*, the train station close to Ana's studio.

Darcey couldn't stop thinking of Ana. Yet, at the same time, she couldn't hide her excitement over the trip, this attempt at putting things right and of finally telling Archie about Nina. There would be no lying anymore.

The detective had been obliging but not completely successful. He was able to locate a former employer but not a current address for Renata. And so there they were, on a plane that smoothly pierced the clouds as it headed to São Paulo. In her heart was a feeling of uncertainty, once scary but now almost familiarly comforting, hinting that life's mysteries could be rewarding, that sometimes only knowing vaguely where you were going could be a good thing after all.

Chapter 31
Eugênia

1940s

Eugênia sat in her tidy living room. It was a space that felt like a lazy afternoon with its shadow-inducing sage curtains and comfortable tapestry couches, the floor lamp in the corner, and the modern art on the walls.

The year 1948 was two months from done, and each day the rising heat made promises that summer was not far ahead. The city of São Paulo had grown to have more than two million inhabitants.

Immense, impressive buildings were sprouting from the ground as if the perpetual drizzle in the city helped them grow like crops. But Eugênia had managed to keep her *sobrado*, her two-story house in the quiet, green neighborhood of Vila Mariana. Dina had passed away of nothing other than old age, and she was missed terribly. So now in the house lived a family of two.

Joaquim rested his head on Eugênia's lap, as he often did when they were not at work, and she figured this was not a bad life after all. Renata, who was turning twenty-six, was pregnant with her first child. She had married a navy commander and lived in Santos, the same port city from where Ana had left them. Eugênia and Joaquim visited often.

Their life was predictable, and Eugênia found pleasure in constancy. In preparing coffee for Joaquim who arrived at six every night. In eating the roast beef and potatoes dish that he made, often on Sundays. In going together to the fashion shows the *maison* organized. In seeing her designs in the occasional magazine.

She hadn't had any children, but that was fine because Renata had been her daughter and had fulfilled that need to nurture that many women confess feeling and that she had surely harbored all her life. That the unlikely love between her and Joaquim had quieted down but remained was as much a surprise as a welcome gift in her life.

Her existence would have been perfect were it not for Ana's absence and for her utter avoidance of anything to do with them. Since Eugênia wrote the letter that revealed everything, Ana had ceased all contact, all correspondence, and all concern for any of them. Eugênia had tried everything and had despaired at times, to no avail.

It had become a one-sided conversation, but Eugênia refused to sever the bond between them. And however conflicted, she wanted to continue to make Renata a part of Ana's life. So no month passed without her sending a letter, a photograph, a little memento, a word of comfort, even in face of Ana's refusal to acknowledge them.

In fragments and pieces, always eternalized in letters, Renata learned to ride a bike, started middle school, turned fifteen and had her debutante ball, received her technical degree, and became a secretary.

And now, she was to become a mother.

"How about I go buy some wine for dinner before the stores close? Maybe we can have some *spaghetti al sugo* with it?" Joaquim's pragmatism interrupted her ruminations.

She stroked his graying hair and smiled feebly. "I think that is a great idea. When you come back, will you check the mail for me? I forgot to do it on my way in."

He kissed her on her forehead. "Will surely do."

Eugênia took his place on the couch, feeling the warmth of his body still insulating the fabric. She reached for a pillow and closed her eyes. Spaghetti sounded perfect. She'd better grate some Parmesan.

But she kept postponing it, the sofa's inviting hug too nice to resist. She didn't resist it either when sleep overcame her. The next thing she knew, Joaquim was kneeling next to her, tapping her elbow gently, handing her an envelope that she didn't fully appreciate at first. Not until the overly adorned "E" became clear and the tail of a stylish "A" materialized in front of her eyes.

After all those years, Ana had finally written to her, and she didn't know if she wanted to read what her friend, her sister, had to say anymore.

Joaquim, noticing her hesitation, opened the envelope tearing the striped line of reds and blues. He unfolded the letter and gave it to Eugênia. She used the residual light of the afternoon to help her decode the words.

Dear Eugênia,

I know this letter is long overdue. Eighteen years to be precise. I lost count of many things, though not of this. Now time only has intermittent meaning in my life. I'm told I only make sense from time to time. I hope I do in this message.

I will be brief. I wanted to thank you for taking care of my daughter as if she were your own. I expected nothing else of you, and I am sorry if my actions changed the course of your life. As for Joaquim, what you said all those many years ago was right—things happen that we cannot predict or control. If your relationship helped you understand me a little better, I will consider that an added benefit. Tell Joaquim, I am sorry for never having told him about the children. I know it must have been difficult for him to stay away from Gus, but I understand why he did it. I think it was best for all of us.

Now Renata. I don't expect she has any good feelings for me. I am glad she at least knows that I exist, even if such knowledge does not translate into any relationship. I have seen her grow—in my mind, in my paintings, in the mementos you have continued to send despite my silence. I have no excuse for my behavior. I made a big mistake a long time ago and I got entangled in the lies I created. I am sorry for all the people that have long been paying for my choices.

Ana

By the way, Raymond once long ago, upon finding your letter, said we could have kept both children. That's how grave a mistake I made.

Eugênia's body contorted into an arch, the pain piercing her stomach suddenly too great to bear. So much wasted life. So much spoiled love.

Joaquim didn't ask for any updates. He didn't ask about the son he had never met. Eugênia knew that hollow would always be there, despite the love for Renata, fulfilling like warm milk, all-encompassing like only love can be.

"I wish I could make her pain go away. All I ever did was try and make life easier for her. The only time I didn't put her ahead of myself was when I chose you." She smiled softly, "I don't regret it one bit."

Joaquim hugged her so hard she thought she heard a rib crack. "I made too many mistakes when I was young to deserve you. And yet, here we are."

She took his hands in hers and kept caressing them until the shadows in the living room grew so big that it was impossible not to realize night had fallen over the city. The crickets were in full activity, and a warm breeze came in through the window.

"I think I'll go make that pasta, after all. Wine?" Joaquim showcased the bottle to her, like a waiter in a restaurant.

"I'd love some."

Eugênia walked outside for a minute. Some kids were playing with a ball in front of her window, just like Renata used to do. She had made it despite everything. Her family was a hodge-podge ensemble, put together with pieces of Ana's life. But it was still her family. She was the thread that connected them, weaving a delicate pattern, with strong stitches of love, loyalty, and devotion. These people over whom she once had no claim were now her whole world, her reason for breathing, for going to work. They were the inspiration for the beautiful dresses she made for others to dance, dine, and be happy.

It was a good life. Despite all the pain, it was a very good life.

Chapter 32
Darcey

1997

"And here you have the Ibirapuera Obelisk. In a minute, we will go past the *Monumento às Bandeiras*, a large Brecheret granite sculpture, a boat being pulled by horses and men. I could've turned back there to go to Vila Mariana, but you said you wanted to see the park."

Darcey translated what was said. They had just arrived at the airport and taken a taxi to the hotel.

"No, this is great. I'm glad to see it," Archie confirmed from the back seat of the taxi, targeting his words at the driver who didn't speak English. Darcey sat next to Archie, still a little self-conscious at his body's proximity.

The driver continued, "The Ibirapuera Park has an area of 1,600 square kilometers and is home to a Japanese garden, museums, a pavilion for events like a book fair. There are also bike trails and a lake. You should spend an afternoon."

Darcey turned Portuguese into English immediately after the words left the man's mouth.

"We will," she said, "after we take care of what we came here to do." She looked at Archie to find any signs of nervousness or hesitation. She only found his familiar solidity.

At the hotel, Archie asked for two rooms. Darcey figured he didn't want to seem presumptuous. They walked down the hall on the sixth floor in silence, his hand brushing against hers as his arm swung back and forth.

She wished to grab it and walk to his room as a couple, lock the door behind them and spend the afternoon lost in the sheets and pillows. But there were things to be done, a detective to meet. She slid the room keycard in its slot and went into her empty room.

"Do we have time to freshen up?" she asked.

"Meet downstairs in twenty minutes?"

She agreed with a nod, though what she wanted was to kiss him until all the air left her lungs.

The detective met them at a restaurant near the hotel. It was an Italian cantina, crowded with families on that Saturday afternoon. Rods of provolone cheese and colorful ribbons hung from the ceiling. The walls were lined with shelved bottles of house wine, and autographed pictures of famous people lent importance to the place.

Darcey and Archie were taken to a corner table. The waiter recommended *Guaraná*, a delicious local soda made with the fruit of the same name.

The detective was punctually late, as was customary in Brazil. He was a small man in a brown suit. Most people were dressed in polo shirts and jeans or khakis, so he stood out. He acknowledged them with a tilt of his head, and walked to the table, steering clear of wooden corners and playing children.

As soon as he was at hearing distance, he said with a smile, "I found her! Here's the address."

"This is incredible!" Darcey said, recognizing the

address. "Renata is back where she started—Eugênia's house."

****

Large pots of ferns framed the front door of Renata's home. After her husband passed away, she had returned to the home Eugênia crafted for her and Dina, who'd been a part of the secret ever since she delivered Ana's twins. It was a friendly house. It invited people in with its green window shutters wide open and a flower garland. A cat sat under a spot of sun by the door and licked its golden paws. The noise of playing children surrounded it. Waving trees lined the front fence.

Archie hesitated, halted a few steps from the house, his fingers in his jean pockets. He took in what he was seeing: a house full of history, full of secrets—a house with a soul.

The cat retreated and startled Archie out of his stupor. He reached for Darcey's hand and squeezed it. She took the lead and knocked on the door. A woman in a low ponytail and white uniform, who looked to be in her sixties, answered the door. Fátima was Renata's nurse, and she clearly knew they were coming.

"She is having second thoughts about seeing you, but I think it would be good for her to talk to young people. She has been a little tired these days, you have to understand."

Darcey translated the woman's words to Archie, who looked back at her as if she had a solution. "What do you figure we should do?"

Fatima opened the door fully and gestured to them. "Come on in, and wait a bit. I'm going to talk to her once more."

"We really don't want to impose," Archie said to

Darcey and waited for her to translate.

"It's all right. Please come in."

The living room of the *sobrado* was covered in knick-knacks—small figurines, a collection of teapots, and photos at different stages of yellowing. The one picture worthy of a silver frame displayed a middle-aged Eugênia and a still dashing Joaquim sitting in a park. A cuckoo clock was tick-tocking the afternoon away, reminding the guests that if they were wasting time, they would not get it back.

Darcey took in the room with all its details. It was like being lost in the past with all its reminders. A voice that sounded like plush velvet broke her concentration. It was a unique sound, and at first it was confusing because it produced English words. Once she figured that out, the words she heard were equally telling.

The voice was saying, "I thought you would never come, Archie, but at the same time I feared you would."

"Mrs—"

"Call me Renata."

"Yes, Mrs. Renata," Archie said as if he were a kindergartner.

She chuckled, but it was a sad chuckle.

"Archie, call me just Renata. Or auntie if you prefer. I am, after all, your great-aunt."

"But how do you know…?"

"Your name? I know much about you. I know you were always Gus's favorite, I know you study law because you are good, and you want to make things right. I know you are devoted to your mother. I even know who this young woman is."

"But when we called, we asked your nurse not to tell you too much. We didn't want to startle you." He was shaking one of his legs rapidly, with an up-and-down movement of the front of his foot.

"And she didn't. She followed your directions. She only told me that two young Americans visiting town wanted to meet me about a research project. And then she told me their names were Darcey and Archie. Too much of a coincidence, don't you think? My brain is old, but it still works. And I am not tired," she said, looking at the nurse and frowning. "I simply didn't know if I was ready to let go of this pain. You know, I kept it encased in one of the chambers of my heart, so it wouldn't take over my life, but I guess I knew the day would come when I would have to open the door and let it go."

By the looks of it, Renata's brain worked much better than their own. She was fast and smart, and she looked at people as if she had an instinctive understanding of who they were. There was something regal about her. The impeccable silver hair, the Bordeaux silk blouse, the long fingers whose nails were polished in a shade of antique rose.

"Sit down, please. I asked Fátima to bring us coffee and *sequilhos*. Do you know what *sequilhos* are?"

Darcey and Archie both shook their heads.

"Delicious corn starch cookies that fall apart in your hand."

"Can't wait to try them," Darcey said, still impressed by how this woman carried herself.

Archie was in another world. Darcey noticed when she looked at him. He was, she thought, trying to make connections in his head.

"Sorry, Renata. But you mentioned Gus. How do you know about my grandfather, about me?"

"Archie, this may come as a surprise to you, and I don't want you to get the wrong idea that we were being deceitful. But Gus and I corresponded all our lives. He was my brother after all. My existence wouldn't be complete without him. He was my twin, you know. Twins have a special bond, even if they aren't identical."

Darcey looked down and tried not to blush, as if that function of her body was subject to her control. Renata's brother had been a far-away sibling, but she had him. Darcey hadn't had the same chance.

"Are you all right, dear?" Renata asked with what sounded like genuine concern.

"I'm fine." Darcey lied. It wasn't the place or the time.

"Here. I want to show you something." She walked slowly to a dark wood secretary whose top was dotted with little glass sculptures. She rummaged through a little drawer and produced a letter folded in four. She gave it to Archie.

Darcey saw his face change—first, surprise in his eyes, then recognition in the way his eyebrows relaxed, and finally tenderness, making a comma of the corners of his mouth. He stood up and took the letter to Darcey when he was done reading.

Dear Renata,

Sometimes I wonder why we don't learn to use the Internet and send the blasted e-mails to each other, but I guess there is a certain poetic element in continuing to write letters, don't you think? How are you? Over here, much good news. Archie is going to law school, and he is so happy. I can't tell what he considers better— getting a chance to study what he likes after struggling with his father for a few years or being able to be where Darcey is. You know I always liked that girl. I hope one day she realizes how much Archie loves her. I hope they can be happy together.

Darcey stopped reading, feeling too embarrassed to continue. She gave the letter back to Renata holding her gaze and mouthing a silent "thank you."

"Did you ever meet? In person I mean," Archie asked.

"No…I guess we were afraid. I'm not sure of what. We were very comfortable with our letters, with distance and closeness at the same time. Our lives were meant for different paths the moment we were born. I was the second, you know? My mo—Eugênia told me. I took everyone by surprise and caused a bit of a commotion."

Darcey sat next to Renata and held her hand. The old woman accepted the gesture, as if saying it was fine, she wasn't going to fall apart. Renata had to live with such knowledge. With distance and rejection. But she had had her sibling. What wouldn't Darcey herself have given to have known her little brother, even if only through letters. She understood Renata as if they were one.

"I loved Eugênia very much. She moved here, cut all connections to anyone but her father, Dina, and Ana so that I could have a normal home. So that I would know I was loved. She became quite famous too. In fashion. Isn't life incredible?"

"When did Ana decide…you know…on this arrangement?"

"The moment she saw we were two and I was a girl. She didn't trust Raymond's love. What a burden to carry. I'm sorry for her. Not trusting is a great encumbrance."

She shook the memories off. "But all of that is in the past, I guess. And it should stay there. I've had a good life. I had Eugênia and my father and then my husband and son. My son travels a lot now. That's why I have Fátima."

The nurse came into the room, the mention of her name magically making her materialize.

"Here's coffee and *sequilhos*." She put a tray with hand-painted china on the coffee table.

"Ah, Darcey. Try this." Renata lifted the plate toward them with a surprisingly steady hand.

The treats were indeed delicious.

Archie stuffed a few *sequilhos* in his mouth. He was pondering, almost in a stupor. And then he seemed to take stock of the room, once more stopping at Eugênia's photo.

"Well, I think you are a very special lady, Renata," he said when he finished eating. When he stood up, he walked toward her and planted a delicate kiss on her cheek. "Very special indeed. I have a great-aunt!"

Her eyes flooded at that, and Archie grew more solemn. "We have something for you. We think it's rightfully yours." He went to a corner where upon entering the room, he had rested a large, flat item wrapped in brown paper. He put the object in front of Renata and helped steady it while she tore the wrapping.

Inside was the portrait of Renata as a child, the one that had graced the living room wall of his house all along.

"She loved you from afar. She always did."

Darcey witnessed Renata's expression change. It was like the shedding of ten thousand layers of doubt and agony, and for a second she saw the woman as the young girl she once was: unencumbered by the weight of so much history.

"Thank you, Archie. This is the best present I could ever wish for."

Later that day, Archie and Darcey sat at the *Trianon*, that same park where Ana sat planning the future that wasn't. They had just visited the MASP, the *Museu de Arte Moderna de São Paulo*.

Darcey was revitalized, her senses heightened as always happened when she was infused with art. She had seen the one painting of Ana the museum owned: it was called "The Market."

The rough grass whose fragrant smell danced around the park was pricking Darcey's legs. The streetlights were just turning on, dusk upon them like a watchful guard.

"So…" Archie took Darcey's hand in his and kissed it. "Have you decided you cannot live without me yet? Can we move on to the next stage of our lives?" He looked at her, a protective hand an awning over his eyes.

"Archie, are you asking me to marry you?" She was smiling, just happy to be.

"No." He made a serious face.

"Oh…that's embarrassing."

He laughed. "I am asking you to spend your life with me in whatever shape or manner you find fit. I'm asking you to not bypass life for fear of how it could turn out. I'm asking you to put up with my shortcomings while I put up with yours. That's all I'm asking."

He paused for a moment, drawing a breath as if he had just come up from under water. "But, if in the process of doing all that, you decide that you'd like to marry me, well, I'm inclined not to say no."

She wanted to laugh but her eyes were marred with tears and if she did, they would overflow. She held his face in her hand, and he rested the side of his jaw in it, as if her palm was a pillow.

"Archie, I can't." She removed her hand slowly.

The smile disappeared from his face, but he didn't speak.

"I can't because I have kept secrets from you, and once I tell you about them, you will not want to marry me. Or be my friend, even."

He still didn't speak. He held her gaze.

She sighed and continued. "I have a daughter. Her name is Nina. She's three. Her father is not in the picture. He wasn't very nice. Not like you." She offered him a sad smile. "I have a daughter, Archie, and I hid this most important part of my life from you."

"I know." He looked up, toward the sky.

"You know?" Her heart thumped inside her chest. How could that be?

"I know. I've known for a long time. It's not like your parents moved to the Far East. People talk. I was waiting for the day you would trust me enough to tell me. I would never not love you because of your daughter. But I have hurt for a long time. Hurt that you would not tell me or that you'd think I would not immediately make her my own daughter if you'd given me that honor."

Fat tears formed again in her eyes and splotched

her legs when she looked down. "I am such a fool. All the time I wasted."

"So will you marry me? Will you give me the honor of letting me be a part of Nina's life?"

His acceptance of her imperfection and of her greatest accomplishment, her daughter, floored her. She wouldn't make the mistake of being proud anymore.

"Yes, Archie. I'll marry you." This time she slid her head toward the hollow of his shoulder and rested there without knowing what to say.

She noticed the noises of São Paulo intervening in the distance: the continuous sound of traffic, the horns of cars, the distant bell of a church, a garage exit chime prompting pedestrians to be careful. They were in the belly of the city. In the middle of things. And she was at peace, perhaps for the first time ever.

Life could be good. She would give it a try.

That night Archie and Darcey forsook the second hotel room.

Chapter 33
Ray

1970s

The nurse came to tell him that Gus had called. The old man smiled inside, looked at the gray rotary phone on the bedroom table. Ray was so proud of his boy, his middle-aged son, though it was hard to imagine him anything other than a young child playing at his parents' feet. What year was it again? 1971, was it? It was hard to tell now that all days blended into scattered hours of awareness interspersed with unavoidable bouts of sleep. After all, he was in his 80s. Alone. Ana had left him over twenty years before.

Yet the memory of that day played in his head like a repeated nightmare. The day no one could find her in the house, and they went around frantically searching the gardens, the road, even the tool shed.

He knew it before it could be known. He believed he had failed her in all the ways he could have failed her, having proclaimed he was so relieved she had a boy the day Gus was born, taking her—a tropical flower—to that sun-forsaken place, removing an artist from the buzz of parties and the adulation of fans.

A grave mistake.

It was only fitting he had been the one to find her, to suffer the terrible blow of losing her.

They were about to call the police when it occurred to him that she had to be in the attic. Her attic, the only sanctuary she ever ran to when life became overwhelming, when she could take the somber house no more. He had looked inside, he had called, but they were beyond calling now. He knew it.

So he went up again, hearing with cheetah ears the creaking of each wooden step, the silence beyond the little annoying sounds. Pitch-black darkness greeted him as he opened the door. A waft of stale air, trapped inside the prison-like attic like a casualty of war, touched his skin and woke it up.

He pulled the cord that turned on the lights and saw the innumerable canvases that leaned against one another as if they needed moral support. On the easel was the picture of the girl.

In a moment of rage, Ray had told Ana they could have kept her. He had been mad. He had been cruel. Cruel beyond belief. He should have taken the blame. For her sake. For everyone's sake.

She would have hated him, and that would have been preferable. Because women have a hard time hating others; they find it a lot easier to hate themselves, to turn all pain inside and to corrode their own souls with self-loathing. Men punch a wall and feel better. Then they go out together for beers and feel even better. Women don't.

He started reminiscing. He saw himself aligning the canvases against a wall. Looking at the elaborate lines, the obvious pain, and the irrevocable confusion distracted him. Oceans, dense forests, gray snow. Navy stripes.

His blood turned to ice in his veins. A lightheaded

giddiness made it hard to discern between the floor and the ceiling. Navy stripes. She looked so quiet and so skinny, lying there on the floor. Immobile. He knew what it meant. The stripes were not moving. The lungs were not filling. All that remained was the old-fashioned dress. One he had never seen before. Silky and fluid lines of white and navy blue. It looked like something from the '20s, from a time long gone. Almost forgotten. But apparently not to her, her brand of time travel quite visible.

He cradled her in his arms. The coldness that had become her. Her heart had simply stopped, too tired of the heartbreak it carried for so long. He swallowed his tears because he had no right to cry. He would suffer in silence, like she did until the suffering and the silence consumed her. His years would be long. His years would be lonely. His years would be filled with the forever memory of her.

Lost in his musing, he fell asleep in his chair. Woke up and fell asleep once more. What day was it again? Not that it mattered. They were all the same unless Gus came to visit. Those were his special days. Other days were just necessary gaps to bridge until Gus showed up again. The nurse brought him his medicines. He swallowed the pills. Swallowed hard.

He touched Ana's portrait with his shaky fingers. She looked at him with challenge in her eyes.

"I'll join you someday," he said to her image. "When I have paid my dues."

The nurse was ready to roll him outside. "A bit of sunshine," she said.

There was no need. There was no sunshine. Not since Ana had gone.

Chapter 34
Darcey

1997

"So did you let sleeping dogs sleep?"

"It is sleeping dogs lie," Darcey corrected.

Lucile blew raspberries through her tensed lips. "What is it that kids say these days?" She paused searching for the word. "Whatever!"

"Where do you get that stuff, Lucile?"

"TV. Where else?"

The things she said were all the more reason for Darcey to love her.

"I'm getting married, Lucile." Darcey suddenly blurted out the words.

The old woman looked shocked for a second, but then she recovered with the expediency Darcey had come to expect. A dash of concern crossed her face. "Tell me the lucky guy is Archie. Please do."

"You can relax, Lucile. It's Archie." Darcey buried her face against the curtain where she had been semi-hidden for the last five minutes. She knew she was blushing like a waltzing debutante.

"Finally!" Lucile lifted her body from the chair with difficulty, her arms too feeble to lever up the rest of her frame. She went to Darcey. "You actually deserve a hug today. For once a wise decision. I knew one day you'd come to your senses. I knew you could fix things."

"Will you be there? At the wedding, I mean."

"I don't have anything to wear. I hardly go out anymore." Lucile picked up a coffee table book and pretended to examine the pictures with a magnifying glass. She didn't even bother turning the book the right way.

"Well, knowing you would say that, I got you this." Darcey stepped just outside and fetched a red gift box that had been conspicuously lying outside Lucile's door. "If you don't like it or the size isn't right, you can exchange it."

Lucile opened the box and looked at its contents as if they were treasure. Inside, a navy-blue dress with a satin collar peeked at her from within the tissue paper.

"It's from Archie too."

The room went very still. Lucile was touching the dress with such care it seemed she was afraid to damage it. And Darcey smiled inside for having been able for once to silence the old woman.

****

Two days later, Julia Northwood was sitting in her living room when Darcey arrived. The painting with girl who now had new meaning and a new identity had been gifted to Renata. The room was almost dark given that only the entrance hall was lit. It was raining heavily, and the sky had turned an unbecoming shade of gray, almost green. At least the air smelled fresh and cool, and it was easy enough to breathe.

"Mrs. Northwood, the day is too dark for no lights," said the maid sneaking up on Julia and giving her a fright, evident in the woman's startled jump.

"Darcey is here. Do you want me to turn anything on?" Mary continued, tidying up invisible messes and straightening pillows that weren't crooked.

"No, thank you. I'll just switch on this lamp. Come on in, Darcey."

Because Darcey had chosen not to be afraid anymore, she spoke first. "To think that for all those years we were staring at Renata not knowing the secret the wall displayed in such vivid colors. It's strange that it's not here anymore."

Mrs. Northwood stood up and walked toward the new canvas, Ana's abstract painting that had been upstairs, and she looked at it more closely, scanning the image from top to bottom. She seemed tired, and Darcey noticed, perhaps consciously for the first time, that Julia was not a young woman any longer.

"I guess you consider your research a success then."

"I do." Darcey stood by her side and focused on the picture too. It was indeed an impactful image, both the pain and the love that had consumed Ana now evident.

"Good. Is that what you've come to see me about?"

"Actually no, but I guess you already suspected that."

Julia turned her upper body around and faced the visitor. "I'm not sure I understand what you mean. Then why are you here, Darcey?"

It took her two Mississippis to answer.

"Archie and I are getting married." Given that Julia Northwood had always blurted out things as she pleased, Darcey had decided to do the same.

"Pardon?"

Darcey repeated it a little more slowly, as if she

were talking to a child. She felt her cheeks blush, a radiating heat that started at the jaw and migrated toward her eyes. She brought the back of her cool fingers to her face, first one side, then the other. "Archie thought it would be nice if I were the one to tell you."

It must have crossed Julia's mind that the pair traveling to Brazil would seal their commitment to one another, but then again, she might have thought Darcey would not defy her, or yet that in the end she would have given in to what Julia had considered her independence and wanderlust.

"Mrs. Northwood?"

"As you can see, I'm still here. Still listening."

"I love your son. I have always loved him. I should have trusted his devotion and my own feelings a long time ago. I will make him happy, and when he is not, I will keep him company until he is happy again."

"Marriages are complicated entities, and they don't age well. Little annoying habits get magnified with time, and the novelty of love, which many times is simply infatuation, withers quickly." She was drinking whiskey and stirred the ice with her index finger. It was an unexpected gesture for such an elegant woman.

"I respect your feelings about marriage, however sad they make me. I of course do not appreciate the fact that you tried to blackmail me over my daughter. And since you've mentioned often enough that Archie should find a nice girl and marry her, it seems that you think the problem is me rather than marriage."

"You are headstrong, and that will accentuate with time. You have a child, which means this would be a blended family from the start. I always thought of a different union for him."

"I see. What about what he thinks?"

Julia sighed. "I just don't know anymore."

"Mrs. Northwood, you realize you come from one such family, right? A good man raised your father. I have the same luck: an excellent, loving man to help me raise my daughter. I am very lucky.

Darcey didn't expect any grand gesture. It was not like Mrs. Northwood would change her mind that instant and recognize she had been unfair. There would be no hugs and warm congratulatory remarks. When Julia called Mary back to the living room and asked her to serve Darcey some coffee, tea, or refreshment to her liking, she got a little more than she could have hoped for.

****

It was uncommon for Darcey to come to Donaldson's door unannounced. But once she was back at the university, she broke her own rule. She asked to borrow Archie's car. When she arrived, she knocked on the door three times and waited while the sun warmed her back.

When he answered, rubbing his eye like he had just woken up, she handed him a carefully stacked manuscript.

"For you."

He grabbed the document while his eyes searched her face for further information.

She wore an air of certainty, her back very straight and her chin in the air. She realized that this posture made it easier to breathe.

"Come in." He made room for her to pass.

She went in without looking back at him and

continued to talk. "It's the first three chapters. About one hundred and twenty pages. There'll be the standard five. What do you think?"

She looked at him teasingly, waiting for his reply, and felt a desire to skip, like a little girl. She had forgotten how good a person could feel.

"But you haven't even defended your prospectus. People usually don't start writing until their prospectus has been approved."

"I'm sure we can take care of that quickly. I have it all here." She pointed at the side of her head with her index finger and walked on, confidence making her step much steadier than she could remember ever being. She had tried to be elegant but assertive, and the move had surprised the scholar into silence and acquiescence. The episode had only strengthened her growing tendency to trust herself and her instincts.

"Sit down." They had reached the living room and Donaldson offered a comfortable rust-color armchair.

"Don't mind if I do." She sank into the chair, crossed her legs, and rested her elbows on them.

Donaldson flipped through the pages of the manuscript, stopping at certain sections and reading with interest. She waited with newly acquired patience.

"Have you cleared this with everyone?"

"Yes, especially with Renata, Ana's daughter in Brazil."

"Ana's daughter?"

"Yes, we found her daughter. The one nobody knew she had."

She stood up and examined the pictures on the mantel. "I'm focusing on art, though. And the incredible historical moment Ana experienced. Her life is only significant as far as its impact on her paintings. I mean, at least for the thesis. Her life matters a whole lot more than that to me. She was really talented." She ran her fingers over a Cézanne reproduction.

"So Archie was onto something?"

"Yes." She answered more to herself than to her mentor. "Archie knows things."

Donaldson scratched his beard and went back to the text.

"I know the next many weeks won't be easy. So much to do. But I'm going to finish my dissertation, and I'll make you proud. And since I'll be ABD, I have everything ready to apply for the job."

"Well, Darcey. I never doubted you could do it. The only person that second-guessed was you. I'll make sure to state how much I trust you'll finish on time in my letter of recommendation. And by the way, Browne is really retiring. It's official."

She sighed with relief. But she didn't wish Browne any harm. There was never anything to be gained by holding on to grudges.

"Stewart." She didn't remember ever calling him that. He had been a good mentor. She hoped in the next phase of her life he would be a colleague and a friend. "I also have an idea I want to run by you. It's important."

He continued browsing through the pages. "I'm listening."

"Good. Here goes. And by the way, Archie and I are getting married. And I have a daughter."

Chapter 35
Darcey

They got married in May when the crystal trees of ice had melted and the green of the grass was like a luxurious carpet under their feet. At the altar, Darcey's eyes unlocked from Archie's long enough for her to inspect the circle of people around them and gauge the mood of the small wedding party.

Nina was the flower girl and wore a yellow dress with a halo of white flowers on her head. Eleanor bit her nails, looking around as if concerned for the casual arrangement, while Lucile used any reflective surface to look at herself and her new dress. Donaldson took in the wedding with great solemnity, as did Julia, who remained mostly still. Both fathers looked at each other with a level of suspicion. They could not be more different from each other—Mr. Mendes affable and kind, Mr. Northwood authoritative and silent. But Darcey and Archie were delighted no matter what, and in the end their delight was what mattered.

Archie had thought of flying Renata over for the wedding. Darcey discouraged him.

"Let things be as they may. These are separate worlds. We may straddle them, but not everyone will follow. It's better this way."

"You're right," he conceded. "Let's send a wedding announcement instead."

Darcey had chosen an off-white dress, simple with lace trimming and loose sleeves. She wore a rhinestone barrette and carried a bouquet of camellias. Her neck exuded a soothing lavender scent.

There were many things to like in her wedding, but the most special for Darcey was the way Archie looked at her, like she was the only woman in the world. Like he couldn't believe his good fortune. Like his life was about to start. She was so grateful for his perseverance, for the fact that he had not given up on her, no matter how hard she had pushed him away. She could allow herself to be sure now. To love, to trust, and to dream.

She took it all in. One breath filled with a memory to last forever. The buttery yellow cupcakes. The white and lilac ribbons. The large tin filled with ice and cherry soda. The quintet of university undergraduates playing. Archie's well-tailored shirt smelling of rosewood and cedar cologne. The sky that had cleared especially for the occasion.

****

Seven months later, graduation day came and went like a dream during a nap. Darcey had skipped the event in high school and in college. Yet she decided that since this was the last time she would graduate, she owed it to herself to show up. She also wanted to allow her parents to take a proud picture. They had done so much for her.

At first, when Darcey came home with the money that Lucile had promised, her mother had refused it. It took a lot of convincing to make her parents agree that nothing was to be gained by being proud. Lucile knew where the money was going. She wanted a reconciliation. It was time they became a family again.

After the wedding, and moving into Archie's with Nina, Darcey dedicated almost every waking moment to her dissertation and her own nascent family. Archie never complained. Instead, he cheered her on. That was what made Archie so special. He and Nina were inseparable, playing on the floor with her toys, walking to the park or having snacks on the couch. Sometimes, he would carry Nina on his shoulders, and the little girl would laugh until Darcey's spirit felt light and new again, and she was ready to work some more.

She cried, she screamed, and she wrote furiously. Donaldson asked for revisions, again and again. Letters danced on the page changing places at times, but she charged ahead. Sometimes, days turned into night only to witness her still sitting at her computer.

Browne had discreetly retired, leaving a position open to be filled by an Assistant Professor. His remaining students would graduate with Darcey.

"Stand here. A little closer to the tree. Now smile. There." They stood outside in the beautiful gardens of the university taking pictures on graduation day.

After, the family celebrated at the little Mediterranean restaurant near the university. Even Lucile decided to come. She ate a pecan-crusted salmon like she had never tasted better food before. She went on to the chocolate mousse cake that had "Congratulations, Darcey" written in white chocolate at the top.

"If I lose my girly figure, you'll be to blame," she teased.

Mrs. Mendes and her sister still didn't talk, but Darcey caught them sharing a smile, and the gesture gave her hope that in time kind words could be exchanged too.

Archie gave Darcey a silver-colored pen with "Dr. Mendes" engraved in the body and complained again about her not having taken his last name. When the time for her campus visit came, a couple of months after graduation, she would be ready. It would take a while for her to find out the outcome, but she was not worried. She already had what was most precious to her.

So they all laughed and had a good time, celebrating until late at night. After that, it was time for Darcey to make an announcement.

And an invitation.

****

Ana Valquíria Eça had lived an incomplete life. She had strayed away from her path. She had been buried for over forty years. Forgotten. Forsaken. Forgone. A few lines in a book or another, a memory on the Northwood wall. In a couple of private collections. Alone in a museum in Brazil.

And then she was reborn.

She lived again through Darcey's relentless insistence. Meetings with the college Dean, negotiations with a couple of collectors, phone calls to university officials. Individually, these efforts might not have amounted to much, but collectively they resulted in a beautiful exhibition in the same gallery that had housed the Latin American show all those months before.

Darcey adjusted one of the small frames. It enclosed a watercolor, two lovers in a passionate embrace. The scene was displayed next to Mrs. Northwood's fortieth-birthday present: a mist of purple, pink, and yellow shades on a large square canvas.

People had started to come in. They looked at the art slowly, as if they were enjoying a delicious cake. What a difference seventy-five years made. In 1922, people had looked at modern art as if aliens from Mars had produced it. They were afraid. What if art changed everything? They weren't ready to risk their ways just yet. They couldn't foresee that the crash of 1929 would do it for them anyways.

"It's a good turnout. There must be two hundred people here." Archie brought her back to reality. He was carrying Nina. "People seem to be enjoying themselves. Ana's art too."

"Yes, it's all as it should be. How could they not like it?" She whisked a lock of hair away from his forehead and kissed the tip of both his and Nina's nose.

Archie never bought her roses. Or chocolate. Much less greeting cards. Late in the fall he showed up dangling a set of keys in front of her and placed them in her hands. He had leased a convertible so that they could go in search of warmer climates, one of those places with no or moderate winters. New Mexico, Arizona, Utah. It was time. She had earned a vacation after working so hard, but they agreed not to be away from Nina for more than a week. They would return the car in Phoenix and fly back home.

Out west, there were valleys and rivers, cacti and pine trees. There were cowboy omelets, salsa and chips, frozen lemonade and churros. And there were roads without end, flanked by red mountains and flowers that had no name and were planted by nobody. "Look, Darcey," he said when they reached a particularly beautiful field full of daffodils.

During her trip a realization came to Darcey like a lightning bolt. His gift to her would never be a dozen roses, nor flowers stolen from someone's yard like Flynn had done. They were not Archie's style. His gift, instead, was all the flowers on the way, all that sky, all those mountains that would not die in a week. His gift to her was the art of always being present, no matter what came to be. He had agreed to be a dad to a child not biologically his, had put up with her inconsistencies, her secrets, her insecurities and denials. He had been there all along.

They were hiking a canyon when she suddenly stopped. "I have a surprise for you. And no, I'm not pregnant. There's time for that. Nina can be an only child a little longer." She searched inside her handbag and produced a simple office paper. "I brought this to show you. Read."

He unfolded the paper and read aloud. It was a letter.

"Dear Dr. Mendes. Thank you for submitting your book proposal. After careful consideration, we are pleased to inform you that we have decided to publish your work. We agree with the title you proposed: *Ana Valquíria Eça: The Story of an Artful Woman*. Please find attached the draft of a contract. Should you have any questions…"

"Darcey! This is wonderful!" He hugged her tight. "I'm so proud of you."

"I'm a little proud of me too." She blushed. "Will you read the contract, make sure it's a good one?"

"Are you asking me as your husband or as your lawyer-to-be?"

"Both, I guess."

"Then both say yes." He kissed her for all that immense valley to see.

The memory of Ana filled Darcey's mind. She would approve, Darcey hoped, and she could not help but mouth a silent "thank you," a little invocation for the extraordinary life that seventy-five years later had saved her own.

Acknowledgements and author notes

While the story and the characters in this book are completely fictitious (although some real historical figures make cameo appearances), the writing of this book has been motivated by my genuine love for Brazil. Therefore, I have tried to create equally genuine representations of the country, mainly through its historic Modern Art Week of 1922, realistic representations of Carnaval, and descriptions of the city of Americana, which is a real place, now a successful textile hub. Where necessary, I have taken creative license with dates and places to fit the plot, but the spirit of the times and the locations depicted should still shine through.

This book is the result of many years of work, finding the right balance between historicism, fiction, and storytelling, and I cannot offer enough thanks to the peers, writers, and friends who helped me so much along the way. I am very grateful to be a part of the Women's Fiction Writers Association, where I have found so much support and joy. To my friends and peers there, I thank you all. My most heartfelt gratitude goes to Kathryn Craft, Margarita Montimore, and Anne Duguid Knol. Your talent is only surpassed by your kindness. To my friends and colleagues Monica J. Casper and Julie Amparano Garcia, you saw the very first spark of the idea for this book and the very early drafts of this work. You always kept me optimistic and on track, and I cannot thank you enough. To the wonderful writers and friends Barbara Solomon Josselsohn and Maggie Smith, you saw the initial idea turn into a full, more mature draft of a book, and because of all the help and encouragement you gave me, this book is yours too. To my great friend and fellow writer Jen Jensen, you always read so much of what I write, and you offer your time so selflessly that I can only be forever grateful. And to my family, everything I do is for you, so too is this book.

And to you, dear reader, you are the reason for books in the first place, and I am so thankful to you for having chosen to spend time with this one. May you always find in books respite and joy.

Patricia Friedrich
Arizona, January 2021

A word about the author…

Patricia Friedrich writes Women's Fiction as herself and historical romance as Eliza Emmett. She is a scholar and professor. Her stories are often about the journeys of women as they make sense of family, love, and their vocations. There is always a bit of mystery too.

Find her on Instagram @eliza.emmett.author and on Facebook

https://www.facebook.com/ElizaEmmettAuthor/
https://www.facebook.com/patriciafriedrich2015

Thank you for purchasing
this publication of The Wild Rose Press, Inc.

For questions or more information
contact us at
info@thewildrosepress.com.

The Wild Rose Press, Inc.
www.thewildrosepress.com